P9-CDU-516

in the rooms

Also by Tom Shone

How Hollywood Learned to Stop Worrying and Love the Summer

in the rooms

Tom Shone

THOMAS DUNNE BOOKS
St. Martin's Press
New York

This is a work of fiction. All of the characters, organizations, and events portrayed in this novel are either products of the author's imagination or are used fictitiously.

THOMAS DUNNE BOOKS.
An imprint of St. Martin's Press.

Printed in the United States of America. For information, address St. Martin's Press, 175 Fifth Avenue, New York, N.Y. 10010.

www.thomasdunnebooks.com
www.stmartins.com

Library of Congress Cataloging-in-Publication Data

Shone, Tom, 1967–
In the rooms / Tom Shone.— 1st US ed.
p. cm.
ISBN 978-0-312-62278-7
1. Literary agents—Fiction. 2. Mythomania—Fiction. 3. Interpersonal relations—Fiction. 4. New York (N.Y.)—Fiction. I. Title.
PR6119.H56I6 20011
823'.92—dc22 2010043594

Originally published in Great Britain in somewhat different form by Hutchinson, Random House UK.

First U.S. Edition: April 2011

10 9 8 7 6 5 4 3 2 1

For my father

acknowledgments

For their comments and encouragement I would like to thank Len and Pat Babb, Rosie Blair, Quentin Curtis, Helen Fielding, Sloan Harris, Nick Hornby, Ian Parker, Emma Parry, Marc Sholes, Gai Shone, Lord Peregrine St. Germans, Lady Catherine St. Germans, and Marcel Theroux—but especially my wife, Kate, who listened to me with such love and patience. I would like to thank the New York Public Library's David Smith and Matthew Sheehy for showing me around the stacks; also Bernard, Bill, Chris, Colin, Darrell, Franklin, Jill, John, Jeff, Mark S., Nat, Scott, Sophia, Violet, and William for their example.

Fixed myself a nice glass of NyQuil.
Dragged a chair over to the window.
Where I watched a pale moon struggle to rise
over Cupertino, California.
I waited through hours of darkness with NyQuil.
And then, sweet Jesus! The first sliver
of light.
—"NyQuil," Raymond Carver

Fake it 'til you make it.
—Alcoholics Anonymous slogan

chapter one

IT WAS A COLD, clear morning, the sun low in the sky, casting long shadows that stretched the length of the sidewalk. My breath formed little clouds of vapor in front of my face that evaporated instantly. I tightened my coat, tucked in my scarf, and fell into step behind a man in a Burberry raincoat, a copy of the *Wall Street Journal* under his arm. Always a safe bet—a man in a Burberry raincoat, carrying a copy of the *Wall Street Journal* under his arm. After nine months in the city, I'd learned to steer clear of anyone with a dog on a leash, a camera around his neck, a baby in a pram, a map in his hand, or a family in tow, all highly likely to commit any one of a number of traffic violations—pulling out in front of you, dawdling, changing lanes without warning, or else just stopping dead on the street. No signal. Just stopping dead, right there in front of you, to gawp, or point, or chitchat, or just hang out, like it was his living room. Nobody *stopped* on the streets of New York. The only reason for you to stop was if you had reached your destination; that was the only real reason, the only valid excuse. Otherwise, you kept going. That was the genius of the grid system: There was always some direction you could be moving in—left, right, up, down, north, south, east, west. The only people who seemed to understand this properly, funnily enough, were the elderly. The elderly in New York were nothing like the elderly in London, inching along the pavement in their multiple layers of wool and nylon. The elderly in New York were wiry, feral creatures, their haunches sprung like marathon runners, their instincts for a gap in the crowd, for some fleeting point of ingress, honed by decades of pounding the streets. In my first week in the city, I had been expertly cut up by this silver-haired old dear in lime green Lycra jogging shorts and sneakers who zoomed just past the end of my nose, missing me by a whisker. I could only gaze in admiration as she disappeared into the midday crowds, elbows pumping. Get behind one of *those*, I figured, and it would be like tailing a fire truck or a police car as it hurtled up one of the avenues. They didn't even look old. They looked young. Only older.

At the end of my street, a heavy refuse truck hissed and moaned, hungry for the black bags tossed into the back by the garbagemen; passersby glanced in, doubtless imagining what it would do to their frail bones, and hurried on. I came to a halt on the corner of Seventh, which was flocked with taxis, beside one of those orange cones belching steam from the subway system. I caught a faceful of cabbagy-smelling steam—what were they *doing* down there?—and felt my stomach roil. The exact dimensions of my hangover, long suspected but so far not precisely demarcated, revealed themselves to me. This was not going to be one of my more productive days.

I was just considering heading north to cross a little higher up, when my phone rang. Fishing it out of my pocket, I saw Caitlin's name flash up in blue on the little LED screen. Fuck. What did *she* want? For a few seconds, I toyed with the idea of not taking the call, then duty, or guilt, or some mixture of the two, kicked in. I flipped open the phone and held it to my ear.

"Caitlin. Hi."

There was a pause before she spoke, and she sounded sheepish when she did. "Patrick . . . hi. . . . I'm sorry to call. I just wanted you to know that I shouldn't have sent that e-mail. What you get up to now is your own business. I'm sorry."

The e-mail, terse with sarcasm, had been the first thing in my in-tray that morning. "Liked your profile on Simpatico.com. Glad to see you're feeling a little more 'chipper' these days—Caitlin." I had groaned when I read it. An actual groan escaped my lips. They really ought to put a warning on those things; I thought: THE FIRST PERSON TO READ THIS WILL BE YOUR EX-GIRLFRIEND. *Then* see how many people called themselves "adventurous" yet "earthy," "spontaneous" yet "considerate," "outgoing" yet "shy" or said that they liked to "laugh a lot," mostly at themselves. If you believed all that you read on the dating Web sites, New York was populated entirely with zany yet grounded twentysomethings engaged in citywide hunts for the best cupcake shop, while laughing at themselves, madly. It was all lies. Most people I knew were too busy working like dogs to embark on spontaneous road trips in custom-painted ice-cream trucks, or to cook blue spaghetti for their art-school friends, or any other of the madcap activities that made up the three-ring circus that was supposed to be your life. *I like to live each day as if it were my last.* How was that any way to live? If I was to live every day as if it were my last, I'd spend the rest of my life drunk, six cigarettes stuffed in my mouth, sobbing down the phone at relatives I hadn't called in ages in a funk of fear and loathing. How was *that* a good way to spend the entirety of the rest of your life? My Wednesdays were bad enough as it was.

"It's okay," I said. "You had every right. It must have been a shock seeing me on that thing. It's not what you think. I'm not using it to go on any dates. It's just . . . window-shopping."

"Window-shopping."

It didn't sound so good when she said it.

"Yes. You know. Fantasy. Pretend. You think I'm ready for someone else? Are you kidding me? Of course I'm not. I just wanted to know what it might be like to feel okay again. Reassurance that I wouldn't feel like this forever."

"Reassurance that you wouldn't feel like this forever."

"Yes," I said, wondering why she was repeating everything I was saying. That couldn't be good.

"I see," she said icily. "So you're not feeling so 'chipper' anymore, then?"

Ouch. Okay. That was embarrassing. *Word That Best Describes Your Current State of Mind.* I'd been trying to strike a note of Cockney insouciance. Cheeky-chappy kind of thing. Allow them to infer how dumb I thought the question, while also hinting at the unusual word choices you got with dating a Brit in New York. Across the street, the light changed, and my little pack of pedestrians surged forward. I racked up a decent pace in the hopes the conversation would follow suit.

"Okay, look, this isn't fair, Caitlin. I was just trying to move on. It's been three months now."

"It's been one and a half."

"No."

"It's been exactly six weeks."

"I thought it was three."

"No."

"Yes."

Turning onto Eleventh Street, I found myself engulfed by a swarm of schoolchildren, all holding hands, jabbering away in what sounded like three different languages. I took immediate evasive action, but it was too late, and I found myself slowing to a virtual standstill. Nobody had told me there would be *children* in New York. I decided the time had come for an experimental note of anger to see where it got me.

"Okay, look, this is ridiculous. You're sounding like it wasn't you who ended the whole thing. You threw *me* out."

"I don't want to go over that whole thing again. That is not true. I didn't *throw* you out."

"You more or less did."

"Can you even tell the truth, Patrick? What happens when you try? Does it hurt your mouth? You're incredible, absolutely incredible. Do you want to know what the worst thing was? It was the fact that you put yoga under 'hobbies and interests.' After all the times I asked you to go. I mean, if the question had been 'Things my last girlfriend asked me to do but I always refused,' that would have been an honest answer. As a profile of *me*, that would have been an honest answer—"

"I'm interested! That makes it an interest!"

"—and baking! Okay, here's a tip. If you're going to put baking as a hobby, then when they ask you about the items you have in your fridge, don't put 'a bottle of champagne' and 'a chocolate bar.' You can't bake with champagne and chocolate."

I thought hard for a recipe that used champagne and chocolate and came up short. Something was bothering me about this conversation, something nagging at its periphery that I couldn't put my finger on. On my left, two schoolgirls had lost hold of each other's hands. I saw my chance and pushed through them.

"You have no idea what I'm up to these days—"

"Well, I'm pretty certain it doesn't involve baking and yoga! Good Lord! The only reason I knew it *was* you was because you put *Albert Speer: His Battle with Truth* as your favorite book. You may want to do something about that. That's not the sort of thing that'll have 'em queuing up at your door in this city. Biographies of dead Nazi architects."

"He was the one Nazi who was man enough to stand up at Nuremberg and—" I began, when suddenly it came to me. But of course! How could I have been so stupid! It had been staring me in the face all along! "Hang on . . . How come you were reading my profile?"

There was silence on the other end of the phone.

"What were you even *doing* on Simpatico.com?" I asked.

An even longer silence, in which I could sense the swell of victory.

"A friend of mine is a member," she said finally.

"Ah. A *friend*," I said jubilantly, feeling the power of my newfound victimhood surging up beneath me like a submarine beneath the feet of a drowning man. "Of course. Right. How silly of me. A *friend*."

"You can believe what you want, Patrick. I gave up trying to convince you of anything a long time ago. That's not why I was calling anyway."

"Oh no?" I asked, feeling the submarine drop back beneath the waves. "Why were you calling?"

"Kira and Mark said you'd asked them out to dinner, and I was wondering if—well, I just think it would be easier if we had a clean break."

"Meaning what exactly? That I shouldn't call them *ever*?"

"I just don't feel okay about it."

I slowed to a halt outside of a pizza parlor on the corner of Sixth Avenue, causing the woman behind me to mutter audibly. I glared at her hunched, miserable back as she passed: Couldn't she see I was having a conversation? "But what will they think if I just disappear off the map like that? Without saying a word? Don't you think they'll think it's a little bit rude?"

"Please, Patrick. Just do this one thing for me."

"But they're the only people I really know in this . . ." I began before trailing off, the memory of what I had written in the *Why*

You Should Get to Know Me section winking at me like the light of an unexploded bomb.

"Okay, okay," I said grumpily. "Whatever you say. I won't call them."

"Thanks. I know this is hard. It's hard for me, too."

"I know. Listen, I'd better go; I'm right outside my office."

Inside World-Famous Original Ray's Pizza, two Hispanic teenagers ladled red gloop into big doughy pizza bases.

"Okay, well . . . take care, Patrick."

Her tone was neutered, inscrutable.

"You, too."

I closed the phone and slipped it into my pocket, going back over the conversation I had just had, probing for weak points in her argument and patching up places where mine could have been stronger. She had dumped me. Maybe she hadn't thrown me out of her apartment, but she had dumped me. And it *had* been three months ago, unless you counted the night we fell off the wagon that time. You couldn't count *that.* And I *had* given some serious thought to a yoga class. The baking, not so much, but nobody told the truth on that thing. It was aspirational: You described the person you *wanted* to be. It was the American Dream—your chance to reinvent yourself. The only time anybody told the truth was in the *What I Am Looking For* section, which was basically the place your last relationship went to die. It echoed with the sound of niggles and peeves. "No workaholics, passive-aggressive, brainwashed Stepford men or Republicans," wrote one girl, Nolita657. "No cynics or assholes, and you know who you are. . . ." It reminded me of that Carly Simon song, the one where she went, "You're so vain, I'll bet you think this song is about you." Okay. First thing. Why would a vain man think *that* song was about him? Surely he'd pick a far more flattering song, "Holding out for a Hero," say, or "Dream Lover," or, if it absolutely had to be a Carly Simon song, "Nobody Does it Better."

I'd always liked that one. But the one song in the songbook accusing him of vanity? I'd almost written to Nolita657 to point all this out, but something had stopped me—a sudden weariness at the thought of slotting into place behind the last guy, even, now that I thought about it, a spooky semblance of Caitlin to the girl's tone. Jesus. Maybe it really *had* been Caitlin. Thank Christ we hadn't gone on a date. I felt a sudden chill, shivered, retied my scarf, and pushed off north toward the office.

chapter two

THE OFFICES OF THE Leo Gottlieb Literary Agency were located in a small redbrick carriage house, just below Gramercy Park. Dwarfed by the buildings on either side of it, it sat a little back from the street, with a small cobbled courtyard to one side, in the middle of which sat a cherry tree; the windows on the first floor were tall and arched, and while the view inside they offered was unremarkable—some stairs, bookcases, a brown leather sofa suite—the overall effect had enough of a gingerbread air to stop the curious, and in the summer it received a steady stream of tourists, asking if the building was anything they should know about. I'd always found it a very American question: "Should I be interested in you?" Usually, Natalie gave them a potted history of the building—how it used to be the stable of a much larger estate in the nineteenth century, and then was turned into an office building sometime in the late 1980s, at the height of the property boom. She told them that Theodore Dreiser wrote *An American Tragedy* a few doors down, in what was now a Pilates studio; and that Oscar Wilde's agent worked in the building directly opposite, now a Spa Belles salon specializing in Brazilian bikini waxes. That usually raised a smile.

She was sitting behind her desk at the base of the stairs when I entered, sorting through the mail. Dressed in her usual palette of grays, her hair fastened back from her face, she didn't look up, sorting the mail into neat little piles on her desk with quick, bird-like movements. She always put me in mind of one of those videos depicting the origins of life: put stuff within a five-yard radius of her and it just started organizing itself, coalescing, synthesizing, ordering, simplifying. I always wondered if it had something to do with her childhood in a Vietnamese refugee camp—her last name, Thị Nghiem, repelled all attempts at pronunciation—but had never felt bold enough to ask. On the filing cabinet to one side of her desk, a poster was tacked up with tabs of Scotch tape: HILLARY CLINTON FOR PRESIDENT. As I closed the door behind me, she looked up, saw me, and called out.

"Morning, Patrick."

"Hi, Nat," I said, unwinding my scarf. "Is Leo in yet?"

I gestured upstairs. She shook her head. "He's not coming in today," she said. "He's got the flu. He said he was taking the day off."

I exhaled loudly, blowing out my cheeks like a trumpet player and peeled off my coat.

"Why? What's the matter?"

"Caitlin just caught me on Simpatico.com."

She waited, as if expecting more. "So? What business is it of hers?"

"You don't understand," I said, frowning. "She read my profile. It was absolutely excrutiating. Just awful." I shook my head at the memory of the evisceration I had received.

"Why?"

"She's not supposed to read that stuff!"

"Why not?"

"Well," I said, a little awkwardly. "I may have . . . embellished things a little."

"What did you put?" she asked, her eyes wide.

"They had a box where you tick your hobbies and interests, and I don't have any hobbies and interests, do I? Well, I didn't want the box to go to waste, so I saw *yoga,* and it made me think of her, and how attractive all that had been to me when I first met her. And all the times she asked me to go."

"That's why you date someone. They complete you."

"Right. One person doing yoga is enough. But then we broke up and—well . . ."

"You needed completing again?"

"Pretty much. So I ticked *yoga*. And *baking.* I've always wanted to do more—"

A key fidgeted in the lock of the front door: We both turned to see Saul letting himself in. Heavyset, hirsute, with dark hair that no amount of combing could untousle, he had square, blockish features and a battered leather suitcase under his arm. As one of the senior agents at the firm, it had fallen to him to show me around my first day; I'd been talking to him about something and he'd gotten this faraway look on his face, as if probing a back molar with his tongue. He looked positively Neanderthal. It had taken me ages to figure out what that look meant. He was *listening,* which was presumably the key to his success with women, despite the fact of his hairiness, right down to his knuckles. I recognized his shrewdness for what it was: a cunning tactic designed to flush you into things you didn't really mean. I'd seen him in negotiations; he was lethal.

"Hey, guys," he called out. "What's up?"

"Patrick just got busted by Caitlin on Simpatico.com," said Natalie before I could stop her.

"No way," he said, drawing near. "What for? Refusing to go back to England?"

"She took me to task for some of the things I wrote," I said, weary resignation stealing over me.

"Like what?"

"He put that he was into yoga and baking," said Natalie.

"Baking!" he yelped. "Why the hell did you put that for?"

"What does it matter?" I said irritably. "I don't know why I'm even on that thing. It's a complete waste of time. It's not as if anybody ever uses it to actually meet anybody, do they?"

"Isn't that what it's for?" asked Saul. "Meeting people?"

"No," I said firmly. "The exact opposite. It's about *not* meeting people. *That's* how it works. You hot-list them. They hot-list you. You send them a wink. They wink back. Then someone actually writes an e-mail, nobody replies, the whole thing fizzles out, and you go back to the beginning again. You see? Now, if you don't mind, I really ought to be getting to work," I said, moving toward the stairs.

"How many dates have you been on so far?" asked Natalie.

"None," I replied emphatically.

"None?"

They exchanged glances.

"Well, there's your problem right there, Patrick," said Saul. "No wonder you think it's impersonal, if you haven't actually used it to meet someone. I hear that helps. Meeting the person. Same with marriage, childbirth. That first meeting just sorta sets the whole ball rolling. . . ."

"That's the way you do it *here*," I said.

"And how do you date in England?"

"You get drunk. . . . You roll into bed with the friend of a friend. . . . You wake up the next morning and decide whether you want to make a go of it or not. It's a lot simpler."

They both smirked.

"How long did you stay last night?" asked Saul.

"Too long," I replied with a grimace.

"You boys went out?" asked Natalie.

"The Paris Review's Christmas party," said Saul. "Patrick was doing impressions."

I groaned at the memory.

"Don't tell me," she said. "Sean Connery, Michael Caine . . . and Borat."

I looked at her, dumbfounded. "How do you know that?"

"You did them at Leo's birthday party," she said.

"I did?"

"Don't you remember?"

"No. I don't. Was Leo there?"

"Of course he was. It was his birthday, you idiot."

"But did he see me doing impressions?"

"Yes. It was him you were doing them for."

"Really?"

"Yes."

"You're getting quite a name for yourself," said Saul, patting me on the shoulder and turning to go.

"Here," said Natalie. "Before you go." She handed Saul a big pile of FedEx boxes; then she handed me my mail—junk mail, mostly, with one brown-paper package bound in string. My usual batch of poems from nutters.

"Don't forget you have an eleven-thirty brunch with Ian Horrocks," she said.

"I thought I'd canceled it."

"That was last week. He called back and you made another appointment, remember?"

"Can you cancel it for me again?"

"Actually, no. I cannot. You take him out. Eleven-thirty. Don't forget."

If there was one thing I had learned since my arrival in New York, it was that the American reputation for a lack of irony was not only undeserved; it was a deliberately propagated piece of misinformation designed to lull the unsuspecting into a false sense of superiority. You walked into the conversation, confident of your superior firepower—not just the cloaking device of irony but the howitzer of sarcasm, the flamethrower of preemptive disdain—only to find yourself completely outflanked and outgunned. My grilling over, I felt grateful for the relative solitude of the taxi, which took the potholes on Broadway at speed, each bump cushioned by the suspension, as soft and spongy as a pram's. The driver, silent and turbaned, wove in and out of the traffic with self-martyring bursts of acceleration that always ended the same way—in a sudden, despairing application of the brakes, as expressive of man's lonely fate in a cruel and indifferent universe as the great operas. I slid around the black vinyl seat, examining the taxi number inscribed in braille on the back of the seat in front of me, wondering what impression it might make on my forehead in the event of a crash. Through the Plexiglas, the cast-iron buildings of SoHo receded in the morning haze, each block milkier than the last. What was that Updike quote—something about New York being the only town that glitters from afar, even when you are in it? It was true: Peer up the avenues, or down the cross streets, and you were confronted with more places you were *not*, right this very second, than in any other city. Even the car horns meant something different here. In London, a sounded horn meant someone had broken the rules: Are you *mad?* In Paris, together with a hand raised heavenward, it sounded a note of philosophical despair: The whole *world* is mad! In New York, it was more personal and to the point: *I'm* mad! Get outta my way! With one last pump on the brakes, as forlorn as Madame Butterfly's final, fluting breath, the cabdriver pulled to a stop outside Balthazar. Ian was already there, standing to one side of the red-tented entranceway, smoking a cigarette. He looked underdressed, as he always did, in faded jeans and a crumpled leather jacket, his neck in desperate need of a scarf. At the sound of the taxi door slamming shut, he turned, saw me, took one last loving puff of his cigarette, and flicked it into the gutter.

"Just enjoying a sneaky little fag," he said, shaking my hand. His hands were freezing.

"Keep your voice down," I said. "That sort of thing gets misunderstood here."

"Wouldn't be the first time," he said, holding the door open as two women came out. "After you, my old cock."

The two women looked at him, then at each other, then walked off.

With its scumbled, faux-nicotine-colored walls, its high ceilings and black-and-white-tiled floors, Balthazar was as perfect a simulacra of a French bistro as could be found in the city, an imitation let down only by the courtesy level of the waiters, who ferried silver trays to the tables and banquettes in crisp white shirts bunched in at the elbow with silver bands. The whole place hummed and clinked with the sounds of midmorning brunch. I was just about to check in with the maître d', when Ian pointed to the long mahogany saloon at one end of the room. A Bloody Mary stood on the corner, half-drained.

"You don't want to get something to eat?" I asked.

"Tied one on a bit too tight last night, didn't I," he said, shaking his head, as if still figuring out how such a thing had come to pass. We headed over to the bar, where Ian poured himself into his bar stool like an amoeba reverting to its natural shape. I had rarely seen him stand upright unaided. He was one of those men who was forever slouching against doorways, or leaning against bars, or draping himself over sofas, as if standing were the most unnatural state in the world for him and only when recumbent could he find his plumb line through the universe, his magnetic north, his raison d'être. I took the stool next to his and ordered a coffee.

"So how are you doing, my old mucker?" he said, leaning over and rubbing my knee. "How's work?"

"You mean apart from the fact that everyone's selling more books than I am?"

"They still haven't found you out, then."

"They will," I said, slipping into the one-downmanship of British conversation as if into a pair of old slippers. "Ian, can I ask you something? Say you were dating a girl and then she broke up with you. And then you called her friends to ask them out for dinner. But she flipped out and said she didn't want you ever calling any of her friends ever again. Would you say that girl was within her rights or completely out of her mind?"

"Is this Caitlin?"

I nodded. "Don't you think that's outrageous?"

He pushed back on the bar until his stool tipped backward, then shook his head and sucked air through his teeth like a mechanic inspecting a dodgy motor. "That's the way it works out here. You offend the chief, you lose the tribe."

"Can't they think for themselves?"

"Were they your friends, too?"

"They might have been. I'll never know now, will I?"

" 'If you can make it here . . .' "

"That's got a downside, though, have you noticed? If you fail out here, then you can't exactly say you were hanging out for the mountain views, can you?"

"*You're* all right. You should try *Time Out* at the moment. They're laying off people like crazy."

"I'm sorry to hear that."

"In fact, I wonder if I could run something past you. It's nothing much. Just an idea I've been kicking around . . ."

Here we go, I thought. Fifteen minutes later and we were still there, my chin sinking deeper into my hand as Ian expounded on the latest book idea he hoped would pluck him from the ranks of *Time Out*'s copyeditors and thrust him, blinking, into the literary limelight. It wasn't quite as bad as his last idea, something called *Next!*—which aimed to apply Bush's notion of preemptive war to the New York dating scene—but it was close: a history of applause, from the ancient Romans and the emperor Nero, who paid people to applaud his terrible singing, through to Mahler, Wagner, and the birth of "the Bayreuth Hush." In Germany, you could clap and boo at the same time, apparently. After a while, I realized he had stopped speaking and was looking at me expectantly.

"What do you think?" he asked.

"Do you have a title?"

"Speak to the Hand."

"Don't you mean *Talk to the Hand*?"

"That's the one. *Talk to the Hand*. What d'you think?"

"Here's the thing," I said, wondering whether it was too early to look at my watch. "The *trouble* is, that whole microhistory thing is kind of winding down right now. I mean, we've had a history of lipstick, plastic, jeans, hair, the pencil, clouds, dust."

"Oh," he said, crestfallen.

"But you know what? It sounds a lot like something Saul might go for. Why don't you send it over and I'll see what he thinks."

"I don't have anything written down as yet."

"Well, when you do."

"Thanks, mate," he said, slurping the pulpy remains of his Bloody Mary. "What are you doing for Christmas? You going back to Blighty?"

"No, I'm sticking it out here."

"Oh yeah? Me, too. We should go out sometime, have a proper British booze-up."

"Actually, I'm trying to cut that out for a bit," I said. "I've been hitting the parties a bit too hard recently. In fact, I should probably be getting back. . . ."

"Of course," he said, drawing a square in the air for the check.

chapter three

THE SUN HAD BURNED away the mist, casting thick shafts of light down the cross streets, which people hurried toward, warming themselves. I decided to walk back to the office, to clear my head and put some distance between me and the conversation I had just had. Ian was all right, I supposed, in his slightly damp way. He was part of a circle of Brits I'd met when I first got out here and whom I'd spent the last few months trying to ease my way away from. It was a little offputting to me, that whole expat scene, lounging around the Soho House, asking the same subset of unanswerable questions: "Do you think you'll ever go back?" "So, are you here for good do you think?" It felt like too much of a backward step, a thin effort at solidarity. We didn't really go in for identity politics, the Brits. We didn't even really think of ourselves as immigrants. The Italians came to America and they got Martin Scorsese and *The Sopranos* and meatballs and Little Italy and Sonny Corleone beating the bejesus out of that guy with a trash-can lid. The Irish came to America and got Saint Patrick's

Day and Tammany Hall and JFK and the railroads and cops so tough that you didn't dare ask them for directions. Even the Samoans had their flag-waving day, the Puerto Ricans their parade. You never heard a peep out of the British. All we got was the chance to look vaguely apologetic on July 4. We were the guys everyone had come here to get away *from*. Our mere presence canceled out the whole point of the place. No matter how Americanized in their manner—no matter how bright and peppy and can-do in their attitude—I always stared into the eyes of my fellow Brits and thought I could determine trace elements of all the old fear and shame and self-excrutiation and furtive self-advancement that I'd come here to avoid. It was a bit like going up to university and running into your old high school buddy: just as you were presenting your brand-new face to the world, a reminder of your knock-kneed past came lurching out of the shadows.

There was no great mystery as to why I was in New York. I originally came out here for Caitlin. We'd first met just over a year ago, in London, at a dinner party thrown by a friend to take my mind off some trouble I was having at the agency where I worked. A new office manager was making life hell for all of us, but I was getting the brunt of it, so Gavin threw a party to cheer me up. I found myself sat next to this petite blond American girl in cashmere and stilettos who leaned into me every time she talked, enveloping me in a tingly haze of eau de toilette. White Linen, I later found out, Estée Lauder's 1978 classic blending jasmine, rose, and berry with bottom notes of moss and amber. Caitlin worked in the PR department of Estée Lauder and was in London for three months to launch a new perfume called Pleasures—another spirited floral, a shimmering blend of lilies, peonies, and jasmine, with bottom notes of *baie rose*. If I had to choose one word that conveyed my impression of her that night, that word would be *shiny*. I'd never set eyes on a woman with such high production values, such finish; they just didn't make them like that in England. For three months, we enjoyed one of those incautious, 60 mph romances that come along every now and again—bus trips home to my flat in Kensington, picnics, strawberries, champagne, Wimbledon, all wrapped up with the drama of her impending return. Our good-bye at the airport was like the last reel of a Meryl Streep weepie.

We tried it long-distance for a while—you've never seen such phone bills—but then, one day in late March, my boss called me into the office and told me about a possible work placement with a sister agency in New York. My time at Smith and Fairfax seemed to be coming to a natural conclusion anyway, so I broached the idea with Caitlin, nervously at first, but then with increasing enthusiasm, as together we imagined tearful reunions at JFK, blissed-out cab rides back to the city, followed by hot, impetuous sex against her refrigerator. I knew that American refrigerators were much larger than their English counterparts, with special chutes that dispensed precrushed ice on demand. Such, anyway, were my thoughts as I finally set forth on the Heathrow Express one afternoon in early May. It didn't quite turn out that way. For one thing, I arrived in the middle of a heat wave. Caitlin's apartment was a lot smaller than I had envisaged, and even with the air-conditioning on full, we were like two monkeys in a hair dryer. She had no room in her jammed closets for even the small suitcase I had packed. For a while we simmered and bubbled, struggling to summon our previous ardor, and on the third day we clashed over garbage disposal and the tensions that had been brewing erupted in a Vesuvial row. That served to break the ice, and for the next few weeks we slotted back into something resembling our old rhythms, although there was a new tone between us—playfully testy, taking mock offense at pseudoinsults, like brother and sister—one that had not been there in London. I couldn't help noticing that Caitlin's forthrightness, which I had been eager to study as an example of that famous American moxie one hears so much about, was more like straightforward bossiness. And why had I never noticed how often she interrupted people? By the end of July, we could barely stand to be in the same room with each other, and after a huge fight about Bono, along the usual lines—she thought his charity work was above and beyond; I thought he was a grandstanding showboat—I moved out. Saul helped me find a sublet on Craigslist, and for the next few weeks I tried to forget about Caitlin and threw myself into my work at the Gottlieb Agency, taking editors to lunch, meeting authors, building up my contacts, just as I was supposed to be doing. She and I eventually patched things up enough to limp on for another few months, but the damage was done. I was furious with her for putting me within a hairsbreadth of being actually homeless on the streets of New York City. Finally, a week shy of the day I was supposed to return to London, I managed to impress Leo with some last-minute edits on some indecipherable technothriller of his about a BlackBerry that warps space-time, and he asked me into his office and offered me a job. Much to everyone's surprise, including my own, I accepted.

There were worse consolation prizes for a relationship going belly-up—a move to New York. As I crossed Washington Square that afternoon, surprisingly empty but for a few figures crisscrossing the sandy-colored paving stones, I found my mood lifting. The sun caught the uppermost branches of the trees, still clinging demurely to the last of their leaves. In the center of the square, the fountain lay waterless; beyond it reared the large triumphal arch celebrating George Washington, through whose legs could be seen the brown ziggurats of Fifth Avenue, and the Empire State Building. It was practically illegal to be down on living in this city, I thought as the large overcoated figure who had been walking ten yards or so in front of me, his hands shoved down into his pockets, leaned over the edge of the fountain and spat into it. *But how disgusting,* I thought, my reactions running into one another: a flare of disgust, followed by a jolt of recognition, before flipping into disbelief.

It couldn't be him . . . could it?

I killed my pace and dropped behind the hurrying figure, who seemed to be headed toward the row of brownstones on the north face of the square. He passed under the triumphal arch and drew up on the other side, by the traffic lights, looking this way, then that, while he waited for the traffic to pass. I drew up behind one of the legs of the arch and took my first good look at him.

His face had filled out a little but still managed gauntness, his eyes disappearing behind deep creases as he squinted in the sun, his hair swept back from his formidable brow into neat track lines of gray, as if he had just showered. He had also grown a beard of sorts, not the intentional kind, but the kind that comes when men simply get bored with shaving. It was streaked with gray, but then, in my experience, authors always chose dust-jacket pictures that knocked a decade off their age. My copy of *Freefall* had to be at least eighteen years old. I'd first bought it while an undergraduate at Bristol; now old and battered, its spine arched to the breaking point, it was one of the few books I had brought with me when I moved here. I squinted again at the tall, brooding figure, my excitement mounting.

It *had* to be him.

The lights changed, and he crossed the road, turning right along the row of brownstones. He walked for about twenty yards, then stopped in front of one of them, pushed open a gate, trotted up some stone steps, knocked on the door, then disappeared inside. I waited a few moments, then drew level with the building, one of those old Flemish brownstones the color of rust, fronted by a small narrow garden strewn with yellow leaves. A small gate, flanked by two stone lions, opened onto some stone steps leading up to a porticoed entranceway, with pillars on either side of a big white door. To one side of the door was a small mounted video camera next to a small copper plaque that read GRADUATE SCHOOL OF ARTS AND SCIENCES. But of *course*. It must be part of the university. He must be teaching here.

The door was buzzed open before I could put a hand to it; I pushed it open, to find a well-lit, modern-looking reception room, at one end of which sat a rather bored-looking security guard behind a desk mounted with video screens, his nose buried in the *Post*. Behind him on the wall was a big bulletin board adorned with flyers: 100 NIGHTS BEFORE COMMENCEMENT DINNER; CARIBBEAN FOOD FESTIVAL; BACK TO THE SQUARE. Approaching, I coughed into my hand and the newspaper lowered a few inches, revealing a neatly trimmed mustache and hooded eyes that radiated the casual insolence of uniformed authority.

"I'm sorry to bother you," I said. "But what *is* this place?"

He looked me up and down, then lowered his paper still farther, revealing a portly gut. "Graduate School of Arts and Sciences," he said gruffly.

"And that man who just came in—does he teach here?"

"Who?"

"The man who just came in," I said, pointing down the corridor.

He shook his head. "He's here for the meeting."

"What kind of meeting?"

"AA meeting."

"Ah."

"You coming in or going out?"

"Oh no, no, I was just curio—"

"Because if you're coming in, you gotta sign the book," he said, bringing a stubby finger down onto the visitors' log on the desk. I scanned the list of names: Godfrey S., Brian L., Prudence K., Douglas K. . . .

Douglas K.

It *was* him.

Behind me, a buzzer sounded. The guard leaned under his desk, pressed something, and three girls spilled through the front door, buoyed aloft on a boisterous wave of laughter. They were about college age, two of them little Britney clones in fur-lined parka jackets and pastel-colored UGG boots, chewing on gum in tandem, like squirrels.

". . . right there in the cafeteria," one was saying.

"Did he put it back?" asked her twin.

"No! It was sitting there on his tray!"

A throaty laugh from the third girl caught the attention of the guard, who set down his newspaper and smiled. She was taller than the other two and a little older, wearing a thrift-storish overcoat in a fawn herringbone pattern, with brown fingerless mittens and a mauve scarf wrapped several times around her neck. Her hair, spilling over the sides, was dark brown or black—I couldn't quite tell which—her skin pale, her cheeks flushed from the cold. I'd gotten into trouble with Caitlin, saying girls weren't wearing makeup when they were, but if this girl was, it was minimal: eyeliner, maybe lip gloss. She was beautiful, but it wasn't an obvious, upfront kind of beauty; it was sleepy, even a little sly, slow to register but once it had, you couldn't take your eyes off her.

"Hey there, Lola, how you doin' today?" The guard beamed.

"A lot better, thanks, Henry," she said, reaching the desk. "I am *so* sorry about yesterday."

"You gotta do what you gotta do," said the guard. "My wife is always telling me to let it all *out*. She says, 'You keep it in, you're gonna get cancer. You gotta let it *out*.' "

"I certainly did that," she said with a wince. "What about you? You booked those flights yet?"

"Uh-huh." He nodded. "Found my Speedos in the closet. Got them all laid out on the bed, ready to go."

"Speedos!" She laughed. "You want trunks below the knee. They don't want to be seeing your knobbly knees in Hawaii."

"Not even when they're knees as pretty as these?" asked the guard, hoisting up his trouser to reveal a few inches of pale, hairy ankle.

"Eww . . ." said one of the Britney twins.

"Even when they're knees as pretty as those," said the girl, laughing and reaching for the pen to sign her name in the log-book, tucking her hair behind her ear as she did so. I stood there, lightly stunned. *She* was an alcoholic? I had no idea they made them so beautiful. It stood to reason, I guessed, but still. When had she fitted it all in?

"I'm sorry—did I butt ahead of you?" she asked, offering me the pen. Her eyes, I saw, were a deeply striated hazel.

"Oh no," I stammered. "I'm not . . . I'm just . . . I'm on my lunch break. I'm not really supposed to be here at all, in fact. I, uh, I saw someone I recognized on the street. Someone I hadn't seen in a while. So I followed him in. I hadn't seen him in a while and I just wondered what he was up to. These days. But he's gone now. So I might as well go, too."

Christ. Pull yourself together, Patrick. She's just an alcoholic. A beautiful alcoholic. She isn't going to bite.

"Someone you know?" she asked, cocking her head, her hair pooling over the side of her scarf. "Do you want to come in and say hello?"

"Oh no, no, no, no," I said quickly, backing off a little. "I wouldn't want to bother him. I mean, I know him, but I don't know him that well. Not personally."

"You don't know him personally?"

"No. Not to speak to. If you know what I mean."

"Oh, I think I know what you mean," she said, exchanging a look with her friends. "*That* kind of friend. Well, tell him there's always a seat for him here if he wants it. As long as he doesn't throw it at anyone. Henry doesn't like it when that happens, do you, Henry?"

"Nope," said the security guard, crossing his arms, his old grumpiness returning.

"Although you don't *look* like the chair-throwing type," she said, looking me up and down.

"Actually, no, I'm not. I'm not a chair thrower. Extremely law-abiding. A rule follower, not a rule breaker. I straighten out piles of books in bookshops. I join the end of any queue, even ones I'm not trying to get to the front of."

She looked at me, a smile dawning. "Well, if you ever feel like unwinding, there's a seat for you if you want it. I'm sorry. For your *friend,* if he wants it."

"C'mon, Lola, we're going to lose our seats," said one of the Britney twins.

She looked back at me and gave a shrug. "Well, it was nice talking to you," she said, hoisting her bag on her shoulder.

"Tell me something," I said. "You meet here every day, do you?"

"Monday through Friday."

"And you have regulars? I mean, you get the same people coming back day after day."

"It can get a little old," she said, lowering her voice. "Take it from me."

"Lola," said both twins together.

"I'm *coming,"* she said, then to me: "Gotta go."

"Bye," I said uselessly as she turned and made her way down the hall, her two friends taking up flanking positions on either side of her, lowering their heads to whisper. They reached the end of the corridor and disappeared through a white door with a thin chicken-wire window, leaving the guard and me in that awkward silence that descends on any two men who have been abandoned by their womenfolk—our source of sunlight, laughter, and swimming-trunk advice now gone. He grunted and picked up his paper. I turned back in the direction of the door, but as I pulled it open, someone pushed from the other side, and our combined force yanked him inside with a surprised yelp. He bounced off me, took a step back, then started dusting himself down, like a cat repairing its pride after a fall. He was short and scruffy, with multiple layers of clothing and dark curly hair of the sort you find sprouting from the tops of chess prodigies or Russian violinists; I could have sworn I saw a small piece of jigsaw puzzle lodged in the thick of it, just above his right ear. He continued to dust down his jacket, saying nothing.

"I'm sorry," I said. "I didn't see you coming."

"It's okay," he said, still not meeting my eye. He pointed outside. "Be careful of that top step."

"I will," I said.

"Something is not right with it."

"Thanks for the tip."

He pulled his jacket down, like a woman adjusting her skirt, and strode off. I stood there, puzzled, for a while—what an odd bird—before heading out the door. As I did so, I heard a wave of laughter, then applause from the room at the end of the corridor. What on earth did *they* have to laugh about? Poor bastards. I hurried down the leaf-strewn steps, grateful for my freedom.

chapter four

I FOUND SAUL IN his office, feet up on his desk, the pages of a manuscript in one hand, a pen in the other. His door was open.

"Ah. Mr. Miller," he said. "The baker."

"Are you busy?"

"Just going over these proofs," he said, waving me in and taking his feet off the desk. "Please."

His desk was even more of a mess than usual: all the pens, staplers, and stationery pushed into the corners to make way for unbound proofs for a book of his called *Voltaire's Wig,* which tracked down the human capacity for optimism to some frontal lobe or cortex. Normally, I envied Saul his home-court advantage for the pulse of his people, but I thought him a little off on this one. The headlines in the *New York Times* these days read like a series of END OF DAYS placards: melting ice caps, home foreclosures, whale infanticides, shopping-mall abductions. I had to say I rather liked this new mood of national despair—it reminded me of Britain under John Major—but the time did not seem to be right for a book telling everyone to think pink and snap out of it.

"How was your brunch with Ian?" he asked.

"A complete waste of time. But you'll never guess who I saw on the way back."

He delved into the rubble of his desk and extracted a green apple. "Janet Jackson?"

"Douglas Kelsey."

His eyebrows rose gratifyingly. "*Really* . . . Where'd you see him?"

"Down at Washington Square," I said excitedly. "I wasn't sure it *was* him at first. He looked a little older, a little grayer, he'd grown a beard. But it was definitely him. Wasn't he supposed to be upstate somewhere, working on a book?"

"Yes, he was. Just outside Woodstock," he said, taking a bite out of the apple. "Until he got doorstepped by Random House's lawyers."

"Doorstepped? What are you talking about?"

"He ran off with his advance," he said through a mouthful of apple. "They had to sue to get it back."

"No."

He nodded. "They'd been waiting for—what? Over ten years. Long past the due date. It got pretty ugly. He started leaving abusive messages on his editor's phone—challenged him to a fistfight is what I heard."

I lowered myself into the chair opposite his desk. "You're kidding me."

"Where have you been, Patrick?"

"What do you mean, where have I been? I've been in London. We don't get so much of the gossip back there."

"This wasn't gossip. It made the front page of the *Times.* His agent had to fire him."

"Who's his agent?"

"Chris Kantor, over at ICM."

"I don't know him."

"Her. She said he went a little loopy up there in his log cabin. All alone in the woods. All work and no play makes Jack a dull boy. Don't you love it when the big ones turn out to be fruitcakes?"

"I used to love his stuff," I said defensively. "I must have read *Freefall* a dozen times when I was back in college. *A Low Moon Over Idaho*. And *The Grenadiers* . . . what a terrific book that was."

"One couple tearing each other apart for four hundred pages?"

"Not every book can be an Oprah book, Saul."

He rolled his eyes. "There he goes. Have you actually read one of Oprah's books, Patrick?"

"No," I said, stiffening my spine, "but I know what I'd be in for if I did."

"Oh yeah? And what's that?"

I looked out the window, knit my brow, and summoned the ghost of the one *Oprah* show I had actually watched, several years before. "Buried traumas . . . sunsets . . . grandmothers . . . quilt making."

"Quilt making!"

"Proud sexual acts."

" 'Proud sexual acts.' And what sort do you prefer?"

"The unproud sort, of course."

He laughed. "So did you speak to the great man? Or was he too busy thinking great thoughts?"

"No. He just crossed Washington Square and then I lost him."

He looked at me for a few seconds, as if sensing my lie. "Shame," he said finally. "I know a lot of people who would like to know where that man is right now."

"Next time," I said.

"Next time," he said absentmindedly, still looking at me oddly.

"Where'd you get the apple?" I asked, getting up to go.

"Natalie didn't give you one?"

"No. Natalie gave you an *apple*?"

"Yeah."

"Huh."

"Anything the matter?"

"*I* didn't get one. What's that about, do you think?"

He thought about it. "I think she only gives them to the agents who can pull their head out of their ass for long enough to see that they are in the business of selling books. As opposed to running a homeless shelter for eighties burnouts. Now if you don't mind, I've got some work to do. . . ."

I'm not sure why I didn't tell Saul the whole truth about where I'd seen Kelsey. I felt embarrassed for him, I guess, also a little protective. His secret felt like my secret, somehow. That's how his work had always felt to me, like the most velveteen of secrets, to be jealously guarded and yielded up to strangers only after careful cross-examination to make sure a welcome audience was assured. He wasn't to everyone's taste. There are two sorts of writers, I've found: the kind who inspires a loose affection, such that when you find out someone doesn't like him, you think slightly less of the writer. Not quite as universal in his appeal as I thought, you say to yourself, nodding sagely and tucking him back into the bookshelf. Then there's the kind of writer who inspires the type of fierce loyalty that borders on a blood oath, so that when you find out someone doesn't like him, you instantly think worse of the someone. Douglas Kelsey was *that* kind of writer. You would hesitate to call him a cult writer, exactly—not with the whiff of patchouli oil carried by that phrase, and certainly not once you learned of his fierce disdain for the seventies, for hippies, drugs, or anything that smacked of the counterculture—but he was the next best thing: a writer's writer, the writer the other writers deferred to and defended, whose neglect they sought to explain in tones ranging from the gently perplexed to the straightforwardly outraged. Some writers cut just a little too close to the bone, they would say. Truth telling doesn't win you popularity contests. His fans wouldn't have had it any other way, of course. For us, the shortfall between Kelsey and his reputation—between his reputation and the place where his reputation ought by rights to be—created a febrile shadowland in which our advocacy could flourish, like mushrooms under a rock.

I'd first come across his work at Bristol, where I was supposed to be studying English literature but instead spent most of my time boning up on proper, living, breathing writers—which is to say, Americans. My best friend, Hugo Davenport, and I would meet up regularly to exchange recommendations and pore over whatever U.S. editions we'd managed to lay our hands on, passing them furtively across the table like samizdat, marveling over their intriguingly Decoish cover designs and interesting ragged pagination—these books looked like they had been ripped from the printers, just as their contents seemed to have been ripped from their authors' chests. To Hugo and I, the superiority of American fiction over the homegrown stuff was one of those facts of life that needed no explanation or elaboration, but if pushed, we might have said something to the effect that Americans tended to write more about real people, in real situations, doing real things, saying and doing stuff that sounded and looked real. The word *real* would definitely have figured prominently. To us, *real* meant waitresses and rodeo riders, checkout clerks and steel workers, returning every night to their trailer homes and subdivisions, where they argued with their wives and drank too much beer and sank into their La-Z-Boy recliners, lit by the ghostly blue illumination of the game shows on TV. You just couldn't write that in England. It was just a story about a person who worked at Tesco and watched too much telly. American reality was just *better* than English reality. Admittedly, neither of us had any direct experience of American reality. We had never worked in a steel mill, or shopped at a Kmart, or reclined in a La-Z-Boy, and for a while we weren't sure how a La-Z-Boy differed from a tall boy—what was with the boys? But that was just it. These stories were more than just the sum of their details. In the right hands, they amounted to anguished howls against the numbing banality of mass-market consumerism, tear-stained songlines sent up from behind the white picket fences of suburban conformity. Hugo and I were a little divided as to which of these two ogres posed the greater threat to Western civilization—the numbing banality of mass-market consumerism or the white picket fences of suburban conformity—but both agreed that if one of those mothers didn't put you down, the other was certain to finish you off.

One night in our second year, sitting in the darkened back room of the Bristol Ram, where we always met, nursing our pints, Hugo slipped a slim novella across the table toward me. "I think you're going to like this," he said simply.

It was a short book, but only in the sense that a walk off a cliff is short. The action covered a single weekend in the life of a Madison Avenue ad executive named Frank Leary. Leary spends Friday getting fired, Saturday getting drunk, and Sunday failing to tear himself away from an NFL play-off in time to attend the funeral of his father, a test pilot and vicious drunk, whose shadow he has struggled to escape all his life. The book begins with a bravura set piece in which Leary, as part of a team-building exercise, participates in a corporate skydive, free-falling from a plane at ten thousand feet, the Massachusetts countryside rushing up to meet him, providing the book with a vertiginous image of a man in moral and psychological freefall. It wasn't the book's plot that held you in thrall so much as its tone—alternately tender and self-lacerating, haggard and heartbroken. "Leary is a classic American malcontent," said the *New York Times* in the blurb quoted on the back jacket, "half in love with the disappointment that besets his outsized dreams, lashing out at the world with wounded scorn before turning his laser-powered insight loose on his own tattered pose of rebellion. Laughter in the dark if ever I heard it."

Turning his laser-powered insight loose on his own tattered pose of rebellion. Reading that phrase, I felt something click into place deep inside of me, like a vertebra snapping back into place. So *that's* what I'd been doing all these years. It just *looked* as if all I'd been doing was studying and getting straight As and winning school prizes and cramming to get into university. It wasn't that I lacked a rebellious streak; I'd just seen through it earlier than most. I eagerly pressed the book on my girlfriend at the time, a freckly economics undergraduate named Anabel, and waited patiently as she made her way through it. Had she gotten to the bit where Leary is arrested for disorderly conduct at the football game? Was she at the bit where Leary finally pries loose the "python of hatred" from around his heart? Or had she reached the climax, where he flees the city, only to get embroiled in an argument with a tollbooth attendant on the Tappan Zee Bridge, a queue of frustrated commuters sending up an angry concerto of horns into the dusk air? Finally, over breakfast one morning, my curiosity got the better of me.

"Finished what?" she asked.

"That book I gave you."

"Oh *that,*" she said, munching toast. "It was a bit of a slog, but I got there in the end."

The thing that had clicked into place deep inside of me came unclicked again. " 'A slog,' " I said, ashen.

"It was just so *depressing.* He hates his wife. Hates his father. Hates his job. He hates *everything.* I couldn't see the point."

"But that *is* the point."

"That he hates everything?"

"But he hates himself more than he hates anyone else. That's the python. Don't you see?"

"Well, that makes two of us then," she said breezily. "I like the dust-jacket photo, though. He reminds me of my brother. I want to give him a cuddle and tell him everything's going to be okay."

At which point, I left the cadre of fans who feel Kelsey's work to be unfairly neglected, and joined the cadre of Kelsey fans who suspect they know why his work is unfairly neglected and feel it connecting up to some deep part of their central nervous system that is best not exposed to the eyes of unsympathetic girlfriends. A cuddle. Good Lord. You didn't peer into the abyss, have the abyss peer back at you, and then climb back down the side of Mount Doom with glad tidings of great joy. You didn't buy Holden Caulfield a puppy and tell him things would seem better in the morning. No, you subjected the world to an all-devouring inferno of such white-hot intensity that you emerged from the other end clutching nothing but ash and embers, and *those* you got to sift for the last vestiges of human hope. Okay, so he wasn't going to be the easiest man to make small talk with once you got to the front of the book-signing queue—what were you going to say? "Um, could you put 'To Binty with love?' "—but then, I didn't have any friends named Binty, and if I had, I would happily have lost them for a book as good as *Freefall*.

I'd caught the book in its second reprint; originally published in 1983, it had been nominated for a Pulitzer, I later found, and optioned for a movie by Oliver Stone, but the Pulitzer went to Alice Walker's *The Color Purple* and Stone let the option slip to make *Talk Radio* instead. It was over ten years before his next full-length work of fiction, 1997's *The Grenadiers*, by which time I was nearing the end of my first year at Smith and Fairfax, where I was up to my armpits in celebrity cookbooks and coffee-table books about pugs. *The Grenadiers* told the story of an American couple vacationing in Europe in an attempt to revitalize their marriage, tormenting each other in a variety of crumbling three-star hotels ("Why do you let a man like that get the better of you, Dick?") before grinding each other to a fine pulp at the San Daniele in Venice. The book was pounded by American critics, one calling it "an accomplished minor novel, from a writer one suspects of systemically denying himself major possibilities"; another said it was "the kind of book that causes people to get divorced." It was better received in Europe, where the book's gloom took on a more lustrous glow; to me, even the book's failure seemed noble somehow, its ragged, unevenly fulfilled ambitions worth a hundred more tidy, well-behaved books. Thereafter, nothing more was heard of him. He refused to do any more book readings or interviews, and was rumored to have holed up in a log cabin somewhere just outside Woodstock to work on his long-awaited third novel, but it never materialized. Each year, his publishers, ever hopeful, announced it in their catalog, and each year it reliably failed to appear. Kelsey seemed to disappear behind the same fulminous cloud of silence that envelops only the very greatest literary talents—Salinger, Pynchon—leaving the rest of us poor, miserable specks of humanity to scrutinize their silence for clues as to what it was we had done wrong. Was it something we did? Something we said?

Leafing through the press cuttings on LexisNexus that afternoon, I was shocked to find much more than I'd expected, particularly from the early part of his career, in the mid-seventies, when he studied creative writing at Santa Cruz under the legendary Raymond Carver. All the other students used to sit around on the floor, smoking joints, their hair long, reading their latest work: muted, minimalist short stories with titles like "Do You Mind If I Smoke?" and "What Do You Want to Talk About?" When it was Kelsey's turn, he read a short story of his entitled "Tomato Soup," about a couple who, on the opening night of their new restaurant, serve tomato soup to a man who the very next day goes on a murderous rampage in the local high school, killing four students and two teachers before turning the gun on himself.

Silence enveloped the class.

"Well, I'm glad you got that story out of the way," said Carver finally, to laughter.

"The harshest words he ever said to me," Kelsey told the literary journal *Quarry West*. (The story later appeared in his short-story collection, *A Low Moon Over Idaho*, the only work of fiction to be found on the bookshelves of Theodore Kaczynski (aka the Unabomber). There was a large swell of articles in 1983, when *Freefall* was published, including a belligerent interview he gave to *Time* magazine, entitled "Kelsey Asks: Where's the Beef?"—in which he ragged on his contemporaries for what he called their "literary anemia," condemning "all these constipated stories in which someone turns off the TV and that's the story," a comment many took to be a swipe at his old tutor, Carver—but then the articles dried up. A few cuts from the trades, but that was about it. The last article in the file was from the *New York Times* and dated April 26, 2006.

> Random House has launched a lawsuit against Pulitzer-nominated Douglas Kelsey for the return of a $300,000 advance, first paid to the author in 1995 for his third novel. "As his publisher of more than twenty years, we are very sorry it has come to this," said Bernard Ableman, a lawyer representing Random House. "We have extended Mr. Kelsey every opportunity to fulfill his contractual obligations and now have a right to defend our interests." The lawsuit was filed on Monday at New York's supreme court, following several months of negotiation, during which neither party was able to come to an agreement regarding the delivery date of Mr. Kelsey's third novel, reportedly a sequel to his 1983 novel, *Freefall*. Originally slated to appear in 2000, the book has appeared in the Vintage catalog every year for the last six years. "It's

long-awaited, like Ahab's whale was long-awaited," said one publicist at Random House, who wished to remain anonymous. "It surfaces every so often to clear its blowhole and then disappears." Mr. Kelsey's agent, Christine Kantor, of International Creative Management, denies that her client has violated his contract, saying only that there was a "disagreement with Random House that we hoped would be resolved without litigation." Mr. Kelsey could not be reached for comment.

I found the whole thing mystifying. I knew the statistics of course—five of America's nine Nobel laureates in Literature had been drunks—but Kelsey just didn't seem the type. He hadn't been found wandering the hallways of the Algonquin naked. He hadn't rolled champagne bottles down Fifth Avenue beneath the light of a wanton moon. He hadn't gotten into the kind of bar fights that made a man feel truly alive. He hadn't murdered his wife or joined the Hell's Angels or run for mayor or any of the extracurricular stuff with which authors traditionally jazzed up their bios. If anything, he gave off a parsimonious, almost priestly aura. In another life, he might easily have been a Quaker. Returning to my apartment that evening, I got down my copy of *The Grenadiers* and flicked to the back. There he was, staring out from his jacket photo with his usual look of hounded scorn.

Douglas Kelsey was born in Minneapolis. He is the author of two novels, *Freefall* and *The Grenadiers,* and one short-story collection, *A Low Moon Over Idaho.* He has been the recipient of many prizes and awards, including a Lannan Fellowship, the Pen/Faulkner Award, and the Ordre des Arts et des Lettres from the Académie Française. He lives in upstate New York.

By the time I got to the end of it, I had made a decision. I was going back to that meeting on Washington Square.

chapter five

ACCORDING TO *PEOPLE* MAGAZINE, Courtney Love credited Mel Gibson with her sobriety. "Mel kept coming to the door with this cheesy grin, going, 'Hi!'" Love said. "I just kept looking at him, going, 'Fuck off!' . . . I know him and he's a nice guy, but it just didn't matter who it was. It could have been Jesus. I didn't care." Huh. I put the magazine back on the table in reception, picked up another, and started leafing through it, much as you do before a visit to the dentist. Colin Farrell had started phone-dating Kate Moss while in rehab in Miami, it said. "Since they're both working on their sobriety, they completely understand the struggle," said a rep. "Plus, they both happen to be very attracted to each other." Lindsay Lohan had also met her latest boyfriend in rehab, a snowboarder who had broken parole by driving drunk in Vegas; they were found making out in the stairwell. "Am with sober friends and feel good ☺ here now wearing marc jacobs pumps and a kate and kass dress," she text-messaged GQ magazine. "Vintage chanel messenger and topshop tights and peace sign earrings from kaviar & kind."

It didn't sound too bad to me. Obviously, you had to give up booze: That had to be pretty intolerable. But the rest of it—the recovery part, the hookups in rehab, the invitations to go on *Oprah* and talk about your struggle—that wasn't too bad. I wondered what it was—what prissy instinct for self-preservation—held me back from a life of balls-to-the-walls addiction. I'd certainly given it my best shot. You were alcoholic just by virtue of being British, of course. All you had to do was propose a nice end-of-week bender, or refuse to go home at eleven because you didn't actually have a gym to get up early for in the morning, and eyebrows were raised here. Nice as it was to receive a compliment, I was really nothing special. Half the job of literary agent consisted of squiring my authors around town while they drank themselves under the table. If anything, I was a paltry example of the species. Once, I was offered a line of cocaine in the Groucho Club by a young British novelist, a client of mine, whose unimpeachably squalid depictions of the London gutter had, for a while, perplexed critics, until he revealed in a *Sunday Telegraph* interview that he had spent his time at Oxford not studying philosophy but mainlining heroin, or, more accurately, a mixture of both. After that, the critics knew exactly what to do with his work: They called it "engrossingly bleak," "monumentally brutal," and "unflinching in its severity." There you go. I was too much of a flincher. I flinched too much. I said no to the cocaine, of course, and then had to sit there for two hours while the idiot raved on at me about Hegel. Everyone knew that drug addicts were deeper people—seers, saints, soothsayers of the human condition—but it put a different complexion on things when it was your job to get them up in the morning, make sure they got to their reading on time, and then comfort them when not enough people turned up. There were two types of men on this Earth, I had concluded: the men who got up in the morning to shrug off their hangovers and pound away at novels that got called "bleak," "brutal," and "unflinching" and the types of men whose job it was to make sure that "unflinching" was spelled correctly on their dust jackets.

Hearing the key in the lock, I turned to see Natalie letting herself in, clutching some shopping bags. She didn't notice me, just closed the door and was almost at her desk when she saw me and stopped, bolt upright.

"Patrick," she said, surprised. "What are *you* doing down here?"

"Just catching up on my reading," I replied, letting the magazine fall to the table.

She peered over my shoulder. "In *People* magazine?"

I got up to help her. "There's a lot of good stuff in there actually. Lindsay Lohan has ninety days sober. Did you know that?"

"Good for her," said Natalie as I took one of the bags from her. "Thanks. Put it over there, would you?"

She nodded toward the small kitchenette underneath the staircase. We both made our way over to the counter by the sink and began unpacking: orange juice, water, coffee, Oreos, but none of the apples Saul had mentioned. "She seems a lot happier now," I said.

"Who does?"

"Lindsay Lohan."

"We're still with Lindsay, are we?"

"She hooked up with this snowboarder in rehab. They were caught making out in the stairwell."

"So?"

I brought out a bottle of Perrier water and placed it on the counter. "Sounds like she's enjoying herself."

"I'm sure she is. A friend of mine got sober a few years ago."

"Really?" I said, looking at her. "How'd she find it?"

She made a face. "I don't know. . . . What a question. Better now that she's conscious?"

"Of course."

"She's a lot more grounded. Centered. She's a great listener. Gives great advice." She continued to unpack.

"Unflinching?"

She frowned. "I don't know if that's the word I'd use."

"You know . . . unvarnished. Straight to the point. Almost brutally so. Gritty. Unflinching."

She shook her head. "No, not really. She's really a lot sweeter to be around."

"Huh," I said, bored. "And that's supposed to be an improvement, is it?"

She stopped unpacking. "It's a disease, Patrick. Not a lifestyle choice. She didn't get sober because she fancied a change. She got sober because otherwise she would have died."

"Of course," I said quickly. "Absolutely. I know that. It's a disease. Everyone knows that. It's definitely the one you want, though."

"The one what?"

"Disease."

"Patrick."

"I'm just saying. If you had to pick a disease, that would be the one to pick. Better than leprosy anyway, or rabies. It's the one the most celebrities seem to get."

"Patrick. It's hell."

"Of course it's hell. Everyone knows that. But afterward, after it's hell. Look what happens then."

"What happens then?"

"You know. You write a book about it, go on *Oprah*. Kate Moss rings you up. . . . If I had rabies, and rabies sufferers even had support groups, which I doubt, but if they did, I don't think I would be getting Kate Moss ringing me up asking to be my best friend."

"What's Kate Moss got to do with anything?"

"Or Mel Gibson. If I had leprosy, I do not think I would have Mel Gibson breaking down my door to be my new best friend."

"You don't think?" she said, smiling.

"Not if I had bits of me falling off, no."

"Not the kind of first impression you like to go for."

"Not really, no."

"Don't you have somewhere to be?"

"I'm sorry?"

"Don't you have places to go, people to see?"

I looked at the clock on the wall: 12:20 P.M.

"Actually," I said, picking up a granola bar and pocketing it, "I do."

The meeting was nothing like I had been expecting. I don't know what I'd been expecting exactly—a roomful of old men in dirty macs, sitting in a circle, smoking furiously. Every now and again one of them would make a run for the door, and the others would rugby-tackle him to the floor, shouting, "It's not worth it, Dave! It's not worth it!" It wasn't like that. The room was spacious and light, like a small art gallery, with bay windows that looked out onto the back lots of the buildings opposite, like Jimmy Stewart's view in *Rear Window*. There were about forty or fifty people in the room; all sat facing the window in two blocks of plastic chairs with an aisle that ran down the middle toward a woman—middle-aged, gabardine coat, gray coiffed hair—who was telling a story about taking her cat to the vet. She didn't have insurance so she'd had to call up her ex-husband to help out with the cost. She'd hated doing it but the cat was her only dependent now, so she'd made the call. "What he thinks of me is less important than the fact that Quincy receives the care she needs," she said. "That was the right thing to do. The sober thing to do."

The room clucked its agreement, everyone's heads bobbing up and down, as I found a seat near the back. Any awkwardness I felt at being there was quickly dispelled by the sheer banality of what I was hearing: Now the woman was thanking the group for the willingness to make the call to her husband. She had prayed for the willingness—or had she prayed for the willingness to be willing? Either way, I couldn't see why they bothered making these meetings open to the public. No one in their right mind would ever want to listen in. I settled into my seat and started looking around the room for Kelsey. I saw a guy in a pinstriped suit and a winter tan with a Bergdorf bag; a big fat black guy in head-to-toe denim wrapped in a mauve Yasser Arafat scarf; a rail-thin woman with a mane of blond hair and bright red talons; some thickset guys who looked like they'd just driven over from New Jersey; a teenager with a floppy blond Mohawk, jabbing away at the video game on his phone. How could *he* be an alcoholic? He looked barely old enough to get served in a bar. I couldn't see Kelsey anywhere. I was just about to give up and head back to the office, when I heard a female voice from the front.

"My name is Lola and I'm an alcoholic."

"Hi, Lola," the room answered in unison.

How had I missed her? I lowered myself back into my seat. She sat halfway down the central aisle, her legs crossed. Her hair was up today, in one of those messy makeshift buns that girls sometimes do, held together with a pencil or elastic band, with loose locks of hair hanging against the white of her neck. Bent forward slightly, she seemed preoccupied with something she had in her lap.

"It's a great topic," she said. "I was *definitely* the last to know. I didn't think I had an alcohol problem. I thought I had a job problem. I kept losing them. Or a boss problem. They kept firing me. This one guy, he wakes me up one afternoon. 'Where the hell are you, Lola?' So I told him I'd been abducted. I told him I'd been abducted and was being held against my will somewhere in New Jersey and could he please get help. . . . He fired me on the spot. He'd called me on my landline."

Laughter filled the room. She shifted in her seat, her left hand reaching out to tug on something—a piece of string of some sort leading down to the bag at her feet—and continued.

"There was nothing special about my last day, nothing special at all. I went to a bar, picked up this guy, woke up the next morning in the middle of God knows where. Looked out the window, didn't know where I was. I'd forgotten to shave my legs. That was always my insurance, you see. Not shaving my legs, because then there'd be no way I'd go home with someone. It never worked. So I sneak into this guy's bathroom and all he has is this old razor—you know, the ones with the blades you insert—so I try to use that, but all I succeed in doing is cutting myself to ribbons. So I'm sitting there in this guy's bathtub—I don't know who he is, or where I am—and I'm bleeding all over the place and suddenly I just stop. I just stop dead. Like someone yanked my batteries out."

The room went very quiet. I would have said it was fairly quiet before, but this was something else again, like a team of audio technicians had sneaked in and removed all the ambient noise in the room.

"I start to cry. And once I start, I can't stop. Because this was not the life I had envisaged for myself when I came here, you know? Not covered in blood in some stranger's bathtub in effing Red Hook or wherever the hell I was."

Some female laughter from the front—sisterly, supportive, or maybe they were just from Red Hook. A strand of hair fell forward into her face; she pushed it back behind her ear, then returned her hand to her lap, where she wound some green wool around her little finger and brought her needles together. *Click-click. Click-click. Click-click. That's* what she was doing. She was *knitting.*

"I got back to the city, went straight to my first meeting, and I haven't had a drink since. I haven't slept with any strangers. I haven't cut my legs up with someone else's razor. I haven't woken up in Red Hook without meaning to. I love my life now. I had no idea it even existed, and I wouldn't change it for the world. . . ."

I felt a tug on my sleeve, and glanced around to find the scruffy little fellow I'd almost run into the day before. He'd scooted up to sit right beside me. His hair sported no pieces of jigsaw today, but he was dressed in more layers of clothing than I'd ever seen on a human being: black peacoat, sweatshirt, shirt, sweater, T-shirt, and those weren't his pajamas under there, were they? He looked like he'd been dressed by a team of overzealous mothers, except that every item of his clothing was about two sizes too big.

"How much time do you have?" he whispered.

"I'm sorry?" I whispered back.

"How much *time* do you have?"

I looked at my watch. "Quarter to one?"

He rolled his eyes like a child being sarcastic. "How much *sober* time do you have?"

"Oh, I'm not sober," I said, sitting bolt upright, offended. "I'm looking for someone. This meeting is open to the public, right?"

"This meeting?" He nodded vigorously. "Yes. Last month we had these students come by to take notes. They were writing their end-of-term papers on us. Me, actually. But then Godfrey brought it up at the business meeting—he said the only people allowed to attend an AA meeting were the alkies. Then Douglas said that if we looked at what the book *actually* said, what the book *actually* said was the only requirement for membership was—"

"Hang on," I said, interrupting him. "Douglas. You mean Douglas Kelsey? The writer."

"Big Doug. Sits at the back. Doesn't like pet talk."

"Pet talk?"

He nodded at the woman who had first spoken, the one in gabardine who'd told the story about her cat. "He can't stand it when they talk about their pets. 'This is supposed to be a fucking AA meeting,' he goes."

As his voice swelled in volume, it caught the attention of the girl sitting directly in front of us, a plump red-haired Goth, who swung around, glared at us through kohl-rimmed eyes, then turned back to the front. My new friend glared back at her, then started tweazling a forelock of his hair between his fingers.

"He doesn't seem to be here today," I whispered.

"No. I'm a writer, too, actually. You know that thing where people say 'what-*ever*'?"

"Whatever?"

"No. Where it goes up at the end—what-*ever.*"

I nodded.

"That was me," he said proudly.

"You . . . came up with the word *whatever*?"

"No. Where it goes *up at the end*. What-*ever.*"

The Goth girl turned around and rested a white elbow on the back of her seat. "Do you think you could talk a little louder please?" she hissed. "Some of us are trying to get sober in here. . . ."

We both stared at the back of her seat and lowered our heads like chastised schoolboys. "Don't mind her," he whispered, extending a hand. "I'm Felix."

"Patrick," I whispered, shaking it. It was warm and a little clammy.

"I like your watch."

"Thanks," I said, beginning to lever myself up out of my seat. "Listen, it's been great talking to you, Felix, but I'd better be going."

"Had enough already?"

"Pretty much."

As I stood up, his eyes followed me up, widening, his face

wearing the expression of a six-year-old boy who had just been told that the Earth's gravity was for losers and that real kids took trips to the moon when the mood took them.

Getting back to the office, I felt strangely unclean, adulterous even, creeping up the stairs carefully to avoid the slight squeak you got when you trod in the middle. Reaching the top, I saw Saul talking to someone at the end of the corridor, by the watercooler just outside Leo's office, and felt a warm lap of relief. At the very least I could get a laugh out of the whole thing. ". . . hard to say," he was saying as I approached. "Two, three years tops? He's not going to be hanging around for too much longer, but I don't think we can count him out just yet. You've seen him with that red pencil; he's still got it—" He saw me and turned. "Hey there, Patrick."

"You'll never guess where I've just been," I said, drawing near.

Saul thought about it. "The Neverland Ranch."

"One more guess."

He gave me an imploring look. "You're not really going to make me do this, are you?"

"Okay, you remember when I came back from brunch with Ian? Well. I didn't tell you the whole truth. What actually happened was I— *Oh* . . ."

Rounding the corner, I saw who it was Saul was talking to and the words died in my throat. My least favorite agent at the firm, Brad Greenwald, stood against the watercooler in one of his trademark pinstriped suits, in a position I knew to be his "You have my complete attention" pose, an effect undermined only by his habit of asking questions solely in order to hear the sound of his own voice.

"Hi, Brad," I said curtly.

"If it isn't the big man himself," said Brad, standing upright.

"Where have you been? We were about to draw straws on who should head down to Balthazar to get you."

"I wasn't at Balthazar."

"It's okay, you know. I'm a great believer in the old British lunch hour. You pad those expenses."

"I wasn't at lunch, either."

"So where were you?" asked Saul.

"Hmm?" I said, turning.

"Where were you?" he repeated.

Quickly, I rallied. "Oh, uh, I was just seeing Ian again to go over that book proposal I told you about?"

He nodded. "And?"

"He actually came up with this blinder of an idea."

"Oh yeah? What was it?"

"I said I would run it past you to see what you thought," I said, glancing nervously at Brad in the hopes he would go away.

"I'm all ears," said Saul, a puzzled smile on his face.

"Oh, it was nothing much," I said. "Just an idea for one of those microhistories. He wanted to write the history of applause."

"Applause?" said Saul doubtfully.

"Yes, you know. Like that one for dust. Except this one would be about applause. Something to do with the emperor Nero. He applauded himself. And then in Germany you can applaud and boo at the same time, apparently. At the opera. Don't you think? Round the whole thing up. Call it something like *Speak to the Hand*—"

"*Speak to the Hand*," said Brad with a snort of laughter.

"It's better than *Genghis Khan: CEO*," I snapped.

"No, no, no," he said, chuckling. "This is what I love about you, Patrick. I think I've gotten too jaded for this business, I really do. I used to be just like you, chasing down every lead, no matter how small. And now look at me." He splayed his hands. "Won't even get out of the office unless I know it's a sure six figures."

"Yeah, well, we can't all have such a fine eye for business manuals," I said, summoning my most withering tone. "It's a very demanding field." My irony went whizzing over his head, although out of the corner of my eye, I saw Saul smirk.

"I'm glad you see it that way, Patrick," said Brad, clapping his hands together. "Not a lot of people do. Well, this has been pleasant. But I should probably be getting back to my desk. I've got an auction to wind up."

"Send me that link, will you?" asked Saul.

"It's done," said Brad, turning on his heel and sauntering down the corridor with an exaggerated show of ease that suggested he knew all too well that he was being observed. I looked away, disgusted for my part in the whole performance, and then when he had disappeared into his office, I muttered, "What a prick."

"Awww," said Saul. "He's just being Brad."

"Did you hear him? 'I used to be just like you, chasing down every crumb from the big boys' table. One day you, too, will have all of this. . . .' "

"Come on. You must have come across guys like him in London."

"True," I said. "But sooner or later someone asks them how these book things work and then they're stumped."

He laughed and we began walking back toward our offices.

"What were you going to tell me?" he asked.

"What do you mean?"

"When you first came up to me. It looked like you were going to tell me something different. Not Ian's book idea. Something else. But then you saw Brad and decided against it."

"No, no, that was it."

"Are you sure?"

"Yes, I'm sure."

He let it go. "You fancy a drink at Hudson Bar and Books later?"

"Absolutely."
"Six?"
"Unless you crack first."

A few drinks with Saul always served to take the edge off things. Floating back to my apartment in a cocoon of boozy warmth later that evening, the city a soft blur of lights through the cab window, everything seemed just that little bit more doable. My job. Brad. New York. Kelsey. In my mind's eye, they all lined up like dominoes: get one and the others would fall. A client like Kelsey would silence Brad, impress Leo, and propel me through the ranks, with the force of a cork out of a champagne bottle. I thought back to the fugitive figure I had seen crossing Washington Square the day before, but all I could summon was a blurry glimpse of his retreating back. The girl on the other hand, Lola. Her I could see, tucking that lock of hair behind her ear, tugging on the ball of wool in her bag, the hypnotic little movements of her hands in her lap. I'd never seen such a pretty girl *knitting* before. It seemed almost penitential, like a nun's rosary beads—penance for past sins. Try as I might, though, I could not imagine her drinking. It was like one of those badly Photoshopped images in the tabloids: The image just didn't gel. It had almost been like she was talking about a wholly different person. I tried to picture her daily routine now and all I saw were lots of white bed linen, prayer mats, houseplants, and camomile tea, the only panic spike coming during her daily dash to a meeting and back, flattening herself against the wall as she passed her local liquor store. It wouldn't hurt to try that meeting again tomorrow. For Kelsey, obviously. She probably only dated snowboarders with a rap sheet as long as their arm, the cheekbones of Viggo Mortensen, and a penchant for whittling driftwood into small but meaningful tokens of their appreciation for Life's Bounteous Gifts. I failed on both fronts. I had neither misbehaved with sufficient abandon nor reformed myself with enough zeal. I was just trying to get home without being tripped up, or found out, just like everyone else.

chapter six

DOUGLAS KELSEY, PULITZER NOMINEE, winner of the Pen/Faulkner Award and the Ordre des Arts et des Lettres from the Académie Française, sat at the back of the room, next to a battered tin coffeepot. Behind him on the wall were hung a series of laminated cards bearing the inscriptions KEEP IT SIMPLE, EASY DOES IT, and FIRST THINGS FIRST in thick Gothic script. Possibly as part of his body's natural defenses against the encroachment of cliché, he had his eyes closed and was leaning back in his seat, his legs crossed, his arms folded, like an airline passenger trying to find the most comfortable spot. I was just wondering whether he really had fallen asleep, when he let out a loud bark of laughter—"*Ha!*"—at something the speaker had said.

The speaker was a stringy guy in his late forties: Peruvian-style woolen hat, with earflaps framing his long, craggy face, mauve CBGBs T-shirt cut off at the shoulders, with tattoos running up and down his forearms, like Iggy Pop. "I knew that normal people did not do that," he was saying. "I knew that normal people did not drink their own cologne at five in the morning with towels pinned up in the windows. I think I just thought, Well, you've been under a lot of stress at work, Brian; just keep an eye on that. Make sure it doesn't happen again." He rubbed his forehead. "Maybe if you just stay off the Chanel Pour Monsieur, everything will be okay again. . . ."

Laughter filled the room. There were more people here today—sixty, maybe seventy people. I'd taken a few more precautions this time, to avoid a repeat of yesterday's entanglement. I'd written my name in the visitors' book, underlining the word *visitor* twice, and found a seat well back from the others, by the door, with a wide swathe of linoleum separating me from the nearest recovering person. The only flaw in the plan, as was only now becoming apparent, was that I would have to sit through an entire meeting before I could speak to Kelsey. He looked as bored as I was. Accidentally, I caught the eye of the scruffy little guy who had tried to befriend me the day before. He gave me an awful little wave, which I returned, awfully, before making a primly censorious show of turning my attention back to the speaker.

"Most days I start off with a quick run-through of steps one, two, and three," he was saying now. "Just to get the channels flowing. I'll do a quick inventory if necessary, maybe a fourth step, possibly a fifth step if I really need to. And I'm living in ten, eleven, and twelve, of course, when I'm not cross-rotating six and seven. I'm just grateful for this simple program. 'A simple program for complicated people' is what my sponsor calls it. . . ."

Somewhere, someone's phone began to ring.

"I don't know where I'd be without it. Actually, that's not true. I know exactly where I'd be. Naked on the putt-putt golf course. Checking into the Chelsea Hotel with a crack pipe and a couple of hookers, turning my 'Yets' into a 'To Do' list. . . ."

People were looking around now, turning to their neighbors, looking for the phone, shaking their heads. I made an ostentatious show of looking around the room for the culprit, only to snare the eye of that scruffy fellow again, who this time was pointing to my feet. I looked away quickly.

"I may think I have problems now, but if I pick up a drink, then pretty soon my problems will be having puppies— I'm *sorry*. . . . But *whose phone is that?"*

The realization didn't come all at once. It was staggered, like a slow-motion car crash. It started somewhere in my stomach, then worked its way up to my chest, acquiring heat and force, before finally reaching my head, still caught in a feeble mime of looking around the room, and which now had to be put into reverse—nothing too fast, maybe some raised eyebrows to demonstrate dawning recognition—there you go—followed by a horrified stare at the coat folded at my feet—perfect, don't stare for long, keep it moving—and now the pièce de la résistance, a "Would you believe it?" shake of the head to accompany the sheer honking irony of the fact that of *course* the phone would have to be mine, because this sort of thing *only* happens to me. My hands, meanwhile, were a blur, scrambling for the coat at my feet, pulling my phone free, then jabbing at it, randomly, repeatedly, hitting anything, until finally, mercifully, the infernal ringing ceased.

For a few seconds I did nothing, just kept my head down and held my breath.

"I think my Higher Power's trying to tell me something," said the speaker, to scattered laughter. "Man, that was horrifying. To have you all listening to me, and then suddenly—gone." He snapped his fingers. "Like my opening night, all over again."

Everyone laughed, harder this time. Something in the room seemed to relax, and when I next looked up nobody seemed to be paying me the slightest bit of attention. The air was filled with upstretched arms, all jostling for attention. The speaker pointed to one—"Yes, Douglas"—and the sea of arms descended again.

"My name is Douglas and I'm a drunk" came a voice from over by the coffeepot.

"Hi, Douglas," the room went in unison.

His voice was low and unhurried—the voice of someone used to being listened to, with a gravelly undertow, like sand being kicked around by a wave. He paused before continuing, rubbing his eye sockets as if massaging himself awake.

"It's a good topic. You know, denial's a funny thing. Bill never mentions it, and now it's everywhere. I was watching CNN this morning. Bob Woodward had just said that thing about the White House in a state of denial about the war. You want to know what they said? They denied it." He let out a single bark of laughter. "Isn't that something? I'd like to have known who had his feet up on the desk when they let *that* one through. Probably the drunk."

People started to whisper. Kelsey leaned back in his chair, unconcerned, relaxing into it. "Did you see him on TV the other night, pleading with us? '*Please* give me more troops so I can stop this war. *Please.* I promise this time I can bring it to a close.' Typical alcoholic logic. Give me more so I can stop. Let me go out so I can come home. But then the whole war is white logic. You start the fight because the other guy was looking at you funny. That's preemptive war for you. It's a bar fight, with millions dead."

People were now shifting uncomfortably in their seats, whispering. There was palpable discomfort—or disapproval. It was hard to read.

"It's always the same. You put an alcoholic in the White House and the country's foreign policy goes in the crapper. It was the same with Nixon. Unwinnable wars against unknowable enemies. Because they're not fighting a war anymore. They're just shadowboxing their disease." His voice rose in volume. "We don't need an election in this country. We need a fucking intervention."

A deathly silence spread throughout the room. Kelsey noticed it, and crossed his arms.

"And I *know* I've just broken the tenth tradition or the second half of the sixth step, and Christ knows what else, but please. *Don't* come up to me after the meeting to tell me." He rubbed his forehead, the side of his face, his jaw. "I've been with my wife's attorney all morning. Going down this laundry list of every last thing I said and did, or didn't say and didn't do. 'Let go and let God,' someone told me in here. Let go and let God *what*? Isn't there a verb missing there? Please tell me this is not what it's come to. Pretending to find puns on the word *God* interesting while my wife's attorney takes me up the—"

"Time!" called out someone from the front.

"I'm out of *time?"* asked Kelsey incredulously.

The speaker tapped his watch.

"Well, that just about sums it up," he said, sitting back in his seat and shaking his head. "Thanks, everyone, for the little rays of sunshine you've all been today. Sunbeams for Jesus, every last one."

There were titters, followed by applause. The meeting was over, everyone breaking up into pockets of excited chatter, reaching for their coats, some hugging and high-fiving one another. The atmosphere was buzzed, like that of a wedding party or the audience after a taping of the Letterman show. Kelsey leaned down under his seat to pick up something and was obscured by the throng of bodies heading toward the exit. I got up and went to stand by the door, my coat over my arm. I soon found myself at the center of a noisy scrum of people, fanning out from the door in an unruly, slow-moving delta; taking a step back to get out of their way, I stood on someone's toe.

"Owww."

"I'm sorry," I said, turning to find the scruffy little guy, who was holding his right foot from the floor like an injured dog. "I didn't see you there."

"S'okay," he muttered. "Nobody ever does. It's fine. I don't mind. Sometimes I don't *want* to be seen. Do you ever think about that? That maybe I *like* being invisible?"

Over his shoulder, I could see Kelsey making his way over to us. "Look, listen, Felix—it is Felix, right?—I was just here to speak to someone, so I can't really talk to you right now."

"I'll speak to you. *I'm* someone."

"Someone else."

He looked hurt. "There's no need to be like that. I was just trying to help. 'Help another newcomer,' they say. They don't say anything about them biting your head off." At the word *newcomer* all the men in our immediate vicinity froze, like men stalking deer.

"I'm not biting your head off," I said. "I'm just kind of busy right now."

"You don't look busy."

"I'm waiting for someone."

"Well, I can talk to you while you wait. Do you want my number?"

"No, I don't want your number. I want. To talk. To *that* man. Over *there,"* I said, jabbing my finger across the room at Kelsey, only to find my through-line obscured by a semicircle of male faces, all standing there beaming at me as if I'd just been given the lead in the school Nativity play. "This is your first meeting?" asked one, a ferrety-looking guy with a ginger mustache. "You're doing great, just great," said another, a portly, bald man in a Duke University sweatshirt, patting me on the shoulder. "It's a miracle you're here, man," said a third, taking my hand and pumping it up and down. "Just to even have made it this far. You're a miracle, a fuckin' miracle. . . ."

It was the guy who'd spoken earlier: the wolverine in the purple CBGBs T-shirt with dragon tattoos running up and down his arms. He looked even more cadaverous close-up, his eyes recessed behind bony sockets, his hair stringy and black, the veins on his forearm standing up like worm tracks in the sand. "What's your name?" he asked.

"Er, Patrick."

"You Irish?"

"No, English."

He pumped my hand ever harder. "God save the queen, man. God save the fuckin' queen. As long as He comes back for the rest of us."

He laughed, and the rest of the men joined in, their faces bright and eager, like children late to a joke but making up for it with enthusiasm.

"Please, there's been a mistake," I said, worming my hand out of his. "I'm not here for myself. I don't have a drinking problem. I'm just a literary agent. I'm on my lunch break."

The men stopped, blinked, looked at one another, then back at me, and broke into loud guffaws.

"Oh, that's good," said Duke University. "I must use that one. On my lunch break."

"A literary agent, huh?" said Ferret. "Not an alcoholic?"

"No. Absolutely not. Not that there's anything wrong with the people who are."

He leaned in and lowered his voice. "Don't worry. I had a big problem with that word, too. I used to just sit at the back and say, 'My name is Joe and I'm not really sure what I am.' Isn't that right, Brian?"

Wolverine nodded. "It's just semantics."

"It's just semantics," repeated Ferret.

Desperately, I looked over their shoulders at Kelsey, just a few yards away now, moving slowly toward the door, and caught the eye of the girl I had spoken to—the knitter, Lola. There she was, walking past with a friend. She saw me, her face lit up, she leaned in to say something to her friend, then she made her way over, my gaggle of fans parting to make way for her. She was wearing a dark blue shirt with a small Japanese-style print on it, open at the neck to reveal a small V of pale skin.

"You came back," she said. "I was beginning to think I'd frightened you off."

"He's been here all week," said Felix.

"You *have*?" she said.

"He still hasn't learned to turn off his phone."

"That was *you*?"

"I'm sorry," I said. "I had no idea. I was looking around, going, What idiot left his phone on?"

"That's *always* a sign that it's yours," she said, and laughed.

"I tried to tell him," said Felix huffily. "He wouldn't even talk to me."

"It had nothing to do with you," I said. "I was just trying to get to *that man*. I'm here to speak to *him*."

I jabbed a finger at Kelsey, who was now almost through the door.

"Why d'you want to talk to *him*?" said Felix disgustedly.

"Doug would be a great person for you to talk to," said Lola, placing a hand on my forearm, leaning in and whispering, "he can tell you which of these freaks to stay away from. In fact, wait here, will you? Don't go anywhere. . . . *Doug!*"

Almost through the door, Kelsey heard her voice, turned, saw her, then waited as she made her way over to him. Taller than she was by a good six inches, he leaned down to hear what she had to say, nodding and listening, then he looked up. For a brief second, our eyes met, then he turned back to Lola, tapped his watch, and shrugged an apology. She turned and mouthed the word *sorry* to me. I mouthed back the words *It's okay.*

"Don't even think about it," said a raspy voice in my ear.

I turned, to find the wolverine smirking at me. "Beneath every skirt there's a slip," he said. "Beneath every slip there's a skirt. What was it brought you in?"

"I'm sorry?"

"What was it brought you in? Your drug of choice? Meth? Blow? Crack? Smack? Or was it just booze and broads?"

The room was almost empty now; all the other men had wandered off, Felix included. It barely seemed to matter *what* I said anymore. The whole situation was fucked. I felt something in me loosen, belligerently.

"Just booze," I said. "Maybe the odd broad."

"No need to say it like that," said Wolverine. "It comes at you in many forms, this thing. Six trash cans, five lids. Cover one up, the other's pulling you in."

"Very much so. Pulling me in. 'Just when I thought I was out,' " I said, doing my best impression of Al Pacino in *The Godfather: Part III*, " 'they pull me back in.' "

"You're never out," he said, stern-faced.

"Of course not," I said. "I was just joking."

"You shouldn't joke."

"Of course not. It was horrible. Hell, really. There's no other word for it. Just pure, unadulterated hell. The booze, the broads. It all blurred into one after a while. Booze, broad, booze, broad. I couldn't tell which was which. Bed, bottle. Bottle, bed."

His face was a picture of dawning realization.

"I knew it! Another sex addict."

"That's a *little* strong," I said quickly. "I wouldn't go so far as to say *addict*. . . ."

He threw an arm around my shoulder. "You've no idea how lonely it can get in here sometimes. I've been praying for someone like you to come along. What do you say we go grab some lunch. You must be aching to open up to someone."

His breath was surprisingly minty.

"Actually, I'm feeling pretty . . . self-contained today," I replied, attempting to wriggle free. "I think I need some time to reflect."

He frowned. "On what?"

"My sins? Maybe I should go somewhere and reflect on them?"

"Bullshit, it's a disease of isolation," he said, tightening his grip. "You're coming to lunch. Come on. Get some solids inside of you."

"Really, I'd rather not. . . ."

"He's not going with you," said a voice behind us. "He's coming with us."

We both turned, to find Felix, standing in the doorway next to the plump Goth girl who had hissed at us the day before. "Sorry, Brian," she said sarcastically. "You don't get this one."

"That's right," I said, finally freeing myself from his pythonlike grip. "I'm going with them. Thank you, though, very much, Brian, for the invitation. Next time, perhaps. . . ."

chapter seven

SHE WAS A VERY strange kind of Goth—short and bosomy, her hair cut into an uneven red bob, her face round, her skin flawless, with racoonish eye makeup. She wore no spikes or straps, harnesses or buckles; her face was not caked in white makeup; she had no metal hanging from her nose, lip, or earlobes; she wore no black. Everything about her screamed black, in fact, except its complete absence, like the silence you hear before a bomb drops in your house. She *was* wearing a T-shirt with SCORSESE emblazoned across it in a metallic hot rod typeface, underneath a thick pink overcoat—I wasn't sure I'd ever seen anyone wear the color pink sarcastically before, but somehow Prudence managed it. That was her name, she said as we descended the steps outside.

"Thanks for saving me back there," I said.

"We couldn't let you go to lunch with crazy Brian," she replied, rummaging around in her bag and bringing up a packet of Pall Mall cigarettes. It was a cold, damp day; the air smelled of wet leaves and cigarette smoke; up and down the steps, people were gathered in small huddles to light up, talk, and shiver. "The last newcomer who went to lunch with him ended up having to pay for his parking tickets."

She lit her cigarette, using me as a shelter from the wind, sucking on it until the tip glowed red. Then she offered the packet to me. "No thanks," I said. "I don't smoke. In fact, I don't . . . I don't belong here at all. I'm afraid I can't go to lunch with you. I need to be getting back to my office."

"Oh, he's got a *job*," she said, miming *impressed* for a millisecond. "Big woo. I'm only going because I want to make sure the others don't talk about me. Where'd they get to?" She looked around at the clusters of people, but Felix seemed to have wandered off somewhere. "He's never in one place for longer than five seconds, that guy. . . . Oh, there he is."

Following her sight line, I saw him, walking along the north side of the square, next to a portly black guy. Felix had the oddest walk—a sort of bowlegged scuttle, rolling from the outer edge of one foot right over to the outer edge of the other and back; he seemed to traverse as much ground sideways as he did forward.

"Will you look at that? Did they ever hear about *waiting*?" she huffed. "Jesus. It's all love and forgiveness inside, and the moment you step outside it's like ferrets in a friggin' sack."

We started walking east, after them.

"This your first meeting?" she asked.

"There's been a bit of a mix-up, actually. I wasn't at that meeting for myself. I was trying to get hold of somebody else."

"Oh yeah? Who?"

"Douglas."

Her eyebrows rose. "What do you want with *him*?"

"Why does everyone say that?"

"Guy's an asshole."

"You know who he is, don't you?"

"When he's not being an asshole?"

"He's a writer. A famous one. He was nominated for a Pulitzer in 1983."

She smiled. "I think he mentioned he used to write. I thought he meant for *TV Guide*."

"Oh no, no, no. A Pulitzer. In 1983."

She released a big plume into the air that was instantly whisked away by the wind. "Well, now he sits at the back of the meeting with his fly open, says nothing all month, and then when he does open his mouth, what do we get? The friggin' war."

"I thought it was interesting what he said," I replied.

"You can't be calling the president a drunk."

"Why not?"

"The next guy coming through that door might be a Republican. Although I doubt it, not at that meeting."

"How long has he been coming?"

"About six months. He got sober upstate somewhere. Some place with deer."

"Woodstock."

"That's it. His dog was always chasing the deer up there. Used to drive him crazy."

"And he, uh, he was definitely a big drinker, was he?"

"What do you mean?"

"I mean he had it bad?"

"You mean, like, did he have the shakes in the morning? Hallucinations? Blackouts?"

"Uh . . . I guess."

"*You can't ask that*." She sounded scandalized.

"Why not?"

"You just can't. You've been watching too many movies. Don't tell me. You think *Leaving Las Vegas* rocks."

"It doesn't?"

"Hell no. You can't fuck with the DTs. I can barely get it on after a Big Mac. Give me *Arthur* any day."

"*Arthur?*"

"That movie was wild. He spends the whole movie chasing Liza Minnelli, finally gets her and marries her, in a *church,* and *he stays drunk the whole time.* They'd never let them get away with that today. Did you see the sequel? He got sober." Her face twisted in disgust. "What's with *that?* . . ."

We turned the corner onto Broadway and found the others standing outside a diner, Felix leaning against the window, talking to the black guy, who was chunky in that way that only African American men seemed able to pull off, dressed in head-to-toe denim, with a turquoise Yasser Arafat scarf around his neck. He was somewhere in his late forties or early fifties, his shaved head showing flecks of gray like carpet lint. "Well, will you look at this one," he said. "All dressed up in his Sunday best. Just like me—keeping it all inside." He peered into my eyes. "Yup. He's got the look all right. Like death sucking on a sponge. Let's get him inside before he expires."

"I can't stay for lunch," I said, "I've got to get back to work."

"He's got a *job,*" said Prudence.

"Well, ain't he the cat's whiskers," said the black guy, looking at me with raised eyebrows. "And has Little Lord Fauntleroy eaten?"

"No, but—"

"Are you hungry?"

"Uh . . ."

"Then that's decided," he said, taking me by the arm and marching me into the diner, with Prudence and Felix bringing up the rear.

"Since when have you ever kept anything inside, Godfrey?" asked Prudence.

"Silence, child. . . ."

It was one of those cheap, nondescript diners that sit on every fourth street corner in Manhattan. I'd been meaning to visit one ever since arriving in the city but once my through line to Balthazar and Pastis had been established, the allure of cheap Formica and parbroiled burgers had receded somewhat. Inside, a slovenly East European waitress walked us past walls hung with black-and-white signed photographs of celebrities from long-dead TV shows to a small booth near the window, hung with a plastic mosaic lamp shade. She issued us menus that looked like they'd been typeset sometime during the Bay of Pigs embroglio, with additions to the menu scribbled in the margins with red- and green-colored pens. Everyone seemed to know the drill and had their orders at the ready: a turkey burger deluxe with extra Gorgonzola for Godfrey, a Caesar salad with no dressing for Prudence, and a vanilla milk shake with extra cherries for Felix. I ordered a BLT. It seemed the hardest to fuck up.

"Hey, guess what," said Prudence. "Hillbilly here wants to know if Douglas had a low bottom."

"He does, does he," said Godfrey. "And what did you tell him?"

"I told him he couldn't ask people that."

"Why not?" I asked.

"It's not a competition," he said. "There aren't judges. It's not *American Idol.* Oh Lord, imagine that—Randy Jackson up there waiting for you to finish. 'Yo, dawg, you were da bomb up there! We got a hot one tonight, America!' "

Prudence bustled forward in her seat to deliver a Paula Abdul love bomb: " 'I fell in love with you ever since I saw you sinking those double vodka tonics in the elimination rounds back in Georgia.' "

It was left to Felix to do Simon Cowell. " 'I'm sorry. That. Is just. About. The Worst. Display. Of alcoholism. I have ever seen,' " he said, slipping into the same Dick Van Dyke Cockney that Americans always did when they imitated a British accent. " 'Either that drink is completely wrong for you or you're on the next bus home. . . .' "

They all fell about laughing. I decided to try a different tack.

"Where did he shoot off to today?" I asked.

"The library," said Felix. "He works there."

"Which library?"

He shrugged. "He works with kids. That's all I know."

"Kids?"

"He's always talking about them. The kids did this today; the kids did that. He's teaching them how to draw."

I had a vision of the redoubtable Pulitzer nominee, up to his armpits in bawling three-year-olds, all of them sticking crayons up one another's noses and spooning oatmeal down the spines of his books.

"I'd advise you to stay well away from that man," said Godfrey briskly. "You'll do each other no good whatsoever."

I turned to him. "Why do you say that?"

"He asks a lot of questions, doesn't he! Because you ask a lot of questions, that's why. And Douglas is precisely the kind of guy who thinks he knows all the answers. He's got a lot of crazy ideas, that one."

"What sort of ideas?"

"The *wrong* sort. Now where *is* our food?"

He twisted around in his seat, his interest in the conversation dead. The waitress was nowhere to be seen; Godfrey soon fell into a conversation with Prudence about cupcakes, while Felix stripped the paper covering from a straw like bark from a twig. He was an odd bird, all right, his many layers of clothing in such disarray that he managed to look both overdressed and underdressed at the same time. He had dark olive skin, almost Mediterranean-looking, with thick, sloping eyebrows that gave fresh credence to the ancient science of physiognomy. If he wasn't mournful to begin with, he certainly was by the time everyone had gotten through asking him if he was okay. He caught me staring at him and stared back.

"You should ask Lola," he said. "She's the only one who likes him. She knit him a scarf."

"What's with the knitting?"

"It's a come-on."

"Are you sure about that?"

"It says, Ask me about my knitting."

"Surely it says the opposite: Don't bother me; I'm knitting."

"Then how come only the best-looking girls do it?"

"She'll never date you in a million years," said Prudence, interrupting.

"I wasn't . . . I was just—"

"Asking about Lola, I know. That's how it starts. Next thing you know, you'll be sharing about her at one of the men's meetings. Then someone will tell one of her friends that you shared about her and she'll ask you to speak at a meeting. She'll ask if you've done your fourth step and how many women were on it. Then your sponsors will step in and tell you to leave each other alone. And you'll ignore them and go ahead anyway. And six months later, you'll be drinking, wishing you'd never met her, or that she'd go back to L.A., so you don't have to divide up the meetings between you, in case you run into each other. Please. Don't go there."

I understood only about one word in ten. "Lola is from L.A.?"

"Her dad wrote that movie about John Travolta and the dog."

"A horse," said Godfrey, correcting her.

"The horse was *Urban Cowboy.* Not that you would know. Studio 54 was still open. You were up to your eyeballs in cocaine."

"That's your disease talking," said Godfrey huffily.

"You're my disease talking. In fact, could you speak a little louder, since I don't think the next table *quite* heard you."

He twisted around to look at the table behind us, then dismissed them with a wave. "They're just civilians," he said. "Like a dog whistle to a cat. . . . They never get anything . . ."

Ten minutes or so later, Felix and I were walking back up Broadway toward my office, the others having already departed. "It's understandable," he was telling me now. "She's very beautiful. But Prudence is right. She'll never go near you. They pick up mentally where you first picked up a drink. How old were you when you had your first drink?"

"Fifteen."

"And when was your last drink?"

"Last night."

"Well, that would be like Lola dating a fifteen-year-old."

"No, it wouldn't, you see. . . ." I looked around to check we weren't being overheard. "Don't think too badly of me, Felix, but I wasn't even supposed to be at that meeting. I was just waiting for Douglas. I'm not an alcoholic."

"What do you want—a medal? Neither am I."

I gawped at him. He gawped back at me. We looked like two goldfish that had run into each other in a bowl we had thought was empty.

"What are you doing all this for, then?"

"My doctors caught me abusing my medication. They said I had to go to ninety meetings in ninety days or they wouldn't let me go."

"Let you go from where?"

"The hospital."

"Ah. And what were you doing in a hospital?"

"I'm bipolar. I stopped taking my lithium. I was working a double shift at the kitchen. They liked it when I stopped taking my lithium because it meant I could work eighteen shifts. But

I was shaking so much, I dropped the plates. They told me to go to the hospital, and then once I got there, they wouldn't let me go."

I understood very little of what he had just said, but I did know that the words *medication* and *bipolar,* used in such close proximity, were never a good sign.

"Don't you have your own meetings to go to?" I asked.

"Don't you start."

"Don't start what?"

"Telling me I don't deserve to be there."

"I didn't say that. . . ."

"No, but you thought it. Go on, just admit it. You don't think pills are as bad as real drugs. God, it's such a racket, it really is. They say it's not a popularity contest, but it is. It really is. It used to be me they made a fuss over. Tomorrow it'll be somebody else—some new golden boy they can show off in front of. Somebody who lost his house. Go on, tell me you lost your house. They'll love you if you lost your house."

"I didn't ask for any of this! You told me that meeting was open to the public!"

"That was yesterday's meeting. That was open. Today's was closed. It was the beginners' meeting."

I threw up my arms in exasperation. "Great. Just great. A beginners' meeting. That is fucking marvelous."

"I don't know what you're complaining about. You're still one sick puppy, either way."

I had nothing to say to that. We both fell silent and continued walking as Broadway began its long slow climb upmarket, the sportswear shops and jean emporiums giving way to the Strand Book Store and Shakespeare & Co. Looking down, I thought I saw the reason for that strange rolling gait of his: The outermost edges of his shoes were worn right down to the soles. It must have been like walking with two wedges of Edam strapped to your feet.

"Do you know where I can buy a chopping board?" he asked suddenly.

"A chopping board? You mean for food?"

"And a watch. I need to buy a watch."

It seemed a bizarre shopping list, the sort of thing a six-year-old might come up with if asked to guess at the sort of stuff adulthood was rumored to require. A chopping board and a watch. Oh, and a suit and a newspaper and a house while you're at it.

"I'm not sure about the chopping board," I said. "The watch—let me see—maybe up on Fifth, in the Thirties somewhere?"

"Thanks," he said, drawing to a halt under the awning of the multiplex on the southeastern corner of Union Square. "I'm this way," he said, pointing toward the statue of Gandhi in the southwest corner of the square, poised as if about to take his message of nonviolent protest into the Diesel Jeans store just opposite. "Here, let me give you my number."

"You don't have to do that," I said quickly, but he was already rummaging around inside his pockets, bringing up a rubber band, a broken Pez dispenser, some change, a piece of string, and finally a pencil and an old receipt. He wrote his number on the receipt, using his leg to write on, the pencil going through the paper many times before he had finished. As much out of politeness as anything else, I fished a card from my pocket and handed it to him in exchange for his number. He took the card and examined it.

" 'Literary agent,' " he read. " 'The Leo Gottlieb Literary Agency.' I'm a writer, too, actually. You know that thing where people say they're having a bad hair day?"

"Uh-huh."

"That was me."

"You came up with that, did you?"

"Then everyone started using it. I'm having a reading of my work in a couple of weeks. You can come if you like."

"I'll try," I said, sticking out my hand.

"Are you going to any meetings this weekend?"

"I don't intend to, no."

"Douglas is qualifying this weekend, I think."

"Qualifying?"

"Telling his story."

My ears pricked up. "*Really?*"

"I think it's the Happy Destiny meeting on Third Avenue. Do you want me to check for you?"

"That would be fantastic."

"No problem," he said, punching me in the bicep a little too hard to be properly playful. "Just stay out of your head. It's a bad neighborhood in there. You don't want to go in there alone."

"I'll do my best."

He looked around to check for pedestrians, glanced both ways, then disappeared into the crowds. Soon, all I could see was his bobbing thatch of hair, then nothing.

chapter eight

NATALIE WAS AT HER desk when I came in, the phone cradled under her ear and Post-it notes attached to her fingers. She saw me and put her hand over the receiver. "Patrick, where have you *been*?" she said urgently. "I've been trying to get hold of you."

"Why? What's going on?" I said, shutting the door behind me.

"Leo's back. He wants to know where you are."

A small alarm bell went off. "When did he get back?"

"Just after lunch. He was a little pissed he couldn't find anyone. 'Where in hell *is* everybody?'—you know how he gets when he's been out of the office for a while. Where *were* you? I tried calling you, but your phone was off."

That had been *Natalie's* call I turned off in the meeting. "Lunch," I said, moving off toward the stairs. "I was at lunch. I'd better go see him. Is he upstairs?"

"Lunch with who?"

"Nobody you know. I'd better go up. . . ."

"Brad's with him at the moment. Why did you turn off your phone?"

"Hmm?"

"Why did you turn off your phone?"

"I didn't want to be disturbed. I was, uh—I wanted some privacy."

"Were you on a *date*, Patrick Miller?" she said mischievously.

Still eyeing the bottom of the stairs but unable to make credible headway toward it, I lowered my head in defeat. "That's right," I said. "I was on a date. From Simpatico.com. Finally decided to give that thing a go."

"You were!" she cried. "*Ohmigod* who with?"

"A girl."

"A girl . . . *Okay*. Good start. You're making some smart choices. What was she like?"

"She was nice. Look, Natalie, I really should get going. If Leo's on the warpath, Brad will be out any moment. . . ." I made another move for the stairs.

"He's not on the warpath. C'mon. Nice is for ice-cream flavors. Give me more."

The only image I seemed able to summon was Felix, sucking disconsolately on his milk shake, his layers of filthy XXL clothing peeling off him, his shoes worn down to cracked leather. "Okay . . . dark hair, lots of it. And lots of layers. Woolens. Handknit. A very downtown, thrift-store kind of vibe going on. Earthy. Grounded."

She frowned. "I'm not really seeing her, for some reason. What does she do?"

"You mean job? I don't know." I had no idea. I had no idea what any of them did. Everything was upside down in there, your most vivid, day-glo secrets tossed about like so much loose change, while the more mundane facts of your existence—your job, your age, your address—took on the glow of intrigue.

"You didn't ask her what she did for a living?"

"The conversation never got round to it."

"The conversation never got around to it or you never got around to it?"

"Both."

She shook her head.

"I should probably get going," I said, moving toward the stairs.

"So, are you going to see her again?"

"Maybe. I don't know. Probably. We'll see."

At which point, whoever it was Natalie was waiting for on the phone came back on the line. "No, that's okay," she said. "No trouble at all. . . ." She shooed me away with her Post-it note–laden fingers. I took the stairs three at a time.

The door to Leo's office was closed, but through it I could hear the *mwarm-mwah* of muffled conversation, interspersed with the sound of Brad's laugh—a highly irritating noise, signaling not hilarity, but deployed in order to signal his recognition that a joke had been made somewhere in the vicinity by an immediate superior. I took a seat in the small waiting area outside, next to the watercooler. The walls were hung with a series of framed black-and-white photographs, all showing him mixing with Manhattan's most vaunted literary lions: Norman Mailer, Susan Sontag, George Plimpton, Sonny Mehta, Nan Talese. Leo appeared the same in every photograph: jacketless, in shirt and bow tie, slightly barrel-chested, his long arms ending in gleaming cuff links. He had a full head of dark gray hair and one of those long, jowly faces that get called "lugubrious," although, as with others of his physiological genus (Walter Matthau, Jerry Orbach, Leonard Nimoy), the rubberiness of his features belied the lizardlike speed of the mind behind it. Ask anyone in publishing about Leo Gottlieb and two things generally happened: First they smiled, maybe remembering a joke or an off-color remark with which he'd livened up a dull publishing party or dinner; then they got a pained, faraway look as they remembered the first round of negotiations they'd ever gone with him. A young author was rumored to have once asked Leo what the most profitable form of writing was. Without missing a beat, he growled, "Ransom notes."

The voices got louder, then swung into clarity as the door to Leo's office opened and Brad backed out of it. "I will, Leo," he was saying. "Consider it done."

"And don't let him get away with all that crap about the final draft not being the final draft," said Leo. "Those deadlines have been in place for over a year."

"I won't."

Brad saw me only after he had closed the door. "Patrick," he said, surprised. "There you are. Natalie was looking all over for you."

"How is he?"

"Where were you?" he asked, ignoring my question.

"Lunch," I said, getting up. "How is he?"

He shook his head. "Not good. Watch your step."

"Why? What's going on?"

"I think you'd better just talk to him."

"Talk to him about what?"

He grimaced. "Just deal straight. Tell him what you know. You know how he hates anything less than full and immediate disclosure. It's never the crime; it's the cover-up. That's what brings us down. Every time."

"But what—"

He cuffed me on the back. "Good luck."

A sinking sensation began to gather as I knocked on the door, the full import of what I had done unfurling in my gut. What had I been *thinking*?

"Come in!" cried Leo.

I entered, to find him on the phone, waving me in with his free hand. ". . . That's what I *told* him. . . . Uh-huh. . . . Uh-huh. Right. Well, *you* try. He needs to hear it from someone in Legal."

He made an apologetic face and pointed to the chair opposite his desk. Leo's office was large and lined with books, the few patches of spare wall space hung with framed clippings from the *New York Times* best-seller list: the agency's most recent successes, already yellowing from a long summer. None of them were mine, needless to say. Leo was sitting behind a large walnut Edwardian desk with an embossed green leather top. It was his pride and joy. He wouldn't let anyone near it, not even the cleaners, insisting on polishing it himself, trotting off every six months or so to some shop on Sixth Avenue to buy the special leather food the desk required. No mistress was ever as well tended to as that desk. Looking through the window behind him, I could see the top of the cherry tree in the courtyard outside bobbing in the wind. Leo was now rolling his eyes and raising his hands to the heavens in a show of impatience for my benefit.

"Yeah, I know. I know. I know. . . . You say that like I don't know. . . . Yes, I do know. . . . Yes—that's what I said. . . . I know. . . . Okay, listen, I've got to go. Give me a call back and let me know what he says. Yes, I know. Okay—bye. . . . Yes—bye. . . . Mmm-hmmm. . . . That's right. You tell him that. . . . Okay, yes—bye."

He put the phone down and held it there, as if it might spring up on him again. "Lord. Another writer who refuses to see the difference between slander and libel."

"That's funny," I said. "Most of them seem born knowing the difference."

He smiled, flashing a full set of ivory-capped teeth, as he reached for a Kleenex from the box on his desk. He blew his nose with a parp.

"How are you feeling?" I asked.

"A lot better, thanks," he said. "Have you had your shots?"

I shook my head.

"You should. It's not like the flu you get over in Europe. This one is serious."

He scrunched up the tissue, threw it in the wastebasket, and leaned back in his chair—a black leather Eames, almost as loved as the desk. "So. Patrick," he said, steepling his fingers. "Tell me what you've been up to, *hmm*?"

I felt my pulse flicker and strained to flatten it. Tom Cruise could do that, I had read somewhere—flatten his pulse at will. "Oh, you know," I mumbled. "Not much. You know how it is the back end of December. Too many parties. Not enough editors with their checkbooks out. I like to get them in the new year, when they're hungover and beginning to panic about where their big books are coming from."

He listened, nodded, then smiled ever so slightly. "That's not what *I* hear."

"Oh no? What do you hear?"

"A little bird tells me you've been on Douglas Kelsey's trail."

"Ah," I said, swallowing, a fist forming in my chest. "Yes, that's right. How did you know?"

"I know *everything*. You should know that by now, Patrick. Did you get as far as an actual meeting?"

The thoughts flashed through my head like a semaphore on a rough sea: *I had been seen. Brad had followed me. Leo knew everything.*

"You know about the meetings," I said weakly.

"You had more than one?"

"Yes, well, he didn't turn up at the first one, so I went back again the next day—"

"He didn't show up at all?"

I shook my head. "No. He didn't."

He frowned. "He was always such an infernally difficult man.

I wouldn't take it personally. I met him a few times, you know, back when he was still buddies with Carver. *So* unhappy. But beautiful hands."

"Hands?"

"Yes, he had these long, elegant hands. Piano player's hands, like Gary Cooper, always drumming away." He drummed the edge of his desk in demonstration. "He couldn't turn the engine off. I always wondered how he got to sleep at night with that head of his. Like putting a porcupine to bed."

He was lost in thought for a few seconds, then came to. "Anyway. I'm sorry, I interrupted."

"Not at all. So I went back again the next day. And there he was."

"Excellent. So what's his story? What's he been up to?"

"Oh, I didn't get to talk to him. But he's going to tell his story this weekend. I'll get it from him and report right back."

Leo's eyes were wide. "You didn't *talk* to him," he said, astounded.

"There wasn't time."

"Not a single word?"

I shook my head.

"Were you *drunk*?"

I frowned. "Of course not. I would *never* do that. Not in a meeting like that."

He harrumphed. "Yes, well. You know what I think about that. It's terrible what's happened to this town. Elaine's serves red wine by the half bottle these days. A half bottle! You're done by the time you've taken your seat!"

What was the old goat talking about? "But you have to see it from their point of view. They're worried about where it might lead."

"Where might it *lead*?" He frowned.

"One guy picked up a drink and the next thing he knew, he

was checking into the Chelsea Hotel with a crack pipe and a couple of hookers. He woke up the next day naked on a putt-putt golf course."

Leo's jaw lowered by half an inch. "*Where*?"

"A putt-putt golf course. Completely naked. He drank his own cologne."

"Cologne," he repeated, stunned.

"Chanel Pour Monsieur."

He blinked rapidly, as if clearing away fuzz. "What on earth are you talking about?"

I froze. "What are *you* talking about?"

"Your lunches with Douglas Kelsey."

"My lunches with Douglas Kelsey," I murmured, feeling suddenly a little numb in my extremities.

"Yes."

For a few seconds we stared at each other blinking. I broke first.

"Oh no, no, no, no, no," I said. "I never got as far as an actual lunch with him. I just saw him on the street."

He frowned. "Saw him on the *street*?"

"Yes, I saw him on the street and that was that. Never saw him again."

"So . . . what were you talking about . . . the crack pipes—the hookers?"

I summoned my closest approximation to a natural human laugh. "Oh, *that*. Hgh. That was. Hgh. That was just a couple of the agents I worked with back in London. They got into a bit of trouble. With the crack at lunchtime, you know. Hgh."

"They got into trouble with *crack*?"

"It's much more of a white-collar drug these days," I said, nodding. "They're in recovery now, poor sods."

He shook his head, processing the information, something still not quite right. It was like watching a boa constrictor try to swallow a deer, the deer working its way down the boa constrictor's neck, until it looked like nothing so much as a deer-shaped boa constrictor. I grimaced my encouragement for this prodigious digestive feat, until finally it was gone. He laughed a little weakly. "Well, you know what I say: Only the Brits really know how to do lunch anymore. Plimpton was the only one who knew how to throw a decent party in this town, and now he's gone."

He harrumphed. "That's a shame about Kelsey. All these business books of Brad's are fine, but you know how light we've been up top lately. We could really do with a decent name like his, we really could."

"I have a few leads," I said. "I'll keep my eyes peeled."

"You do that," he said, rocking in his chair, the sure sign that he was beginning to get bored. I felt a flood of relief. "You going back for the holidays?"

"No, I'm sticking it out here."

"Good for you. Go see a show. Get those shots."

"I will, Leo—thank you. Are we done?"

"Yes, we're done," he said. "Go on. Scram."

My shirt, damp with sweat, peeled away from my back as I got up. I was almost at the door when he spoke up again.

"Oh, and one last thing, Patrick."

"Yes?"

I turned around.

"Stay off the crack, there's a good boy. It never leads anywhere good."

"Of course, Leo. . . ."

I closed the door behind me with a soft *kerrlunk*.

chapter nine

I'M TELLING YOU, SAUL, he was trying to sabotage me."

"No, he wasn't. He was just having fun with you."

"Is that what you'd call it? Just as I'm about to go in to see Leo, telling me about how angry with me the old man is and how I should come clean with him right away?"

"Come clean about what?"

"Nothing. That's the point. It screwed up my meeting with Leo."

"How? Sounds to me like someone has a guilty conscience."

"I'm British," I said grumpily, "we feel guilty about everything."

It was a Friday night and already dark as Saul and I walked up Irving Place toward Gramercy Park. The sidewalks glistened with rain, reflecting back the neon lights of the cafés and bars, already packed to the gills with the Friday-night crowd: office workers letting off steam before heading home, bridge and tunnelers, getting their evening started. Through the thick crenelated glass of

Pete's Tavern could be heard muffled whoops, hollers, and the *bmm-bmm-bmmm* of a bass line.

"It's just depressing is all. I mean, if that's what Leo wants in his agents, then why is he employing me?"

"Maybe he woke up one day and thought, How about a completely useless Brit on the payroll."

"You're joking, but that's how it feels. The butler effect. The accent is nice. I sound good on the phone, but God forbid he let me near any real, actual clients."

"I'm sure that's how he sees it."

"It is! I represented Booker nominees in London! Okay, one Booker nominee. But an actual, living, breathing Booker nominee. Here, I'm lucky if I get bloody *Talk to the Hand.*"

"Then why *are* you here?" he asked.

That shut me up. There was never any answer to that. Or rather, there were too many answers to that, none of which seemed quite right. Even the weather seems to have followed me over, I thought dismally as we rounded the corner onto Gramercy Park, where the trees swayed in the wind, their branches illuminated orange by the streetlights. Up ahead, the lights of the National Arts Club spilled out onto the sidewalk, the windows crammed with drinking, talking, smoking silhouettes. My stomach fluttered with that mixture of excitement and dread with which I approached any large gathering. Leo was right: The days were long gone when Manhattan's literary set lost themselves in nights of marathon debauch, waking up at dawn in the arms of a total stranger in the fountain of the Princeton Club. No publishers threw decent parties anymore, opting instead for the more cost-effective literary lunch, attended by eager young professionals far too worried about slipping a rung on the corporate ladder to dare getting bent in public. But the party at the National Arts Club was a firm fixture in the Christmas season. The previous year, Saul had told me, the organizers had had to cancel the National Arts Club event on account of being "too partied out." I knew kindred spirits when I saw them, and had been angling for an invitation ever since.

It looked a little like one of the swankier members-only places you get in Mayfair: an imposing sandstone mansion with a pillared entrance, big glass doors, a marble lobby where you checked in your coat, red-carpeted stairs leading up to the second floor, where a series of interconnecting drawing rooms held the bulk of the guests, all shouting loudly to hear themselves over the noise of everyone else's shouting. Every bit of wall space was crammed with paintings, sculptures, statuettes, vases, mirrors, and lamps, as if someone had taken a bunch of Edith Wharton characters, locked them in a room, told them to redecorate, then not let them out for a century. I saw some faces I recognized—a publicity girl here, an editor there—but most were unknown to me. We made a beeline for the bar, where a small rugby scrum had formed beneath a beautiful stained-glass skylight. We stood and jostled and elbowed and waited and eventually snagged an order from the beleaguered barman for two glasses of wine.

"This reminds me," said Saul. "Liz and I have decided to go ahead with our Christmas party."

"Is Caitlin coming?" I asked.

"No, you're good." Liz was Saul's girlfriend; she and Caitlin knew each other.

"Then I'm there."

"Listen, I know we were busting your balls the other day, but are you okay?"

"Okay about what?"

"Caitlin."

"Oh Christ yes."

"I don't know, you've been through a lot this year. Breaking up with her. Changing jobs. Moving to another country. You never seem to talk much about it."

"There's not much to talk about, is there?"

"Of course not. I didn't mean . . ."

"I know what you mean. . . ."

"If you ever needed to unload or anything."

"I'm good, but thanks anyway."

I looked away. As incomplete and unsatisfactory as the whole exchange was, I was almost grateful: Who knew what lay beyond a conversation like that. Wobbly chins? Tears? Ardent declarations of friendship? I was just so ill at ease with all the forms of male bonding they had out here—high fives, backslaps, knuckle bumps, Giants games, beer commercials. There were just so many things to fuck up. Only alcohol helped. Just one gulp and my Englishness started to evaporate. Two and I felt loose-limbed, windswept, sun-kissed. Three and I felt like John Wayne, busting through saloon doors with Katharine Hepburn slung over my shoulder. Our glasses of wine arrived; I slurped mine greedily.

"Hey, isn't that Christine Kantor?" said Saul.

I followed his gaze across the room. "Who?"

He pointed. "Douglas Kelsey's old agent. You were asking about her the other day."

Standing in front of the tall bay windows was a woman in maybe her early fifties; champagne flute in one hand, talking animatedly to two men in dark gray suits who had their backs to us.

"Do you want to say hello?" asked Saul.

"Yeah, why not," I said, taking another swig to steel myself.

It was slow, hot work getting there. As we drew closer to the window, I began to notice something odd happening to all the conversations, speakers tripping over their own stories, listeners agreeing with things they hadn't properly heard, laughing at punch lines that hadn't yet arrived. It was like the conversation of six-year-olds, or movie extras rhubarbing for the camera. Then we reached the window and I saw the reason why: The two men talking to Kantor were Bret Easton Ellis and Jay McInerney, no longer young, Ellis pale and jowly, McInerney as tan and leathery as a football. For the room at large, it was a little like seeing the Joker and the Penguin together again.

"—had no idea," McInerney was saying as we approached. "She just waited until the words were out of my mouth and then put me on hold. *Beeep.*"

They all laughed.

"Chrissie?" said Saul. The woman turned and, without missing a beat planted a kiss on Saul's cheek, as if she had seen us all along. "Saul, darling man. How *are* you?" She had blond-gray hair, immaculately coiffed, and was wearing a sharp gray suit over a sweater and pearls—attractive, in the slightly impenetrable, matte manner of powerful women. "You know Bret and Jay. . . ."

"Of course," said Saul, extending his hand. "Sorry to interrupt. This isn't the 'I love you' story, is it?"

"Afraid so," said McInerney.

Saul turned to me. "Jay was dating these two women back in—when was this, the early nineties?"

"No, no. *After* my divorce. Jesus."

"One evening, one of them phones him up, gets him to say how much he loves her. He gets an incoming call. Puts the first girl on hold. It's his other girlfriend, the cookery writer. Now *she* gets him to say 'I love you.' He's like, What in hell is going on? He puts her on hold, goes back to the first one, who asks him, 'How *much* do you love me?' Then he realizes. They'd found out about each other. They were on conference call. He'd been punked."

Everyone fell about laughing.

"It's funny until your eleven-year-old reads about it on *Gawker,*" said McInerney.

Everyone laughed some more.

"Christine, I wanted to introduce you to someone," said Saul. "This is Patrick Miller. He joined us last year."

She turned and took me in with a quick glance, then extended her hand. "Very pleased to meet you, Patrick."

Her hand was cool and papery to the touch.

"Saul says if I want to know anything about representation in this town, you're the woman I should speak to."

She smiled at Saul, who was already in conversation with the two authors. "Well, that is very sweet of him to say, but really *he's* the one you need to talk to."

"We were talking about you the other day, in fact. Didn't you used to represent Douglas Kelsey?"

A small flicker of something passed over her face, like an aircraft shadow over summer lawns.

"Why? You haven't run into him, I hope," she said, and laughed.

"I was just wondering what happened to him."

She blinked twice, in rapid succession, as if wiping the question from view. "How long have you been in New York, Patrick?"

"Almost a year."

"Well, you've landed on your feet with Leo, who is one of the last gentlemen in this town, and Saul—well, everyone loves Saul. The only way you could possibly improve on your luck is to stay away from clients like Douglas Kelsey." She leaned into me and whispered, "One of the heartbreakers, I'm afraid."

"What happened? If you don't mind my asking."

"Not at all," she said, once again in firm possession of her spirits. "He got into a fight with Random House over that novel of his. He wanted more time; they refused. He wanted more money; they refused. Then he started making all these terrible telephone calls to his editor, calling him every name under the sun. All behind my back, I should add. You know how well *that* always goes."

"They sued."

"Yes, they did. He had to sell his house to pay them back. He was extremely bitter about that. Personally, I think he was just looking for an opportunity to pull the plug on the whole thing."

"What do you mean?"

"His marriage, his life up there. Just walk away from everything. You've read *The Grenadiers,* I take it."

"I didn't know whether it was autobiographical or not."

"Oh, they're always autobiographical, Patrick. Like vultures on their own lives. God, when I think of what he put that woman through. All that stuff about Carrie having 'unpardonably thick ankles.' It was very hurtful to her."

I chose my words carefully. "He wasn't in any other kind of . . . trouble?"

She looked at me quizzically. "What do you mean?"

"I don't know, drinking, anything of that nature?"

Her eyes narrowed to slits. "Whatever makes you say that?"

"Nothing," I said quickly. "It just looks—from the outside at least—as if there might have been something else going on."

"You must never go on the way things *look*. Heavens, *I* used to drink more than he did." She swirled the champagne around in her glass. "Douglas was always terribly abstemious. Always went home early, never stayed up late." She laughed dryly and glanced over my shoulder at the others.

"Is that right?"

She nodded.

"So what happened to the book? Did he ever finish it?"

"I've no idea. One of my colleagues rang him up a few months after the lawsuit was settled to see if he still wanted to sell it. You want to know what he said? I'll always remember this. He said he'd rather inject liquid cholera." She laughed. "You see? Completely crazy."

Somewhere in my pocket, my phone started ringing. I fished it out, to see a number I didn't recognize.

"Please, go ahead," she said curtly.

"It's okay. I don't need to—"

"We're done, I think," she said, cutting me off and turning back to the others. I was left facing the back of her charcoal gray jacket. I flipped the phone open and held it to my ear.

"Hello?"

"Oh . . . Thank God . . . Thank God you're there, Patrick. I'm sorry, I didn't know who to call, but this man just threatened me. I had to call someone."

"Who is this?"

"All I did was ask him where I could buy a watch, and he just started shouting at me. 'Do I look like the kind of guy who sells watches to people?' It was horrible, just horrible."

"Felix?"

"I had to leave after that. I'm standing outside now."

"You'll have to slow down. I can't hear you very well. Outside where?"

"McDonald's."

"What were you doing in McDonald's?"

"Looking for someone to sell me a watch."

"I don't think you're going to get that in McDonald's. Where are you now?"

"Uh . . . West Thirty-third Street."

In the background I could hear the roar of traffic.

"What about the avenue?"

"Fashion Avenue. You see, now what's that?"

"That's Seventh. It's what Seventh calls itself when it gets up that high. You want to be on Fifth, two over. If you want to buy a watch. Okay?"

"Oh. Fifth. Okay. Thank you."

"You're welcome," I said, feeling the rare satisfaction of having given an accurate set of directions in New York. Normally, people heard the accent and their eyes just glazed over.

"Where are you?" he asked. "I can hear voices."

"I'm at a work party."

"Work party. Well, be careful. I looked into that meeting tomorrow, by the way. It's on Third Avenue and Sixth, just up from St. Mark's."

"Is it? That's great, Felix. Thank you," I said, turning to face the bay windows that looked down onto the square. Through the rain-flecked glass, I could see the trees swaying in the wind, as if pushed by unseen hands; overhead, the clouds, illuminated pink by the streetlights, hung low over the city, like a blanket. "Felix, can I ask you something? That thing that everyone was talking about today, about there being no judges."

"That's right."

"So there's nobody on the door? Nobody checking to see if you're legit or not?"

"Oh no. You saw it. The only requirement for membership is the desire to stop drinking."

"That's it?"

"That's it."

"What about actually stopping? Don't you have to stop?"

"No, they're sometimes drunk. One guy sang Christmas carols."

"And what about actually being an alcoholic? Isn't that a requirement?"

"Oh *no*. Nobody thinks that, do they? There was this one guy? Albert? He used to make the coffee all the time. Then someone asked him to speak, and he gets up there and starts telling this story about how his wife died of cancer and how awful it was and how lonely he's been. I mean, he did the best with what he had, but it was pretty clear he was coming up a little empty, if you know what I mean. He was like, 'Was that all right? Did I do okay?' Everyone was like, 'You did great, Bert. You did great. . . .' "

"They didn't throw him out?"

"Oh no. He still comes to meetings. Chairs one on the Upper West Side, I think."

"I see."

"I'd better go. My phone is about to run out of batteries."

"Oh. Of course."

"You can call later if you need to. We don't have to do this alone. Stay close to the pack. Stick with the winners."

"Thank you, Felix."

I closed my phone and slipped it back into my pocket but remained standing at the window. It wasn't like I hadn't lied for my work before. I'd once pretended an interest in golf in order to schmooze a Cornish thriller writer, and I'd wangled membership in the Groucho Club purely by putting Damien Hirst as my sponsor, even though I'd only met the guy once to talk about a potential book. The Groucho Club and Alcoholics Anonymous were very different types of organizations, of course, one dedicated to the task of getting blotto seven days a week and the other to, well, not. But a club was a club and rules were rules. If what Felix had said was true, it wouldn't even be that much of a lie. I definitely didn't think I was an alcoholic and I did want to quit drinking, if it would get me closer to Kelsey. Kind of. I'd definitely been hitting the parties a bit too hard since Caitlin and I broke up. I qualified on both counts. It was like how you couldn't be accused of stealing from a Communist, because they didn't believe in private property.

"Who was that?"

I spun around to find Saul standing right behind me.

"What?"

"On the phone. You were talking for some time. Who was it?"

"Uh, nobody. Just a friend."

"Is everything okay?"

"Yeah, yeah. Why wouldn't it be? I'm just . . . Actually, you know what? I'm kind of tired. It's been a long week. I don't think I'm going to stay that long."

"But we've only just gotten here!"

I looked at my glass of wine. It seemed a shame to waste it. I figured that maybe I should sober up at the end of the evening, not the beginning. Yeah, that made much more sense.

"I'll get the next round, shall I?" I said with a grin.

chapter ten

HOW AM I DOING for time?" asked Kelsey.

The boy sitting next to him, no more than a teenager, in a purple tie-dyed T-shirt, looked at his watch. "Five minutes?"

Kelsey nodded. "I'm almost there. Almost at the pearly gates . . ."

Somewhere, someone snorted. It was a much bigger meeting than the others I had been to, situated in a church basement somewhere in the East Village—I hadn't even known the place existed until I looked it up on the map. Even though it was a Saturday morning, there had to have been some two hundred people, sitting in three large banks of plastic chairs, as if at an auditorium. It could almost have been one of Kelsey's book readings, with some spilling into the aisles, where they sat cross-legged on the cool stone; others loitered by a large trestle table bearing coffee and doughnuts, or behind the pillars at the edges of the room, at the tops of which were perched a series of stone gargoyles. The air was cool and smelled of bleach. On the white-washed stone wall behind Kelsey hung a series of commandments written in thick Gothic script. On the table in front of him were a cup of Starbucks, a small dark blue book, and a microphone, which was connected to a small PA system, such as you might use at a church bingo game, amping his voice tinnily around the basement.

"I wish I could sit here like one of those smiley, happy people we seem to hear from so much in here and tell you that I quit drinking and got everything back. With me, it was all in reverse. I got sober, and within a year I had lost everything—my work, my wife, my agent, my house. Like a fire that hadn't quite burned itself out. The only message I have for the newcomers is 'brace yourselves.' You think that if you take these principles out into the world and try to practice them in all your affairs, you're going to be *welcomed*? You think a hedge-fund manager can sell derivatives in a spirit of love and service? Or that a divorce attorney can afford to preach forgiveness? You think a secretary of defense who told nothing but the truth would last longer than five minutes? Hmm?" He picked up the blue book sitting in front of him. "Make no mistake. This book is not a design for living. This is not a book for the peace bringers and basket makers. This does not tell us that the meek will inherit the earth. This book is a plan for *war*."

He shook the book at the room, then sat back in his seat and crossed his arms. "But that's probably more than enough from me. I'd like to hear what you guys have to say."

The room burst into prolonged and enthusiastic applause; there were even some whoops and cheers. Kelsey fought a losing battle not to smile. As the noise died down, the air filled with hands. He pointed to someone in the front row and the arms descended, revealing Godfrey's big bald black dome in the front row.

"Hi, my name is Godfrey and I'm a gratefully recovering alcoholic and addict."

"Hi, Godfrey," chorused the room as one. They packed a fair punch, all together like that.

"Thank you for your honesty today, Douglas. I know you've wrestled with this program, but today I heard a lot of honesty, a lot of acceptance, a lot of growth."

Kelsey grimaced infinitesimally.

Godfrey twisted around in his seat. "I *did*. He's a *lot* better than when he first came in, believe me. He was crazy as a coot when he first dragged himself through that door. Like a fist looking for a fight. Too twisted for color TV. His engine was running, but there weren't nobody driving!"

The room laughed with each turn of phrase. Kelsey, meanwhile, was staring down at his fingers drumming on the table—*thrum, thrum, thrum*—looking as if a small team of dentists had started work in the back of his head.

"I don't mean to take your inventory, child," continued Godfrey, his accent hiking further south than usual. "But you've got to give up on all this war talk. You must be reading a different big book from the one everyone else be readin', because there ain't no talk of war in that book. That's just untreated alcoholism, that is. The war's in here." He tapped the side of his head. "In that alcoholic head of yours."

Thrum, thrum, thrum went Kelsey's fingers on the desk. He leaned forward and tapped on the mike. All the heads turned his way, like those of spectators at a tennis match.

"I don't normally like it when people do this, but since it's me stuck up here today . . ." He paused and rubbed his beard. "You know, I've found one thing to be true and it's this: If you sit in meetings long enough, you'll hear just about everything attributed to 'the disease of alcoholism.' Thinking too much, not thinking at all. Feeling too much, not feeling a thing. Being too up, being too down. Being too much of a perfectionist, never getting anything finished. Being too domineering, being a doormat. . . . After much thinking, I've concluded that the main thing we all have in common is that we drink too much. There're only two types who come in here, the sad and the mad, and we count it progress when the one becomes the other."

This time, the laughter broke his way.

Everyone turned back to Godfrey.

"Well, in that case, you are *definitely* making progress," he quipped.

The room erupted.

For a moment, it looked as if Kelsey was going to say something else, but he didn't; he just shrugged and smiled to himself while the commotion died around him. Then the air filled with arms, but before he could pick anyone, the boy next to him spoke up. "We're going to take a fifteen-minute break," he said. "We'll go back to a show of hands at twelve-fifteen." Before he'd even finished the sentence, people were up out of their seats. Kelsey stood up to receive a small line of well-wishers who began to line up by the wall to his left; he shook their hands and listened to them with a patience honed by many a book signing. It was an older crowd than before, slightly rougher-looking, with more tattoos, more shaved heads; but everyone seemed to have a strangely beatific smile on their faces, and the ones who didn't were soon surrounded by people with concerned looks on theirs. There's no need to draw this out, I thought. Just get in, get his number, and get out. Short but sweet. I was halfway across the room when I saw Lola partway down the queue, talking to a tall, bald hipster in a tartan short-sleeved shirt and Peter Sellers–style spectacles. She looked very grave, nodded at what the guy was saying, then saw me and waved me over.

"It makes a big difference to someone with a needle in their arm," the hipster was saying as I drew near. "What are *they* going to think if they hear that? He *has* to think of the newcomers." Lola nodded again. She was wearing Saturday-morning gym clothes—hooded blue sweatshirt, slacks, sneakers—and her hair was down today, just grazing her collarbone. "Patrick!" she said, reaching out to hook her hand in my elbow. "How great to see you. Have you guys met each other? Scott, this is Patrick. Patrick, Scott. We were just talking about Doug's qualification. What did you think?"

"What did *I* think?" I said, touching my chest. "Well, let me see. I thought it was excellent. Yes. I would go so far as that. I would say it was excellent."

She nodded, a look of encouragement on her face, like a TV interviewer spurring on her subject.

"Uh," I said, gathering my thoughts. "I thought it was powerful. Extremely powerful. A powerful examination of one man's battle. And it *is* a battle. Did he say that? Yes, he did. A war, in fact. Yes, that's what he said: It's war, not a battle. I guess it can be both." I laughed, but it came out a little higher than I might have liked. "Lose the battle, you lose the war. You can't have a war without a battle. . . . It doesn't really matter which comes first. Either way, it's not pretty."

The two of them both wore a lightly stunned expression.

"He's new," said Lola apologetically. "He has . . . What do you have, Patrick? Three days?"

"You're kidding me," said Scott. "Why didn't you say? How are you feeling?"

"Not too bad," I replied. "All things considered. I mean, not great, obviously. I've seen better days. But not bad."

He gave me a sympathetic look. "I know. It's up and down at the beginning. Your brains are like scrambled eggs. It gets better; it really does. Here, let me give you my number."

"You don't have to do that," I said quickly, but it was too late. He already had his phone out and we were exchanging numbers. What was it with people giving you their number in recovery? You only had to catch their eye and they were all over you with promises to call and invitations to lunch and God knows what else. Didn't you ever just get to be unhappy in a corner somewhere, ruing a life misspent? We had taken one step closer to Kelsey, who was now talking to a large Hispanic Hell's Angel wearing a leather jacket adorned by sheriff's badges, a long gray ponytail halfway down his back.

"Call me, okay?"

"I will."

"We don't have to do this alone."

"I know."

He backed off, miming taking a phone call. The moment he was out of earshot, I let out a long sigh. Lola sniggered.

"You should see your face," she said.

"What's the matter with it?" I asked.

"Nothing," she said, wiping the smile from her face. "Scott can be a little hard-core."

The Hell's Angel stepped aside, and Kelsey saw us for the first time. "*Here* she is," he said, throwing his arms wide and drawing Lola into a hug. "My favorite sober woman."

"I never knew you were such a jerk to your wife," she said.

"I'm paying for it now," he replied, pulling back but staying in her arms, drinking her in. A surprisingly sharp shard of jealousy bisected my midriff.

"No matter how much it is, it's not enough," she said. "That was some bad shit you pulled. *Bad* alcoholic."

"I know," he said, grimacing. "Which reminds me: When are you off to see your father?"

"Next week."

"How do you feel about it?"

"Nervous. More about what I'm going to say than anything he might do."

"You're going to do great. You know that, right? Just say your piece and get the hell out. Don't let him pick a fight. Don't engage."

She shook her head and mouthed a silent *no*. "Hey, I want you to meet someone. This is Patrick. He has, like, one day."

Finally we were face-to-face. He had the kind of features that a sculptor would love: rough-hewn, ugly-handsome, his gray-blue eyes deeply recessed beneath a brow as wide as it was high, a wraparound of bony skull. He looked well-weathered, grizzled, solid but fugitive, his eyes alighting on different parts of me all at once, like a bird hopping from spot to spot. He held out his hand, his grip surprisingly soft. "Piano player's hands," Leo had told me, "like Gary Cooper's."

"Nice to meet you, Patrick," he said. "I'm sorry you got to hear me with only one day. How are you feeling?"

"Like my brains are scrambled eggs."

He smiled. "They say you get 'em back at five years."

"Get what back?" I asked.

"Your brains. . . . Isn't that right, Lo?"

"That's what I hear," she said.

"She outranks us," he said to me behind his knuckles. "Stand up straight when she addresses you."

"Ah," I said, straightening my spine. "I'm a big fan of *yours*, actually. I must have read *Freefall* over half a dozen times when I was at college. I hope you're still writing."

He paused, wonder on his face. "I'm sorry," he said. "I didn't mean that literally. You can stand any way you want."

"Oh," I said, slouching again.

"He really is new, isn't he?"

"I almost lost a girlfriend over that book," I continued. "And your second one, *The Grenadiers*? I don't understand what happened with the critics. *I* could see what you were doing. Dirty realism had become a complete blind alley by that point. What was your term for it? 'Literary anemia'? You were trying to give it a lifeline back to the work of Yates and Fitzgerald. *Any* fool could see that."

He held my gaze for a few seconds, taking me in. "Who did you say this little threat to sobriety was again?"

"Patrick," said Lola.

"That's very kind of you, Patrick, but there's only one book you need be concerning yourself with right now, and that's *this* one." He picked up the small dark blue book from the table and handed it to me.

"What's this?" I asked.

"You are holding in your hands the single most useful piece of American prose since the Bill of Rights."

It had no cover, no name, no author, nothing, just page after page of Bible-thin paper. Some passages were underlined in red pen; others sported scribbled marginalia. "Interesting," I said, handing it back to him. "But what about the novel you were working on in Woodstock? What happened to that?"

"No, you can keep that," he said, refusing the book.

"But it's your copy."

"He wants your number, as well," said Lola.

"Of course," he said, reaching for his jacket. "But just so you know: If it's a sponsor you're looking for, there are plenty of men out there who work this thing a lot better than I do."

"That's nonsense," said Lola. "He's talking nonsense. You sounded great today, Doug."

"Oh, you stick me up there, I'll sing," he said. "He was probably not even going to ask me, were you?"

"I do have a few questions," I said as he took the book from me and leaned over the table to write his number in the back. "Your novel for instance. The one you were working on. What happened to that?"

"It's sitting in a drawer somewhere."

"I'd love to read it."

"You already have."

"What are you talking about?"

He handed me back the little blue book. "Just now. My qualification. It's much the best version of that story, believe me. No *adjectives*. No *adverbs*. It's all nouns and verbs in recovery, you'll find."

The woman behind us in the queue—short, elderly, in a gray shawl—pushed forward to take his hand. "I loved what you said about growing up on military bases," she said. "My father was in the navy, and it was exactly the same for us, exactly the same. I can tell you used to be a writer."

He shrugged helplessly. The conversation was at an end. We beat a retreat to the snack table on the other side of the room; just beyond it lay the big oak doors that led back up to the street.

"Do you want a tip?" asked Lola.

I nodded.

"You should backcomb your hair a little and squeeze into some cutoff jeans. I don't think that jacket is going to cut it with the hard-core groupies."

"You're saying I came on a little strong?"

"Just a little. People normally leave that stuff at the door."

"What stuff?"

"Work."

"Ah."

"Hey, Pru!" she called out. *"Guess who I found!"*

Turning from the snack table, a plateful of doughnuts in one hand, licking the fingers of the other, was Prudence. She was wearing a bright yellow cocktail dress with a floral print that, upon closer inspection, turned out to be a pattern of tiny skull and crossbones. *"Finally* you get his attention," she said. "I know you've only just escaped the jaws of your own personal hell, Patrick, but do you think you could pay a little more attention to your environment? We were waving at you for *ages*."

"I was listening to Douglas."

"Looked like the onset of a vegetative state from where we were sitting. You'd better have some coffee. We've still got an hour to go."

"Actually, I think I'm probably going to split," I said, nodding the way of the door.

"Aww, c'mon. I was just messin' around."

"You know what, Pru," said Lola. "I don't think I'm going to stick around, either. I've got some work this afternoon."

"On *Saturday*?"

She made an apologetic face. Prudence looked back and forth between us, her eyes narrowing. "You're going to do this, aren't you? You're really going to leave me to listen to this lot whining about how triggering they find the eggnog."

"Sorry," said Lola.

"You rats . . . Okay. All right. Give me a minute. I'm coming with you."

As we headed for the door, a bell rang, calling the meeting to order.

chapter eleven

It was one of those unseasonably warm days you sometimes get in December, the sun chalky and diffuse through the branches of the trees; all over the city people were performing mini-stripteases, shedding clothes on the street, the subway. The steps leading up from the basement were mossy, the railings entwined with ivy, the church situated halfway down a street of residential brownstones. At one end, the traffic on Third Avenue was a speedy blur. We all headed that way, feeling the unfamiliar sensation of the sun on our backs.

"Did that hit the spot, Pru?" asked Lola.

"I liked the cross talk at the end. That was old-school."

"You mean that argument he had with Godfrey?" I asked.

"They're always at it," said Prudence. "Like Godzilla versus Mothra."

"Godfrey and Douglas don't really get along," explained Lola.

"Why not?"

"He thinks Godfrey is too evangelical. He sponsors a lot of

guys. Speaks at a lot of meetings. Douglas thinks it's a personality cult."

"He doesn't have any problem with personality cults," said Prudence. "He just wants them to be about *him*."

"You should have heard the questions Patrick was asking him," said Lola.

"I just wanted to know whether he was still writing."

"Probably got nothing to write about now that he's left all his angst back there in the woods. It's like Elton John. . . . Did you get that, by the way? How picturesque the whole thing was? The snow. The deer. The woods. Jeez. It's bad enough hitting bottom without trees being involved."

"Pru has never left the city," said Lola.

"That's not true. I went to Arizona. That was outside the city."

"That was *rehab*. You never left the compound."

"Hang on," I said, interrupting. "What do you mean, Douglas is 'like Elton John'?"

"He never did anything good once he sobered up," said Prudence. "Same with Clapton. Never did anything as good as 'Layla.' "

"That is unfair and you know it," said Lola. "What about the Chili Peppers? All their best albums were done clean . . . *Mother's Milk . . . Blood Sugar Sex Magik*."

"James Taylor," countered Prudence.

"Rufus Wainwright."

"Too many sound tracks. Billy Joel."

"Lou Reed."

Prudence narrowed her eyes.

"Which album?"

"*The Blue Mask*. That was beautiful."

"Okay. I'll give you that one. *One*."

"You are such a rock-press snob, Pru. What about live performances? I saw Cat Power while she was still out there, and it was a *mess*. She staggered onstage, played three chords, asked the audience if anyone had any lipstick, wandered off, never came back . . . Now, she gets up there and she sings her heart out. And the press are all like, 'I preferred her when she was all drunk and slutty.'" Prudence cackled. "That's when you know they're in trouble. When they start saying things like 'Here are the songs that mark my journey.' That's when you know the record is going to suck balls."

Lola exhaled loudly, glanced heavenward. I felt my exasperation build and break, like a wave.

"But this is just awful," I said.

They both looked at me.

"What's awful?" asked Prudence.

"It doesn't matter which one of you is right. Either way, it's awful. Douglas is a writer, a great one. He doesn't take . . . *dictation.* His work is his work. Nothing changes that. I mean, say he just doesn't believe in God? He's tried, he's really tried, but no. Nothing happening. Nothing he can do about it. Just doesn't. Sorry."

They both exchanged glances.

"Who said anything about God?" asked Lola.

"That's what this is all about, isn't it?" I said. "That's what it says on the wall. God. That's what everyone talks about all the time."

"I wouldn't get too hung on that stuff," said Lola. "I know one guy who made his Harley-Davidson his Higher Power."

"Someone else I know chose her Magimix blender," said Prudence.

"Her *Magimix*?" I asked, incredulous.

"Yup," said Prudence.

"And people fall for that, do they?"

"Fall for what?" asked Lola.

"Being patronized like that. 'We know that the whole God thing is kind of scary, so why don't you make it something nice and familiar and cuddly, so you won't be scared.' I mean, come *on*. At least have the guts to say it like it is. If you don't believe in God, at least call Him that so you know what it is you're not believing in, but a Magimix. That's just . . . that's . . ."

"I'm not sure I can carry on this conversation with you, Patrick," said Lola, slowing to a halt on the sidewalk. Prudence, too, slowed to a point just beyond her. We were just a few yards from the pedestrians and traffic streaming up Fourth. "Why—what—," I stammered.

"I mean, how could you *say* a thing like that? I really don't understand it."

"Don't understand what?"

"How could you sit through a meeting like that and not feel the presence of *something*?"

"Well I . . ."

"Maybe not God with a beard, but *something*, something larger than you and me, larger than all of us. Something lifting us up, binding us together, drawing us toward all that is good and right and true in the world."

"Okay. Look," I said, estimating the distance to the nearest pedestrians. "I'm not saying I didn't feel anything. In fact, I may well have felt something, come to think of it. A little twinge. More than a twinge. A tug."

"A tug?" she said hopefully.

"Definitely. Look, Lola. I didn't mean to offend you. I have the greatest respect for what you people get up to back there. It's just that it's a little beyond anything I've ever experienced, so I tend to get a little—Well, you don't even really want to know how it seems to me. . . ."

"I think it's best if you just go," she said, shielding her eyes behind her hand, as if unable to even look at me.

"You're not serious."

She nodded, and her shoulders began to shake.

"I'm sorry. I . . ."

At first I thought she was crying, and went to comfort her, but she fended me off, her head lowered, her face hidden behind a shaking curtain of hair. Then I looked over at Prudence and saw her trying to hide a smirk behind her hand. I looked back at Lola, who was still shaking, fighting hard not to laugh, but then she looked up at my face and lost it; then Prudence did, the two of them letting rip with high hoots of laughter that left them breathless and weak, hanging on to each other for support.

"Very funny," I said.

"That was . . ." said Lola.

"Help me . . ." said Prudence.

"Oh God."

"No. Please don't . . ."

"Just stop."

"A tug . . . He felt a tug. . . ."

That seemed to bring Lola to. "Oh no, that's not cool," she said, straightening up. "I'm sorry, Patrick. That was not cool. It was just . . . the look on your face. . . . I couldn't help myself. . . ."

"You got me," I said.

"I kind of lost it at the end."

"No, you were good."

"You're very kiddable, you know that?"

"I always thought I was a cynic."

"Cynics are the easiest. You're *dying* to believe."

We made it the rest of the way to Fourth Avenue in silence, jaws easing and rib cages subsiding. When we reached the corner, Prudence stopped. "I'm this way," she said, lifting her arms to indicate readiness to hug. Lola complied, wrapping her arms around her and squeezing her tight. "Are you going to the dance this year?" she asked her.

"I haven't made up my mind. It kind of blew last year."

"Yeah. I guess."

"You?"

"I'm going to be in L.A."

"Oh yeah. That's right. Good luck with that."

"Thanks," she said, then, remembering something, exclaimed, "Paul Westerberg!"

"When was *his* last album?"

"Okay, then what about Ryan Adams?"

"He's got less time than Patrick. I'm not hearing many big names here. Unless . . ."

Lola narrowed her eyes to a squint.

"Is she . . ." coaxed Prudence. "Dare she . . ."

"Okay . . ."

"She is, she's going for it!"

"Aerosmith," said Lola defiantly.

Prudence let loose a low cackle. "If I can get Aerosmith out of her, I *know* she's on the ropes. All right you hosers. Later, Hillbilly . . ."

She turned north up Third Avenue, giving us a metalhead salute over her shoulder as she went. It was one of those stretches of Third that looked like it had been thrown together in a hurry: a health clinic, a tanning salon, a laundry, a cinema, a pastry shop. A few blocks down, a series of spindly cranes shot up into the sky from a building site, hoisting not the girders of a building but the central tower of another, even bigger crane, which eventually would be used to construct a skyscraper. Boxes within boxes.

"Are you trying to get away from me or something?" asked Lola.

I spun around to find her scrutinizing me.

"No, no, no, not at all," I said a little too quickly. "I was just . . . I was just trying to get my bearings."

"Where you headed?"

"West Tenth and Bleecker."

"I can walk you as far as Broadway."

"Okay."

And so we set off south, toward the construction site.

"You've had that conversation before," I said.

"Yeah. She knows how to push my buttons. The fact is those guys don't really have any choice. You can't pick up any royalty checks if you're dead."

She laughed. All the unease that had been bubbling under since this conversation began came to the surface like boiling milk up the side of a pan. "Lola," I said abruptly. "There's something that I need to tell you."

"Shoot," she said.

"The fact is. . . . I'm not really decided about this whole thing. It may not be really right for me . . . at the end of the day."

"It's not for everyone."

"Right. Exactly. It was more of an experiment than anything. An experiment to see if I needed it or not, and the fact is, I'm beginning to realize that I probably don't. False alarm."

"Don't make up your mind too quickly."

"No, of course not, but I guess what I'm trying to say is you shouldn't be too surprised if I don't really stick around for *all* that long."

"Don't get too attached, you mean?" she said, arching her eyebrows.

"No. God no," I said, feeling my face flush. "That's not what I meant at all. . . ."

"It's okay, you're safe. That one-year rule is there for a reason. It's not to protect you guys. It's there to protect *us*. You're like little wrecking balls, you guys. You come in, you get sober, and the first thing you see you think is your mother. Like baby ducklings. Could be some old boot. A tractor."

It was as good as I was going to get. I let it go.

"I don't think you're anything like an old boot," I said.

"Why, thank you," she said.

"And I promise you you're nothing like my mother."

"Well, that's something, too."

"You're a lot wider around the hips, for one thing."

She looked at me, outrage dawning, then pushed me off the curb as we rounded the corner onto St. Mark's. It bustled with Saturday-morning shoppers heading in and out of the record stores, T-shirt shacks, tattoo parlors, and bong palaces. The air smelled of barbecue sauce and incense. In the window of one shop stood rows of T-shirts with messages like BUCK FUSH and FUCK MILK GOT POT? Outside the store stood racks of sunglasses and umbrellas, the shopkeeper as confused by the weather as everyone else.

"How's she like you living in New York?"

"My mother? Calls me every time the threat chart on CNN goes above orange. I explain to her that I have more chance of being electrocuted in the bathtub than I do of being killed by a terrorist."

"How's that go down?"

"She tells me to clear my bathroom of all electrical appliances."

"Yeah, right. How long have you been out here, Patrick?"

"Just under a year."

"Oh, you really *are* a baby," she said, looking at me. "How come you moved?"

"I was offered a job."

"You couldn't get a job back in London?"

"Yes, of course, but . . . it's just a bigger pond, isn't it?"

"And what was it about the other pond you didn't like?"

That flummoxed me. "It's not that I didn't like it; it's just . . . normally when an American asks me that question, I just say something with the words *dream* and *opportunity* and that gets me off the hook."

"Oh, he's funny," she said, as if reporting the conversation to a third party. "And that works for you, does it?"

"What?"

"Telling people what you think they want to hear."

She smiled and reached up behind her head, bunching her hair with one hand, then rolling down the rubber band she had bunched on the knuckles of the other in one well-practiced motion, then shook her newly bunched hair free. Her ears were pierced several times, I saw, but she wore no earrings.

"Is that what you think I'm doing?"

She ignored my question. "I always like to find out the reasons people come to New York—the real reasons, not the ones they give. They're always a little off."

"How do you figure that?"

"You go to a place like Boston, it's normally because you have a pretty good reason to go to Boston. Maybe your sister lives there. Maybe you have a job. You go to Pittsburgh, well, you'd better have a pretty good reason to go to Pittsburgh." She laughed. "But all the people that are left—all the people who don't have a very good reason to be anywhere? They come to New York. I think it's all the choice. It saves having to make up your mind."

"Actually, I came out here for a girl," I said.

"You did?" she said, her interest level rising.

"I met her in London. We thought it was something more. So I came out to stay with her."

She winced. "How'd that work out?"

"She chucked me out after three months."

"Three months," she said. "Not bad. . . . She'll be first on your amends list."

"My what?"

"You draw up a list of all the people you've harmed over the course of your life and you make amends with them. You don't have to worry about that now. It comes later."

"I've got absolutely *nothing* to apologize to Caitlin about," I said, feeling a small swell of anger. "She threw *me* out."

"It's not an apology. It's an amends. Okay, so look, I haven't spoken to my father in four years, not since I quit. I came in convinced he was the one who had done this to me, that he was responsible for everything. So I spent the night in jail once because *he* refused to put up bail. But the fact is, *I* totaled his car. I also stole a lot of money from him. So *I* need to make amends. It's not an apology. I'm just there to set the situation right."

"But that's crazy."

She looked a little shocked. "How so?"

"Atonement for your sins. That's the idea?"

"You're a little judgmental. Has anyone ever told you that?"

"That's a judgment, too, you know. Calling me judgmental."

"And a smart-ass!" she said, laughing and shaking her head. "Jeez. Are you ever going to get a lot out of this. Wait till you've had the stuffing knocked out of you a few times and *then* we'll see how you sound."

"Well, that isn't going to happen, I'm afraid."

We reached the corner of St. Mark's and Fourth, the wider avenue arriving out of nowhere, cutting the buildings high and narrow. On the traffic island in the middle sat a large burnished-steel cube sculpture. On the other side of it, the Astor Place Barnes & Noble; beyond that, the traffic streaming down Broadway. Lola saw a fire hydrant on the corner, placed her foot on it, and proceeded to retie her sneakers. "I'm this way," she said, nodding down Fourth.

"I know where to go from here," I said.

She remained intent on her laces. "Do you want to know something my father once told me?" she said. "He said the reason the fire hydrants in Los Angeles were yellow was because they served Sprite and the reason the fire hydrants in New York were red was because they served Coke."

"And you *believed* that?"

"I was seven."

"I think I knew that at seven just from watching *Sesame Street*."

"You got *Sesame Street* in the UK?"

"Yes, we did," I said with mock indignation. "On these things called TVs. They're powered with this thing called electricity. In houses. With hot and cold running water. You didn't invent everything."

"Well, we invented the TV, I know that much."

She swapped feet on the fire hydrant. I stared at her hard. "What are you talking about? It was John Logie Baird."

"John Bogie *who*?"

"John Logie Baird."

"Is that supposed to be, like, the name of a *person*?" She laughed.

"The man who invented the TV."

She shook her head. "No way. It was Philo Taylor Farnsworth."

"Philo who?"

"Taylor Farnsworth. The guy who invented TV."

"It was John Logie Baird."

"Stubborn *and* wrong."

She laughed, stood up and kissed me on the cheek. I caught a whiff of that clean, plain smell of hers. "Don't go anywhere, Patrick. It would be a shame to lose you. You're an original."

She turned and walked away. I stood there for a while, watching her walk down Fourth Avenue, her hair swinging behind her, feeling something ticklish and rotten in my chest, like the first swell of a toothache. The other pedestrians moved around me like fish around a diver. But it *was* John Logie Baird, I thought, coming to and moving off.

chapter twelve

BY THE TIME I reached my building, I knew I was in trouble; by the time I had let myself into my apartment, I knew I was in big trouble. Lying to someone about work was one thing, but lying to someone you liked, that was another. And lying to someone who made all the molecules in your body jazz around like a pinball machine every time you thought of her, well, that was another thing altogether. I knew from the moment I had first laid eyes on her that this girl spelled trouble. I knew that any possible move in her direction would spell complete disaster. She was a no-fly zone, a black hole, a rip in the space-time continuum. So what did I go and do? I only went and hung out with her after a meeting and had a conversation—a proper conversation, a great conversation, in fact, the kind where you flirt and bait and switch and tease, in the course of which she had bunched her hair up behind her head with one hand, revealing pink pierced but unadorned earlobes and soft tendrils of hair wreathed in the nape of her neck. Was she *trying* to make this more difficult?

She had to. She had to know. It was always something I thought I could tell about a girl: what proportion of her life she had been admired. Some bend in the light, a haze in the air around her, an extra beat in her reaction time, which she waited for the world to fill. It was important information to have—it told you how much attitude you were going to get, but there was something about Lola that was throwing my calculations off. She had the friendliness level of a girl half as attractive. She'd certainly called me on my shit, although normally girls only pointed out that stuff three months into a relationship, and it was generally a sign that the relationship was about to end. That was the way it worked. It was like witnesses to a massacre: You didn't want anyone who had seen all that stuff hanging around. But Lola had found out all that stuff within six minutes of talking to me, and it hadn't been the end of the conversation; it had been the beginning. She hadn't said it to be insulting; she had said it in the same way that you'd say that the sky is blue or that water is wet, like it was just a fact, and maybe not the most important fact. I'd never been spoken to like that before. There was some mixture of the girlish and the grown-up to her that I hadn't encountered. Some of the things she said sounded like they came out of the mouth of a seventeen-year-old, others like they came out of the mouth of a seventy-year-old. It was as if she'd skipped the whole middle chunk of her life, the bit everyone spends learning about boring things like mortgages and jobs and breakfast cereals.

I knew what had taken that chunk out of her, of course, and that thought brought my pacing around my apartment to an abrupt halt. Nothing could ever happen between us. I knew that. For something to happen, I would have to tell her, and to tell her . . . well, I couldn't imagine it. It was like quarks and protons. One heard tell of their existence, but one couldn't actually see the things. I had to concentrate on Kelsey. Putting the kettle on, my thoughts ran back to the chastened, grizzled figure I had seen at the meeting this morning, this most private of men forced to cough up his pound of flesh for a bunch of complete strangers. I had thrilled, momentarily, at the mention of his old creative writing tutor at Santa Cruz, the one who had drunk even more than the students and sometimes slept it off in Kelsey's car—Raymond Carver! I'd felt like shouting. That was Raymond Carver!—though no one else in the audience seemed to know or care. After that, we were deep into the thickets of his marriage. He couldn't work without the feeling of her hands on his shoulder in the morning, he said. He used to plead with her for an opinion of his work, only to turn on her when she finally delivered it. One time, he even went back over their first love letters with a red pen, editing them for sentiment. Then he had quit drinking, and things seemed to get worse. First he realized he had fallen out of love with her and told her so. She left a week later. He came home from a long walk and thought the house had been burgled. Then he noticed that only her stuff was gone.

"The first gift of sobriety," he joked. Then he hit a block with his book. That's when he'd really panicked. He made a "whole bunch of phone calls I shouldn't have made"—I was assuming those were the ones to his editor that sent everything south. He got sued, sold his house, paid them back, moved back to New York. He hadn't sounded angry about any of this, just weary. "The fire hadn't burnt itself out," he said. "It still had a little ways to go." I didn't know what that meant. When you stopped drinking, weren't things supposed to get better? I got up, boiled the water, made myself a cup of tea, and retreated to the sofa with that book he'd given me. Opening it at random, I read:

> There was a sense of victory, followed by such a peace and serenity as I had never known. There was utter confidence. I felt lifted up, as though the great clean wind of the mountaintop blew

through and through. God comes to most men gradually, but His impact on me was sudden and profound. I was soon to be catapulted into what I like to call the fourth dimension of existence. I was to know happiness, peace, and usefulness and a way of life that is incredibly more wonderful as time passes.

Jesus Christ.

I'm not making this up. It was all like that, all sappy extended metaphors—"the road of Happy Destiny," "the Sunlight of the Spirit," "the Bridge of Reason," "the Shore of Faith"—and boy! The exclamation marks everywhere! To convey the joys of sobriety! I was just about to hurl the book across the room, when my phone rang. It came as quite a shock. Gingerly, I picked it up.

"Hello?"

"Patrick. What's up?"

"Saul! How nice to hear from you!"

"Are you okay?"

"Yes, of course I am, I'm great! It's just it's nice to hear from you, that's all!"

"What are you up to?"

"Oh, uh, just catching up on my reading."

"Anything good?"

"Definitely not. One for the slush pile."

"I'm heading down to Hudson Bar and Books to meet Nat later for a drink. I said I would give you a shout to see if you wanted to come."

In the apartment block opposite, people house-cleaned, watched TV, and unpacked shopping while the sky behind them deepened to a dark magenta. I could do with a drink; that book was doing my head in.

"Absolutely," I said. "Give me twenty minutes."

* * *

"Let's see, Updike's an Episcopalian. Roth isn't practicing. Mailer kind of got God, but only at the end, and it was a very Mailerized God. And Salinger went all Zen on us, of course. . . ."

Saul stirred his whiskey sour as he tried to answer my question. We were sitting in one of the back corners of Hudson Bar and Books—narrow and dark, with a long beaten-copper saloon. Crisply shirted barmen tossed cocktails back and forth over their shoulders, while the patrons, arrayed around small round candle-lit tables, sipped from large balloon glasses of wine. Deep maroon shadows swam with the aroma of cigar smoke and cognac.

"What about more fringe stuff?" I asked him. "Cults. That kind of thing."

"Well, DeLillo made mincemeat of the Moonies a couple of novels back. Most writers are too busy playing God themselves to get religion. Why? What is this about? You got someone who looks like cracking?"

"Not exactly. I was just wondering whether any career has survived a brush with that stuff—"

"Okay, you know what?" said Natalie suddenly. "This isn't going to work for me. If I'd known you guys were going to talk shop, I would have stayed home."

We both looked at her, shocked.

"Of course," said Saul.

"Absolutely," I said.

We looked at each other, then back at Natalie, then back at each other again, then down at our drinks. The noise of the bar seemed to swell around us, drowning out any possible topics of conversation, our heads as empty as beach balls.

"You really don't have a clue, do you, either of you?" she said. "You can yak all day long about overseas rights, or translation rights, or who sold what to whom, but you've absolutely no idea what a normal human conversation goes like."

"Of course we do," protested Saul. "But you just killed off the conversation."

"It died an unnatural death," I said.

"Exactly, Patrick. An unnatural death. There has to be a period of grieving."

"A decent interval at least."

"At least."

We both grinned at each other. Behind us, a woman guffawed at something her date had just said, leaving us in an even greater pool of silence. Natalie patiently tapped her drink with her straw. "O-*kay*," she said. "Be like that. Saul, perhaps you'd like to ask Patrick what his holiday plans are."

"She's not really going to do this, is she?"

"Looks like it."

"Patrick, d'you have any holiday plans yet?"

"No."

He upturned his palms.

"Patrick," she said. "Saul and Liz will be celebrating their two-year anniversary in January. Perhaps you'd like to ask him how he does it."

"How you do it, Saul?"

"No idea," he said, knocking back a slug of his drink. "Two years, huh? Thanks for reminding me, Nat."

"Okay, now you're both just being difficult. What about that new girl you've been seeing, Patrick? How's *that* going?"

"What girl?" asked Saul, looking up.

I shook my head, swished the dregs of my drink around my glass. "There's no girl."

"What do you mean?" said Natalie. "You took her on a date. You were going to see her again, you said."

Saul's surprise spread across his face. I looked from him to her, then back, then down at my drink. "It's just this girl I saw. It can't go anywhere. Does anybody want another drink?"

"You've been keeping this very quiet," said Saul, drawing closer to the table. "I *knew* you were up to something. So, what's she like? Party girl? Bimbo? Slutbox?"

Natalie shot him a look.

"What?" he protested. "You should see the girls he pulls up on that thing. 'Things I Find Sexy: Sweat.' 'Things I Find Sexier: Sweating together.' 'Things You Will Find in My Bedroom: Me.' "

"Okay, calm down," I said, trying to kick him under the table. "That was just a joke. I didn't meet up with any of those girls. I was just . . . after Caitlin . . . I felt like . . . Okay . . . guys . . . can I ask you something? This is serious. Do you think that . . . I behaved badly with her in any way?"

"With who? Caitlin?" asked Saul.

"Yes. Do you think I owe her an apology?"

"You don't owe that girl anything," said Natalie, always my fiercest defender in this regard. "Why? Who said that you did?"

"Nobody. It's just I've been so busy blaming her for everything, I wonder if . . . I don't know. If that's the whole story."

"I'd have thought she owed *you* an apology."

"That's sweet of you, Nat, thanks. It's just . . . Oh, forget about it. It's nothing."

"What's eating you, Patrick?" asked Saul.

"It's just . . . sometimes I think I moved out here . . . too lightly."

" 'Too lightly.' "

"Yes. Have you ever felt like that? Like you made a really big, important decision but you weren't really there for it? You signed off on it at the time, but looking back on it, you see that you weren't really there. Like someone else was really doing it and you were just along for the ride. Sometimes I feel like that. Like I packed my bags, but not me, if that isn't too weird."

"Where do you think you are?" asked Natalie.

I looked up, to find the same concerned look on both their faces. "Oh Lord," I said. "What am I even talking about! What a loon! I am so sorry, guys. Getting all existential on you like that . . ."

"No, no," said Saul. "You made a big move; that's not nothing. . . ."

"What are you guys having?" I asked. "More of the same?"

I took their orders and made my way to the bar, where I laid my elbow, a twenty between my fingers, and breathed a sigh of relief. That was close. I was going to have to watch myself. Saul was onto me, I could tell. I was acting weird and he could see right through the weirdness. I needed a drink. One of the bartenders, shaking a cocktail, gave me a nod; somewhere in my jacket, my phone started to buzz. I got it out and, this time, recognized the number.

"Felix," I said. "Thank God."

"Why thank God?"

"I'm having a tough time here."

"What's going on?"

I sank onto the bar, lowered my voice. "I went to that meeting you told me about—where were you, by the way? I looked for you, but you weren't there."

"I overslept."

"Oh. Well, anyway, I went, and afterward I got to talking with Lola. So we're walking and talking and really hitting it off, you know. I mean, she patronized me, insulted me a little. Do you know she actually told me she thought I owed Caitlin an apology?"

"You mean an amends?"

"Yeah, that's it. Can you believe that? She'd only been talking to me for five minutes."

"You might want to think about it."

"About what?"

"The amends. Lola would never date a guy who hasn't done his ninth step."

"Do you listen to anything I ever tell you, Felix? I'm faking this whole thing! You know that, right?" The bartender arrived; I mouthed the words *whiskey sour* and held up three fingers. He nodded and turned to the wall of liquor bottles behind him, pulling out a bottle of Jim Beam.

"It's still a very alcoholic thing to do," said Felix. "That doesn't mean you don't need this."

"Nobody is telling me that. It's me who—"

"You've earned that seat," he said, a catch in his voice. "You belong there as much as anybody, and nobody can tell you otherwise. . . ."

"They're not, Felix. I—"

"Nobody can turn you away from that door, nobody, you hear me? Nobody."

He sounded on the verge of tears.

"I hear you, Felix, I hear you. Jeez. Calm down. Why do you even care?"

There was a pause before he answered. "Because you're the only remotely normal person I've met in there. All the others are like little pod people. They're always saying they want normies to do the program anyway."

" 'Normies'?"

"Civilians. Normies. 'If only the normies did this, maybe the world would be a better place.' "

"How obnoxious."

"It's what they say. I've even heard Lola say it."

"You have?"

"Uh. Yes. Many times."

"So what exactly *is* an amends?"

"It's when you go back to someone you've wronged and offer to make it up to them."

"What if the person has wronged you?"

"You still make the amends."

"Why?"

“I’m not sure. Something to do with forgiving yourself? I can’t talk for much longer, actually. *America’s Next Top Model* is about to come on. Do you watch that show?”

“No.”

“You should. They get these models and get them to dress up as circus freaks and then they rip them to shreds. ‘Your skin needs a little work.’ ‘You’re too hoochy.’ ‘You weren’t smiling on the inside!’ They’re very mean.”

“I’ll try to catch it,” I said as the bartender arrived back with three whiskey sours. I hung up and dug around in my pocket for another twenty. Maybe it wouldn’t be such a bad idea, I thought as I waited for my change. See what I’m up against. I might even get something out of it—kind of a “clean as you go” arrangement. Plus, there would be the look on Caitlin’s face. I took a hefty swig of my drink. The idea got better the more I thought about it. The bartender came back with my change; I left him a hefty tip.

chapter thirteen

OKAY. *BUSINESSLIKE AND BRISK.*

Do not expect any particular reaction.

She is a spiritually sick person, too; she just doesn't know it.

But don't point that out. You're there to sweep your side of the street, not hers.

It was one of those cold, crisp Sunday mornings that made you feel every inch of your lungs. My insides felt tarred and feathered; my temples pounded. I'd gotten far drunker last night than I'd intended to. The Bowery was almost empty but for the refrigerators, sinks, and stoves that stood outside the restaurant-supply stores, their stainless-steel surfaces glinting in the sun, as if some natural disaster had shoved mankind toward extinction while the Earth repopulated with kitchen appliances. Wincing in the glare, I made my way down the street, the memory of the conversation I had had the night before coming back to me in fits and starts. I'd caught her just in time: In a few days she was leaving to see her family in Pennsylvania. She had sounded surprised to hear from me, suspicious. The only time she could meet for brunch was today, she'd said, and suggested a place near her apartment that we'd been to many times before. A narrow alley-way, bedecked with hanging baskets and Christmas lights, led to a quaint, Dickensian window, the panes steamed up with the cold. Inside, couples leaned into one another across their tables, while young waiters, some with patchy scrublands of beard, ferried breakfast and coffee. The walls were hung with a gallery of stuffed animal heads—a deer's, a ram's, a bear's, a goose's, all bearing the expression of stunned perplexity worn by all stuffed animals. In the corner was the head of a boar who looked like he had, until a few moments ago, been happily grubbing in the dirt for truffles and was now most disgruntled to find himself hanging on a wall above my ex-girlfriend, Caitlin, while she perused the Sunday *New York Times*. She was wearing a gray turtleneck sweater and a fawn jacket; she'd had her hair cut into a neat blond bob: a postbreakup cut. She didn't see me until I was almost upon her.

"Oh," she said, her hand going to her neck. "You gave me a shock."

"I tried waving, but you were reading—ah, your favorite." She was reading the "Style" section of the *Times*.

"What's that supposed to mean?"

"You always read that section first."

"I started with the *Book Review*, actually," she said, putting it away officiously. If there was a more misleading advert on TV than the one for the *New York Times*, showing a happy young couple, cozying up in bed with their favorite sections (Him: "I like to start with 'Arts & Leisure' "; her: "I like the magazine"), I did not know what it was. This most romantic of rituals had, for Caitlin and me, been a weekly ordeal, prickly with defensiveness and denial.

"Like your haircut."

"Thank you," she said, cupping the bottom of her bob with her hand. "I'm not used to it yet."

"It's nice."

"Thank you," she said again.

"So," I said.

"So," she said, raising her eyebrows, looking down at the table.

"Thanks for seeing me."

She frowned. "Of *course* I'll see you. How are you?"

"I'm great, thanks. Just great. And you?"

"Well, like I said, I'm having a packing nightmare at the moment. Not just my suitcases but the presents for everybody. I've got to get it down to two bags. And *no* liquids. Isn't that absurd? What are you doing? Are you going home?"

"Actually, no, I'm staying here."

She tilted her head. "Really? Miserable. What are you going to do on Christmas Day?"

I was about to reply, when the waiter appeared between us, dispensing menus. I hated the way New York waiters did that, just butted right in. "We have an excellent eggs Benedict with a delicious hollandaise sauce made with fresh Devonshire cream," he said. "Also, a crispy chicken salad made with fresh endives, Stilton—"

Caitlin held up her hand. "It's okay. I know what I want. I'll have the scrambled eggs with lox—the eggs not overdone, please, with just a little milk—and some whole-wheat toast—not dark, just lightly toasted—and a glass of orange juice and a coffee."

He scribbled to get it all down. "I'll have an English muffin and coffee," I said, handing my menu back to him.

"Excellent," he said, taking the menus and leaving us in silence, as if absconding with our conversation. Caitlin looked around a little awkwardly.

"I'm sure you must be a little confused as to why I called you," I said.

"If this is about the other week, I think I've already apologized."

"No, no, no, it's not that. It's more . . . well . . . I've been doing a bit of thinking about my conduct while we were dating and I've come to the conclusion that it left a lot to be desired."

She cocked her head curiously. "Well, that's very sweet of you, Patrick. I really appreciate that. Truly I do. But what are you talking about, exactly?"

"Well. Uh. Nothing specifically. But in general. I think I need to take more responsibility for myself, for my own actions, and stop blaming other people so much."

"Blaming people."

"Yes."

"Meaning me."

"It wasn't entirely your fault. No one person can be responsible for destroying another person's happiness so thoroughly. That person has to choose to be unhappy, don't you see? It wasn't your fault. It was my choice."

She blinked twice, in quick succession. "I'm sorry," she said. "I thought you said you wanted to apologize to me for something."

"I *do*. For blaming you."

"Blaming me for *what*?"

I tried very hard not to roll my eyes.

"Let's not go there, shall we?"

"'Let's not go there'? But you brought it up!"

"I didn't bring it up."

"Yes, you did! You called me up last night, drunk, I might add, and more than a little weepy, and you're all 'Caitlin, I need to see you. Caitlin, I need to apologize for something.' I think, Okay, a little weird, but okay. I turn up. And the thing you want to tell me, the thing that's burning you up, is that you *forgive me*?"

Her nostrils flared when she said this. The couples on either side of us had fallen silent, leaning across their tables and grasping hands and whispering, shielding themselves from the failed relationship in their midst, like sheep from a wolf.

"Look, you're taking this entirely the wrong way," I said a little haughtily. "I just wanted to sweep my side of the street is all."

"Sweep your *what*?"

"Clear away some of the wreckage of the past."

" 'The wreckage of the past,' " she repeated.

"That was a poor choice of words. You're not a piece of wreckage, obviously. . . ."

"Patrick . . . Look at me."

"Yes?"

"Is this an *amends*?"

I froze. They didn't tell me what to do if you were rumbled. I nodded, tentatively.

"You're in *recovery*?"

I blanched.

Her jaw fell open by half an inch.

"A lot of people are these days," I said.

"But Patrick, this is ridiculous. You don't drink *that* much."

"Not anymore I don't," I said, seeing the waiter approach with our breakfast and lowering my voice. "It's not how much you drink. It's how unmanageable your life gets. I don't see why you find it so hard to believe."

"But you're the biggest control freak I know!"

"Internally."

" 'Internally.' "

"Yes. Internally."

"Enjoy!" said the waiter, placing the plates on the table, looking at our faces, and then beating a hasty retreat. Caitlin stared at me, saucer-eyed, which was certainly better than staring at me with her nostrils flared. I needed to consolidate my advantage. "Excuse me for a minute, will you?" I said. "I need to speak to someone."

Getting up from my chair, I walked a couple of yards to the

breakfast bar, behind which a row of cappuccino machines gurgled and hissed. I perched on one of the stools, got out my phone, and dialed Felix's number, checking that Caitlin was within hearing range. The phone rang seven times, then went to a voice message: a long stretch of silence, punctuated only by the sound of Felix's breathing, followed by the beep. Damn.

"Felix. It's me, Patrick. If you're there, pick up. I really need to talk to you. I'm having a bit of difficulty with that thing we talked about and I need some advice on what to—"

Clunk. He picked up.

"Felix? Thank God. Listen, I'm having some problems on this end. Is this a good time? Can you talk?"

Silence.

"Felix? Hello? Are you there?"

"Yeah," he said finally. "I guess." He sounded devastated, lethargic.

"What's going on?" I asked. "Are you okay?"

He loosed a long, weary sigh of the kind emitted by sleeping giants, lesser-known deities of the forest, and Easter Island monoliths.

"She's gone," he said.

"Who? Who's gone?"

"The most beautiful girl to ever walk that catwalk. And they just threw her away like she was a piece of garbage."

"What are you talking about, Felix?"

"Didn't you watch it?"

"Watch what?"

"America's Next Top Model."

I glanced nervously at Caitlin, who had begun buttering her toast.

"Er, yes, I did see that. It was very sad, Felix, but I've got a situation here and I need your help—"

"She had hypothermia! They put her in a swimming pool and

told her to smile with her eyes, and she did. She smiled with her eyes for so long, she got hypothermia, and then they blamed her for not knowing her limits. Tyra's gone too far this time. She's gone too far."

"That's awful, Felix, but," I began, then suddenly saw my opening, like a chink of daylight in rubble. I raised my voice slightly. "Of course she went too far, Felix. That's the whole point. None of us knows his limits. We smile with our eyes, but not in our hearts. And then before you know it—bam. We're out. Blue with hypothermia."

"I guess."

Caitlin had stopped buttering her toast now and was resting her knife on her plate.

"It's a tragedy that she's gone," I continued. "But maybe there's a lesson to be learned there. Because that could be any one of us. It's a day at a time, Felix. That's all we ever have, one day."

"She skipped off the stage when she left. Did you see that?"

"I'm sure she's gone to a better place."

"You think?"

"A much better place."

"You mean the reunion show? Or . . . or . . . maybe a guest appearance on *The Hills*? Do you think she'll make a guest appearance on *The Hills*?"

"Almost definitely, but I can't talk long, I'm afraid. I'm in the middle of that amends we talked about."

"How's it going?"

"Oh, you know. It's painful, but that's the truth for you."

"Call me later."

"I will."

"Keep it real."

"I will. Oh, and get yourself a new outgoing message, Felix, for God's sake. You sound like you're stalking yourself."

Slipping the phone into my pocket, I returned to our table

with as much nonchalance as I could muster, respread my napkin on my lap, and started buttering my muffin with what I hoped was the simple gratitude of a man happy for a plate of hot food in front of him. "Your scrambled eggs will get cold," I said, pointing at Caitlin's plate with my fork.

"Patrick."

"Hmm?"

"Patrick, look at me—"

I looked up. Her face was a picture of molten compassion. She reached out and cupped my hand in hers. "I am *so* sorry. God, you must think me terrible. I can't believe I was such an idiot. I had no idea, just none. Was it the breakup?"

"I'm sorry?"

"Was it the breakup that made you hit bottom?"

"No, no, of course not," I said, appalled by her narcisissm, withdrawing my hand. "It was a long time coming, but it's all over now. Long in the buildup, quick in the finish. All better." I started buttering my muffin again.

"But it all makes so much sense, now that I think about it."

"Makes sense of what?"

"Your behavior."

I froze. "What behavior?"

She smiled. "Oh, you know. The grandiosity, the self-pity, the mood swings, the self-absorption."

"Self-absorption?"

"There's more to life than just making deals for books, Patrick."

"Of course there is. I know that."

"Oh yeah? Like what?"

"Well, the books themselves. They're much more important than the deals for the books."

She smiled, shook her head.

"And the people who write the books. They're much more important than the books, and the deals for the books. And then there's everybody else. The people the books are about, the real people."

Her smile turned sad. "You really have no idea, do you?"

"How can you say that to me, Caitlin? Of course I do. I didn't come out here for work. I came out here for you."

"No, you didn't."

"Of course I did."

She shook her head. "We *both* know why you came out here."

I felt a quick cooling sensation in my gut. I started gathering my napkin. "Look, I really appreciate you coming out here to see me at such short notice, really I do. But it's best to keep these things short and to the point. I should probably be heading back." I pushed my chair out.

"Hang on," she said. "Aren't you supposed to ask me if you've forgotten something?"

"I don't think so," I said, looking around for the waiter. "That must be another type of recovery. Overeaters Anonymous maybe."

"Yes. I'm certain of it. My father is sober, or had you forgotten? You're supposed to ask me if there's anything I'd like to add."

I sank back into my chair.

She cleared her throat and began.

"You live in such a complete dreamworld, Patrick. Which would be charming were it not so insulting to the people around you. I thought it was charming, once upon a time. It was when I first met you. You seemed to live in your own little world, and it seemed such a nice place to be. It took me a while to realize it's just your way of getting what you want."

"But that's not—"

She held up a hand. "You see, this is just the problem with you, Patrick. You never listen. You never do. And you can convince yourself of just about anything. You told yourself this wonderful romantic story about how you came out here for me, and how heartbroken you were when it all ended."

"I was. . . ."

"But that's not the reason you came out here, Patrick. And you know it. You came out here because you almost got fired."

I felt my cheeks flush with anger. "That is not true."

"It *is* true, Patrick."

"I didn't get *fired*."

"That's what you told me."

"I was being overdramatic."

"Well, whatever happened, you were in a bad way when I met you. I didn't quite realize it at the time, because I was so bowled over by all the attention. It's kind of heartbreaking when I think about it, because I really did believe it was me you were interested in, not New York."

"I was."

"No," she said angrily, shaking her head, her eyes filling with tears that wouldn't fall. "The reason you left had nothing to do with me. It was because everything was beginning to fall apart around you and you wanted out, just like you always do. You fled, Patrick. You ran. That's why it's so great you're doing what you're doing now. Really. You're going to meet such great people. Totally in touch with their humanity, you know?"

I let the insult go. Above Caitlin's head, the stuffed boar's head looked much as I now felt. So this was what recovery was about, was it? Breaking up a second time, only this time more insultingly? Caitlin exhaled noisily, like someone who has just come off a Stair-Master. "Wooo!" she said. "That was—wow—that felt—woow—great! I wasn't . . . I wasn't too hard on you, was I?"

"No. That's what it's all about. Hearing the truth."

"So tell me everything! You have to tell me who you've met. . . ."

chapter fourteen

It just went to show how stupid I had been ever to trust her. I'd had a weak moment, confided in her, and look what happened: It got taken down to be used as evidence against me. They hadn't been about to *fire* me. What happened was this: I'd received a new novel from one of Smith and Fairfax's best clients, the South African writer Richard Blomkamp, gone out to celebrate, and when I woke up the next morning the manuscript was gone. I retraced my steps to the Groucho, the minicab firm that ferried me home—no luck. It wasn't a fireable offense. It was lost for only a couple of weeks. Eventually, Blomkamp tracked down a previous draft of the book, one that he ended up preferring and using. The problem was not him. The problem was our new office manager, who had been making notes on my various indiscretions ever since she'd arrived at the office at the beginning of the year—an overlong lunch here, a missed morning there. The loss of the Blomkamp manuscript was exactly what she'd been looking for: an opportunity to read me the riot act and hang me out to dry in front of our boss. Yes, it had been the single most unpleasant afternoon of my life; yes, I had for a period feared that maybe, if I didn't play things right, I stood a small chance of getting fired. But your mind plays strange tricks on you in a situation like that. A few days later, Gavin threw the dinner party at which I met Caitlin, and then I was New York bound. There had been no reason to tell Leo or Saul or Natalie about any of my indiscretions in London. If Leo had seen in me the qualities that made for a great agent, then Leo had seen those qualities. I wasn't making *them* up. It had been a clean slate, a fresh start, a second act, all that. That was the whole point of this country, wasn't it? Standing on the corner of the Bowery and Delancey, beneath the awning of a bodega, I punched the last digit of Douglas Kelsey's number into my phone and plugged my finger in my ear to block out the noise of the traffic. My anger gave me just the kick of brazenness I needed to make the call. He answered after the fifth ring, his voice low and bleary, like I had just woken him up.

"Hello?"

"Mr. Kelsey?"

"Yes?"

"This is Patrick? We met at the meeting on Saturday? You gave me your number."

"Sure. Lola's friend. How are you?"

"I wonder if we could talk. I just had an amends backfire on me."

"Who was it with?"

"My ex."

"Ah. She didn't play ball."

"She demolished me."

"And now you're wishing the genie could go back in the bottle? Look, nobody said this was going to be easy, Patrick. You don't come out of this smelling like roses. You can't count on getting any particular reaction. They might accept what you say, or they might rip you a new one; it doesn't matter because— Hang on . . . *What in hell's name are you doing making an amends with only three days?"*

"Uh—"

"Jesus Christ. You see, this is exactly what happens. The evangelicals get you guys whipped up into a frenzy; then out you go and run slam into a wall. You don't feel like drinking, do you?"

"I don't feel one hundred percent."

"*BILLY, NO!*" he shouted suddenly. "Excuse me," he said, and disappeared from the line, to be replaced with the sound of some scuffling, then something that sounded like furniture being dragged across the floor. *"Billy, no. Let go— That's it—there you go—go lie down— LIE DOWN!"*

He came back to the phone. "I'm sorry. I'm going to have to take this dog out before he destroys my sofa. Where are you?"

"On the corner of Bowery and Delancey."

"You're not far from me. Do you know Sarah D. Roosevelt Park? It's not far from you. Why don't you meet me there in about ten, fifteen minutes. I'll have a big black-and-white mutt with me."

Sarah D. Roosevelt Park turned out to be a thin sliver of parkway, with trees, a basketball court, and a children's playground, sandwiched between Christie and Forsythe streets; a long, narrow traffic island, really, surrounded on all sides by the sooty tenements of the Lower East Side. Crossing the road, I saw Kelsey call out after a black-and-white dog, which was racing around the perimeter of the basketball court, chasing pigeons. Unlike their British counterparts, the pigeons didn't fly away, merely circled lazily and then alighted on a spot a few yards distant, only to be chased again. As I approached the court, the dog looked my way. Kelsey turned and saw me; he waved and headed over. He was wearing the same thick overcoat I had first seen him wearing, over some beaten-up Timberland boots. "Here he is," he said when he reached me. "Our British loose cannon."

His dog skidded to a halt at my feet and started biting at my sleeve. He looked like he had some German shepherd in him, but had a puppy's oversized joints and paws.

"If he bites you, stick your fingers down his throat," said Kelsey.

"Stick my fingers down his throat?"

"Teach him biting is no fun— *Billy!*"

The dog immediately lowered itself and slunk to a revolving position around my heels. "My wife's dog," he said. "Now I'm stuck with him. It's probably best if we sit down."

He motioned to one of the concrete benches at the edge of the basketball court. "So tell me what happened. What was the amends for?"

"I felt guilty, I guess."

"About what?"

"About the fact that we broke up."

"Your part in it being?"

"I'm sorry?"

"Your part in it. The thing *you* did wrong."

That stumped me.

"You don't do amends out of *guilt,* Patrick. Lord, if this program and I am in agreement on anything it's the supreme uselessness of *guilt.* This isn't therapy. It's not about sitting around and exploring our feelings about the many and manifold ways we feel bad about ourselves. It's the exact opposite. It sounds like you've got this completely in reverse. It sounds like you wanted an amends from *her.*"

"It wouldn't have hurt."

He laughed.

"You haven't met this woman," I said. "She's absolutely impossible."

"So what were you doing with her?"

"What do you mean?"

"Well, if she's as impossible as you say, then you have to ask yourself, What was I doing in the relationship in the first place?"

We reached the bench and sat down, wrapping our coats about us. Some distance beneath our feet, a subway rumbled, rattling the metal mesh around the court; above us, a series of cumulus clouds scrolled between the rooftops, as stately as blimps, giving the impression you were witnessing the rotation of the Earth. Across the park, Billy barked at a pile of leaves. Kelsey crossed his legs and wrapped his coat around them.

"I don't really know. I guess I thought . . . I don't know what I thought. She was just so . . . together. I guess I liked the way I looked in her eyes."

"Women can never save us, Patrick. Only we can do that. Did you read that book I gave you?"

"I tried."

"What did you think?"

"Can I be honest?"

"I'd like it if you were."

"I thought it was the worst book I've ever read."

He looked at me for a few seconds, as if deciding something. "Well, Bill's no Steinbeck. That's for sure. There's nothing original to any of it. He filched the whole thing. It's just religion's greatest hits." He spread his arms and sat back on the bench. "Look, I know it's painful. You're clearly smart. That's just going to have to be your cross to bear, I'm afraid. Smarter men than you or I have tried to figure this thing out and failed, Patrick. Cheever spent his entire time in rehab correcting everyone's grammar. Did you know that? Berryman sat in meetings reciting Chinese and Greek poets, the silly ass—he couldn't even get through the Serenity Prayer without deconstructing the goddamn thing. A complete waste of time. This program lacks the coherence of even a redneck cult. You can practically smell the shoe leather coming off everything Bill wrote."

I stared at him. "So why do you *do* it?"

"Because for some reason that nobody has yet been able to work out, it stops us all from drinking ourselves into a ditch."

"But you don't believe in it."

"It has very little to do with what I believe. What I believe is neither here nor there. No sentence will lose you friends faster in AA than the one that starts 'I think . . .' It's like a dog masturbating against your leg. It's honest, but how useful is it, exactly?"

He laughed. Across the park, Billy looked up. He was standing at the bottom of a children's slide, at the top of which were perched two toddlers, bawling, too terrified to come down. He resumed his barking.

"Why did you stop writing?" I asked him.

For a long while he said nothing, just stared into space. A few streets away, a siren sounded: a slow rise and fall, with an occasional mad *whoop-whoop* turkey gobble, like the sound of a tape being chewed up. I was beginning to think he had not heard me, or was at least going through with a pretense of not having heard me, when he said something.

"Tell me. Have you ever heard Lola share?"

Feeling a constriction in my chest, I nodded.

"It's quite something. Just rattling off the first thing that comes into her head. She has no idea who she's talking to, you see. Most people put a hand up and they think they're talking *to* someone—their father, maybe their mother, their shrink, their first pet. They're trying to impress, or persuade, or project, or cajole. She's not talking *to* anyone. She's just taking a shower, washing all that crud away. You should try it sometime. You'll be surprised by how little you have to say."

He smiled.

"I don't understand what this has to do with your work."

"Only two things happen when writers get sober, Patrick. They get sloppy or they get soppy. Hell, even Bukowski ended up writing about his cats. His fans were very disappointed. They were like, 'What happened to all the whores?' "

He let out a bark of laughter. "Look, I'm glad you called, Patrick, but you can see why I'd make the world's worst sponsor, can't you? You call me up and I do nothing but talk about myself . . . *Billy!*"

For a second, Billy faced a decision: go to Kelsey or continue to chew the boot of the homeless man lying on the benches. The decision held him in its grip for a few seconds; then, reluctantly, he let go and trotted over.

"We should be getting back," said Kelsey, unwinding the leash he had in his pocket.

"Of course. I'm sorry for hijacking your Sunday."

"No need to apologize. It helped me more than it helped you probably. Just promise me one thing, will you?"

"Yes."

He looked at me intently. "Slow down. This is heavy machinery you're operating here. You're not supposed to do it all in a day. You'll kill yourself."

"I'd like to see you again sometime."

"Sure, although I have a day job these days." He said it with evident amusement.

"Where?"

"The public library on Fifth Avenue."

Billy arrived at our feet, his wet nose heading straight for Kelsey's lap. "Hey there, Billy boy," he said, ruffling his ears. "And stop thinking about this stuff so much. It doesn't repay much head-on analysis. You want to know the best novel written on the subject of alcoholism, in my opinion?"

"What is it?"

"*The Shining*. Do you want to know why?"

I nodded.

"Because it doesn't know that's what it's about," he said.

"I didn't know Stephen King was, uh . . ."

"One of us? Oh yes. Complete garbagehead. Coke, Valium, Ny-Quil. Says he can't even remember writing *Cujo,* he was so loaded. It's not alcoholism that creates great novels. And it's not sobriety. It's *denial.*" He attached the leash to Billy's collar and stood up. "Come on, let's leave this man alone, shall we, Billy boy. . . ."

chapter fifteen

I'M TELLING YOU, NAT, it's a cult."

"Don't be ridiculous. It's not a cult. Nobody's taking any money from anyone."

"No, they brainwash them for free. They're quite open about it. It's all about submitting your identity to the will of the group. You completely forget where you came from, who you are."

"They're only trying to help."

"Yes, but at what cost? They lose all sense of self. It's just the program this and the program that. Then they have to get up in front of the group and testify to what a difference the program has made in their lives."

"But the program has made a difference in their lives, hasn't it? They're not on the streets anymore."

"Yes, but I'm not so sure that being paraded up and down in public like that is any good for them, either. Some of them cry. They get up there in front of the judging panel and it's too much for them. They just break down."

"Is that right?"

"Yes, it *is* right. You should hear some of the things Tyra Banks says to them. 'You weren't smiling on the inside. Smile with your eyes. . . .' She's like the anti-Oprah."

"They're models, Patrick. I think bitchiness comes with the territory."

"That doesn't mean they're not human beings."

It was the last week before the holidays and we were on the ground floor at Saks, its high, cavernous ceilings filled with the hum of a hundred decisions and the scents of a dozen perfumes, all atomized and recombining to form a single scent, Eau de Department Store, with top notes of Givenchy, Dior, Chanel, and bottom notes of Obsession and Notorious and Unforgivable. We were Christmas shopping for Leo and his family, something Natalie did every year. Sometime in late December, she told me, Leo would always arrive at the office, huffing and puffing and complaining about the Christmas crowds, or the ID you needed to get into FAO Schwarz these days, until Natalie volunteered. She liked the chance to get out of the office, she said. I'd grown a little tired of it, too, recently; it seemed filled with people asking me what I was up to or what I was working on. I couldn't put my finger on why, but even the most basic exchange of pleasantries left me feeling frazzled. On either side of the aisle, the tanned, smiling salespeople stood, hoping to catch our eye. "Brown Sugar Body Polish, sir?" "Scott Barnes Body Bling, madam?" "Shock Therapy Super Minty Concentrated Body Wash?"

"Just keep your head down and don't catch their eye," said Natalie, pointing down the aisle. "Gloves are at the end here."

"Natalie. Can I ask you something?"

"Of course."

"Would you say that I lacked humanity?"

She stared at me. "I'm sorry?"

"Humanity. Would you say that it was a quality I lacked."

"What kind of a question is that?"

"An honest one?"

"You don't think it's a little broad? What's this about, really? Who have you been speaking to?"

"No one," I said, sullenly.

"C'mon. You don't just suddenly start in with questions like that unless you've been talking to someone."

Immediately to our left, a saleswoman came up from behind her desk, smile already in place, wielding a tube of apricot exfoliant; for a second, I thought of catching her eye and allowing myself to be drawn in, then thought better of it. Nobody I knew needed apricot exfoliant. I had a sudden memory of that clean, plain smell of Lola's, like conditioner, or moisturizer, and felt the toothache in my chest swell up to a dull throb.

"Caitlin," I said.

"Caitlin?"

"Yes."

"What are you doing talking to *her*?"

"She's not *that* bad, Nat."

"What do you mean, 'not that bad'? She dragged you all the way out here and then she dumped you."

"That's not the whole story."

"What do you mean 'not the whole story'?"

"It's not the whole story. I had other reasons for moving here."

"Of course you did. You dealt with the whole thing brilliantly. Getting a job with Leo, finding an apartment . . ."

"No, I mean I had other reasons back home. A situation."

"What kind of situation?"

I felt a little hot and light-headed, as you do when you are about to throw up. "An almost getting fired type of a situation," I said quietly.

"So what?"

I looked at her.

"I don't . . ."

"Why are you telling me this?"

"Because I almost got fired."

"But you didn't."

"Only because I didn't stick around to find out."

"Leo gave you a job, didn't he?"

"Yes, but it was on false pretenses."

"False pretenses how?"

"I didn't tell him about any of this. He looks at me and sees this, I don't know, young British hotshot, but it's all rubbish. I'm here by the skin of my teeth. I shouldn't be here at all, in fact. I should be back home clearing up the mess I left behind me."

Something told me I had been talking for too long. I found Natalie's eyes like saucers. "Are you crazy?" she asked.

"I'm not feeling so good at the moment actually, Nat."

She came to a stop in the aisle. I drew up in front of her.

"Patrick, listen to me. You are completely self-sabotaging. All that stuff, whatever happened to you before—it's all in the past. It's gone. Nobody cares in the slightest. You're in New York, for heaven's sake. Nobody even cares what happened last week, let alone last year."

I was reminded of what Lola had told me about New York being the place for the people who were left over, the ones with no clear idea of where they wanted to be, and smiled.

"What's so funny?"

"Nothing. You're absolutely right. Of course you are. I need to forget about that stuff. What's done is done."

"Exactly."

"God, what an idiot you must think me!"

"No, not at all," she said. "You just need to relax a little bit, Patrick. Enjoy what's going on around you, you know?"

"It's always been my problem. A complete inability to enjoy

what is bang smack in front of me. You're right. I need to move on. Keep moving. Forget about it."

"Patrick . . ."

"C'mon, let's go get those gloves."

I tried moving off, but she stayed stock-still.

"What's the matter?" I asked her.

"That man," she said, pointing over my shoulder. "I think he just called your name."

"What man?" I said, turning.

Looking down the aisle, I could see only women shoppers, smelling their wrists, rubbing their cheeks, cocking their heads into mirrors. Then, peering between the shoulders of two women, I saw a bobbing red hunting hat and a hand hoisted above everyone's heads, waving. Something formed in my chest, like quick-setting cement.

"I don't see anyone," I said. "Let's get going. . . ."

"He just called your name," said Natalie, refusing to budge. "I'm sure of it."

"I don't think so. C'mon, Natalie. We can't be all day at this. We'd better get Leo his gloves—"

"PATRICK!"

The cry was unignorable this time.

"Yes, he is. He's calling your name."

I knew instantly who it was moving through the crowds like a bowling ball through skittles; finally squeezing his way between two shoppers, Felix saw me, his face lighting up. He looked ever more derelict than usual, if only because he had made the unwise decision to smarten up: he was wearing a secondhand tuxedo with tattered piping over a hooded sweatshirt, and some huge gray plaid pants that looked to be supported by suspenders alone; the flaps of the hunting cap were pulled down over his ears, his hair sprouting from the bottom of it like weeds. He looked like a homeless person with a big day in court.

"That woman just called me something nasty," he said, arriving at our feet.

"What are you doing here?"

"I won't repeat it."

"What are you doing here, Felix?"

"Shopping . . . What are *you* doing here?"

"Uh—" Before I knew what was happening, Felix extended his hand to Natalie. "I'm Felix," he said. "Natalie," she said with a smile. He performed an elaborate bow that put his backside out into the path of an oncoming shopper; she tutted and moved around him.

"Maybe we'd better keep moving," I said. "Felix, it was lovely running into you, but we've got to get going."

"Where are you going?" he asked.

"We're going to the glove counter," said Natalie. "Do you want to come?"

"That's not a bad idea. I need some new gloves."

And just like that, it was decided, my heart sinking with each step as the three of us set off up the aisle toward the glove counter. Felix wasn't exactly cut out for the traffic, hopping this way and that in an attempt to remove himself from everyone's path, an effort doomed ultimately by the necessity of occupying physical space himself. He looked like he was performing a rain dance. I kept my head down, trying to avoid Natalie's eye.

"Hey, Patrick, I'm glad I ran into you," said Felix. "I was going to call. I've heard some good news. You know my poetry reading I told you about? It's happening. This Saturday."

"Poetry reading?"

"Yes. At the Poetry Club on the Bowery. Can you come? Lola's coming."

"I really don't know, Felix. I . . . I'll try."

"Who's Lola?" asked Natalie.

"She's just this girl we both know," I said quickly.

"Oh yeah? What girl?"

She had a mischevious look in her eye that I didn't like one bit.

"Just a mutual friend who's a girl."

"And how did you guys meet?"

"You mean Felix and I?"

"No, you and Elvis Costello."

"We met in the rooms," said Felix.

"The *rooms?"* asked Natalie. "What rooms?"

He turned to me, a worried look on his face. "Is she a civilian?"

"The *Writer's* Rooms," I said quickly. "You know, that place on Broadway."

"Oh shit, I'm sorry," said Felix, hunching his shoulders apologetically.

Natalie looked back and forth between us. "What's going on?" she asked.

"Nothing's going on."

"What's he sorry for?"

"What are you talking about? He's not sorry, are you, Felix?"

Felix said nothing, slunk down further.

"I heard him," said Natalie. "He said you'd met in some rooms somewhere and then he called me—a 'civilian,' I think it was—and then he apologized. What's he apologizing for? Why am I a civilian? What's going on?"

"Nothing is going on," I said calmly. "It's just . . . Look, the Writer's Rooms can be a kooky kind of a place. You know what writers are like. It's very hard to get in, and once you're in, everyone has their own lingo to talk about the outside world. 'Civilians.' That's what they call people from the outside. Felix was. . . ."

I came to a halt in the middle of the aisle. Felix was nowhere to be seen.

"He was right here. Right next to me."

"Patrick, who *is* he?" asked Natalie intently.

"I told you: He's a writer."

"Bullshit."

"He is! He sent me a manuscript a few months ago and it wasn't very good, so don't press him on it, will you? He's very sensitive about it. Please?"

"Who *is* he, Patrick?" she asked again.

Finally, I spotted Felix, half an aisle away, talking to a salesman who was holding out a vial of something for him to sniff. I strode over and grabbed him by the elbow.

"Does this smell like cannabis to you?" he asked, holding up his hand for me to smell.

"A blend of patchouli, cannabis, and rose," the salesman said, correcting him. "Cannabis Santal eau de parfum by Fresh. One hundred and forty-five dollars."

Felix sucked air through his teeth. "Do you have any samples?"

"Felix, come on," I said, hoisting him back into the aisle. "We haven't got time for this. Don't catch their eye, okay? That's the trick to this place. Just keep your head down and don't let them catch your eye."

"It's as bad as Gracie Square," he muttered as we resumed our march toward the glove counter. We walked in silence for a while.

"Patrick tells me you're a writer, Felix," said Natalie.

"That's right. You know when people say they're having a bad hair day?"

"Yes."

"That was mine."

"You came up with the expression 'bad hair day'?"

"Yep," he said proudly. "Then everyone started using it."

"That's why you need Patrick," she said. "To chase down those royalties. What is it these days, Patrick? A dollar a word?"

"Bad. Hair. Day," said Felix. "That's three dollars."

"And when were you in Gracie Square?"

"During the summer. I wasn't there for long. A few weeks."

"What were you doing there?"

"Watching TV, mostly."

"TV?"

"*American Idol, Project Runway, Top Chef, Being Bobby Brown.*"

"Anything else?"

"*The Bachelor. America's Next Top Model—*"

"No, I mean did you do anything besides watch TV?"

"Not really. My friend Tobias? He took all the chlorpromazine they gave him and stored it under his tongue. Then he ate it all in one go. It gave him an erection that lasted for four days. You know those ads that say 'If you have an erection that lasts more than four hours, consult your doctor'? Well, his lasted *four days*."

A hospital. They were talking about some fucking hospital.

"So you made friends in there?" asked Natalie.

"Yeah, but we haven't really stayed in touch."

"Why not?"

Felix rolled his eyes. "Because crazy people aren't so good at writing."

"*Gloves!*" I exclaimed. "Look! Moleskin gloves!"

The girl behind the counter looked genuinely pleased to see us.

Fifteen minutes later, Natalie and I were standing outside the store, listening to the drumbeat of the rain on the striped awning above; next to us, the Salvation Army brass band shook the water from their trumpets and trombones. It was already dark, Fifth Avenue lit up with long strings of light, like pearls; on the corner stood the store's concierges in full-length maroon coats, flagging down passing taxicabs with whistles. Felix had already disappeared into the teeming crowds, his pockets bulging with samples swiped from the store, cucumber body balm, avocado-stone shower gel, cocoa-bean facial scrub.

"He's not really one of your writers, is he?" said Natalie. It wasn't really a question.

For a few seconds, the urge to come clean came at me with surprising force. "What's Gracie Square?" I asked her.

"A psychiatric hospital on the Upper East Side. An expensive one."

I nodded. "He mentioned he'd been somewhere like that," I said.

"You're not in any trouble, are you, Patrick?"

I looked at her sharply.

"Trouble? What kind of trouble?"

"I don't know. Drugs. Anything like that."

I stared at her, marveling at her weird, inverted perspicacity. "No, no, no, no, no, it's nothing like that. Lord no."

"Well, what *is* it, then?" she said, stung.

"I can't tell you."

"Why not?"

"Because there are some people I need to speak to first."

"Some people? Patrick, are you sure you're not in any trouble?"

"Why would you think that I'm in trouble?"

"Oh, I don't know," she said. "Maybe it's something to do with the fact that we haven't seen you in the office for the last two weeks. And when you are in, you're hiding from everyone. And when you're not hiding from everyone, you're running around town with frigging Rain Man over there."

"I'm sure this all must look very strange to you, Nat, but I can assure you there's a perfectly good explanation."

"So what is it?"

"I can't tell you right now."

"Does Saul know?"

"No, absolutely not," I said anxiously. "You absolutely must not tell Saul about any of this."

"Any of *what*? What would I tell him? I wouldn't know what to say. I don't *know* anything!"

"You mustn't even tell him that."

"This is absurd."

"You know what I mean."

"No, I don't actually, Patrick. I don't know what you mean."

"It's not bad news, I promise. It's good news. It could be *very* good news. I promise you'll be the first to know, okay?"

She held up her hand. "Don't want to know."

"I'll tell you as soon as I—"

"Tell it to someone who cares."

"Here, let me help you with those bags—"

"You suck, Patrick Miller. You absolutely suck."

Getting into her cab, she mouthed the words *You suck* one more time through the window. I smiled and waved, but as the cab pulled away, I felt something tearing inside of me, as if I had lost both something very precious and the last opportunity I would ever have to get it back. A block away, the spires of St. Patrick's Cathedral rose up into the darkness, dwarfed by the sheer glass surfaces of the skyscrapers on either side. This had gone on long enough, I thought.

The time had come to act.

I stuck my hand out for a cab.

chapter sixteen

DESPITE THE BEST EFFORTS of the Dutch, Manhattan is not flat. Take a walk up or down the avenues; you'll find yourself ascending and descending a series of bumps and hillocks, slopes and swells, as if a giant were trapped under the ground, pummeling upward—remnants of the massive glacier that once covered the Hudson Valley, scouring its riverbed with rocks brought down from the Catskill and Adirondack mountain ranges, before packing them down into the marbelized bedrock that makes the city's skyscrapers possible; it's why the buildings are tallest at the middle and bottom of the island, where the rock is deepest. The New York Public Library sits atop a saddle of land that once boasted rolling hills, pine forests, bears, wolves, and mountain lions; a Swedish naturalist who came to the city in the early eighteenth century remarked that the din of tree frogs was so great that conversation was impossible. Kelsey would tell me all this during one of our long telephone conversations in the months to come. A keen natural historian, he was fond of the irony that this most ersatz and man-made of cities was made possible only by a geological accident. "A big chunk of ice," he would say in the tone he reserved for such marvels. "Isn't that something? This whole place made possible by a big chunk of ice."

It was raining on the afternoon I first visited him at the library in late December—hard, cold, driving rain that seemed to fly in horizontally under your umbrella. In Bryant Park, the chess tables sat empty, the trees bent double by the wind; at the street corners, small lagoons of water formed, forcing people to step around them or leap over. I hurried quickly up the steps to the library, past the two stone lions, Patience and Fortitude, on either side. At the top of the steps, a few people took shelter from the rain behind tall stone pillars. I shook off my umbrella and pushed through the bronze revolving doors, to find an empty reception hall with a long red carpet that led to a small desk, at which sat an elderly lady doing the *New York Times* crossword; I approached and coughed into my hand.

A gray perm tipped back, revealing a beaky, inquisitive face.

"Excuse me," I said. "I'm looking for Mr. Kelsey."

The gray perm nodded as she scanned the list in front of her.

"Kelsey . . . Kelsey . . . Ah, yes," she said. "I thought so. He works in the stacks." She pointed up the marble steps to her left. "Up the stairs to the second floor; take a left, then a right. Ask for him in the reading room. They'll show you where to go." I trotted up the marble steps to the reading room, which turned out to be as long and deep as an Oxford dining hall, with high, vaulted stained-glass windows, chandeliers, and row after row of oak tables, at which sat a dozen or so people, hunched over books lit by small reading lamps; the only sound was the rustle of pages being turned, or the occasional cough. At the near end of the room was a high oak bench, at which sat a row of librarians like magistrates; behind them was a small administrative area, where their colleagues worked at desks, separated off from one another by thin partitions. I approached one of the librarians, his balding head bent to the task of filling out a small pink slip, and was just opening my mouth to speak when he held up a finger. "One moment," he said.

He finished filling out the slip, rolled it up, and inserted it into a cylindrical metal canister, rolling his chair back and spinning around to insert the canister into a long pewter gray pneumatic tube that ran from the ceiling to the floor; he snapped shut the lock, and with a soft *schwuuucking* sound, the canister disappeared down the tube. The librarian pushed his chair back to me. He had one of those babyish Karl Rove–like faces, which made the sprouts of gray hair on either side of it all the more incongruous. He resembled an aging egg. "Can I help you?" he asked.

"I'm looking for Mr. Kelsey. I believe he works here."

"Not here. He's on the seventh floor. Is he expecting you?"

"I'm a friend of his."

He raised an eyebrow, keeping it aloft for a few seconds, as if wonders would never cease. "Follow me," he said, leading me to a hinged portion of the bench and lifting it so I could walk through. People raised their heads from their desks as I did so, peering at me like brontosauruses disturbed while grazing, before returning to their work. Inset in dark wood paneling on the far wall was a small elevator—the old-fashioned sort with an iron grille you slid open. With a little grunt of effort, the librarian pulled it open and gestured for me to step inside, then stepped inside himself. There was barely enough room for the two of us. "Let me see," he said, scanning the row of buttons. "Seventh floor, seventh floor. Ah, here we go. . . ."

"How can there be seven floors?" I asked him. " Aren't we on the top floor now?"

He punched one of the buttons. "Seven floors *down,*" he said as the elevator began its descent with a lurch. "The stacks are located under the park. They blew it out with dynamite. It was the only place they could store one million books." He eyed me suspiciously. "You're not a trustee of the library, then?"

"No, I'm not."

He seemed visibly to relax. "Ah. That's how he came to us, you see. One of the lifers died. Another friend of Mr. Kelsey."

"*Lifers*?"

"Most of the other librarians have been here thirty, forty years. Rick had been here fifty-five years, I think it was. . . . It was very sudden, very sad. Liver failure."

"So Douglas took his job?"

"He met one of the trustees at the funeral and, well, there you have it. What will be, will be." He sealed his lips in a manner suggesting the practice of great restraint. "Not that I mind that kind of thing, but it puts some people's noses out of joint."

"Of course," I said.

We rode the rest of the way in silence but for the clanking of the elevator cables, then came to a halt with a knee-bending bump. The librarian slid the grille open again. "Watch out for your head," he said. I stepped out into a low-ceilinged walkway hung with ducts, pipes, and yellowish fluorescent strip lights. There was a slightly antiseptic smell in the air, like oil paint, and it was freezing cold, our breath fogging up in front of our faces. We were standing at some kind of junction, with long corridors stretching off in four directions before disappearing into darkness; they had to go on for several city blocks at least. Off each of the corridors ran row after row of book stacks bearing leather-bound books from ceiling to floor, although looking down, I found that we were walking not on solid floors at all, but on long marble gangplanks stretched atop steel girders; peer between the walkway and the book stacks and you could just see the floors below. It was like walking through the middle of a giant Erector set.

"Douglas keeps these books in order," I said.

"Just the Slavic section. He has an affinity for the Russians.

But then we knew that from his own work. Not that he ever talks much about that. Keeps himself to himself mostly. We've asked him out to Mulligan's many times, but he always turns us down. . . ."

Suddenly, a hooded figure zipped across the corridor in front of us. It moved so fast, I barely had a chance to see what or who it was before it disappeared down one of the book stacks. *"Hey!"* exclaimed the librarian, hurrying to the end and peering down it.

"Who was that?" he called out.

There was no answer. Looking over his shoulder, I dimly made out a figure in the distance, scything along like an Olympic skater. It had to be on skates or Rollerblades of some sort.

"Who is that?" he called out again. *"Is that Shakira?"*

The figure straightened and slowed.

"Sor-*reee*," came a sheepish voice.

"How many times have I told you to keep your speed down!"

She stuck a foot out behind her, swung left, and disappeared. The librarian huffed and turned back to me. "I tried to put a stop to this, but he said it was the only way we could keep up with Google. It's a lawsuit waiting to happen if you ask me."

"This was Douglas's idea?"

"Yes. He seems to forget they're just kids. We had to cordon off the comic-book section last year because he let them read at lunchtime. He's been trying to get them to graffiti his desk."

"Kids?"

"We get them from the local colleges."

"He works with kids," Felix had told me. "He's teaching them how to draw." The pieces of the jigsaw were beginning to fall into place. Much the same thing had happened to Raymond Carver. He'd gotten sober and gone to ground for a year. When someone asked him if he was writing anything, he said he "couldn't see the point." But then look what happened: He got remarried and published his best work. Elmore Leonard said that attending meetings had made him a "better listener." I thought I could see the connection there: Both were flinty minimalists who wrote short declarative sentences with low centers of gravity. Minimalists seem to do better out of this than maximalists. It was the geniuses, the magic realists, the florid encyclopediacs who suffered. The poet John Berryman wrote a whole series of poems about his Higher Power ("Under new governance, Your Majesty"), and a novel about his recovery ("a bloody philosophy of both history and Existenz, almost as heavy as Tolstoy"), which were slaughtered by critics for their "contradiction, special pleading, and vagueness." Clearly, comparing yourself to Tolstoy was a bad sign; if it had to be a Russian, Chekhov was a much safer bet. Writers from the North did better than writers from the South. Short-story writers did better than novelists. And fiction writers seemed to do better than poets. Everyone did better than the poets. The poets were screwed. Presumably, if you were a poet from the South with a tendency to run on a bit, you might as well walk into a bar right now.

"This way," said the librarian, turning down one of the book stacks. At the far end, a small reading light illuminated the gloom. Sitting at a desk in a thick overcoat, a gray woolen hat pulled down over his ears, was Kelsey. A series of pneumatic tubes similar to the ones I had seen upstairs descended from the ceiling to his desk, on which lay several piles of books, a mug of coffee, and a newspaper. He appeared to be doing the crossword. As we got closer, the view widened: His desk was surrounded on three sides by stacks of wooden drawers. It looked a little like a cramped boat cabin. Finally he heard us approach and looked up.

"Patrick," he said. "This is a surprise."

The librarian looked at me. "He wasn't expecting you?"

"Everything's fine, Sam," said Kelsey. "I told him he could drop by." The librarian stood there for a few seconds with a cheated look on his face, and was rewarded with the glimpse of another figure flashing by, several book stacks away. "*Did you . . .*" he began, then walked over and peered down the book stacks. "*Who was that?*" he called out.

There was no answer.

"*Who was that?*" he called again, louder this time.

There was a pause; then a young man's voice piped up: "Don't know."

"Don't you try and pull that. I saw you. I know who it was." He turned back to Kelsey. "Who was that?"

Kelsey shrugged.

"Can you ask them to keep their speed down, Douglas? One of them almost ran us down on the way here."

"I'm sorry, Sam. I'll ask them."

"They *are* just college kids."

"I know. I know."

"It's nothing short of criminal what they let you get up to down here."

The librarian glared at him one last time, then walked off. "Always a pleasure, Sam," Kelsey called out after his retreating back, and shook his head. "Please," he said, indicating the seat opposite his desk. On its side, someone had scrawled "Impeach Nixon."

I took the seat, tightening my coat around me. "Why is it so cold down here?" I asked.

"It's our old friend, Books Versus People. The books like the cold temperatures. The people not so much. The books win. If you'd told me you were coming, I would have told you to dress up."

I got the point.

"Ah. Well. I'm sorry to drop in on you so unexpectedly, but I've been thinking about some of the things you said during our last conversation."

"Uh-oh," he said, leaning back in his seat and cradling his hands behind his head. "What's on your mind, Patrick?"

"We were talking about writers getting sober. Everyone's work goes off, you said. They either get sloppy or they get soppy. But what about Carver? He got sober and his work got better."

"You came here to talk about *Ray*?"

"He didn't do it immediately," I continued. "For the first year, he did nothing. All he did was go to bingo halls and eat doughnuts."

He smiled. "I know. He used to invite me to go with him. He always said the cheating was more fun than the actual game." His hands fell from behind his head. "I'm sorry. Am I missing something here?"

"There's a fallow period. Don't you see? That's all this is," I said, looking around the book stacks. "It's not that you're finished. You can't be. You can't just fall off the radar. You're just recharging; that's all this is. You may even be getting better, but you haven't been writing, so you don't know that yet. Don't you see?"

For a long while he said nothing, taking in what I had said; the only sound was the humming of the air ducts. Then his eyes narrowed.

"Who are you?" he said matter-of-factly.

I was at the edge of the waterfall.

"Okay," I said, swallowing hard. "My name is Patrick Miller. I'm a literary agent. I work for the Leo Gottlieb Agency. Before that, I was in London, with Smith and Fairfax. I was there for five years. I moved here last year to work for Leo. I know I should have said something earlier, but what I did, I did out of a profound love of your work and my complete horror at finding that you had given up writing. I need you to know that."

My voice sounded thin, weak.

"A literary agent," he said.

"Yes. I know you're not writing, but I want to urge you to reconsider that for a moment, if you'll just thi—"

He held up his hand. "Whoever said I'd given up writing?"

I stared at him.

"But you did."

"I said no such thing."

"They get sloppy or they get soppy, you said."

"I didn't say it had happened to *me*."

"So you're . . ."

"A page a day for the last three years. Quite good going, if I do say so myself. It's amazing what a clear head in the morning will do for you."

"But Christine Kantor . . . she said you'd quit."

All the good humor vanished instantly from his face.

"*She* didn't send you, did she?"

"No, no, no, I work for Leo Gottlieb. Christine has nothing to to do with this. She just told me—"

"*What* did she tell you?" There was steel in his voice now.

"She told me that you'd had a big fight over the book. She said you'd gone a little crazy up there in the woods."

"Do I seem crazy to you?"

"Not at all."

He smiled. "Well, that's something. What else did she say?"

"She said you were never much of a drinker. That you were just looking for an excuse to pull the plug on your life up there."

He thought about it, turning something over in his mind. "Look, far be it from me to call Christine on her drinking. Only she can do that. Let's just say she was a little blind to what was going on with me, and when I quit, she was horrified. Then things started getting a little . . . bumpy and she fired me."

"You've been working on the book all this time?"

"Yes."

"But that's wonderful news."

"It is for me. I don't see what it has to do with you."

"Well, I understand you may not need an agent right now, but at some point in the future you will," I said, reaching into my pocket for a card. "And I'd be honored if you would think of considering me."

He shook his head. "I couldn't possibly ask you to be my agent."

"Why not?"

"You have no idea what a relief it's been to fly off the radar all this time. I'm not late, because there are no deadlines. I'm not letting anyone down, because no contract has been signed. It's been bliss. I feel like I've lost thirty years. Plus, you also happen to be completely insane."

"I'm sorry?"

"You're only—what?—a few weeks off the booze? Your brains are still mush. I hate to pull rank like this, but it's the same for everyone. It's nothing personal."

"Oh, but you don't have to worry about any of that," I said, "I'm not really doing any of that anymore."

"Doing what?"

"The meetings."

"You're not drinking again?"

"No, no, no, no," I said, feeling my forehead prickle, despite the cold. "I'm just not going to meetings anymore. I don't think I ever really needed them, to be honest. I overreacted. I thought maybe I did, but I don't. False alarm. Overreacted. Just like I always do."

I laughed, but it hung in the air, while he eyed me suspiciously.

"You may wish to reconsider that."

"Quite possibly."

"And it's none of my business. But look. I'm sorry you've wasted your time coming here today. I don't need an agent just yet. Please give Leo my best. Is he still married to that beautiful woman?"

"Catherine."

"Not Juliet?"

"That was the previous one."

"Oh. I'm sorry to hear that. When did that happen?"

"I'm not sure. I know he's been married to Catherine for five years."

"Five years, huh." He rubbed his chin. "Isn't that something. Well, give Leo my best anyway."

"I will. Maybe I could leave you one of these," I said, reaching inside my jacket for my card.

He took the card and read it.

"And maybe I could call you in the new year and check in with you again."

"If it's my book you're after . . ."

"Just to see how you are."

"You really don't take no for an answer, do you?"

"I'll let you get back to work."

I shook his hand and left.

chapter seventeen

"You found him *where?*" asked Saul, hauling a bag of ice from his fridge and depositing it on the stainless-steel counter with a crunch. Through the kitchen door could be heard the chink and chatter of his party guests.

"The New York Public Library. He works there as a stack supervisor," I explained. "It's quite extraordinary actually, Saul. The stacks are seven floors under Bryant Park. Just row after row of books. He's got the pages on roller skates, or Rollerblades, or something. He says it's the only way they can keep up with Google."

He frowned. "But what's he doing down there?"

"I think he just got burned out. Wanted a break from the bear pit. You know how bad it gets sometimes." I laughed. "I can't say I blame him. I do wonder sometimes if we don't get a little hollowed out by this business. I mean to say, it's easy to lose sight of what's important. When everything is up for negotiation, how do you know what is true?"

"Oh boy," said Saul, breaking open the bag of ice and pouring it into a silver punch bowl that was filled with pink liquid. "The agent who doesn't think he's in a business meets the author who thinks he's too good for publishing. . . . Leo's going to be delighted. You heard him the other day, about how light we were getting on top."

"Let's not go there *just* yet," I said quickly. "He hasn't said yes."

"But he's out of money."

"Yes."

"And he's still writing."

"He's been working on the book all this time."

He finished pouring the last of the ice into the punch and stirred it with a wooden spoon. "Well, my understanding of these things is a little rocky, but generally when you take a penniless author with a book to sell, and you get him together with a publisher who wants to give him money, something usually cracks."

I smiled. "We'll see."

"Would you do me a favor and open one of those bottles?" he asked, pointing to one of a flotilla of champagne bottles on the counter—beaded with condensation, ice-cold. My stomach fluttering at the thought of my first drink in two weeks—two weeks!—I picked one up and began untwisting the wire and foil cap.

"I *knew* you were up to something," said Saul.

"What do you mean?"

"You've been acting shifty all month. Natalie thought it was this girl you've been seeing."

"Oh, right . . . *That* girl . . . There was no girl."

He laughed. "I *knew* it was bullshit. I told her. I thought you were back in touch with your old firm in London. I thought you had buyer's remorse and were heading back. . . ."

"No, no," I said, scrunching up the foil cap, my mind snagging on Lola. I'd been able to think of little else recently. Lola ascending the steps of the church. Arguing with Prudence. Pegging back her hair with one hand, leaning over to kiss me good-bye. I'd gone over these images so many times, they had begun to fade, like overthumbed photos. All had the capacity to leave me a little breathless, but one was calming: a side view as we walked along the street, her ear transluscent in the sun, nodding at something I'd said. She did that, I'd noticed: nodded while you were talking, partly out of encouragement, like a TV anchor encouraging a reluctant interviewee, or as if confirming something to herself. When you had her attention, you really had it, but there was a watchfulness to her as well that I envied. When I thought of the two of us that day, I saw myself as a rat scurrying this way and that around a maze, while she looked on, amused. I was like one of those absurd herky-jerky figures in an old silent movie, running around at double speed, while she just calmly got on with her day. Even arguing with Prudence, her voice had had none of that strangled quality mine gets when I am trying to convince someone of something—she just batted the ball over the net to see what came back. It was a low center of gravity thing. It was as if she'd worked out some way to use half as much energy as the rest of the world to complete exactly the same tasks. I'd missed my one chance with her; that much was clear. There was only one way anything could ever have happened between us, and that was if I had had the good sense to walk away from the whole thing the moment I met her. Then, maybe a few months down the line we might have run into each other on the street. And we'd both be a little flustered and surprised and she'd ask me how I was. And I'd say Fine, what about you? And she'd say I was a little worried about you; you just disappeared. And I would go: Oh, you mean the meetings? I would chuckle, and say the same thing I'd told Kelsey, that I'd just hit a bad patch, that it was just a false alarm, better safe than sorry, and then I would tell her all about it over dinner. I would tell her the truth, and she would be scandalized and amused in that unshockable way of hers, but she would recognize a fellow traveler when she saw one: a fallen angel, an accidental sinner, a faulty human being sitting in front of her in all humility, submitting himself before her judgment, her forgiveness, her . . .

Somewhere, a gun went off. I looked down and saw champagne spuming over the top of the bottle onto my fingers. On the other side of the kitchen, Saul came up from his crouching position. "Holy crap, Patrick."

"I'm sorry," I said, looking around for a glass.

"Here," he said, handing me a champagne flute. "When you've finished emptying that on the floor, maybe you'd take it through for me?"

"Of course. I'm sorry. I'm feeling a little tightly wound tonight, for some reason."

"Maybe you could do with a glass of that yourself."

"I think you're right."

Our bottles and punch bowls in hand, we pushed through the swinging doors into the living room. Saul's apartment was a large open-plan SoHo loft with parquet floors, exposed brick walls, the kind of place that elicited openly voiced envy from guests. At one end, an elevator opened directly into the living room; at the other were a fireplace, an emerald green sofa suite, and big arched windows with a view of SoHo's rooftops and water towers. It was the last weekend of December and a snowstorm was due to be rolling into town, so Saul had told everyone to arrive early. The room was already half full. I recognized a couple of the other agents from the agency, including Brad, huddled in a work circle. A few conversational groups away, propped against the mantelpiece, talking to two girls, was Ian Horrocks.

"You didn't tell me Ian was coming," I said.

"Did I have to? What's the matter?"

"I just haven't gotten back to him about that proposal."

"The history of applause."

I rolled my eyes.

"You know it's not *that* bad an idea."

"Please. It's a terrible idea."

"Ah, I see. Gets his first whiff of a Pulitzer nominee and he's too big for his old friends."

"I just don't think this country is quite ready for a book about applause yet. The political climate, I mean."

"Still in the booing stage?"

"Exactly," I said, spying a couple standing drinkless behind the sofa. "Here we go. . . ."

"It's okay. You don't have to bother with th—" Saul began, but it was too late: I was already upon them.

"No, we're good," said the guy, holding up his hand.

"You sure? I'm not sure how much of it we're going to have left later."

"No, really," said the guy, pointing the bottle neck away with his finger. He looked vaguely familiar to me: shaven head, black Peter Sellers glasses, blue V-neck sweater, white T-shirt, chinos. Maybe it was the look: Banana Republic Anonymous. I turned to the girl standing beside him: petite, mousy hair, flowery dress over jeans.

"Where's your glass?" I asked her.

"I don't have one."

"Saul, she doesn't have a glass. Do you think you could pay a little more attention to your guests?"

"It's okay," said Saul, exchanging a look with the girl. "Have you guys met, by the way? Scott, this is Patrick. Patrick, this is Scott and his wife, Lindsay."

"No, I don't think we have," I said, swapping the bottle from my right hand to my left. "Nice to meet you."

"We've met," said the guy.

"Really?" I said, frowning. "I don't think so." We shook hands.

"I'm pretty sure of it. You're a friend of Bill's, aren't you?"

"Bill? No, no, I don't know any Bills."

"Yes, you do," said the guy, giving my hand a squeeze. *"Bill."*

At which point, the penny dropped with a ghastly little *whoosh*. The guy whose hand I was shaking was the same guy who'd been standing in line with Lola at the meeting where Kelsey spoke. My heart started a gentle fibrillation. "Oh, *Bill*," I said. "The guy who wrote the . . . the guy who started the whole . . . But of *course*. Why didn't you say? *Bill.* Of course."

"So, you *do* know each other?" said Saul, looking back and forth between us.

"Yes," I said. "We do."

"So who's Bill?"

It was Scott's turn to look concerned. "Oh, I'm sorry," he said. "Saul, do you mind if I have a word with Patrick on my own?"

"Sure," said Saul, smiling perplexedly as Scott took me by the elbow and wheeled me toward the windows. "I'm sorry," he whispered. "I hope I didn't blow your anonymity back there. I thought Saul knew."

"Oh no, he doesn't know anything."

"You may be the wiser man. I told in the end. It helped to have someone who could cover for me at lunchtime."

We came to a halt in front of one of the arched windows, outside of which the snow was coming down in soft, silent waves. The building looked as if it were sailing upward. I placed the bottle of champagne on the windowsill, where it stood illuminated by the streetlights, the bubbles like those of a descending whale.

"Well, I don't have to worry about any of that stuff," I said. "I'm not going to meetings anymore."

"Oh."

"It's okay, Scott, really. I wasn't really serious about the whole thing. It was just a lark, really. Not a lark. An experiment. To see if I needed it. Which I don't. Thank God. I thought I did, but it turns out I don't. Which is good news, in a way. Tells you the system works. There are rejections as well as acceptances. 'That one, that one, that one, not for that one . . .' "

I laughed, but found only the faintest of smiles cracking his face.

"Of course," he said. "I was the same way at first. It took me a while to accept that I really needed it. And the meetings can be very strange. I think we forget that sometimes, how goddamn weird the whole thing is for newcomers."

"No, no, no," I said. "You don't understand. I really didn't need it. You see . . . Okay, look, don't think too badly of me, but I was just pretending. I was only going to meetings so that I could meet someone. It was a work thing. Terrible, I know, but I'm not"—looking around, I lowered my voice—"I'm not an actual alkie. Not that there's anything wrong with the people who are!" I laughed. "I've got nothing against you guys. On the contrary, I would say that I really like the people I've met. Some of the nicest, smartest, most attractive people I've met since arriving in New York. I'm not quite sure what that says about me!" I laughed again. "Actually, you know what, I think it may have something to do with all that self-deprecation. 'What do I know? I'm just a stupid alcoholic, thinking my alcoholic thoughts. . . .' When I first heard that, I thought, Wow, it sounds just like my friends back in London, only they don't use the word *alcoholic;* they use the words *stupid arse.* 'Oh my God, I can't believe I've gone and done it again, what a stupid arse.' You see?"

He had the look of a parent whose three-year-old is poised, ready to insert his fingers into a light socket. He glanced nervously at the bottle on the windowsill.

"Oh for goodness' sake," I said, grabbing the bottle. "This wouldn't do anything to me. I could drink the whole bloody bottle and it wouldn't do a thing to me."

"Put the bottle down," said Scott quietly.

"I'd be drunk, of course, but just normal drunk. Not falling down in the gutter. Just drunk drunk. Like a normal person."

"Put the bottle down, Patrick," he said, his tone sterner this time.

"I don't need to put the bottle down! Don't you get it? *I'm not an alcoholic!*"

Suddenly, there was a flurry of movement as Scott lunged for the bottle. I pulled away, hoisting it out of his reach. His other hand shot out, circled my wrist, and dragged it down until the bottle was held, trembling, between us, like two men in a Clint Eastwood movie wrestling over a gun, just standing there, motionless, locked in silent standoff, our faces in tight little grimaces as we battled for control of the bottle.

"Let . . . go . . . of . . . my . . . hand. . . ."

"Put . . . down . . . the . . . bottle. . . ."

"Let . . . go. . . ."

"Put it . . . down. . . ."

"Let . . ."

"Put . . . it"

". . . go."

". . . down."

At which point, a thick spume of foam rose up the neck of the bottle and overflowed all over my fingers. Scott immediately let go of my wrist and without thinking I licked the sticky foam from my fingers. As I did, I heard a low groan escape Scott's lips.

"Oh for goodness' sake, look at me, Scott. Do you see anything happening? Hmm? Do I look as if I'm about to sneak off and down the whole bottle on my own somewhere?"

"No!" called out a voice to our left. I turned, to see Ian Horrocks weaving his way toward us with the diligent air of a man attempting not to appear too drunk. "Do not sneak off with that bottle! I've seen you do it too many times before, Patrick Miller! You are not doing so again!"

He arrived and slung his arm around my shoulder. I could tell from the weight he was putting on me that he was already disgustingly drunk; he felt like a sack of potatoes.

"I don't know what you're talking about, Ian," I said testily. Then to Scott: "I don't know what he's talking about."

"You're always running off with the booze, you bloody alkie! I said, 'Where's the bubbly?' Saul goes, 'Patrick's got it.' 'Farking 'ell, that's the last anyone will ever see of it. He's like the Bermuda Triangle, that one. I'd better go get it before it disappears.' "

He laughed loudly and hoisted his empty glass. "Fill 'er up." Feeling Scott's beady eyes on both of us, I reached for the bottle in the window, attempting to shrug Ian off at the same time. "I wasn't running off with it," I said. "I was just pouring it."

"Well, you haven't been doing a very good job, have you? Where's his?"

"Don't worry about him," I said.

"Why not?"

"It's okay," said Scott. "I hope you don't mind. . . . I'm going to leave you two. . . . I think Lindsay's looking for me."

He gestured toward the other side of the room, smiled, and removed himself. We both watched as he made his way across the room to his wife. The party was beginning to fill out now, fresh infusions of guests flowing from the elevator every few minutes. Somewhere, someone had cranked up a Daft Punk track. There were sporadic outbreaks of dancing, like little pools of mercury seeking to become one. It was starting to seem mightily oppressive, this room, with all its people and noise and chatter, each conversation with a different set of attendant complications, each requiring an infernal calculus all its own. I began to wonder whether Felix's poetry reading was really such a bad idea after all. He didn't expect me to be someone or say something, or do anything other than just turn up. Ian finished pouring himself a glass of champagne.

"Where's your glass?" he asked.

"Do you know what? I don't have one yet."

His face softened in deepest sympathy. "We can't have that, mate. Let's go find you a glass. Come on. . . ."

I followed him obediently across the room, heading toward the kitchen. I felt glassy and absent, as if all the willpower had been emptied from my body and I were looking down on myself from a great height, curious as to what I was going to do next. It wasn't entirely unpleasant: like sitting on the sea floor, watching the ocean froth and foam overhead. Other people's ideas seemed just as good as mine. None of mine seemed to come to anything. Best simply to do what I was told. I saw Saul ahead of us, silhouetted by the lights of the kitchen, talking to Brad and the other agents. Something jogged in my memory.

"I'm sorry I haven't read your proposal yet, Ian."

"I haven't sent it."

"You haven't?"

"That's probably why you haven't read it, you plonker."

"Oh . . . well . . . that's all right, then."

He laughed as we joined the others.

"You found him!" called out Saul.

"Over by the window. You don't have a glass, do you?"

"Hang on," said Saul, disappearing briefly into the kitchen and coming back with a champagne flute. He handed it to Ian, who then proceeded to pour clumsily, the glass immediately filling with foam. "Ah," he said. "Just wait for it to go down a bit."

"It's okay," I said.

"You sure? It's mostly fizz."

"It's fine. Just give it to me."

He handed me the glass, which felt cool and nicely weighted—there was more champagne in there than it seemed.

"I think a toast is called for," said Saul. "Since we're all here now."

Everyone in our circle raised their glasses.

"The new year," said Saul.

"The election," said Ian.

"A new president," said Brad.

"The new president, whoever he may be," said Saul.

"Or she," said Ian.

"Or she," said Saul. "The new president. Whoever he, she, or it may be."

We clinked glasses. I held mine to my lips and was just tipping it back, the foam just brushing my mouth, when we heard the cry across the room.

"HOLD IT!"

I froze. I knew instantly who it was without turning. I could just feel the two of them, beetling across the room toward me without actually having to see them. For one thing, I could see it on the faces of Saul and Ian and Brad: a gallery of open mugs and dropped jaws as Scott and Lindsay marched up behind me and spun me around to face them. Lindsay plucked the glass from my hand. Scott laid his hands on my arms and peered deep into my eyes.

"I'm sorry, but we can't let you do this to yourself," he said.

"Play the tape, Patrick," urged Lindsay. "Just play the tape through to the end."

"It wasn't going to do anything," I said weakly.

"Do you need a meeting?" asked Scott. "I think you need to go to a meeting."

"Sober feet," urged Lindsay. "Let those sober feet do the walking."

"I don't need to go to a meeting."

"What's going on?" asked Saul, appearing at my elbow.

"Nothing, it's just . . ."

"Tell him, Patrick," said Scott sternly, then, more softly: "Patrick. I really think you should tell him. Make things easier for yourself."

"Tell me what?" asked Saul.

I shook my head. "I don't know what you're talking about."

"Patrick . . ."

I pulled free of his grasp. "I don't know what you're talking about! I don't know what he's talking about, Saul! These people are lunatics! They think they know me from somewhere, but I've never laid eyes on them before, I swear!"

Scott and Lindsay exchanged glances, like two forgiving disciples: Forgive him, for he knows not what he does.

"Patrick," said Saul. "What is going on?"

On the other side of the room, the elevator door pinged and opened, a fresh batch of guests spilling out, unraveling their scarves, brushing snow from their coats. Like someone who has been drugged wrestling himself awake, I launched myself through the party toward the elevator, not looking left or right, not looking back, not even when I heard my name being called behind me, just pushing on through the wet coats and furled umbrellas until I reached the elevator with a clatter, and punched the button marked LOBBY with an open palm. With a lurch, I began my descent.

chapter eighteen

THE SNOW WAS COMING down heavily now, wave after wave, a thick aerial bombardment absorbed the moment it hit the ground. There were few cars on the roads and even fewer people until I reached the Bowery, flocked with a bedraggled Saturday-night crowd, slowly making their way through the snow like a retreating army. It was only ten minutes or so from Saul's apartment to the club where Felix was supposed to be reading. From the outside, it looked like a cross between a café and a pub, with temporary scaffolding, beneath which a small crowd had taken shelter from the blizzard. I pushed past a spindly young man with a long chain dangling from his back pocket, a young woman with white hair shivering beneath a skimpy five-dollar umbrella, her fishnet stockings laddered. The front window was plastered with brightly colored flyers: LUCKY'S LIVE POETRY NIGHT: A MUSIC AND FREE-VERSE FUSION THAT WILL INSPIRE! *10:00 P.M. LITERARY DEATH MATCH NYC, EP $6–$10. ALL-NITE POETRY JAM!* There, huddled in the doorway along with the others, was Felix, his deerstalker rimmed with snow, his usual layering of jackets, shirts, and coats splayed open at the neck, revealing a small triangle of pale flesh. He appeared lost in thought, then saw me and his face lit up.

"Patrick! I thought you weren't coming!"

"What are you doing out here?" I asked.

"It was too hot inside," he said. He looked down at his feet. "I needed to cool down."

"What about your reading? Have you done it yet?"

"No, not yet," he said, shaking his head. He started shifting from one foot to the other, casting anxious looks up and down the street.

"When are you on?"

"Uh, not long. I thought you were going to your friend's party?"

"The whole thing was a disaster."

"Oh yeah? What happened?"

I ran my hand through my hair, then cupped my forehead, staring at the ground. A Snickers wrapper had been stamped down into the snow.

"Saul asked me to serve drinks. And I ran into someone from the program."

"Ah," said Felix.

"It gets worse. So he takes me aside and I explain to him that I wasn't doing it for real, but he's having none of it, of course, and then this friend of mine Ian shows up, completely drunk, and accuses me of stealing the champagne. So I go off with him to try to shut him up by having a drink with him, and then the first couple—the sober guy and his wife—come screaming up to me. 'God, please, Patrick, please don't do it,' right in front of everybody. Saul, Ian, Brad, all the guys I work with." I shook my head. "It was awful, Felix. Just awful, the whole thing. Although do you want to know what the weirdest thing was? Right in the middle of it, for a moment I was completely calm. Not calm. More . . . numb. Like I was looking down on my body from a great height, watching what would happen next. Nothing I said or did seemed to matter anymore. It was entirely up to everyone else. Does that sound weird to you?"

He was looking right through me, his eyes focused on some point behind my back. "Sounds like my mornings," he said.

"What the fuck am I going to do?"

"What are you going to do?"

"Yes. What am I going to do?"

"Is there anything you can do about anything right this second?"

I thought about it. "I guess not, no. I'll have to speak to Saul in the morning, though, and explain everything. A great conversation *that's* going to be."

"I always knew that party was going to blow."

"Yeah? Well, you were right."

"This was the place to be."

"Of course it is," I said, and put a hand on his shoulder. "How are you feeling?"

"Sick."

"Don't worry. Once you get started, it'll be fine. Where's your work?"

He patted his pockets as a couple appeared in the doorway. I flattened myself against the doorway for them to get inside, the door letting out a blast of warm, beery air, the *boom-boom* of a bass drum in the background. "Do you want to go in?" I asked Felix. He nodded and we headed inside, finding what appeared to be an empty coffee shop, in one corner of which was hung a maroon velvet curtain draped from floor to ceiling. Behind the curtain could be heard the *boom-tss-boom-tss* of the music. Parting the curtain, we pushed through into the next room—big, dark, and filled with people. The room was long and cavernous, illuminated by a series of red lightbulbs hanging from the ceiling, with a bar against one of the walls, crowded with people—young, downtown, bills in hand, all vying for the bartender's attention. Beyond the bar lay row after row of collapsible chairs in front of a small stage area with microphones, speakers, and a PA system pumping out The Smiths. Immediately to our left, a burly-looking guy with a shaved head, a goatee, and multiply pierced ears removed the straw from his mouth. "Six dollars, please," he said.

"Each?" I asked.

"How many of you are there?"

"Two," I said, turning to look for Felix, only to find him gone. "Where'd he go?"

He shook his head.

"Well, he's somewhere," I said, handing over a twenty. "I'll pay for the two of us."

The man fished out a small black tin box, rattled around in it, handed me back my change, then brought out a small potato press and imprinted my knuckle with a small pineapple. I thanked him and headed into the room, threading my way through the bodies, before coming to a standstill at the outer perimeter of people pressing against the bar. I was just about to join the throng, when I felt a tug on my left sleeve and turned to find Felix standing there.

"Where did you get to?" I asked.

"I had to go to the men's room."

"Don't wander off like that again without telling me. I thought I'd lost you."

"Sorry. I saved us some seats at the front."

He pointed to the stage, and I followed him. The first row of seats was filled with the performers and their girlfriends or boyfriends; you could tell the former by the intense, worried look on their faces, and the latter by their look of weary patience. These open-mike events could be pretty nerve-racking. Felix showed all the usual signs, glancing nervously around the room, tripping over people's feet as he led the way to two empty seats by the wall.

"You've done this before?"

"Only at sober camp."

"Ah. Well, it's exactly the same. Just take your time. Don't rush. People are here to listen. Let them."

He nodded absentmindedly, twisting around in his seat to check out the room.

"Felix."

"Uh-huh."

"Where's your material?"

He began rummaging around in his pockets. Who knew, maybe Felix would turn out to be one of those New York street savants one read about so much, eccentric and encyclopedic of memory, well known among the local shopkeepers for the notebooks he had spent the last few decades filling with nothing less than an oral history of the city—its odds and ends, flotsam and jetsam, bums, hustlers, and hobos. The kind of thing that had critics queuing up to call it "raw," "gritty," and "unflinching." I tried to remember what he had been addicted to. Pills didn't really cut it, not to launch a decent literary career. What you wanted was crack. In fact, not even crack was enough these days. Look at that guy Frey: He had crack in the bag, but had needed aggravated assault, a handful of DUIs, *and* a root canal without anesthesia, just to get people's attention. Felix had come up from his pockets clutching a Pez dispenser, an elastic band, and what looked like laundry receipts, all bearing minute scribbles.

"Felix. Can I ask you a personal question? What did you say you were addicted to?"

"Pills."

"Which ones?"

"OxyContin. Percocet. Ativan. Klonopin. Benzos. Mustn't forget the benzos—mother's little helpers. Oh, and diet pills. Ephedrine."

"Diet pills."

"I used to weigh two hundred and fifty pounds."

I stared at him. "You're kidding me."

"No, I'm not kidding you."

"Two hundred and fifty pounds. That's . . ."

I cupped the air on either side of me with my arms.

"It's big, I know; you don't have to rub it in."

So *that's* why his clothes were all so loose-fitting.

"Anything else?"

"Not enough?"

"No, no, not at all. More than enough."

But it was too late: I'd lost him. He had burrowed down into his seat, his arms folded, staring straight ahead at the stage.

"Felix, I think you're a drug addict, okay? I think pills are a very serious thing indeed. As bad as heroin, as bad as crack. Maybe even worse, because nobody even thinks of them as being all that dangerous. . . . I mean to say, that's what makes them so insidious. Because they seem so inno— That's not the word I'm looking for. They're not innocent. Not at all. That's my point."

Felix had shrunk even farther down into his seat, turning up the lapel of his jacket, as if hiding from someone. "Keep talking," he said.

"Keep talking? I'm not sure I have that much more to say. Look, Felix, you shouldn't pay any attention to anything that comes out of my mouth. What is going on? Why are you . . ."

The bouncer with the goatee arrived in front of us, beckoning Felix up with his finger. "Hey, you, time to go."

Felix shook his head.

"I'm not going to say it again," said the bouncer.

"What's going on?" I asked.

Felix said nothing. I looked at the bouncer. "What's going on?" I asked him.

"This guy knows what's going on," he said. "C'mon, buddy, out of that seat before I throw you out of it."

"There's no need for that," I said, getting up. "Look, I'm sure there's been some sort of misunderstanding. . . ."

"There's been no misunderstanding," said the bouncer. "I told this dude he can't read. I showed him the door, and here he is again. Like a bad penny."

"Is this true?" I asked Felix, who merely tightened his crossed arms.

For a few seconds, everyone held their positions; then two things happened in quick succession: The bouncer reached down to grab Felix by the arm and Felix leapt up out of his seat and whipped into a position somewhere behind my back. "They told me I could read," he yammered. "I asked them and they told me I could read. I wouldn't be here otherwise. I only came because they invited me."

"Who invited you?" I asked him.

"The people in the café."

"The people who run the café have nothing to do with the people who book the poetry," said the bouncer. Then to me: "I've been through all this with him. He says someone out front invited him to read. One of the waitresses. But we've got a whole selection procedure for booking these guys." He hiked a thumb at the row of anxious faces. "They send in their work. We read it. We send them a letter back. They all bring those letters tonight or they don't get to read."

"Felix, is this true?" I asked.

I heard not a peep from behind my back.

"You see?" said the bouncer.

"They didn't say anything about a letter," said Felix sulkily.

"That's because the waitresses don't know a thing about any letters! It's got nothing to do with them! I don't know why I'm even arguing with you about it. I want both of you out—"

"Hi, Lola," said Felix.

I spun around, my pulse racing, and there she was, the girl I had made into a movie star in my head, standing there in her overcoat and green Wellington boots, a thick gray scarf, her hair tucked up beneath a tweed cap, a slight flush in her cheeks from the cold, a frown creasing her forehead. "Hey, Patrick," she said. "What's going on?"

"Felix thinks he's reading his poetry. This guy says he doesn't have the right letter." My heart was doing back flips.

The bouncer nodded.

Lola turned to him. "He's been talking about nothing else for weeks. He invited all his friends. Are you sure you can't let him read?"

The bouncer shook his head. "I can't. It wouldn't be fair to these guys."

"How about one poem? It doesn't have to be very long. You've got some short ones, haven't you, Felix?"

Felix nodded.

"There you go. How about that? How about he reads his nice short poem and then we'll take him home?"

The bouncer shook his head.

"Please," she implored.

The bouncer shook his head again. Silence reigned, nobody budging, just scanning the faces of the others to see if they would budge first.

"That's okay," said Felix finally. "I don't want to read in this place anyway. The toilets stink."

What little flexibility Lola had injected into the proceedings was removed immediately. "Okay. Let's get moving, you guys," said the bouncer, ushering us away from the stage with raised arms. We moved off, filing back down the aisle between the two banks of chairs, past the bar, toward the tall velvet curtain and the exit. The bouncer followed us all the way to make sure we got there, then held the curtain open for us to troop through, like schoolchildren caught raiding the pantry. Felix went first, then Lola, then me.

"Are we the only ones who turned up?" she whispered, holding the curtain open for me.

I nodded.

"Oy."

Outside, it had stopped snowing and the crowd of people collected under the scaffolding had dispersed. Little eddies of snow swirled across the deserted road; a traffic light swung in the breeze. Some distance away, a woman let loose a bloodcurdling scream; I looked up, to see a man running up the street, while the woman bent to scoop up a retaliatory snowball. Funny how similar they sounded: Americans being raped and pillaged and the sound of Americans just horsing around.

"Well, *this* turned out to be a fun Saturday night," said Lola brightly, tightening her coat around her.

"I'm sorry," said Felix.

"We almost had him there until you brought up the toilets."

"He wasn't going to let me read."

"I still think I coulda swung it."

"You just have a problem working out who's in charge, Felix," I said. "That's all."

"What do you mean?" asked Lola.

"He tried to buy a watch in McDonald's once."

"I didn't want to buy a watch there. I wanted him to tell me where I could."

"Right. You were lost. So you asked this guy, who was just a cashier at McDonald's. He didn't know what you'd been through. He didn't know you were lost. Same with that guy back there. He didn't get how excited you were when you came in. It's not his job to get it. His job is just to do his job. He didn't mean anything by it."

"Whose side are you on?" he asked.

"I'm not on anybody's side. I'm just saying you shouldn't take it personally."

"I think I want to go home now," he said grumpily.

"Where's home, Felix?" asked Lola.

"Avenue B," he said, pointing east.

"I'll walk with him," I said.

"I'll come with you," she said. "I'm not ready to go home just yet. You guys are my Saturday night."

"Apologies," I said.

"No need."

She linked arms with both of us and we set off across the Bowery, the snow coming up to our ankles.

"How was L.A.?" asked Felix.

"Warmer than this," said Lola.

"And your dad?"

"Not so good, Felix, not so good."

"What happened?"

"We were supposed to be going for lunch, but he's got this new girlfriend. She's a masseuse called Suzi. Don't you think that's kind of tacky? Dating your masseuse."

"Is that how they met?"

"Actually, no. No, they met at one of his scriptwriting classes. She was one of his students."

"Maybe she'll write a movie about masseuses."

"Maybe. Or maybe she'll just stick around and screw things up for me whenever I come to visit. So I get there and he's already got a bottle open, and I'm like, 'I thought we were supposed to be going for lunch, Dad,' and he goes, 'But we have lunch for you here,' and I go, '*Daad,*' but friggin' Yoko Ono's standing there staring at me, so what can I do. I sit down. I eat lunch. I try to get him on his own later, but he won't let her out of his sight. 'Ooh no, don't leave me alone with my daughter.' Jackass."

She laughed.

"That's too bad," said Felix.

"Yeah, it is, Felix. It really is. I didn't get to say anything I went there to say. It really makes me wonder what the point of the whole thing is, you know? Like why do we bother?"

"Don't ask me."

"I'm just glad to be home. I was so pleased to get your message. I really needed to get out of the apartment. Sorry I didn't get to hear your poems. What were they about?"

"One was about that girl—you remember, Patrick? The one who got hypothermia."

"The one they kicked off for not knowing her limits."

"Kicked off what?" asked Lola.

"*America's Next Top Model.*"

She laughed. "You wrote a poem about one of the girls on *America's Next Top Model.*"

"She was the most beautiful girl who ever graced that catwalk. And they kicked her off for getting hypothermia. She was too good for them. That's what the poem was about. Her being too good for them."

"I've been doing some thinking about that show, Felix," I said, "and I've come to a few conclusions."

"Oh yeah?"

"You know how all that stuff seems so unfair—the way they keep changing the rules, or only inventing them once they've been broken?"

He nodded. "Uh-huh."

"Well, I don't think the unfairness is an accident. I think it's deliberate. It's designed to impart an almost visceral feeling of unfairness. And I think that unfairness has to do with how Tyra Banks sees the world. I think she's exactly as unfair to those models as she feels people were to her when she was coming up through the ranks. Man hands misery on to man."

"Model hands misery on to model."

"Exactly."

"I might have to use that. That's a good line."

"It's Phillip Larkin's. You may have to credit him."

"Patrick's my agent," said Felix proudly.

"I didn't say that."

"But you might be."

"Only if you credit Larkin."

Lola laughed. "I think you two have been hanging out too much," she said. "One's as crazy as the other. Like Tweedledum and Tweedledee . . ."

Felix's street was completely empty, the cars covered in duvets of snow, the fire escapes fretted with thin white stripes, the trees on either side leaning over to create a bower that ran the length of the street, down to the lights of a distant bodega. Without conferring, the three of us headed into the middle of the street, where virgin drifts of snow glowed orange in the streetlights. It looked almost phosphorescent. The only sound was the crunch of the snow under our feet, and the distant hum of traffic. Above us, through the branches of the trees, the low-hanging clouds appeared pink, lit up by the city lights; and through the clouds, the light of a thin crescent moon. When I went back over this scene in the days and weeks to come—as I was to do many, many times—this was the moment that stood out as the point of no return, the point at which I could still have pulled back, and walked away with my sanity intact. The real tests in our lives do not come with big flags announcing "This is an important test. Pay attention. You must get this one right." Instead, they slip by as innocuously as a missed turning, or a paper cut. It can be quite some time before you notice you are lost, or bleeding. Approaching the bodega on the corner, we heard the tinny sound of an old Motown song playing on a radio. Felix drew up beside a small gated doorway with a box of busted buzzers, their multicolored wires dangling loose.

"Will you wait till I get up to the top?" he asked, rummaging around in his pockets for his keys. "Sometimes the lock jams and I'm shut in."

"Shut in where?" I asked.

"In the corridor. Between the door and the apartment."

"You should probably see your landlord about that."

He rolled his eyes, as if this was the dopiest thing he had ever heard; the lock tumbled and he let himself in. Lola and I were left in silence; I couldn't help noticing that she was wearing earrings: two thin silver hoops. She caught me looking at her and smiled.

"You're really good with him," she said.

"With Felix?" I asked.

"Everyone else treats him like a toy. Their new bipolar buddy. He can be pretty charming. He's smart. He agrees with everything you say. I get it. But then something happens, as it always does, and they tend not to stick around for very long."

"He doesn't seem that bad to me."

She smiled. "That's just it. You don't talk down to him. And you don't talk around him, either. You meet him head on."

The praise brought on a surge of guilt. "Listen, Lola. There's something I need to talk to you about. Something I've been meaning to tell you."

"Oh yeah? Shoot."

I put my hand across the doorway and looked down at the step, staring at it for a while before speaking. "I've done something stupid."

When she realized that nothing else was going to be forthcoming, she said, "Don't worry. I've been there."

"I don't think so. It's really stupid."

"Then I've *really* been there," she said, and laughed. Then she saw my face. "Oh sweetie, I'm sorry. You look so serious. It's okay, you know. Whatever you've done, it's okay. You know that, right?"

She wore such a sweet, sympathetic expression that I had to look away. "You don't understand. I've been lying to you about something. You remember the first time we met, at that meeting on Washington Square?"

She nodded.

"Do you remember our conversation? What you told me about the meetings. What time they were, when they happened. Do you remember?"

She let go of a lungful of air, her puffed cheeks slowly deflating. "Is this going to be about the program?"

"Yes," I said. "It is. Kind of. You see—"

She cut me off. "Do you mind terribly if we don't have this conversation, Patrick? Not tonight. I know I shouldn't say this, but I'm sick to death of hearing about the program. Seriously. I know I shouldn't say this, but how about just for one night we try it, huh? Just for one night."

"I'M IN!"

It was Felix shouting down to us from the top floor.

We both craned our necks but could see nothing, just the corner of the building against the cloudy night sky. We walked out into the middle of the street again. Then Lola tugged on my sleeve and pointed him out: a small figure waving from one of the top windows.

"We see you!" she hollered, her hands cupped around her mouth.

"I'm in!"

"That's great, Felix!"

"Thanks for waiting!"

"Anytime!"

"I'm going to brush my teeth now!"

"You do that!"

"Night, night!"

"Night, Felix!"

"And thanks again for everything!"

"You're welcome!" we both hollered.

The window slammed shut.

"I didn't see any models," she said.

"Maybe they're waiting behind his shower curtain."

This time, her laughter pushed her off balance. Her arm shot out to grab mine, pushing me off balance, too; for a second or two, we both seemed to teeter, then we regained our footing, and before we knew it, we were both standing in the middle of the road, clinging to each other for support, her rib cage rising and falling against mine as she struggled to regain her breath.

"What did you want to say to me?" she asked.

"Hmm?"

"The thing you wanted to say to me before."

Somewhere inside of me, a fierce battle was being waged. I could almost hear it—the distant clash of bayonet and musket—but then it was gone, lost in the low hum of the traffic.

"Vladimir Zworykin," I said.

She frowned. "Come again?"

"The man who invented the TV."

Her eyes widened. "It was a *Russki?*"

"It was a simultaneous invention. It happened everywhere all at the same time. John Logie Baird invented the television in the UK. Your guy phyllo pastry whatsit—"

"Farnsworth."

"Right. Farnsworth invented it for you guys. Vladimir Zworykin invented it for the Russians."

"I don't believe it."

"It's true! It's like simultaneous jokes. What you have to imagine is that around the 1920s, a lot of people started to think that something square in the corner of the room, showing electronic images, might, you know, be a good idea. And enough people in enough places thought like this to pull the television into existence in all these different countries."

She laughed. "I can't believe you actually looked this up."

"We had a bet."

"I was joking."

"I was curious."

"As to whether you were right or not?"

"We were both right."

"Why do I get the impression I should be grateful for that?"

She looked at me slyly. I knew instantly that if I held her gaze, one future would unfurl, and that if I looked away, another, altogether different future would happen. Then, almost as quickly, the moment was gone and we were kissing, my hands finding her waist, hers mine, pulling each other in until nothing seemed to exist outside of the warm cocoon created by our bodies and our coats that not even the cold December air could touch.

chapter nineteen

HER BEDROOM WAS SMALL, dark, the bed strewn with rumpled sheets, the floor with discarded clothes. A pale blue light seeped through the window, across which a white shawl had been hung as a makeshift curtain; beneath the window, an old iron-ribbed radiator hissed gently. On the wall opposite us were two posters, one for a Jenny Lewis and the Watson Twins concert, the other a silk-screen print of Barack Obama facing heavenward, above a single word, HOPE. A door led through into the bathroom.

"Patrick," she said.

"Mm-hmm."

"Come here."

I rolled over. She had her head propped up on her hand, her elbow in the pillow. "There's something I want to tell you," she said, looking at the sheets in between us. "I'm not sure how you're going to take it. . . . But this thing always follows me around and it always comes up sooner or later. So I'm just going to come out with it."

Her hand started smoothing out imaginary creases in the sheet. "It was during my second year at UCLA. Things were just beginning to go wrong for my dad. He was defaulting on my college fees. We were having these massive fights. I was spending more and more time away from home, and I started dating this guy. At least I thought we were dating. I mean, I knew what he did, but I didn't mind too much—the other girls, they were just business. That was work. And then one night, one of them didn't show up. Ricky had this massive freak-out. 'Ohmigod, what am I going to do? She's my best girl. Ohmigod, she's really screwed me this time. What am I going to do? We don't have any brunettes.' " She paused and swallowed. "So he asked me. And I said yes."

"Said yes to what?"

"It was so stupid of me," she said, ignoring my question. "I didn't know *what* I was doing. No idea. He tells me to stand on this corner, and I get the wrong corner. I could have sworn he said Bonnie Brae and Sixth. I was supposed to be on Sixth and Union." She shook her head. "You don't need to know the whole story, but basically I got myself arrested."

"Arrested for what?"

She looked up at me, winced. "For soliciting."

"For . . ."

She was keeping a close eye on my face to see how well I was taking it. "You're shocked, aren't you?" she said.

"No, no, not at all. . . ." I felt dizzy.

"I only did it a few times. It was just to pay my college fees."

"Of course you did. To pay for your college fees. It's perfectly understandable."

"Are you sure?" she said, wrinkling her nose. "Because you look a little sick."

"No, no, no. I understand. You needed to pay your college fees. Your dad defaulted with his payments."

"I just got unlucky is all. They told me the wrong corner. I could have sworn he said Bonnie Brae and Sixth. . . . Do you want me to open a window or something?"

"No, I'm fine, really I am."

"I can't bear it. You look terrible. Hey, Patrick. It wasn't really me that happened to. You know that, right?"

"Right. You must have to go to somewhere deep inside."

"No, I mean it happened to someone else."

"Right, almost as if it were someone else."

She reached over and put a hand on my shoulder. "No, Patrick. Look at me. It really was a different person that happened to. It wasn't me. It was my sponsor."

"Your . . ."

She nodded. "My sponsor. Glenda."

She held on to it for as long as she could, but it was too much even for her. Shrieking, she dived under the covers.

"That is not funny," I said to the empty room.

The covers shook and heaved.

Eventually, I got bored of staring at the empty room and dived under to exact retribution. With a shriek, she dived deeper, wriggling away from me as I burrowed toward her; after much pursuit, I caught her by the waist and pulled her close, still wrapped in sheets.

"Don't do anything to me," she begged, breathless. "Please, please, please, please, please . . ."

"I thought you really did—"

"You thought I was a ho?" she said, twisting around in the bed, her face flushed. "You thought I was a crack ho."

"I didn't say that."

"And you were willing to let it go."

"I don't know about that."

"So sweet."

She kissed me on the end of the nose. "Oh, he's still mad. I've got some major ass-kissing to do, I can tell. . . . Do you want some more tea?"

I nodded sulkily. "Yes, please."

She rolled over to the edge of the bed and leaned over to fish for some clothes, her back pale and long, a small tattoo at the base of her back that looked like a piece from a mah-jongg set. She came up with a tartan dressing gown. She stood up, pulling it on. "Put some music on if you like," she said, flicking her hair over the collar. The moment she stepped outside the room, it seemed empty. I got up, went to the window, and parted the shawl. Snow covered everything in a thick white blanket—the street, the cars, the fire escapes, the chimney stacks, the water towers—but the sky was solid blue; at the end of the street, the sun was just beginning to peek over the rooftops. It was clearly going to be a glorious day, and yet I felt sick with the toad sitting in my stomach—big and fat and gnarly, like one of those cane toads you get in Australia. He had been with me all night, Lola already asleep beside me while I sat there, bolt upright, tracing the progress of a small block of moonlight across the wall.

From the kitchen, a kettle whistled. I hunted around for my jeans, pulled them on, and padded through into the kitchen, tucked into the short arm of an L-shaped living room. Lola's apartment was one of the smallest I had ever seen, the rooms tall and narrow, with ornate cornicing in the corners of the high ceilings. Lola was standing over the stove, turning off the flame beneath a beaten tin kettle before dropping tea bags into two waiting cups. "One, two," she said as she did so. She often did that, I had noticed: commented on the most prosaic of actions, as they were happening, as if to double-check that they were. On the refrigerator to her left, a handful of photographs was pinned in place by magnets: Lola with her friends, at a beach, in a car, being hugged by an older man.

"Is that your dad?" I asked.

"Oh," she said, turning, her hand going to her neck. "You gave me a shock. . . . Yes, that's him. That's Bruce."

I looked at the photo again. He had luscious, almost womanly features, with a red-gray beard; she fit under his arm as if she'd grown there.

"He's a screenwriter."

"Used to be. Now he just collects residuals and gets drunk all day."

The toad inside of me let loose a loud belch.

"Lola," I said.

"Hm-hmm."

"There's something I need to tell you."

She replaced the kettle on the burner.

"I tried to tell you last night but . . . well, everything went so fast."

I walked over to her; she turned to face me. "Oh God," she said.

"Oh God what?"

"I knew this was coming."

"Knew what was coming?"

"Our 'Come to Jesus' talk. Look, Patrick. You need to know something, too. This. This isn't something I've really done in a while. Don't get me wrong. I'm pleased you're here. Really pleased. I'm enjoying myself. But I'm a little appalled at myself, too."

"Why?"

"Sleeping with a newcomer, dumbo. It's not done. None of my sponsees will be able to look me in the eye again. I'll be shunned, an outcast." She placed an arm on my shoulder. "I guess what I'm saying is, I like you a lot, far too much to ever let this happen again. It really was very selfish of me."

"No, no, no, no, no. You don't get it. You didn't sleep with a newcomer. I'm not . . ."

My voice trailed off, the toad lodged in my windpipe.

"I've done a bad thing," I said.

She placed her other arm on my shoulder, lowered her head seeking eye contact. "It's okay," she said. "Just spit it out. What's going on?"

I concentrated hard on what I had to say.

"Okay, so I told you I'm a literary agent?"

She nodded.

"Well, the fact is, I've been going to meetings to sign up Douglas. That's what I've been doing all this time. I saw him crossing the square and I followed him into the meeting. That first time I met you, and I said I was just there for my friend. Do you remember that?"

She nodded again.

"I was talking about Douglas. And you said to come back again the next day, so I did. And he was there that time, but when I tried to get to him, everyone leaped all over me. You came up to me and told me you'd get his number for me. Do you remember?"

"Uh-huh," she said, her hands dropping to my waist, where they remained.

"And so I went back a third time, to hear him tell his story. I had to find out what had happened to him, don't you see? No one seemed to know where he was. That's the one I feel worst about, the one where we met up afterward. That was the only meeting where I actually intended to lie."

Her face was wearing the kindest, most sympathetic expression I had ever seen on a human being. I'm not kidding. It was the face of an angel.

"Oh Patrick," she said. "Is this what you've been burning up to tell me?"

"I know I should have told you earlier."

"Oh please. In L.A., people use the meetings to network all the time. It's where you find all the fucked-up creatives. Except my father. So if you want to meet the fucked-up creatives, that's where you go."

I groaned. "You don't get it. That's the only reason I've been going to meetings. To sign up Douglas. I'm not an alcoholic."

Everything went superstill. Her face wore the expression of a telephone operator whose console had just lit up with calls and she didn't know which one to put through first.

"Why would you say that?" she asked.

Her voice was soft, contained, like someone shrinking themselves in the presence of a bear.

"Because it's true."

She shook her head. "It's not true, Patrick. Don't say things like that."

"I don't know what to tell you. It's true. I've been lying to you."

She looked at me imploringly. "This isn't funny anymore, Patrick. Please stop it."

"I'm not trying to be funny."

"Then why are you saying what you're saying?"

"Because . . ."

"No, it's *not* true, Patrick. Don't keep *saying* that. You're just hurting yourself. I want you to stop."

"I'm not hurting myself."

"Well, you're hurting *me*."

"Lola . . ."

I made a move toward her, but she pulled up her arms like a boxer, backing away, then turned and walked out of the kitchen, around the corner, and into the living room. I stayed frozen into position by the refrigerator, reeling. More out of reflex than anything else, I set about finishing the two cups of tea that stood on the counter. Pouring the boiled water into the cups, I saw that my hands were shaking slightly. I stirred sugar into the tea, and kept on stirring, and when I couldn't reasonably go on stirring any longer, I took the two cups of tea into the living room.

She was curled up on the sofa by the window, a small two-seater draped with an Indian-style paisley coverlet, her feet tucked up underneath her. Next to her was a large potted palm; on the wall behind it, a blurry lozenge of light was slowly making its way down the wall. She saw me and patted the seat next to her. I walked over, handed her the cup of tea, and sat down. From the TV opposite, our reflections came reflected back to us: two figures on the sofa, silhouetted by the window behind us. They looked weighted, submerged, like two statues at the bottom of a pool.

"I should have told you before. I know that. I've known that ever since we went for that walk. That's when I knew I was in trouble. That's why I stayed away from you. I couldn't be around you. Not without telling you. I had to tell you or just walk away. Just walk away from the whole thing. Then I might have given us a chance. But I didn't." I shook my head.

"I never intended it to get this far. You have to believe me. I didn't even intend to start lying, not at first. It just happened. Felix told me that meeting was open to the public."

"Felix *is* crazy. You do know that, don't you?"

"He has his problems. . . ."

"'His problems,'" she repeated. "Three months ago, he was wearing arm restraints in a lockdown ward on the Upper East Side." She laughed. "I was like, Well, he seems like a nice guy, but he's also drawing all the crazies out of the woodwork. I didn't stop for a second to think that included *me*." Her hand went to her chest.

I turned to her. "So you believe me?"

"Believe that you're crazy?"

"Believe that I'm telling you the truth."

She looked at me for a few seconds, incredulously, struggling to keep herself from smiling. "Okay, so you're a literary agent."

"Yes. That's right. Good."

"And you've been going to meetings solely to sign up Douglas."

"Yes."

"Not because you have a drinking problem."

"No."

"You saw Douglas crossing the street and you thought, I know what. I'll follow that man into an AA meeting and then pretend to be an alcoholic so that I can sign him up as my client?"

"Well, it never came to me as a plan like that. I was in the meeting and then suddenly everyone jumped me. There was Felix, and there you were, and everybody was telling me how great I was and before I knew what was happening. . . ."

"You were in recovery." She was smirking.

"Yes. That's right. I was weak. A moment's weakness and—*boom*."

"Why didn't you just call him up?"

"I'm sorry?"

"Why didn't you just look up Douglas at the library? Why go to all this trouble?"

"I didn't know where he worked! I didn't even know he was in New York. Nobody does. He just disappeared off the radar. I had to find out what had happened to him, don't you see?"

"And did you?"

"Did I what?"

"Sign him up."

"He said he didn't need a literary agent right now."

She laughed, her hair falling forward, creating a dark tent on either side of her face. When she came up she was holding the bridge of her nose. "I'm sorry, I shouldn't laugh, but you do know how completely nuts this sounds, don't you? You say you want to sign up Douglas. That it's all been about him. Then what are you doing *here*, for heaven's sake?"

"What am I doing *here*?"

"Yes. With me."

"I haven't been able to stop thinking about you since I first met you."

"Oh no, leave me out of it, mister. This has nothing to do with me."

"But of course it has to do with—"

I was interrupted by the sound of my phone from the next room, ringing through muffling layers of clothing. It rang once, twice, three times.

"Don't you want to get that?" she asked.

"It's probably just Saul."

"Saul," she said, as if repeating the name of a visitor from another planet. "And does Saul know about any of this?"

"No."

"Did you tell any of your friends?"

I shook my head.

"Why not?"

"Because . . . they'd think I was crazy."

"It might be worth thinking about," she said, then caught my expression and wiped the smile from her face. "Look, Patrick, sweetheart . . . Nobody does what you did unless they're unhappy with their lives. Believe me, I've been there. You're talking to a girl who used to lie all the time, twenty-four hours a day, seven days a week. Lied to my parents, lied to my teachers, lied to my boyfriends. I lied just because I could, because it was easier than not lying, because it was the only way I could think of to get the world off my frigging back. I know what it's like. It's exhausting. It's miserable and it's isolating and it's exhausting. Aren't you wiped?"

It was weird: The moment she said it, I felt a wave of tiredness hit me like the undertow of a retreating wave. At the base of her neck, I noticed a small blue vein, as pale and delicate as streaking in marble.

"I don't have a drinking problem, if that's what you're suggesting."

"I didn't say you did."

"But you think it."

"I don't think it really matters what I think, do you?"

"It matters to me."

"Well, it doesn't much matter to me. Either you're a raging alcoholic in complete denial who is about to relapse or you're a complete sociopath who lies his way into AA meetings. Either way, I don't come out of this whole thing with my taste in men vindicated."

She laughed.

"You think I do this sort of thing all the time, is that it?"

"Do you?"

"No, not at all. This is the first time I've ever done anything like this in my life!"

"Then maybe you want to ask yourself why you started now? I mean, what is it with me, Patrick? Why do I only attract the fuckups? Do I have a big sign above my head saying 'Only fuck-ups need apply'? Is it some kind of pheromone I give off?"

"You do smell good."

She considered it. "Yeah, but it can't be just that. You put them anywhere within a ten-mile radius and I still find 'em. You can put him in a suit and a fancy English accent and stick him in an AA meeting and I will sniff that sucker out. How do I do it?"

"Maybe it's some kind of sixth sense?"

"Yes, I really think it must be something like that. A sixth sense. Yes. Very good. I like that."

"Lola," I said, moving toward her.

"Oh no," she said, pushing me away. "Do you want something to eat? I don't know about you, but I'm famished."

"Enjoy!" The waiter placed a plate of doughnuts next to our coffee on the table and retreated. Lola reached across and fished out a sugar-dusted one; she was still wearing her fur-trimmed Puffa jacket, over a navy blue roll-neck sweater; she had a small triangular scar, I saw, on the back of her left hand, just above her thumb. I continued my point.

"Did you know the *Guardian* once asked him for his books of the year and when he said he had no books of the year, they published the space blank? That's how much his opinion was worth to them."

"Wasn't that just a waste of space?" she asked through a mouthful of doughnut.

She licked her fingers. "You should try these doughnuts. They're good."

"I'm not very hungry," I said. "The point is, he was—is—a very important figure for a lot of people. Look, I've seen him in meetings and he stands out a mile, and it's not because he's famous or because I read his books in college. It's because he's unhappy. And he's unhappy because he's not doing what he was put on this earth to do."

"Which is?"

"Write."

"But you said he was writing."

"Publish, then," I said. "He can't just write for himself."

"Why not? Maybe he needs to. Maybe he's spent his entire life writing for other people and now he needs to write something just for himself."

"He's *always* written for himself."

"You sure about that?"

"Positive."

"Every time you talk about him, you sound like you're talking about yourself. Have you noticed that?"

"What are you talking about?"

"Just what I said. Whenever you talk about him, it's like you're taking about yourself. I don't know why, since I don't know you well enough, but for some reason the sight of Douglas being humbled really gets to you. You know what you remind me of? You remind me of a child who hears his mother in labor and goes, 'Who's hurting Mommy?' Nobody's hurting 'Mommy,' Patrick. He's just going through changes. It's our job to stand well back and let that happen."

"I'm just trying to help him is all."

"You don't think you're in a *little* deeper than that?"

I groaned. "Let's not talk about Douglas. We're just going to go round and round in circles."

"I'm perfectly happy," she said, taking another bite of a doughnut; pink icing cracked and fell to her plate. Her phone began to ring. She fished around in her bag, brought it up, and looked at the number, still chewing.

"I'm sorry, I'm going to have to get this."

"Please . . ."

"Dee. How are you, honey? How'd it go? . . . No . . . Uh-uh . . . You did? . . . Oh, okay. I'm sorry I didn't get back to you sooner. . . ."

I leaned back in the banquette and gazed out the window. The sun was coming over the rooftops now; shapely dunes bounced back the blue of the sky; a block away, a man made progress down one of the avenues on a pair of skis. Fishing out my phone, I found two messages and four recent calls from Saul. Shit.

"I thought so," Lola was saying now. "Okay—don't worry about it. . . . Have you eaten? I can meet you for lunch if you like. . . . No trouble at all. . . . Okay . . . all right—Duck Soup at two. I'll see you there. I love you."

She gave me an apologetic wince as she replaced the phone in her bag. "Sorry."

"I'd like to see you again."

She looked surprised. "Are you going somewhere?"

"I have to clear up some things with my friend."

"You don't think we have a few issues?"

"All the more reason to see each other again. Hash them out. That's what issues are for—hashing. Otherwise, why have them?"

"And what are they, do you think?"

"No idea, but I'll try to figure it out and tell you the next time I see you."

She shook her head, staring at me as if mesmerized. "God," she said. "The urge to fix you is almost overwhelming."

"I don't need fixing."

Her face crumpled, a little sadly. "No, you don't, do you?"

chapter twenty

"You want some coffee?" called Saul from the kitchen.

"Love some!" I called back.

"Milk? Sugar?"

"Both!"

His apartment was dark, the blinds drawn. There was a slight stickiness to the floor. When I hoisted the blinds, a scene of ashen devastation was revealed, every table and shelf littered with empty bottles, crushed cans, glasses, and plastic cups; cigarette butts bristled from ashtrays and swam in half-full wineglasses, soaking up red wine like gauze stanching a flesh wound. The air stank of beer and ash. Fighting a losing battle with my schadenfreude, I started clearing away bottles from the dining room table. Sobriety had to knock at least fifteen years off you. It whisked you back to that magical time when you got a head start on every day, throwing off your Superman duvet cover, stepping through the debris of your parents' parties to wolf down Cocoa Puffs and bolt out the door. Saul appeared in the kitchen door bearing two steaming cups of coffee: Tousle-haired, clad in a white bathrobe, visibly hungover. He mosied over and set the cups down on the table while I cleared more space, cutting a swath through the forest of bottles on the table. He sat down, saying nothing, his silence like some ritual, a precursor to appeasement talks between nuclear nations.

"How'd it go after I left?" I asked.

"Great," he grunted, taking a sip of his coffee.

"I'm sorry I had to run out on you."

"What happened? We were worried about you."

"Well, I am in one piece. As you can see." I beamed brightly.

"That's terrific, Patrick. What the fuck happened?"

"You didn't have anything to worry about, really, Saul. I just had someone I needed to see." I peered at him, trying to ascertain what, if anything, he knew. "Why were you so worried?"

"Well, ordinarily I wouldn't have been worried. You're always bolting off. But Scott and Lindsay seemed to think that you might be in some danger. I said to them, 'What kind of danger?' They go, 'Mortal danger.' I go, 'Mortal danger.' Then they give each other this funny look. 'What is it?' I go, and that's when they tell me."

My throat felt a little dry, so I took a sip of my coffee. "Tell you what?"

"Let me see—what did they say? Oh, that's right, they said that you were in an extremely vulnerable state right now since you had only a couple of weeks of sobriety under your belt. Which was weird, since I didn't even know you were sober. I said that, but they told me you'd been going to meetings for the last month, and things had been going great until last night. You were acting very impulsively, they said. They were worried you were close to a relapse. I said to them, 'Are you sure? I mean, I know he drinks a lot, but that's just because he's British. . . .' "

I held up my hands in surrender. "Okay, okay," I said. "All right. Enough. I hear you."

Behind me, a large clump of snow, melted by the sun, detached itself from the roof with a soft *floop* sound and slid past the window.

"The first thing you need to know is that I'm not an alcoholic."

"I never thought you were."

"It's just that a lot of people seem to think I am."

"And why would that be?"

"Well," I said, with the air of a man whose next words might be "I'm glad you asked me that." I stared at the tabletop, which was rimmed with crescents of red wine. "I didn't find Douglas Kelsey at the library like I said. I found him in an AA meeting."

"And what were you doing at an AA meeting?"

"I followed him in. And I went back a couple of times to hear his story. Which is absolutely amazing, by the way. If the book is anything like his qualification, it's going to be sensational. Do you know that nobody's ever written a great American novel about alcoholism? He says it's like staring at the sun—it can't be done. Although he seems to think Stephen King came close in *The Shining*."

"I didn't know King was an alkie."

"Complete garbagehead. But Douglas's book is bound to be better. How can it not be? A writer of that caliber? A return to form for Kelsey *and* a no-holds-barred confession as to what he's been up to all these years. It's sure to get serialized, don't you think? Maybe *Vanity Fair* would go for something like that."

"*Woooah*, ease up a little, Patrick," he said, raising his hands. "Go back to the bit about attending AA meetings."

"I only went to a couple."

"A couple."

"Okay, three. Three and a half."

"And you stopped drinking."

"Of course I did. I'm not *that* bad."

"I didn't say anything about 'bad.' "

"That night with you and Natalie in Hudson Bar and Books. That was my only slip."

"Well, if we'd known you were attempting to get sober, we would never have asked you out, would we? When did all this start?"

"Middle of December."

He nodded. "That's when it all began."

"That's when all *what* began?"

He gave me a look. "Patrick, you've been acting like a complete fucking lunatic for weeks now! I thought you were having an early midlife crisis. Nat thought it was that girl you kept going on about. I *knew* that was bullshit. I *knew* it."

"Well . . . actually, Saul," I said, tracing the arc of one of the wine crescents with my forefinger, "there is a girl. That's where I was last night. With her. That's where I went."

"And she knows you're not . . . like her."

"I told her this morning."

"This *morning*. You slept with her and *then* you tell her."

"I tried to tell her before, but it all went so fast."

"Oh man. You are something, Patrick."

"What do you mean?"

"She must've been mad as hell."

"Actually, she took it quite well, all things considered."

"All things considered? All things considered? You mean considering that honesty is only the most important thing in the world to recovering alcoholics?"

"It's not the *most* important thing," I said, bristling.

"What are you talking about? It's only the central tenet of the whole program. You can fuck up any which way you like, but if you lie, you're toast."

I shook my head. "I don't think so. I'm pretty sure I would have noticed if that was the case. A small part of it maybe. Most of it's about staying nice and upbeat. Not honesty. The opposite.

It's very English, actually. It's all backbone and stiff upper lip and self-deprecation and putting a brave face on things."

"Saul?" A sleepy female voice came from the bedroom. It was Liz, Saul's girlfriend.

"Yes, sweetheart?" he called out.

"I hear voices."

"It's just Patrick . . . He's alive!"

There was a pause.

"That's good . . . Do I smell coffee?"

"I'll bring you some when I come back in!"

"Thank you!"

"I'm sorry about busting in on you like this," I said, gathering myself. "I'll leave you be."

"So how'd you leave it?"

"She said to call her. Do you think she meant immediately, or in a week or so?"

"I meant Kelsey. How did you leave it with Kelsey?"

"Oh. He said he'd think about it."

He looked at me with a look of soft marvel in his eyes. "Unbelievable."

"What?"

"Absolutely unbelievable."

"What?"

"You are."

"Why?"

"Leo's going to be delighted."

"Not a word of this to him, Saul. Kelsey's not in the bag yet."

"Okay," he said, getting up from the table. "But he *is* going to be delighted."

We both made our way to the elevator.

"So, what do you think?" I asked him.

"What do I think about what?"

"What do you think about Lola? What do you think I should do?"

"How the hell would I know? How did you leave it with her?"

"She said I could call. But did she mean immediately, or in a week or so?"

"I would give it a bit of time to cool off."

"She really wasn't very angry, Saul. I know it sounds weird, but she's not like that. Not like Caitlin. She's very calm. It's some low center of gravity thing they teach them. You know, like when you throw a cat, they always land on their feet?"

"Uh-huh."

"She's like that."

"A *cat*."

"Never mind," I said glumly as we reached the elevator.

Saul punched the button. "Just give it some time. She'll see you're basically a decent guy. It's not like you do this sort of thing all the time."

"No, right," I murmured.

The elevator arrived and the doors opened. "God, I can't believe Scott did that."

"Did what?"

"Broke my anonymity. The dick."

Saul looked at me with fresh amazement.

"Stop it, Patrick. Just stop."

How could I possibly explain to Saul when it all felt so strange to me? What had happened between Lola and me felt as fabulously strange as a piece of moon rock. As many times as I had played out the scene in my head, it bore no resemblance whatsoever to what had actually transpired. I'd pictured tears, rage, fists, followed by recriminations, reconciliation. That's how it went with normal people. That's how it would have gone with Caitlin. Jesus. I'd have been lucky to have gotten out of that apartment alive if it had been Caitlin I'd lied to. Instead, I'd got incredulity, followed by amusement, concern, even compassion. It was genuinely mystifying to me. It was like I'd pushed on a door I'd long thought locked, only to find it swinging open into a room that I'd never known existed. What did you do in *this* room? I didn't know, only that I couldn't wait to go back there and that I'd count down the days until I could call.

As Christmas approached, the city emptied of all but the most hardened stragglers, negotiating the streets in ski masks and goggles. The snowfall had set some kind of record, in the everybody-wins manner of American records—the second deepest snowfall in the third week of December since 1978, or some such—creating deep banks between the sidewalk and street that you had to clamber over, like an amateur mountaineer. I stayed home for the most part, stocking up on groceries and cleaning products; my apartment was a mess of socks and cereal packets, as if someone had been sneaking into the place while I'd been away. Lola's had been messy but clean; mine was tidy but dirty—hers with all the clutter out in the open, where you could see it; mine with all the grime hidden away, invisible to the naked eye until you got in good and close.

On Christmas Day, I phoned my parents to thank them for the Paul Smith shirt they had sent me and did my best to reassure my mother that I was not about to become terrorist roadkill. Despite the blandishments of adulthood, my parents' image of me remained locked at the socks and marmite stage—their son barely able to complete his own laundry. If only they could see me, I thought as I laid into some particularly stubborn stains in the bath, the sort of thing that normally remained untouched until a female relative came to visit. It was now a few days after Christmas. The taps were running and I was soon lost in my usual thickets of multiple choice about Lola—wondering whether I was thinking about her too much, and if so, then whether catching myself accidentally thinking about her counted, and if it did, then what about dreams, and if I was to be held accountable for those, too—when the phone rang.

At first I didn't hear it, but then I turned off the taps, and froze. I was rewarded with another ring; and bolted for the bedroom, sending bucket and cleaning products flying. My phone. It took me an agonizing five rings to track my phone down and free it from my coat, but eventually I held it in my hand, struggling to calm my breathing as I punched TALK.

"Hello?"

"Patrick?"

"Yes?"

"It's Douglas Kelsey here."

I was stunned and—strange to say—a little disappointed. "Mr. Kelsey. How nice to hear from you. How are you?"

"Terrible, since you asked."

"I'm sorry to hear that."

"Although I don't think I can claim to be any worse off than any other citizen of this godforsaken country. I don't suppose you saw the *New York Times* this morning?"

"No, I can't say I have."

"They published transcripts of these interviews with the man at the Justice Department who told the president he could go ahead and torture those detainees. Someone asked him if the president was entitled to crush the testicles of a small child in the fight against terrorism. Do you want to know what he said? 'It depends on why the president thinks he needs to do that.' Isn't that something? Crushing the testicles of a small child. It depends on what side of the bed our beloved leader got up that morning."

"That's shocking."

"It's the first real sign I've seen that this country's days are numbered. The side that tortures always loses. Without exception. I've always known the end was coming, of course, but still, to see it with my own eyes in the newspaper this morning, that's another thing altogether."

I didn't know what to say to that, puzzled as to whether he had really called me up just a few days after Christmas to talk about the president's legal right to crush the testicles of small children. The number of comebacks available to me were limited, to say the least. "I can only imagine" was what I finally managed.

"Yeah, well. What are we going to do about it. Nothing. I've had some bad news this end, Patrick. You know that I'm in the process of divorcing my wife."

"Yes, I did know that."

"I won't bore you with the details, but I've just heard that I have to pay Carrie half the money I got from the sale of my house."

"I thought you used that money to pay back your advance from Random House."

"I did. I have to find two hundred and fifty thousand dollars on top of that. That's the amount of emotional cruelty she was judged to have suffered from being married to me."

"Oh, Douglas, I'm sorry. That seems terribly unreasonable. What are you going to do?"

There was a long pause.

"Okay," he said finally. "Here's how this would work. You wouldn't be my agent exactly. I just want this one book sold."

"I understand."

"And I don't want it sold before the end of the tax year, or it shows up on my return and she gets half of that, too."

"Of course. Can I ask you something? How would you feel about my going back to Random House?"

"Things got very ugly there, Patrick, I don't mind saying. My editor and I almost came to blows."

"Yes, I know, but he's gone now. Your old editor? He left to set up his own press in Mississippi a year ago."

"I hope a tornado picks off his kids."

I laughed, uneasily. "Hah! Well—my point is, it's a fresh slate there now. I'm sure they'd be delighted to hear from you. What do you say I start out there? We've got good contacts with the new guys there, and I also happen to know they're a little short on new fiction this year."

"Sure, why don't you try them, but don't be surprised if they slam the door in your face."

"I'm sure that won't happen."

"We'll see."

I had hung up the phone before I realized I had completely failed to address the subject of the meetings, how we had met, my lie. A feeling of doom gathered in my gut. I would straighten out the details with him the first chance I got. How about that? The next time I saw him, I would straighten the whole thing out. I called Saul with the good news.

chapter twenty-one

THE RAIN RAN DOWN the taxi window in jerky rivulets that pooled into one another and, pooling, plummeted. Through the window, the city streaked and blurred, the bluish gray gloom lit up with red clusters of brake lights and the gaudy neon facades of Times Square. It all looked unfamiliar to me—alien, hieroglyphic, vaguely threatening, a little as it had when I first arrived. Up on a giant screen that spanned the side of a building, a woman blew a kiss toward me; a few buildings down, a giantess in a nurse's uniform slapped a doctor across the face. On the other side of the cab sat Saul, his elbow wedged into the window. He'd become a closed book to me since my revelations over the holidays. I'd thought that coming clean with him would bring relief, maybe some comradely joshing, and there had been some teasing, but it soon ran dry, to be replaced by a slight wariness around me. It was nothing you could put your finger on—a few skipped beats in our conversations, an occasional quizzical look, as if to see what I would do next: start dribbling soup down my shirt, turning lamps on and off at precisely measured intervals. That was the first sign I had that what I had done was beyond the pale—the fact that it was beyond the reach of even Saul's sarcasm. I thought telling the truth was supposed to make you feel clean. That's what they called it: Coming clean. It didn't. It made you feel dirty.

The cab drew to a halt outside the Random House building on the corner of Fifty-sixth Street and Broadway. A sleek gray monolith with smoked-glass windows, it jutted up into the cloudy January sky. The lobby was marble and glass, its high ceilings echoing with the sotto voce hum of employees taking their coffee breaks, visitors signing in with the security guards, the guards phoning upstairs for clearance. Bearing freshly printed stickers identifying ourselves, we made our way to the elevators, silent and whip-fast. You almost didn't notice you were moving until you felt your stomach gently nuzzling the bottom of your rib cage and heard your ears pop. We were met on the twenty-seventh floor by a gangly male editorial assistant with an intense postgraduate manner; exchanging barely a word, he swiped us through some big plate-glass doors and led us down a long corridor with carpet the color of muesli and tables bearing the occasional halogen-spotlit orchid, past offices with doors just slightly ajar, revealing editors at their desks, some with phones wedged under their chins, one bouncing a ball against a wall. Saul received nods from those he knew, blank stares from those he didn't, the latter looking up like deer interrupted in their grazing. It all seemed oddly formal to me, like a rehearsal for a scene in Kabuki theater. I had spent so long tramping down mossy steps to dingy church basements, with their statues and gargoyles and smell of old books and wax, a whole other New York lying right under everyone's nose, hidden in plain sight, that I had forgotten this other New York existed: this city of concrete and steel and plate-glass windows. It was a little like returning to the city, only to find it transformed into Tokyo.

The boardroom was long, with a large ebony table that ran the length of it, surrounded by high-backed black leather chairs. Saul sat down and opened his briefcase; I walked over to the window, pressing myself against the glass and peering out. Directly opposite, the skyscraper on the next corner vented steam into the air, the clouds writhing for a few seconds before disappearing; suspended between two white masses, the building looked almost to be hanging in thin air, like one of those cartoon characters who should by rights be falling but hasn't realized it yet. I had a sudden vision of Lola under the bedcovers, her limbs wrapped in white sheets, and caught my breath. I was seeing her this evening. It seemed we had waited too long, long enough anyway for my thoughts to have taken a dive toward the tortuous. She'd sounded busy and breathless on the phone. Why was it that girls always did that? Sounded busy and breathless on the phone when you called them, their voices so redolent of the rich, packed life you dimly hoped to be a part of but which at present you were cruelly excluded from? Did they think we needed reminding? American girls drove the point home with particular force: "What's up?" they'd ask, casually. You mean *apart* from the fact that you've just spent the best part of two weeks counting down the days when you could call them, going over what you would say in endless permutations, dialing their number umpteen times before plucking up the courage to punch the last digit? And now they ask you, "What's *up?*" like you had some other news to report? Some topic of conversation other than them? Putting down the phone afterward, I wondered whether it was possible for a human being to obsess about someone so much that he literally emptied himself out; whether if you burrowed through me, you would find nothing but Lola thoughts, Lola feelings, Lola conversations, running on Lola power. To speak back to her, she first had to speak to me. To tell her about my life, she first had to become a part of it. To be free, I first had to be forgiven. Everything else was just birdsong—Swahili.

I heard the door behind me and turned to see the two editors I'd spoken with on the phone earlier entering the room. They saw Saul and their faces lit up.

One hour later and we had a deal for Kelsey: a tentative deal, to be sure, more a deal to make a deal on March 1, when the timing would not draw the attention of his wife's attorney, but a deal nonetheless. Everyone at Random House was delighted at the prospect of Kelsey's return; only one of the editors had had any dealings with him before, and he expressed his deep embarrassment over the lawsuit, blaming the overzealous tendencies of the company's legal department. They were a little suspicious of making an offer on a book they would not be able to read for another few months, even in partial manuscript form, but after retreating to one of the adjacent rooms for a few minutes, they came back with an offer of $250,000. They wanted to make it $400,000 for two books, but I demurred, explaining that Douglas did not want to be tied down so far in advance again, given what had happened before. They exchanged glances, and we shook on it. Crossing the lobby just under one hour later, Saul was impressed. "That was old-school," he said. "Spit and a handshake."

"Thanks for the introductions. You didn't have to come with me, you know."

We reached the revolving doors and pressed through to the outside, where a stiff wind had picked up, howling up and down the avenues. "Actually, Patrick," said Saul, tightening his coat, "I kind of did."

I came to a halt just in front of him. "What are you talking about?"

"Don't get freaked out about this, okay, but yesterday I was present at a meeting where Brad expressed the opinion that maybe you were a little too . . . junior to handle Kelsey. And maybe if Leo wanted a more trusted pair of hands on the account—"

"That little fuck."

"It's okay, it's okay! Leo shot it down instantly. The old man believes in you. He really does."

"But you came along to hold my hand just in case?"

"I just wanted to make sure you had your back covered. That's all."

"My back covered."

"I know you didn't have anybody on the inside at Vintage, so I came along to make sure you did."

I stared at him, suspiciously. "Thanks . . . I think."

I stewed for most of the cab ride back to the office, wondering if that was the reason Saul had been so distant with me recently, before realizing that it mattered little what Brad said or did: Kelsey was mine and no one was taking him away from me. Opening my briefcase, I went over the materials the editors had given me—a complete copy of Kelsey's correspondence with Vintage over the years: a 2003 letter from Christine Kantor asking them for more money, followed by their refusal; a similar letter dated 2004, and again in 2005, this time for more time, followed by another refusal. Finally, there was a long letter from Kelsey himself, handwritten.

Dear Alex,

I've been up all night thinking on this, and nothing but this, so help me. Next to my wife and Christine, you have been the most important individual in my life, and that's the honest to God's truth. If I have any standing or reputation in this world, it is because of you. I know that you have waited long and patiently for this book, longer than anyone ought while still retaining their sanity. But she's changing direction under my feet and I need to follow her. Sorry to be so cryptic—you know how much I hate that—but everything has changed for me up here, not just the book. I beg you for more time. Can you blame it all on me and get me out of the contract someway? And then decide next year what to do? Alternatively, I could always return the money and we would pick things up again a few years down the line, but you know how much I would hate to do that. As I say, I owe you so much. You've already put in many days and nights on this. But I'm damn near going out of my mind over this. I'd better go before I embarrass myself any more.

Much love, Douglas

It was clear to me that he had not told anyone at Random House about getting sober. I wondered why; they were in the publishing business, but they weren't inhuman. The last letter in the file was dated April 2006, just a few days before the lawsuit was issued. It was from his editor, and short.

Your performance on the phone last night was an appalling piece of self-destruction—ugly, demeaning, and sad. Your rage should be directed elsewhere, Douglas. As for your threats of violence, bring it on, my old friend. You'll find me as energetic in this as I have been in everything else.

"Anything good?" asked Saul.

"Oh nothing," I said quickly, slipping the letter back into my briefcase. "Just a thank-you note."

It was hard to tell whether Kelsey was pleased or not: He took the information in silently, harrumphing when I mentioned their embarrassment over the lawsuit. "Not embarrassed enough not to do it," he snapped. For someone who'd just secured a book deal, he was in an awfully bad mood. I put it down to his divorce and got on with the rest of my afternoon—or rather, going through enough of the motions of the rest of the afternoon while rehearsing what I was going to say to Lola. I wanted to thank her for the good grace she had displayed when I dropped my bombshell the other week. I wanted her to know that she came out of the whole thing extremely well, even if I didn't, and that I would perfectly understand if she wanted to put the brakes on things, so as to accommodate the long, slow process of rebuilding trust. No. Scrub "long" and "slow." That made it sound too much like a prison sentence. The quick, pleasurable task of rebuilding trust didn't sound right, though. Breezy, pleasurable. No. Maybe ditch the adjectives altogether. The *task* of rebuilding trust. That was better. A task. To be manfully executed, with the minimum of fuss, like chopping up logs to keep the family warm in winter. That was the tone to strike, I thought, as I made my way to the bistro on Sixth Avenue where we were meeting. The sidewalks were flocked with people heading home after work, the sky a cool dark blue. There wasn't much snow left on the roads, but what there was had been carved and recarved into mountainous wedges of gray ice by the side of the road. The bistro was small and dark, with a bar waiting area that led into the main restaurant, the walls hung with Gauloises posters and large gilt mirrors, their mercury backs flaked and peeling. I took up a position at one of the bar stools, and ordered a vodka tonic. Then, worrying what it would do to my chances of getting kissed, I downed it in a few swift gulps. God knows what stunts my face pulled when I saw Lola waving through the window.

"Sorry I'm late," she said, a little out of breath, wrapped in her usual array of scarves and mittens. "I was almost out the door when a new client walked in."

She planted a kiss on my cheek.

"What is it you do?"

"Real estate. I'm a Realtor. What's that you have there?"

"A lemonade."

She squinted at the blackboard above the bar. "I'll have a green tea, I think."

The bartender turned and disappeared.

"What about you?" she asked. "How was your day?"

"I spent most of it trying to secure some money for Douglas."

"He agreed to be your client?"

"Yes, he did. Now, look, Lola," I said, putting my hand on her elbow. "I know you had some concerns about the two of us working together, and I want you to know that I completely hear you. Especially given my behavior recently, which even I concede has been abysmal, beneath even the standards I—"

"That's great, Patrick. Just great. You must be really pleased."

"I'm sorry?"

"You must be really pleased. That's exactly what you wanted, isn't it? A deal for Douglas?"

"I thought you had some reservations. . . ."

"That's one of the reasons I was so pleased to hear from you. I want to apologize for that conversation we had in the diner. The one where I told you to stay away from him. I had no right to say that."

"But of course you did."

She shook her head. "It was none of my business."

"But of course it was your business. After what I did, I mean . . ."

The bartender came back with her cup of tea. Lola gave my arm a squeeze and pointed to one of the round marble tables by the window; we gathered our drinks and resettled as more people came in through the door and took our seats at the bar. On our table was a small candle; the window was frosted glass and was carved with the name of the bistro; looking through it, we could see the flashing headlights of the passing traffic.

"This is all backward," I said. "You're not the one who should be apologizing to me. I should be the one apologizing to you."

"For what?"

"For what I did."

"You didn't do anything to *me*."

I stared at her, dumbfounded. "But Lola, I sat there in meetings, many meetings, lying to all those people, lying to you. . . ." I shook my head. "I know I can't ask you to forgive me all at once. I realize it's going to take time. Maybe more time than I have a right to ask for. But I'm a good guy, really. I just need you to give me the chance to prove it."

She looked at me over the rim of her teacup.

"Have you finished?"

"Uh . . . I think so."

"You're talking to the wrong girl. I couldn't care less. There're only a few things I care about in there, and one of them is hanging on to the respect of my sponsees, because they're the ones who keep me sober, and one of the ways I do *that* is by not sleeping with newcomers. So you see, I really *do* need to apologize to you, whether you like it or not."

She took another sip of her tea.

"Newcomers," I said.

"Yes. Sleeping with. Big no-no."

"You mean me."

"Yes."

"But this is crazy. I'm *not* a newcomer."

"I thought you were and I still went ahead and slept with you anyway. Because I was pissed at my dad. Because I'm profoundly selfish and even after five years of sobriety I still lack the ability to say no to myself. Apparently."

She reached across the table and cupped my hands in hers.

"I wish we had met five years ago. I think we could have had a lot of fun, I really do. If there's one thing I've learned about people who don't know themselves very well, it's that you're like lightning rods: Stuff happens to you. It can be very exciting to be around, but I can't be, not anymore. Are you sure it's not an active alcoholic you're looking for, rather than a recovering one, because we're really not much fun. We're very boring."

A sick feeling had begun to gather in my chest. "I don't want any alcoholic. I want you."

She shook her head. "No. You just think you do."

"You're telling me what I *want*?"

"I'm just saying that there's a difference between what we want and what we need, and I don't trust your ability to tell the two things apart."

"And the difference is?"

She frowned. "Okay, look, say we got into a relationship. I'm sure it would be fun for a while, for three, maybe four months tops, but then you would wake up one day and decide that it's not me you really want, and then it would be my heart in the gutter, don't you see?"

"You know that for a fact, do you?"

"No. But I have to call it like I see it."

She twisted uncomfortably in her seat.

"And what about that conversation we had?" I said. "That means nothing to you, I suppose."

"What do you mean?"

"That conversation we had. On your sofa. The morning after. I thought that meant something. It did to me anyway. Maybe you have conversations like that all the time, but I certainly don't."

She looked at me incredulously. "We had an honest conversation, Patrick. That's all."

"And I'd like to have more," I said beseechingly.

"We're having one now."

"I don't like the way this one is going."

"We don't get to pick and choose."

Something about the way she said it stopped me in my tracks. "Someone put you up to this, didn't they?"

"No."

"They did, didn't they? Someone told you to do this."

"No, they didn't."

"Yes, they did. Your sponsor. Your sponsor told you to do this. What to do, what to say."

She said nothing.

"Christ Almighty, the hold these people have over you is amazing. It's like *1984*! It's like Big Brother bearing down on poor Winston Smith and whatever the fuck her name was."

"Please stop, Patrick, before you say something really stupid."

"Stupid? I'll tell you what's stupid. Doing exactly what you're told by a bunch of people who spend their entire time getting together in a series of crummy rooms to decide who the hell is holier than thou on this particular Tuesday. Any other words of wisdom you'd care to impart to me before I go?"

She looked me right in the eye. "Be careful, Patrick. You're in a lot of trouble."

"Trouble. What are you talking about? What kind of trouble?"

"The kind you don't know you're in until it's too late."

I wasn't staying to hear any more of this. I got up and left.

chapter twenty-two

It didn't go so well, then."

"No, it didn't, Felix."

"I'm sorry."

"It's okay."

"You look terrible."

"Thanks."

"No, really, you look terrible."

We sat on tall stools in the window of a café on Second Avenue, Felix swaddled in his usual seven-layer cake of loose, filthy clothes, his feet dangling like an errant schoolboy's while he wolfed the remains of his brownie. The crumbs of the cookie and chocolate croissant he had already devoured sat on his outermost lapel. Behind us, a row of cappuccino machines hissed and gurgled.

"I just don't get it, I really don't. 'I don't know myself.' What's that supposed to mean? I'm the world expert on myself. I just don't happen to like myself; that's the difference. I don't see any good reason to go shouting it from the rooftops is all."

"If God had meant us to tell the truth, why didn't He make it more fun?"

"I'm sorry?"

"Why didn't He make it more fun? More like an orgasm. Then we'd do it all the time."

"I'm not following you."

He took a bite of his brownie. "She's not Snow White, you know. You should hear some of the things she shares about. They used to have this competition at UCLA—who could break up with a guy for the lamest reason. Lola never lost that title once in three years. She broke up with a guy for owning fewer than five hundred CDs."

"Fewer than five hundred CDs?"

He nodded. "Another time, she broke up with a guy for naming a font after her. A *font*."

"I did a lot more than name a font after her. Jesus." I shook my head. "After the way I behaved. I get it, I do. If she had the balls to say 'I hate you for what you did, so please never see me again,' I'd get that. I'd understand anger, but instead she's all 'I think you're great' and 'I'm not judging you' and 'you're in trouble.' The way she talked you'd think *I* was the one with the alcohol problem, not her."

He shrugged. On the other side of the street trooped a line of Hare Krishnas wearing raincoats over their robes, which they struggled to keep from flying up above their shins.

I looked at my watch. "I guess I should be getting back to the office. Where did you say you were going?"

"The Strand."

"I'll walk with you."

We made our way to the cashier by the door to present them with our check. There was one person ahead of us in the queue.

"I've got it," said Felix.

"Got what?"

"What if you started drinking again?"

"I'm sorry?"

"What if you started drinking? Would she have you back then?"

"I don't think so, Felix, no."

"What about crack? Any fool can get addicted to crack. Even *Brian* got addicted to crack."

"No, Felix. I don't want to get addicted to crack."

Handing over the check, I made an apologetic grimace to the cashier; she took my twenty and handed back my change. I wrapped myself in my coat and headed outside, holding open the door for Felix. Up and down Second Avenue, shopkeepers shoveled the snow away from their patch of sidewalk with plastic shovels; others scattered sand. Farther up, a new type of deicing truck scoured the gutter, sucking up the snow through a nozzle at the front and ejecting it as water from a chute out the back. We both started walking north.

"Why not?" he murmured.

"I'm sorry?"

"What's the matter with crack?"

"What's the matter with it? It's bad stuff. That's what's the matter with it. Okay? I'm feeling bad enough as it is. Jesus."

"I'm just trying to help."

"Really? Because from where I'm sitting, it sounds like you're just trying to make stupid suggestions."

"What's stupid about it?" he said sullenly.

"Okay, here's what's stupid about it. One, I don't want to get addicted to crack. I'm sorry, but there it is. Two, I don't think it would impress her very much. Weirdly. And three, it's just plain nuts. Which is what I must also be for listening to you all this time."

The moment it had left my lips, I knew that I had gone too far. Felix stuck his hands down into his pockets and stepped up his pace, pulling out ahead of me on the sidewalk. "Felix," I said, but he only sped up some more. "Hey, slow down," I called out, as he opened up a gap of four yards, now five, beetling along the street. I scrambled to catch up but found myself slipping on the ice.

"Hey, Felix, I'm sorry, okay?" I yelled, drawing the attention of one of the store managers with his shovel. He looked up at the commotion, then recommenced shoveling. Felix was almost half a block away now. He reached a large sycamore tree, turned, and disappeared into what looked like a small garden. I broke into a jog and soon drew level with one of those small squares that dot lower Manhattan: a fountain in the center, ringed by benches and trees, iron railings, a quadrangle of brownstones. Felix was sitting on one of the benches in the center, staring at the fountain, his arms crossed. He heard me coming on the gravel path; jamming his hands even more firmly into his armpits. I took the seat next to him and for a while we said nothing, just stared at the fountain. It was completely iced over, twigs and leaves frozen in place; on the other side of it was a statue of a man with one leg.

"Listen, I'm sorry about what I said back there."

"You live in your head a lot. Do you know that?"

"I know."

"Do you?" he said, turning to face me. "I'm not sure you do. I know *I'm* crazy. That's the difference between us. You don't."

I exhaled, watched my breath evaporate in front of me. "You may be right. The way I've been acting lately. Even *I'm* shocked. It's just . . . For a moment back there, when we first woke up together, I thought I had her. I knew what it felt like to be forgiven by her. Or thought I did. And then . . ." I shook my head.

"Was there a horrible blue light creeping in through the window?"

I looked at him. "How did you know that?"

"What about the birds? Were the birds singing?"

"I don't remember any birds."

"I hate it when you hear the birds. That's when you know you've fucked up big time. When the birds start in like that."

He'd lost me. "Whatever," I said.

We stayed staring at the fountain for a while; then his hand sprang over, palm upward. "You owe me a dollar," he said.

"What for?"

"You used my word."

"'Whatever'?"

His hand clenched and unclenched. "Two dollars."

I leaned back to dig into my pockets. "You're the only one of my clients who gets richer while I get poorer. It's supposed to be the other way around."

I handed over two crumpled dollars, which disappeared into his pockets faster than a ferret into its hole. He shivered and rubbed himself. "I'm cold," he said. "I think I'm going to go now."

"I think I'm going to stay here for a bit."

"Suit yourself. You really ought to buy yourself a new jacket. That one looks like it's about to fall off you."

"I'll see what they have in the sales."

He got up and held out his hand. At first I thought he wanted me to shake it, but he shook his head, held his palm higher. A high five. He wanted a high five. I brought my hand up against his and—bingo—brought off a satisfying slapping sound.

"Stoked," he said.

"Speak to you later."

"Stay out of your head, Patrick."

"I'll try."

I watched him as he loped off.

He didn't seem that crazy to me. He had his blind spots, of course, but then, so did everyone; his were just a bit bigger than everyone else's. I never got very far with working out Felix's story; it seemed to change from day to day. Sometimes there were four brothers; sometimes there were three. Sometimes he had gone to Harvard, sometimes to Yale. His family were rich; I knew that much. They lived on the Upper East Side, hence his presence in Saks that day; his mother had taken him to lunch at Le Bernadin. He was certainly the snobbiest near-homeless person I'd ever met, forever dispensing fashion and fragrance advice from the gutter. Why was it that the people who told you that you had to "be yourself" or "know yourself" were always the ones who had such solid, definite selves to go off and be? You never heard them say, "I got to know myself better, and guess what? I turned out to be a real asshole." Presumably, you weren't supposed to go off and be true to *that* self—your asshole self. It was some other self you had to go off and be true to. You were a lumberjack, or a deep-sea diver. An alcoholic deep-sea diver. A drug-addicted lumberjack. How could those people fail to be real? They had a lot to get real about. What had I got? I didn't have any big secrets. I was just secretive. That was different. And sure, it was a complete waste of time. I knew that. That's why I'd come to America in the first place. They'd invented this thing called self-esteem over here. The women all watched *Oprah* and read books about emotional intelligence, and spent time getting along with themselves like a house on fire. Not all American women, obviously. Caitlin's emotional intelligence had turned out to be straightforward bossiness. I hadn't needed to travel halfway around the globe for that. But Lola, she was the real deal. In her eyes alone, I found some kind of solution. I had tried and I had been found wanting, and the worst thing was, I could see her point. I would break up with me if I had half the chance. Where was *my* support group? I guessed I was looking at him, scurrying up the street with two dollars of my money.

chapter twenty-three

AND SO BEGAN THE final phase of my involvement with Douglas Kelsey. I should say, before I go on, that we are still talking to each other and harbor no ill will for what happened. "Might as well blame each other for the weather," he says, although I happen to think the weather *did* have something to do with it. When snow first arrives in New York, the effect is magical, transformative, covering everything like icing on a cake. But as December turns into January, the Christmas trees, now bald, are ejected ignominiously onto the streets, and the snow turns to ice; the city takes on a more ingrown, fractious aspect. The winter starts to seem less like a season that looks like letting up anytime soon and more like a state of mind that will never be shaken. Looking back at that whole period now—from my late-night calls with Kelsey in January to our final confrontation in the woods below Hunter Mountain—it seems to have taken on the slurred, slow-motion quality of a nightmare, like the last few glimpses of oncoming traffic before a crash. I can say I didn't intend for any of what happened to happen, but intentions, as we know, are not worth much; it is by our actions that we are judged, and my actions during those months were not governed by anything much besides the intense conviction that any program that encouraged beautiful Californian Realtors to break off their relationships with mendacious British literary agents could go screw itself.

If *Oprah* came on the TV, I turned it off. If I found myself approaching a church—and they were all over the place in Manhattan, once you started looking—I hurried quickly past. At work, I treated the self-help submissions to even curter dismissals than usual, taking great pleasure in turning down a book of recipes inspired by the great religions of the world, entitled *Daily Bread*. And when the junior senator from Illinois I had seen on Lola's wall scored a string of victories in the Democratic primaries, I scanned the eager faces of his supporters, with their childishly credulous placards bearing the words HOPE and CHANGE, and thought I could see the connection: yet another moonfaced cult.

"He can't win," Kelsey told me. "He'll have to pry that nomination from her cold, dead fingers. That's the thing with the Clintons. They're always the last to leave the room. They *outlast* everyone."

He didn't own a cell phone, but he was a great fan of his landline, and certainly liked his conversations long. If I returned his calls at home, I would make sure I ordered a pizza before doing so. Once he phoned me, jubilant with the news that two NASA astronauts had ignored the twenty-four-hour bottle-to-throttle rule and flew the space shuttle *Challenger* drunk.

"Isn't that something?" he said. "Isn't that the goddamnedest thing? Drunk, with two million pounds of solid rocket fuel up your tail."

From there, it was but a short step to the most recent news from Iraq, and the administration's failures therein, and from there to the alcohol levels of the presidents past and present, from Grant to Nixon, and its impact on U.S. foreign policy. "A drunk is the last person you want managing an asymmetric fight," he told me once. "Alcoholism is asymmetry in excelsis. All that happens is they end up shadowboxing their disease. A bear swatting at shadows."

"But Forty-three isn't drinking, is he?"

"It would almost be better for everyone if he *were*. At least then the beast inside of him would be fed and watered. Instead of having to go off and pick fresh fights."

I know I should have taken the opportunity to come clean with him about attending the meetings, but somehow the moment never seemed quite right. When we have gotten to know each other just a little bit better, I told myself; when there isn't quite so much at stake. Instead, I relayed to him the latest news from the world of publishing—the deals, the divorces, the firings, the hirings—for which he had an insatiable appetite, sharpened no doubt by the fact that he had spent the last five years living in self-imposed exile. Other than the interns at the library and his divorce attorney, I don't think he spoke to another living human being besides myself. Talking to him sometimes felt a little like debriefing a refugee from a desert island, or a coma survivor. I felt like I was feeding a man who had been on a hunger strike. The one subject you did *not* want to get him on was his wife's attorney, the mere mention of whom evoked in him a desire to outperform every insult he had previously thrown at the man. Very occasionally, like catching sight of the dorsal fin of a whale, I caught a glimpse of his book, a sequel of sorts to *Freefall*, which caught up with Frank Leary, now in his fifties, attempting to flee the city for upstate New York, where a Walden-style self-purification comes spectacularly off the rails when he is joined by his wife and son. It was going to be very different book, he said, from *Freefall*, less radioactive with self-loathing, lit from within by moments of unforeseen grace and the possibility of redemption.

I relayed what news of it I could back to the office, where I was the hero of the hour, singled out for praise by Leo, and showered with congratulations from the other agents. I grimaced through most of it as best I could, pointing out that nothing was in the bag yet, that no contract had been signed, a fact that was not lost on Brad, who brought it up at our monthly staff meeting.

"I'm sure Patrick knows what's he doing," said Leo. "Patrick's playing the long game. Some writers need a little finessing. A little courtship. Lord knows, he worked in London for ten years. You know what *they're* like."

"Ming vases," said Brad.

The table fell about laughing.

"It's perfectly reasonable," I said testily. "He's just been through this divorce. The last thing he wants is more paperwork."

"I met him a few times, you know," said Leo, rocking back in his chair. "Such an unhappy man. I always remember his hands. He had these long, elegant hands, like a piano player's, always drumming away on the table, like he was waiting for something." He drummed the table in demonstration. "The liquor, most probably. That man could knock it back. What do you say we get him in for lunch one of these days?"

"I don't think so, Leo," I said quickly.

"Don't think we could loosen him up with a nice bottle of Chablis?"

"I don't think that would be a very good idea. Not yet. Maybe later. Once I've got everything in writing."

He looked at me for a few seconds, then let it go. "Whatever you say. Just keep us in the loop."

"Of course."

Closing my office door half an hour later, I found myself longing for the day when I would hold a finished copy of Kelsey's book in my hand and could be done with the whole wretched business.

In the last week of January, a small article appeared in *Publishers Weekly*. It was small, only about a hundred words. If you didn't comb that magazine like a hawk, as I did every week, you would almost certainly have missed it, but there it was, toward the back of the January 31 issue, just to the left of an advert for the new Danielle Steel:

> Reappearance Act—Douglas Kelsey, the "patron saint of bankrupted idealists" (*Time*), returns with his first work of fiction in more than ten years, a sequel to the Pulitzer Prize–nominated *Freefall*, his 1983 novel about a Madison Avenue advertising executive gone AWOL. The book has been long awaited: After Kelsey failed to deliver in 2006, Random House instigated a lawsuit against the author for the return of his advance. No deal has yet been signed for the new novel, but Random House is in the frame, according to his agent, Patrick Miller, of the Leo Gottlieb Agency. "We are delighted to be representing Douglas," said Mr. Gottlieb. "He is the last of the old guard, one of the few writers brave enough to take on our American tragedy in all its gory glory."

I read it, reread it, then walked through Saul's office, dropped the magazine on his desk, and scanned his face as he worked his way through it. "Your first mention in *Publishers Weekly*," he said, pushing it back across the desk. "Congratulations."

"What does Leo think he's playing at?" I hissed.

"What's the problem?"

"I told him: no press. What was he thinking?" I picked up the magazine again. " 'One of the few writers brave enough to take on the American tragedy in all its gory glory.' What does that even *mean?*"

"He probably got a little corned up at lunch. You know how he is. I don't see what you're so uptight about."

"It looks like I've gone yakking to the press about a deal that hasn't even been done yet."

"It's just *Publishers Weekly*. He probably doesn't even read it. Quit griping."

I retreated to my office and read the article again. Maybe it wasn't *so* bad. My name was featured quite prominently. It was only a hundred words. The whole thing would be dead in a few days. I put the magazine away and returned to my work.

The first call came in at 10:30: an editor from HarperCollins who'd seen that Kelsey hadn't signed with anyone yet. Were we taking offers? No, no, I explained. The book wasn't being put up for auction, but if we decided to, he would be the first to know. I put the phone down and returned to my work. The second call came through at just a few minutes before 11:00: an editor at Knopf who had heard that I was taking bids on the new Douglas Kelsey novel. No, no, I told her. Sadly, we were not taking bids, but I would let her know if we changed our minds. Finally, just before lunchtime, I got a vexed call from one of the editors at Vintage I had met with, worried about all the talk he was hearing about Kelsey's book going to market. Beginning to sweat a little now, I reassured him that there was no auction going on, everything was fine, Kelsey was in the bag, et cetera. I went to lunch, feeling the irony of the whole situation keenly: These were publishers I had spent the best part of the last year trying to get an in with, struggling in some cases even to get my calls returned, and now my phone was ringing off the hook with offers for a book I could not sell. I returned to the office one hour later, to find Natalie brandishing a handful of Post-it notes, all bearing offers from a half a dozen publishers—one for $250,000, another for $330,000, and a two-book deal with Knopf for $500,000. I returned to Saul's office and fanned them out on his desk.

"Wow," he said. "Dougie boy's got some fans."

"What do you think I should do?"

"Why don't you call him and see what he says?"

"I can't do that."

"Why not?"

"This is not what he wanted."

"He doesn't want half a million dollars?"

"He didn't want any publicity. He's trying to get that money past his wife's attorney."

"Why don't you just call him and say we've had some more offers. What do you think?"

I started pacing up and down in front of his desk. "Maybe. I've never met anyone with faster instincts for when he's being hustled."

"He didn't see you coming. He can't be *that* sharp."

"Funny," I said, and returned to my office. I stared out the window—perfectly round, like the portholes of a ship—for a long time, trying to decide what to do. Finally I picked up the phone and dialed Kelsey's number.

"Patrick. I was just about to call you. Did you watch the debate last night?"

"I caught some of it."

"Did you see what he did when the Farrakhan question came up? 'It's not enough that you denounce the man's views; you must reject his endorsement.' Did you hear his response? 'If you think that *reject* is a stronger word than *denounce*, then I both reject and denounce.' Just like that. The old rope a dope. Like Ali."

"That's very interesting. Douglas. Listen. I have something

I want to ask you. Would you be at all interested in putting the book up for auction?"

"Why?"

"We had a few offers this afternoon."

"How does anyone know about it?"

"There was a piece in *Publishers Weekly*."

"An article?"

"It was Leo. He got soused at lunch I think and—"

"Close it down."

"Okay. I will."

"Close it down immediately."

I replaced the phone receiver and returned to my work. It was beginning to get dark outside when my phone rang again. "Just out of interest," said Kelsey this time, "how much were they offering?"

"The best was five hundred thousand from Knopf."

"Christ."

There was a long silence.

"There's no need for me to turn them down immediately. Why don't we sleep on it and see how we feel in the morning?"

"Sleep on it," he repeated a little numbly. "Okay, yes, that's a good idea. Why don't we do that."

When I next looked up, it was completely dark outside and most of the other agents had gone home. I packed up and went downstairs, to find Natalie at her desk; I thanked her for her help, said my good-byes, and was almost out the door, pulling on my coat and scarf, when her phone rang.

"The Leo Gottlieb Literary Agency," she said. "This is Natalie."

She listened, then held her hand over the receiver and mouthed, *It's K-e-l-s-e-y.*

I groaned.

"Shall I ask him what it's about?" she whispered.

"It's okay; I know what it's about," I said, retracing my steps wearily and gesturing for the phone. "Give it here," I said, putting the receiver to my ear. "Douglas."

"I don't think I can sleep on this, Patrick. It's just too much. I think we should decide now."

"Okay, so what's your answer?"

There was a long pause.

"It's no."

"All right. I'll call them in the morning and tell them." There was another long pause. "Douglas? Hello? You still there?"

"This is fun for you, isn't it?" he snarled.

"I'm sorry?"

"Tossing a grenade into my lap like this and then watching me squirm. Go now. Just walk away, why don't you. It's what you people do best."

I wanted to shout at him, No, actually, this is not my idea of fun, Douglas, actually. Not standing here talking to you on the phone when I could be home watching the season finale of *America's Next Top Model*! But I didn't. Instead, I said, "I'm not going anywhere. I'm standing here talking to you. Do you want to talk about it some more? Over dinner maybe?"

More silence.

"Give me half an hour," I said wearily. "I'll pick you up."

As I headed out into the night, I remembered Lola's last words to me—"You're in a lot of trouble. . . . The kind you don't know you're in until it's too late." I pushed them from my mind and hailed a cab.

chapter twenty-four

KELSEY'S APARTMENT WAS NOT far from the basketball court where we had first met, in one of those old Lower East Side tenements that used to house a family of twelve Prussian peasants, plus their sewing machines. The first floor was given over to a haberdasher's called Gentlemen's Fashion, Inc., in whose window a group of mannequins stared awkwardly into different corners like people avoiding the issue. The buzzer emitted an electrified squawk when I pressed it, followed by a burst of static. The door opened onto a large landslide of junk mail, a dimly lit hallway with tin-plate ceilings, and walls the color of deep nicotine. He was two floors up; I could tell which one from the scratching and whimpering coming from the other side of the door. A latch slid back and the door opened a crack to reveal Kelsey holding his dog back by his collar, the animal's paws pedaling the air furiously.

"No, Billy, back," said Kelsey. Then, to me: "You'd better come in."

I entered, bending down to ruffle Billy's ears. He leapt up

onto my knees and gave me a wet lick across the mouth. "Give me a second. I'll get my coat," said Kelsey, and disappeared down the corridor.

The apartment was medium-size, with sagging floorboards and furnishings that looked like they had last seen the sunlight on VE day. The hallway I was standing in abutted a large living room, whose walls were piled high with paperbacks in tall, teetering piles. On the TV set in the corner, a football match was playing; opposite it, a battered sofa, long and narrow, in the style of the fifties, was slowly losing the stuffing in its arms. Kelsey reappeared in a doorway, pulling on a coat. "Billy!" he barked.

Billy released his hold on the sleeve of my coat and slunk off to the sofa, whose arm he proceeded to gnaw sulkily. "The Saints have fumbled the ball twice now," admonished the commentator on TV, where a mass of bobbing black and white helmets rammed into one another beneath waves of sleet and snow. "They have gotten nothing at all going since that Brees-to-Henderson completion on the second play. . . ."

"You been following the game?" asked Kelsey.

"What? Me? Oh no," I said. "Is it a, uh, big game?"

"Bears versus the Saints. The Saints can't seem to hang on to the ball."

"Who can't?"

"The Saints."

"The Saints are your team?"

"Hell no. The Vikings. The Bears put them out in the playoffs. I was hoping the Saints could exact a little retribution, but they can't seem to hang on to the goddamn ball."

He stared at the TV as if personally betrayed. The ball shot up into the air, up and up through the waves of snow, before it disappeared into the stands. He swiped at the screen disgustedly and turned it off. "There's a Korean place not far from here where we can go. Do you like Korean?"

"Sounds good."

We had a job getting out without Billy, but after a certain amount of pointing and hoisting and pushing, Kelsey finally closed the door and we made our way downstairs.

It was a cold, clear night, the stars thick in the sky. Following Kelsey's lead, we walked south, past fabric shops and haberdashers, poultry markets and bodegas, the side of the buildings encrusted with posters for old boxing bouts, an advert for Hersh's rabbinical wine (JUST ASK YOUR LOCAL RABBI). The gentrification that had taken over the Lower East Side like moss seemed to have stopped just short of his street.

"So what did it say in *Publishers Weekly*?" he asked finally.

"It was entirely flattering. It had that quote from *Time,* calling you the patron saint of bankrupt idealists, and then a quote from Leo, saying how much he was looking forward to the new novel and something about you tackling the American tragedy in all its, uh, 'gory glory.' "

"All its *what*?"

"It was a little fruity, I know. I think he got a little soused at lunch."

He shook his head. "This is exactly what I didn't want, Patrick. I can almost see Vogel's greedy little eyes lighting up."

"Who?"

"My wife's attorney. Did you know that when the Nazis annexed Austria, they took over all the Jewish businesses and sold them off for nothing? Vogel's great-uncle took over the Vienna Hofbraü for three million schillings. He kept the Wehrmacht pumped up on its beer for the remainder of the war."

"I didn't know that, no."

"He'll have no compunction about taking that money. None whatsoever."

"Look, I'm sorry about the article. I'm sure he can't have read it."

"Everyone else seems to have! We've got an auction on our hands!"

"I tried to shut it down. I told everyone who called, 'No, we're not taking this to market,' but they didn't seem to believe me, or they spoke to one another, or something; before I knew what was happening, I had half a dozen offers on the table."

"Good Christ."

I could feel my annoyance rising. "They were decent offers. You're being a little unreasonable, Douglas . . ."

"I knew this was a mistake. I *knew* it." He shook his head. "Have you thought about going back to meetings again? Because this? This mess? This is classic dry-drunk behavior."

"Is that right."

"Yes, it is. Trapped in a speeding car with no steering wheel."

"Well, that's very odd seeing as I am, in fact, no kind of drunk. Seeing as I was, in fact, pretending, solely in order to sign you up, although quite why, I am seriously beginning to wonder."

My outburst over, silence descended on the conversation, the only sound the crunch of our footsteps on the gravelly ice. Up ahead, a laundromat cast its yellowish light out onto the street; just beyond it, a red neon strip light spelling out the word EAR—presumably BAR in better days. When I looked at him, Kelsey was staring at me with wonder in his eyes.

"You're not an alcoholic."

"No."

"But you've been going to meetings."

"Yes."

"To get ahold of me."

"Yes."

"Bullshit."

"Do you know I don't really care whether you believe me or not? I know what's true, and that's all that matters."

There was a long silence.

"Well, isn't that some thing," he said, and let out a single hoot of laughter. "Isn't that the goddamnedest thing."

"So fire me if you like. I'm past caring. This book has already cost me more sleep than any book has a right to."

"And you did all this for me?"

"It was the only way I knew how to get to you."

"But nobody does all that for a *writer.*"

At which point, a volley of shouting erupted from the bar up ahead. *"REGGGIE BUSH!!!!!!! GOOOOOOOO!!! BUSH!!!! GGGOOOOOOOOO!!!!"* It was one of those small, dingy dive bars that sits on every street corner in lower Manhattan, its windows packed with neon beer logos—Heineken, Corona, Budweiser—and a big blackboard sign that read COLD OUTSIDE. WARM AS FUCK IN HERE. $6 ALL HOT COCKTAILS—IRISH COFFEE, HOT TODDIE, HOT PEPPERMINT ROD. Peering through the pebble-thick windows, Kelsey muttered, "What the . . ."

"RRRUNNREGGGIERUNNNN!!!!!!!!!!!!!!!!!"

The shouts were louder this time.

"Do you mind if we go in for a second?" he asked.

He didn't wait for an answer, pushing in through the black double doors. I waited for a few seconds, bewildered, then followed him inside. The bar was small, dark, and noisy, with a TV hoisted high at one end of a wooden salon, casting its spectral blue light on the upturned faces of the men below; and the moment you walked into the place you knew it was just men. Some were on their feet, some sat at the bar, and some sat at tables, but all were trained on the TV like gundogs. "An amazing play by the Saints!" trilled the commentator as a player in white performed a somersault beneath a barrage of beer cans. "Even though they're still trailing, it seems they have this game by the neck right now . . ."

The cheers dying in their throats, the men retook their seats, turning to one another to talk about what they had just seen. Kelsey pushed through the thickets of bodies to the bar, where he secured a corner for both of us and flagged down the bartender, a jowly, thickset man with a beard and a bandanna, who was polishing glasses.

"What just happened?" Kelsey asked him.

"Bush runs a little wheel route down the sideline. . . . Has the ball lofted right onto his chest by Brees at the thirty. Bush just *guns* it. Like he hit the turbo button."

"They finally showed up, huh?"

"Looks like we just got ourselves a game. Can I get you gentlemen anything?"

"Two Cokes," said Kelsey, taking one of the high stools by the bar, immediately transfixed by the game. The ball was moving quickly now from player to player, all in white, all advancing steadily up the pitch. "He's at the twenty-nine! The Saints are starting to look good!" sang the commentator. Suddenly, a man broke through a wall of men in black and lobbed the ball up into the air, the ball tumbling end over end through the sleet and snow before it hit the ground and bounced off, uselessly, into the stands.

"Oh for Crissakes," said Kelsey with a disgusted swipe of his hand.

Over by the window, five bruisers in baseball caps erupted in loud, raucous cheers. Kelsey glared at them as the bartender came back with our Cokes.

"What are they doing here?" he asked him.

"Been here since three," replied the bartender. "Just ignore them. That'll be five dollars."

Kelsey peeled off a twenty. At the other end of the bar, in a small room illuminated by a single green lightbulb, a group of young Hispanics prowled a pool table, dusting their cues and joking. When I turned back, I found Kelsey looking at me the way you might a species of purple jellyfish that had just washed up onshore.

"Are you *sure* you're not an alcoholic? Because it's a very common delusion, you know. You're there just to study, or observe, or because you like the people."

"Absolutely positive."

"No one in your family has a drinking problem? Mother? Father?"

I shook my head.

"No history of embezzlement? Fraud? Any gambling debts?"

"No."

"And no one smelled a rat?"

I shook my head. "No."

"What about the evangelicals? Godfrey. Did you come across Godfrey?"

"Yes, we went out to lunch. I tried to tell them the truth, but they all just thought I was in denial."

"Of course they did," said Kelsey with a chuckle. "Your 'disease' talking. I tried to tell them; you can't say I haven't tried."

"Tried to tell them what?"

"They've pathologized the life out of this thing. It never used to be this way. But then along come the rehabs and money enters the picture. People start shelling out money for a cure; they want to know what they're being cured of. So suddenly there's all this talk of a disease. 'The disease of alcoholism.' Except if it's a disease, then what are the symptoms? So they ask a few questions. 'Hey, buddy, you ever felt hungry? Angry? Lonely? Tired?' Why of course you have. 'What about restless, irritable, and discontent?' All the time. 'Then you must be an alcoholic.' It's just like those questions you get in those little leaflets from Scientologists. 'Do you suffer from self-centered fear?' " He snorted derisively. "As opposed to what? *Un*self-centered fear? The selfless kind? How do they know how much fear runs through an average human heart, hmm? How do they know? They have an instrument to measure it? Someone forgot to tell Tolstoy he was out of a job."

"I'm not really following you."

"This is the human soul they're cutting up, with little plastic knives. How do they know? How do they know enough about normal people to pronounce themselves so different?"

Somewhere inside of me, an alarm bell went off. Something was wrong. I couldn't put my finger on what it was but something was wrong. I felt it the way an animal feels fear. Suddenly, I wanted to be out of there.

"Hey, Douglas. What do you say we go looking for that restaurant? Hmm? I'm getting pretty hungry."

He looked hurt. "But we've only just gotten here!"

"I know, but I thought you just wanted to find out what happened. . . ." I nodded at the TV set.

"Let's watch one more quarter," he said, "just to see if they can turn this game around; then we'll go get something to eat. How about that?"

"But . . ."

"There we go. Now we're talking. Let's see what these boys can do. . . ."

He cuffed me lightly on the shoulder and turned his attention back to the screen. It was snowing heavily now, the teams almost indistinguishable from each other: two seething masses repeatedly clashing, retreating, withdrawing, and clashing again. A shunt was followed by a collision, the collision by a smash, the smash by a shunt, at which point a red flag went up.

"PENALTY!!"

Cheers from the table behind us.

"ROCK THEM LIKE A HURRICANE!! ROCK THEM LIKE A HURRICANE!!!"

Kelsey turned to stare at them, his face a picture of disgust.

"Jesus Christ," he said, a little too audibly for my liking. "People *died* down there."

"Down where?" I asked quickly, trying to get back his attention.

"New Orleans. I have relatives who live in Baton Rouge. They had to be evacuated."

"Of course. Katrina. What a mess *that* was."

He looked at me, frowned. "Are you okay?"

"Yes, why?"

"Because you're acting awfully funny."

"You know what it is? I think I'm feeling a little low on sugar. I was really counting on that meal. . . . We ought to think about moving on soon."

"*I want to watch the rest of the game,*" he said through gritted teeth.

"I thought you said just one more quarter."

"What are you, my wife? I just got rid of the other one. I *want*. To *watch*. The *rest*. Of the *game*."

At which point, the bartender wandered over and leaned over conspiratorially.

"That was no fumble," he said. "I don't care if the guy dribbled the ball like a basketball before he was tackled. If he regained possession before his knee went down, that was no fumble."

"You know who that is, don't you?" said Kelsey. "It's Terry McAulay's crew. They enjoy screwing the Saints. Remember when they played the Giants? McAulay's crew did that game, too. They gave the Giants fourteen penalties in the first half."

"You mean the first game after nine/eleven?"

"Same referee."

"And what's the matter with that field?"

"You live in Chicago, for crying out loud. Install some turf and get over it."

They beamed at each other. "You sure I can't get you gentlemen a proper drink?" said the bartender, clearing away our glasses.

"A double scotch for me," said Kelsey. "Basil Hayden's. No ice."

"Basil Hayden's . . . I don't think we have any."

"Yes, you do," said Kelsey, pointing to the banked rows of liquor bottles stacked against the wall, illuminated from behind, like a mountaintop village seen at night. "Right at the top there . . ."

My head spun around so fast, it felt like it would snap off.

"What the fuck are you doing?" I hissed.

"What does it look like I'm doing? I'm ordering a drink. Same for him, too."

"Coming right up," said the bartender.

"Douglas, no."

"I've been thinking about this," he said. "Here's what I think. I think we take the offer from Knopf. The only problem, as I say, is going to be keeping the money away from Vogel. But if you could work the same magic you worked before, then there's no reason we shouldn't accept it."

I shook my head. "No, Douglas."

"No? Why not? I thought you'd be pleased."

"Not the deal . . . the drink."

"The drink is to celebrate the deal."

"And are you sure that's such a good idea?"

"Oh *please*. You think one drink is going to hurt me? 'The insiduous insanity of the first drink.' Don't tell me you bought all that crap. I hit a bad patch in Woodstock. My marriage was breaking up; the book was going badly; I was drinking too much, sure. Who wouldn't? There's nothing to do up there *but* drink. But I stopped, didn't I? It got a little much, so I stopped. Things are completely different now. My divorce is done. The book is going well. And I've got a big chunk of change coming my way, thanks to my excellent new agent."

He slapped me on the knee as the bartender arrived back and placed two tumblers on the bar in front of us. "C'mon, one drink," he purred. "Then we'll hit the road and go get that Korean."

"No."

He looked at me, softening. "What do you think is going to happen? You think I'm going to sprout hairs and start howling at the moon?"

"Of course not."

"Besides, I'll have you with me. If anything starts to go wrong, just can just pull the cord. 'Douglas. I want to go home.' Done. We're out of here."

"What are you even asking me for?" I said miserably. "If it's all so okay, why do you even need my permission?"

He looked at me a little blankly for a few seconds, then smiled. "I knew there was a reason you were my agent," he said, scooping up the tumbler and downing it in one gulp. He let out a little "Ah" of satisfaction, wiped his mouth with the back of his hand, replaced the tumbler on the bar, and gestured for the bartender to refill it. "Same again, please. . . . Man, that was good."

I stared at the glass in front of me. A tumbler with two inches of liquid, in which the lights of the bar were flattened, stretched, and reflected back like a little golden galaxy suspended in amber liquid. Out of the corner of my eye, I saw Kelsey down another shot and plant his glass back on the bar, then motion for the bartender to leave us the bottle. Then he noticed me.

"Goddamn—Patrick—are you— Don't tell me they've got *you* worried, too?"

"Of course not," I said, embarrassed.

"That is something. You are something, you know that?"

I picked up the tumbler and downed it.

I felt nothing, just the trickle of fiery liquid spreading out from my chest. He poured me another.

"I'll bet you never tasted anything like this before."

"What is it?"

"Basil Hayden's."

"It's very good."

"King of the bourbons."

He looked the most relaxed I'd ever seen him, as loose-limbed as a newborn lamb, his eyes clear with wonder. For the first time, I felt what it might be like not to be frightened of this man, and to get to know him. He wasn't that bad, not really; behind the grumpiness, he had the very same salad of neuroses as every other author I'd ever come across. Looking at him now, his gestures rangy and expansive as he talked shop with the bartender, he struck an avuncular, almost beatific figure, much more like the author I had idolized all those years ago, the one who had written such supple sentences about the overcrowded heads and hearts of men so far from happiness, or home, that it was all they could do not to laugh.

The bartender left to deal with another customer. Kelsey turned back to me. "So tell me something," he said. "What did you make of the whole higher power thing? Isn't that a hoot? D'you ever notice how similar everybody's gods are? They say you can choose anything you want, but everyone ends up choosing exactly the same thing. 'Someone nice who'll love me for who I am.' Their first pet. Their mom, before the divorce. The God of the Old Testament, minus the plagues. No mention of the children He kills for disrespecting the prophet. Or the seventy people He wipes out for accidentally looking at the Ark of the Covenant. Or the stone wall he brings down on twenty-seven thousand while they are retreating from the Israelites. While they are *retreating*. You don't hear much about *that* in meetings. . . ."

Up on the screen, a player in black had broken free from a massive scrum of limbs and was haring up the field, pursued by men in white. "This looks ugly for the Saints," fretted the commentator. "They aren't even trying to keep the Bears out of the end zone now. . . ."

Kelsey waved it away, annoyed to be so interrupted.

"You want to know why? Because they cannot admit for a single second that there might be something destructive about the creative impulse. That to create something, you must first burn down the house. Burn it to the ground. 'I form the light and create darkness, I bring prosperity and create disaster; I, the LORD, do all these things. . . .' "

The noise in the bar started to swell as the announcer intoned, "Jones goes left, then reverses field, goes to the left and circles the Saints' defense. The Bears are going to take the points anyway. They can't get 'im. . . . And . . . touchdown! Bears eighteen, Saints fourteen!" The bar was on its feet again. The table behind us erupted:

"WE WILL! WE WILL! ROCK YOU!!
WE WILL! WE WILL! ROCK YOU!!
WE WILL! WE WILL! ROCK YOU!!
WE WILL! WE WILL! ROCK YOU!!"

Slowly, Kelsey turned around to face his tormentors. The men were on their feet now, too, high-fiving one another across their table, their faces puce. "Crumbling like a levee!" shouted one, to laughter. "It must be all that water on the ground," said another. "They're all confused!"

Kelsey looked about to explode. "Hey, can you have a little respect?" he said loudly. "People died down there."

The table fell silent. I shrank down into my bar stool, staring at the bottle of whiskey, as if, by sheer power of thought alone, I might be able to transfer myself inside the bottle. It looked a lot safer in there.

"How about we go get that food now?" I asked.

"People died down there, Patrick."

"I'm more worried about the people who are about to die right here."

"You talking to me, old man?"

The voice came from behind us, from the table by the window.

"You heard me," said Kelsey, not turning around.

"I'm sorry, I didn't quite catch that," said the voice.

"Apology accepted."

"C'mon, Douglas, let's just go," I said, putting my hand on his arm. My heart was beating so hard I could feel it lifting my shirt away from my chest. I caught a glimpse of Kelsey's antagonist: heavyset, wearing a Bears sweatshirt, with a bristly crew cut, a roll of fat at the back of his neck, his hand cupping his ear, ignoring the entreaties of his friends.

"Hey, asshole, you got something to say, you can say it to my face."

"He's coming over here," I whispered.

"I'm not going anywhere," muttered Kelsey in reply, pouring himself another slug of whiskey. The Bears fan was almost upon us now, reeking of booze and bad aftershave.

"Hey, asshole. I was talking to you."

A hand descended on Kelsey's shoulder, puckering his jacket. He gave a little grimace and slowly, ever so slowly, turned around in his seat until he was face-to-face with the Bears fan.

"I'm sorry if I offended you," he said, wiping his mouth. "I have relatives down there. I didn't care much for your song."

"Is that right?"

"Down in Baton Rouge."

"You want to say something, you say it to my face."

"I think I just did. I didn't much like your song."

"Douglas," I hissed.

The Bears fan didn't look at me, just kept his eyes on Kelsey. The patrons on either side of us had, meanwhile, quietly edged away; a little way off stood the bartender, monitoring the situation.

"Leave him be, Alex," called out one of his friends from the table. "He didn't mean nothing by it."

"Come back here, you moose," said another, to laughter.

Something in Kelsey seemed suddenly to give way. "Look, I'm sorry. It was just a misunderstanding. I have a big mouth. Can I buy you a drink?"

The Bears fan squinted at him, his eyes like raisins in dough. "You sure about that?"

"Yes, absolutely. We're just trying to watch the game. We couldn't help but hear you and your friends. I spoke out of turn. I'm sorry."

"That's all we were trying to do, too. Watch the game."

"I know, and I'm sorry."

"Just keep it to yourself next time."

"I will. Lesson learned."

"All right."

"So we're good?" asked Kelsey.

"We're good."

"You sure about that?"

"Yeah."

"Really, truly, properly sure?"

The man frowned.

"Because if we're good, do you think you could remove your fat fucking fingers from my shoulder?"

For a few seconds, nobody said or did anything. Everything was hushed, as if someone had pressed pause on the whole scene: Kelsey on his stool, the guy with his hand on Kelsey's shoulder, looking at him intently, processing what he had just heard. Then he got a concentrated look on his face, as if he had just remembered something, and turned as if to go.

What happened next happened fast.

Kelsey's head spun around, his whole body rocking back on his stool, the stool tipping, his left elbow catching me straight in the gut, winding me. Something wet hit my forehead. Then my stool, too, started to tip, the ceiling swimming into view—I saw a chunky wooden chandelier with slim tulip-shaped bulbs against black stucco—then there was nothing at my back and I was falling, my arms flailing, until I hit the ground, and my head felt as if someone had just driven a nail into it.

Above us, all was commotion. I kept my eyes closed, feeling for the back of my head, and when I opened them, the first thing I saw was Kelsey, lying next to me on the ground, a puzzled look on his face. The men stood in a circle around us, but they weren't doing anything, just looking down, as if expecting us to come up with something. We're just lying on the floor, I can remember thinking. What are you looking at *us* for? Then Kelsey rolled over onto his front and got up onto his knees, rubbing his jaw and smiled to himself. Then he looked over at me and mouthed something, but I couldn't hear it over the shouting. He raised himself onto his feet, his hands on his knees, his head down, as if catching his breath for a moment. Then he looked up, steadied himself, and charged.

The bar seemed to explode. I rolled into a fetal position, my hands covering my head, only to receive a draft of cold beer to my chest. Someone's foot caught me smack in the ribs and I curled up tighter. All around me, feet scuffled. *"I want that motherfucker out,"* screamed someone at some point. It took a while for all the noise to die down, and when it did, I let go of my head, opened my eyes, and saw someone reaching down, extending a hand. I took it and was hoisted up into a standing position.

"Are you okay?" asked the owner of the hand, one of the young Hispanics from the pool table.

"I think so," I said. I felt dizzy.

"Do you want to sit down?"

I nodded and was led over to a stool by the bar. I kept my head down, cupping my forehead with my hand, and when I brought it down again, it was smeared with what looked like black ink.

Blood.

Kelsey's.

He was nowhere to be seen.

chapter twenty-five

YOU TOOK HIM TO a *bar*?"

"He wanted to watch a football game. We were looking for somewhere to eat and we passed this place and he just dragged me in."

"And that's where you got into a fight with the Bears fans."

"Yes."

"And you don't know where he is now?"

"I checked the other bars in the area, went back to his apartment—nothing. No. I have no idea."

I leaned forward in my chair and cradled my head between my palms, as if hoping to massage the answer out of them. My temples pounded, like someone was yanking on my spinal column, tugging on every vessel and ventricle in my brain. I felt like a walking sack of blood. It made no sense to me—I hadn't drunk *that* much—but I put it down to the knock on the head I had received; the welt I had back there had come up nicely. "You have no idea what he was like, Saul," I said. "I'm telling you. I've never seen him like that: manipulative and bullying and mean. Just vile. Absolutely vile."

"I've heard it can be pretty bad for them. Drinking. Same with bars—generally frowned on in those circles. It's very boring of them, I know, but what do I know. You're the expert."

I looked up at him. "I've had enough of these bloody people, I really have, Saul. They seem normal enough, and then you brush up against them and—boom—they turn into fucking werewolves right in front of your eyes—"

"I think you did a little more than brush up against him, Patrick."

Looking through Saul's window at the apartment block opposite, I could see a woman watering a plant; I felt sick with envy that somewhere in this world there were people whose most pressing concern was to water a plant. "Fuck," I said. "What am I going to do?"

"You'll find him. You should probably go tell Leo, though."

I stared at him. "No. No way."

"Patrick, you *have* to. One of the agency's biggest clients goes missing, and you're going to say—what? That you misplaced him? What exactly?"

"I don't know. I'll think of something."

"You'll think of nothing. You're telling him right now."

I knew he was right. I protested some more, but only half-heartedly. What I really wanted to do was go home and pull the bedcovers over my head until I felt human again, but a few minutes later, I found myself walking down to Leo's office, past the black-and-white portraits of Manhattan's best and brightest, feeling like a man going to the gallows. This was it, I felt certain. This was a fireable offense. Peering through the frosted glass door to Leo's office, I saw someone in there with him. I knocked, heard Leo's voice—"Come in"—and opened the door to find Brad standing at Leo's shoulder, going over some contracts on his desk. Leo put down his pen, staring up at me anxiously through his bifocals. I felt newly conscious of my rumpled clothing, and its stale odor of beer and sweat.

"What's going on?" asked Leo. "Are you okay? Sit down, why don't you."

"I'd prefer to stand. I have something I need to tell you. Some bad news."

"What is it?"

"It's Douglas. I've lost him."

"You've *lost* him?"

"We went to a bar last night to talk over some offers we'd gotten from Knopf and HarperCollins, and we got a little drunk and, well, one thing led to another and we ended up getting into a fight with some football fans."

"A fight? Are you hurt?"

"No, no, it was more of a scuffle really, but when I came up, he was gone, and I haven't been able to find him since. I've looked everywhere."

"He's probably just sleeping it off somewhere," said Leo, removing his spectacles to give them a clean. "Lord. I don't think I've heard of a decent *fight* since Mailer kicked the bucket. There was that thing between Crouch and Peck, but Crouch didn't deck him, did he? He didn't finish off the job."

Leo pounded his fist into his hand; Brad shook his head.

"No, Leo, you don't understand. You see. . . . He's . . . he's an alcoholic."

"An *alcoholic.*"

"Yes."

"How do you know that?"

"I didn't find him at the library like I said. I found him at an AA meeting. I'm sorry for lying to you. I think I was too ashamed. It was the wrong thing to do, I can see that now; I should have told you."

They exchanged glances.

"What were you doing taking him to a bar?" asked Brad.

"He wanted to watch the football game," I snapped. "We were supposed to be going for dinner to talk through this deal, so we—"

"You mean the Bears game?"

"Yes. He wanted to see the Bears lose. They put his team out or something."

"Will wonders never cease?" said Brad. "Patrick does football."

"Leave the boy alone, Brad," said Leo. "He must be feeling terrible. Are you sure you're okay?"

"I'm fine, Leo, thank you," I said, clasping my forehead. "I've got a bit of a headache, that's all."

"Why don't you sit down. We don't want you passing out on us. Do you want a glass of water?"

"It's okay, thank you," I said, sinking into the seat opposite his desk.

"Get Patrick a glass of water, Brad?"

Brad moved off to the small refrigerator Leo kept in the corner of his office. It was stashed with mini bottles of liquor, filched from various airlines—his midafternoon pick-me-ups.

"I'm okay, really," I said, "I just took a knock to the back of the head when I went down."

"When you 'went down.'"

"This guy took a swing at Douglas, and he went over, and then we both kind of went down. . . . I'm really sorry, Leo. I'll find him, I promise. . . . Thanks, Brad."

I took a bottle of Evian from Brad. He nodded and returned to Leo's side of the desk. "You'll do no such thing," said Leo. "You're in no fit state to conduct a manhunt. You're going home."

"What are you talking about, Leo? I don't have any time to waste. I have to find him before he does real damage to himself. . . ."

"And it's thinking like that that led to your relapse. I'm not risking you with another. Go home and say your prayers or call your sponsor or whatever else it is you're supposed to do."

In another life, I might have felt more surprise at what he had just said, but by now it barely registered—just another mess to clear up, another correction-in-waiting. "No," I said wearily, rubbing my eyes. "I wasn't going to AA meetings for myself. I followed him in. That's all."

For a moment, there was silence.

"Oh," said Leo. "Well, what are you doing lounging around my office, then? Get on the phones! Call the police. File a missing person's report."

I leaped up out of the chair as if scalded. "Not the police, Leo. Please."

"Do you have any better ideas?"

"The hospitals. I haven't called the hospitals."

"Well, get on it, then. Jesus Christ. This is not looking very good, Patrick. This is not looking good at all. He might sue. You realize that, don't you? He'd be perfectly within his rights."

"I know," I said, getting up from the chair. "Just give me a week, Leo. I'm sure I can find him."

"Three days."

"Five."

"Three."

"I should know better than to negotiate with you," I joked.

"Just find him," he replied tersely. "We'll deal with everything else later."

I backed out of the office, closing the door behind me with a soft *kerlunk*.

"How'd it go?" asked Saul, who was standing by the watercooler. He tossed the magazine he was reading into one of the chairs.

"Terrible."

"What did he say?"

"It was bad."

"What did he say exactly?"

"He gave me three days to find him before he calls the police."

"Oh boy."

"You see? The fucking police."

"It's okay. I've seen him like this before. He gets all riled up, but he calms down again."

"No, Saul. I don't think so. You weren't in there. 'Just find him,' he says. 'We'll deal with everything else later.' "

He took the information in. "I'm sure he meant nothing by it."

"Really? It sounded pretty meaningful to me, Saul. I mean, shit—what am I going to *do*? He's going to fire me. I absolutely know it. Even if I do find him, he's going to fire me."

"He didn't say anything of the sort."

"He didn't need to. He could barely bring himself to—"

At which point, the door opened and out walked Brad. He saw us and wiped the grin from his face. "Wow," he said. "That was. . . . I don't know what that was. . . . Are you sure you're okay, Patrick?"

"He's fine," said Saul.

"That was quite a story. If there's anything I can do to help, just say."

"Thanks, Brad, but I got it."

"Seriously. If you need someone to cover for you while you're out of the office. . . ."

"What are you talking about, Brad?" said Saul.

"At lunchtimes," said Brad. "If he needs anyone to cover for him at lunchtimes."

"It's okay, Saul, I can handle this myself. . . . What if I did? What if I liked nothing better than to hunker down with a nice crateload of crack at the end of a hard week and smoke the whole lot? Would you have a problem with that, Brad? Hmm? Would you have a problem with that?"

"I think *you* would be the one with the problem," said Brad.

"You miserable little—" I said, taking a step toward him. He actually flinched, before Saul stepped in between us, his hand on my chest. "Okay, both of you, cool off," he said. "Brad, why don't you leave us alone for a bit. Hmm? I want to talk to Patrick on my own."

Brad raised his hands in mock innocence. "I was just saying . . . "

"Yeah, well, you can say it to someone else."

"I was just messing with you, Patrick. You know that, right?"

"Fuck off," I said.

He looked surprised, then annoyed, he then slunk off down the corridor—

"Someone's been hanging out with Ernest Hemingway for too long."

"I'm sorry, Saul."

"Fine by me. There's just one thing, though: I don't think crack comes in crates. I think it comes in vials."

"But the vials have to come in something."

He smiled. "C'mon, let's go get some lunch. You look like you haven't eaten in days. . . ."

That afternoon, I called St. Vincent's, Beth Israel, Lenox Hill, Bellevue, New York–Presbyterian, all the hospitals in downtown Manhattan, then all the hospitals in upper Manhattan. No luck. Returning to his apartment block, I found the street rudely oblivious to the events of the previous night, bikes threading in and out of the pedestrians, delivery bags hanging from their handlebars, while shopkeepers stood guard outside their shops, smoking cigarettes. I buzzed Kelsey's apartment until my thumb was sore: no response. I was just wondering if I could clamber up the fire escape without drawing too much attention to myself when I saw a face peering at me from between the mannequins in the storefront below. He ducked out of sight almost as soon as I saw him. Walking up to the door of the shop and peering in, I saw roll after roll of fabric stacked from ceiling to floor, a thin path cutting through the middle to a cash register at the back of the shop, where I saw my elderly gentleman in a dapper gray Nehru tunic, looking at his nails. I made my way inside, a small bell sounding as I did so.

"You come for dog?" he asked a little fearfully.

"I'm looking for Mr. Kelsey. From the second floor?"

"No see him. *You come for dog?"*

"No, I'm not here for any dog. I'm here for— *Shit, Billy."*

"Yeesss. Billy!" he said triumphantly. "Very bad to leave Billy for such long time."

"Is there any way of getting up there?"

"One moment. *I get keys."* He disappeared into the back of the shop and reappeared a few moments later holding a jangling set of jailer's keys, counting through them one by one.

"Have you seen Billy's owner, Mr. Kelsey?"

"I not see Mista Kelsi for *long* time."

"Do you know where he might have gone?"

"Noooo," he said, shaking his head. "Maybe he see wife. Maybe go on holiday. Maybe he go skiing." He grinned at his own joke.

"I don't think he can have gotten very far."

"You think? What about *car*?"

"He has a *car*?"

He nodded vigorously. *"His car gone."*

It was the car that did it. Up until that point, I had nursed the slim fantasy that I might be able to find Douglas, nurse him back to sobriety, hang on to my job, not be ejected from the country and returned in shame to London to receive the insincere condolences of my friends. But a *car*? My head filled with smoking Land Cruisers, shattered dolls, smashed picnic hampers. I was reminded of a comic strip I'd read as a boy, in which scientists traveled back in time to save the dinosaurs, only to step on a butterfly and return to find out they'd accidentally wiped out mankind. That's how I felt. I hadn't understood half of what Kelsey had told me the night before—about diseases and Tolstoy and God and the Israelites—but I understood one thing, and that was the visible effect my revelation had had on him. I had faked the program. That meant the program could be faked. Which had led him to the possibility that maybe he, too, might be faking it. I had entered through some unforeseen hole in the back of the tent, bringing with me news of the outside world, praise, fresh air; and he had bolted back through the hole I had made. The effect of my lies had been viral. "I was like, Well, he seems like a nice guy, but he's drawing all the crazies out of the woodwork," Lola had told me. "I didn't stop for a second to think that included *me*." I groaned out loud at the thought of her, and of her warnings, which I had so roundly ignored. I thought briefly of calling my friends back in London to prepare them for my inevitable return, but instead, I called Prudence.

Actually, I called Felix first, but he was worse than useless: He suggested I leave a trail of miniature vodka bottles in the street, then pounce when Kelsey showed up. He did, however, have Prudence's number—I could hear loud R&B in the background when she picked up, and what sounded like the noise of a kitchen. I told her what had happened and she listened, interrupting me every so often to ask questions. What was he drinking? How many times did he get hit? What time did I lose sight of him? What kind of car did he drive? "A Chevrolet," I told her. "A blue Chevrolet Caprice."

"You mean one of the old cop cars? Those things are fast.

That's eighteen hours. Ignoring the speed limit. That puts him no farther south than Virginia. Somewhere on the eastern seaboard anyway. Maybe Canada, although I doubt it."

"Christ."

"You'll find him. You have one huge advantage in this game. You know that, right?"

"What's that?"

"He's drunk and you're not. When I escaped from rehab the first time, I made two mistakes. First, I dug my way out under the wire fence. I didn't need to do that. The gate was open. Completely fucked up my nails. The second was, I always went back to the same place. Shot up, passed out, forgot I was supposed to be on the run—my parents picked me up there every time. You see? We're not criminal masterminds. We're too habitual."

"I'm sorry, Prudence."

"What are you sorry for?"

"What I did."

"You think I care? I think it was wild. Don't lose your contempt now, Patrick, not when you need it most. It will help you find him. . . . *No, that's not it!*" She suddenly started speaking to someone else. "*What did I say? . . . I said cold-pressed virgin coconut oil. Do I have to walk you to the store and put your hand on the right friggin' can myself?*" She came back to me. "I'd better go. The douche I work with has just bought the wrong ingredients."

"Thanks so much for speaking to me."

"Don't be a jerk. Just think, People, places, and things."

"People, places, and things?"

"That's what they tell us to steer clear of. The people, places, and things that remind us of our old lives. So if you're off to the races, they're your first stop."

I closed my phone and slipped it back in my pocket. *People, places, and things.*

People, places, and things.

People, places, and things.

Then it came to me. It wasn't much, but it was at least a place. A place where Kelsey had done the bulk of his drinking. A place you needed a car to get to. Most important, it was a place I hadn't looked yet, and I didn't have too many of those.

chapter twenty-six

MANHATTAN DOESN'T REALLY THINK of itself as an island; that's how much of an island mentality it has. You don't get to drop anchor or throw down the gangplank; you don't get to see it rise up out of the mist as your canoe gently bumps shore. What happens, most commonly, is that you approach the city by one of the looping overpasses, the Manhattan skyline briefly visible beyond the Brooklyn rooftops; then you head into one of the bridges or tunnels, the girders or green fluorescent lights blurring past overhead, and the next thing you know you are shot out like a pinball into screaming, belching bumper-to-bumper traffic. There are no halfway houses—it's either long shot or close-up, admiring the skyline or dodging some guy's side mirror. By necessity, the mental attitude such a place encourages in its inhabitants is somewhat strange, lying somewhere between shell-shocked solipsism and a defensive crouch. It doesn't take long—days, sometimes just hours—for you to forget that anything else ever existed beyond this Darwinian death match, although some may dimly recall a more tranquil way of life that didn't require the combined skills of an Olympic toboganner and a speed-chess master. Such memories are, however, fleeting and should generally be extinguished if any progress is to be made. Occasionally, one hears of places farther afield, from those who have made the trip to Long Island, enjoying a day or two of sandy beaches before enduring the grueling six-hour crawl through fuming traffic to get back, by which time they have generally ingested enough carbon monoxide to cancel out whatever dim therapeutic value the trip might have promised in the first place. Occasionally, too, you hear rumors of people making an even longer journey, by air or train, to a far-off land of strip malls and televangelists, polygamist cults and spree killers, a land ravaged by hurricanes and populated by Republicans, otherwise known as "America"; but the general thinking seems to be that while this unpleasant addition to the otherwise-fine island of Manhattan may have been necessary at some point in the nation's history, it should now be avoided if at all possible.

There's another more practical reason why so few people ever leave: It is physically impossible. You can certainly try. You can gather your documents and rent a clean-smelling blue sedan from a hire firm called Rent-a-Wreck in Chelsea. You can plan your route carefully on the map, and decide, not unreasonably, that the West Side Highway—that long ribbon of road that runs up the west side of the island—looks like a good bet. It is straight and simple and takes you north toward the George Washington Bridge, your chosen point of disembarkation from the island. You buckle yourself in, start the car, and pull out gingerly into traffic; you take your first pothole and laugh, disapproving of its high pitch but reasoning that, with time, it will come down to resemble normal human laughter; you see the turning for the West Side Highway, get into a lane, pull up by the traffic lights, and wait, feeling a swell of panic at the speed of the cars zooming past. They want you to do *that*? The lights change, you pull out, and the next thing you know you are gunning it down a six-lane concrete highway, separated from oncoming traffic by the flimsiest of divides, with an eighteen-wheeler up your tailpipe and a grip on your steering wheel rivaled only by that of the Boston Strangler.

After that, all bets are off. The highway bears about as much relation to a normal road as Einsteinian space-time does to normal Euclidean geometry, and as much resemblance to the map that just plastered itself to your back window as it does to the family tree of Kunta Kinte. The Henry Hudson Parkway? The West Side Elevated Highway? The 9A north? Are they the same road? Why does every road have a dozen names? Meanwhile the turnoffs are speeding past you, like a taxi meter clocking up a monster fare—14th Street, 30th Street, 57th Street, 79th Street, 95th Street, 125th Street, 158th Street—every wrong turn punishable with an immediate and irrevocable lurch into Harlem. But somehow you avoid turning your car into a gasoline-soaked fireball for—oh, five, ten, fifteen minutes. You feel you are getting the hang of things. The ridges of the tarmac beneath your wheels beat out a soothing rhythm. You may have only the faintest clue where you're going, but you are alive and *driving*, goddamn it, and gosh, there's the Hudson River on your left, sparkling beautifully in the sun, and there are the skyscrapers of Midtown rising above the rusty ironwork of the Meatpacking District. A billboard for the new Adam Sandler picture floats by; you relax your death grip on the steering wheel, lower yourself gently into your seat and turn on the radio.

". . . That was Van Halen's 'Jump,' back when Eddie was—well, let's just say back in better days. In fact, I've got a letter here Eddie recently wrote to his fans. I'm going to read it to you. 'I would like Van Halen fans to know how much I truly appreciate each and every one of you,' he says. 'Without you, there is no Van Halen. At the moment, I do not feel I can give you my best. That's why I have decided to enter a rehabilitation facility to work on myself, so that in the future I can deliver the one hundred and ten percent I feel I owe you and want to give you. . . .'" I turned the radio off.

It didn't take long to leave the city, the buildings of New Jersey dropping away to make way for trees and fields as the road split smoothly into a dual carriageway. On the right, a steep bank led down to the Hudson River; on the other side of the river, an Amtrak train ran north along the shoreline. I put on a burst of speed, thinking I could beat it, only to see it pull inexorably ahead.

After an hour or so, the sun disappeared behind the mountains and the road began to rise, cutting through rock faces that angled up steeply on either side, the patches of snow joining up to form an even blanket, the birch trees making way for towering firs that crept up to the side of the road. Spring might be on the way in the city, but up here it was still winter. Even the place names sounded ominous—Beaverkill, Ashokan, Willowemoc—like the kind of places you managed to leave only by gnawing off one of your own legs.

As darkness descended I flipped on my headlights: snow streamed through the beams like moths. I began to wish I'd taken Saul up on his offer to accompany me. After another twenty minutes, I saw the lights of a tollbooth up ahead. I chose a lane at random, drawing up to one of the booths, to find a woman in a blue uniform and a coonskin hat nursing a steaming flask of coffee. Rolling down the window, I felt a blast of icy air scoop out the car's warmth.

"I wonder if you can help me," I said. "I'm looking for, uh, Pine Lodge Lane?"

She held out her hand for the map, flipping it through ninety degrees, tracing routes with her finger, before handing it back. "You're going to want to get off Eighty-seven at the next junction. Just follow the road around until you see the church. You take a right at the church and go up the hill—it's pretty windy, so don't let it kick ya—just keep followin' it and followin' it until you get to the Harley-Davidson garage, and then you're going to take a right. That's Pine Lodge Lane. You can't miss it. Just look out for the motorcycles."

But for the lights of an occasional liquor store, the last leg of the journey was in complete darkness, my headlights picking out the dimmest of spots on the road ahead. The snow was coming down thicker now, flying right up at the windshield before swerving off to the side. I killed my speed, hunched forward in my seat. The road turned narrow and windy as it ascended the hill, overhung with a canopy of firs that blotted out the stars and moon. I saw no signs of a Harley-Davidson garage, and after ten minutes of hairpin bends, the road began to descend again. I pulled over to the side, checked my map, decided that I had overshot, and turned around, driving even slower, my nose just inches from the windshield. This time, just as I was about to reach the top, my headlights caught a flash of something metallic off to the left of the road: the rear fender of another car, jammed into a snowdrift at the base of a tree. I backed up, my exhaust fumes steaming red in the back window, pulled in, parked, and got out.

The air was cold, clear, and eerily quiet after the noise of my engine. Through gaps in the trees overhead, the moon shone with unusual brightness, illuminating the snowy fields beyond the trees a radioactive blue. Behind the back wheels of the other car lay long spumes of dirt—the driver had obviously tried to accelerate his way out. I walked up to the license plate: EXPLORE MINNESOTA. 10,000 LAKES. A Chevrolet. It *looked* blue, but then, everything looked blue in this light. I walked around to the front.

The fender was jammed into the snow; wrapped around it was a long metal pole. Brushing off the snow, I followed it down to a flattened metal sign that read PINE LODGE LANE.

That's why I hadn't seen the turnoff. On the other side of the tree, I could just about make out a narrow dirt track in the forest. I returned to my car and was almost there when a large dark mass broke away from the side of the road. I froze, my mouth filling with an acrid metallic taste, as if I had run my tongue down the blade of a sword.

Whatthefuckwasthat?

It was large and black and moved swiftly across the road, with a heavy, rolling gait that put you in mind of a large body of water, before disappearing into the trees on the other side. My heart pumping, I climbed quickly back into my car, shut the door, locked it, and started the engine before any other patches of darkness decided they wanted to break away and cross the road, too. I was halfway down Pine Lodge Lane, the branches scraping my roof, my tires yo-yoing up and down inside their hubs, before I eased off on the gas. Slowing down to read the mailboxes—17, 19, 21, 23—I saw the number I was looking for. I took the turn off the track, up a steep driveway, before reaching a small clearing, in the middle of which stood a low two-story wooden chalet with walk-around decks, an adjoining garage, and a Jeep Cherokee parked outside of it. I pulled up beside the Jeep and got out, the muscles in my legs feeling heavy and knotted. There was a smell of wood smoke in the air, and a thin tendril of smoke made its way from the top of the house.

Sounding the doorbell, I heard voices, movement, and the door opened, revealing a woman in her early fifties: dungarees, dishwashing gloves, short gray hair, owlish round face that bore a puzzled expression.

"Can I help you?"

"I'm really sorry to bother you, but I'm looking for the man who used to own this house before you. Mr. Kelsey? Douglas Kelsey?" My voice sounded odd to me after two hours of driving.

"Sure, I remember Mr. Kelsey," she said, looking me up and down. "We haven't seen him since he moved out. . . . Why on earth did you think he might be here?"

"I think that's his car at the end of the drive," I said, pointing back the way I had come.

"Is that so?" she said, peering over my shoulder. "We didn't know who left that there. Damn near took down our road sign. You can't take these roads in a two-wheel drive. Not at this time of the year."

"Who is it?" A male voice came from somewhere in the back of the house.

"We got a young man!" she called over her left shoulder. "Says he's looking for Mr. Kelsey!"

"I'm his agent," I said.

"It's his agent!"

There was silence.

"Why do you think he'd come back here?" she asked me.

"I don't really know, to be honest, but he's gone missing. And he often talked about this place and how much he regretted having to move. This whole thing must seem totally ridiculous. I'm sorry to bother you. Do you think I could leave you my card? And if you see or hear from him, maybe you could give me a call?"

"You're his agent," she said, reading the card.

"Yes."

"With the Leo Gottlieb Agency," she said, continuing to read.

"Yes."

"And you just drove all the way from the city?" I nodded. She gave me a pitying look. "And now you're going to drive back?"

"I might stay in town. You can't recommend a bed-and-breakfast, by any chance?"

She studied me, as if considering my request.

"Well, you don't *sound* like you're from Chicago," she said finally.

"Chicago? No. I've never been to Chicago."

"He said there were some men from Chicago who wanted to kill him."

I stared at her. "You've *spoken* to him?"

"He's upstairs," she said, opening the door. "Why don't you come in before we lose all our heat."

I felt a flood of relief.

"Oh my God, thank you! Thank you so much!"

"Henry, will you check if the trash is in or out?" came the voice from the back of the house.

The woman poked her head out the door, than called back over her shoulder, *"It's in!"* She turned to me. "It's the bears. If we leave the trash out, we wake up with chicken carcasses and yogurt cartons all over the lawn."

That's what I'd seen.

I needed no more invitations to go inside. The house was messy, folksy, and warm, with a fireplace set beneath a large brick chimney, logs piled waist-high on either side of it, and embroidered wall hangings depicting houses, streams, a Jamaican flag. In the corner of the living room stood a pile of wood planks and loops of snaking orange cable; through an open door could be heard the whine of an electric drill.

"I'm Henrietta," she said, extending her hand.

"Patrick."

"Can I get you something to drink?" she asked. "Coffee? Beer?"

"A beer would be wonderful."

"I think we've still got some left. . . . *John, he's having a beer. Do you want one?"*

There was no reply.

"He's probably got his headphones on," she said, leading the way around the chimney to the kitchen on the other side. It was hung with tin pots and pans; a chipped wooden counter in the middle looked like it had once been a carpenter's work table.

"When did he get here?" I asked.

"Two nights ago," she said from behind the refrigerator door.

"I hope he wasn't any trouble."

"Not really. I mean, he took down our sign, but he seemed the worse off, if you know what I mean. We asked him in, but he said no, that he wanted to go off on a walk. An hour later, John opens the door to see where he is and he's passed out on the porch. Comes to, proceeds to drink us out of house and home, then falls asleep again. John had to put him to bed."

At one end of the kitchen, a wooden staircase led up to the second floor. She came back with two opened bottles of Heineken.

"Thank you," I said. "So did he say why he was here?"

She shook her head. "No. I mean, we were both pleased to see him, obviously, but no, I don't believe he told us that."

"What about this morning? He didn't tell you what his plans were?"

"Oh no. He didn't get up this morning. He's been in bed since he got here."

"He's been asleep *for two days?*"

"Isn't that right, hon? Been asleep since he got here?"

"Yep," said a voice behind us.

I turned, to find a stout, red-faced man with longish gray hair, and a neatly trimmed mustache; he was wearing denim overalls and had a pair of old-fashioned headphones, big and bulbous, slung around his neck.

"Excuse me if I don't shake your hand," he said, wiping his hand with a rag. "I've been stripping wood."

"I always knew he'd be back," said Henrietta. "What did I say when he left? I said, 'That man is not finished here.'"

"Oh, Henry."

"I did, too! They sold in such a hurry. It just didn't feel right to me, somehow. Like the painting in the bedroom. Do you remember? Half the room was plain eggshell white; half was a creamy off-white. Like he was trying to get something right and then—just stopped dead. Only half the wall done. Who paints half a wall and just stops dead?"

"Someone in a hurry to sell a house?" said her husband.

"That's not what it looked like. It looked like a man who'd been told he had ten seconds to evacuate. I said to myself, That man is going to be back."

Before long, I was hungrily devouring one of Henrietta's bacon and tomato sandwiches, answering her questions about whether this was my first trip to the area and what was it like to work with a man like Mr. Kelsey, prompting some eye rolling from her husband, but which I answered as best I could. I told them about the bear I had seen and the strange metallic taste I'd had in my mouth afterward.

"Bitter-tasting?" said John. "Like a piece of lemon peel? That was adrenaline. If she didn't have any cubs with her, you were probably okay. And don't, whatever you do, offer them any ice cream."

"Ice cream?"

"Please, John, no," said Henrietta.

He leaned over and put an elbow on one knee. "A couple of summers back, we had a young woman who thought it would be a good idea if her son fed the bear an ice-cream cone. Bit the child's head clean off." He drew a finger across his neck.

"You see?" said Henrietta. "Now what is the point of a story like that, really?"

"Like a scoop of ice cream," he said.

"He tells that story to everyone," she said. "And then complains that tourism is down."

I made a show of asking about B and B's in the area, but they would hear none of it. Within the hour, Henrietta was showing me to my room, a slanting attic bedroom, right next door to where Kelsey lay sleeping, adorned with posters for Jay-Z, Band of Horses, and Grand Theft Auto. The window looked out onto the small clearing on which the house stood: the snowy lawn, blue in the moonlight, ringed by fir trees that swayed in the wind like silent sentinels, and just beyond them, the dark shadowy mass of Hunter Mountain. The perfect spot to write a book. Or drink yourself to death. I wondered which Douglas Kelsey I was going to be waking up to in the morning.

chapter twenty-seven

DOUGLAS REAPPEARED AT JUST after ten o'clock the next morning. Henrietta was in the kitchen, making some coffee, while she told me about her sons, both of whom had recently left for college; it was nice to have a full house again, she said. We both heard a creak on the staircase and turned to see two feet slowly making their way down the stairs, clad in moccasins. They were followed by a pair of dungarees, and finally Douglas, dressed in clothes two sizes too large for him. His hair tousled, a confused look on his face, he seemed to be occupying about 15 percent less body space than before, moving gingerly, slowly, toward us, as if concentrating very carefully on all the new distances involved.

"Morning!" sang Henrietta. "Can I get you some coffee?"

"Thank you." His voice was croaky—barely audible. The flesh around his right eye was inflamed, yellow-brown, just beginning to turn purple. Taking a chair at the table, he looked at me blankly, as if trying to remember who I was.

"How long have we been here?" he asked.

"Two days. You got here a couple of days ago. I got here last night."

He blinked. "How did I get here?"

"You drove."

"Ah," he said, nodding slowly.

"You don't remember?"

He frowned. "I remember being in the bar with you. And that guy taking a swing at me. Are you okay?"

"I took a knock to the back of my head," I said, feeling for my bump. "You got the worst of it."

I pointed to his eye. He reached up to touch it but got the wrong eye. I shook my head and pointed to his other eye. He got it this time, wincing sharply, then picked up a knife from the table and held it up in front of his face, turning it this way and that to catch his reflection.

"Where did you go?" I asked him.

"I'm not sure. I remember the fight. I remember us being thrown out of the bar. Then going to the second bar, the one with the loud music."

"I didn't go to a second bar with you."

"You didn't?"

"I lost track of you after the fight."

"You didn't go with me to another bar? With loud music? And red walls. I remember it had red walls. It was your idea, I thought."

I shook my head. "Absolutely not."

"That is strange. I can see you there."

I shook my head again.

He rubbed his jaw.

"Huh. Well. I don't remember anything after that. The next thing I knew, I was driving. Someone had just sounded their horn. It woke me up. I was on the interstate. I saw the signs for I-87 north and figured I had to be coming here."

He fell silent.

"You don't know why you're here?"

"How did *you* know I'd be here?"

"I don't know. Lucky guess. You don't know?"

He shook his head. "And there I was, hoping you would be able to tell me."

I looked at him, dumbfounded.

"And there I was, thinking it was my French toast," said Henrietta, setting a large coffeepot and two mugs down in front of us.

"Ah well, now there is *that*," said Kelsey. "I would never say no to French toast. . . ."

We were soon lost in the business of breakfast. If our host sensed any peculiarity about the whole situation—her two sons having left for college, to be replaced, a few days later, by the previous owner of their house, shit-faced, and then his frantic British literary agent—she did not let on; whether because this sort of thing had happened to her before or because she was one of those people who believed it best to be prepared for all eventualities was hard to tell. I was grateful for the semblance of normality she brought to the proceedings. If the conversation we had just had filled me with unease—how could the man not know where he'd been, and how could he imagine he had been to another bar with me?—then the conversation we were soon to have made me feel even uneasier. I felt a little like someone fast approaching a visit to the dentist or taxman. I was relieved when the talk finally turned to lunch—"John'll be back by then. Will you stay?"—and Douglas demurred.

"Oh no, we've got to be getting back to the city," he said. "What do you say, Patrick?"

"I'm not sure your car is going to make it."

"Something happened to the car?"

As soon as he heard what he had done to their sign, Douglas disappeared into the workroom, came back with a toolbox, and we both headed down to see what could be done with the car. It was a bright, windy day, the branches of the trees hung with tiny icicles that shimmered in the sunlight. At the bottom of the drive we found his car, wedged into the snowbank.

"Douglas," I said. "About what happened—"

"I don't want to talk about it," he said curtly, his head in the engine.

"But—"

"Not now, Patrick."

He gave me a look and I let it drop. The car was a write-off, the engine black, the pistons burned out. He'd fried it trying to reverse himself out. He'd also let some of the air out of the tires in an attempt to gain traction, but he'd succeeded only in completely deflating them. After getting back to the house, he spent twenty minutes calling the local garages, until he found one that could come and pick it up; someone would come first thing the next day. "If they have the parts, I should be able to come pick it up in a couple of weeks," he told Henrietta, pulling on his coat out on the porch. "Is that okay?"

"You'll drop in again, I hope."

He made an embarrassed face. "I don't think so. I've caused enough trouble."

"No trouble at all," she said, peering at his black eye. "Are you sure you don't want to get that looked at?"

"I'll see my doctor as soon as I get back to New York. Thank you." He grimaced, zipping up his jacket. "You ready, Patrick?"

I nodded. I could see he could not take much more of this. Walking toward my car, I sprung the locks with the opener: *bloop-bloop*. Henrietta stood on the porch, waving.

"Jesus," he muttered. "Like we'd dropped in for a round of golf."

"They seem like nice people."

"The Sieberlings? Oh, they are. They're fine people. Fine people . . ."

The way he said it made it sound as if the world divided into the fine people, the not so fine people, and the people so far from fine that they can only laugh and that he fell firmly into the latter category. We buckled up and reversed back down the driveway, the snow falling in soft *fwwmps* as we brushed the branches. I turned the car around and set off down the track to the road. Drawing up at the turning, I flipped my blinker right to take us back to the highway. "Do you mind if we head into town first?" asked Kelsey. "There's someone I want to say hello to."

"Sure," I said, puzzled.

Woodstock was a lot smaller than I'd expected. A single main street led up a gentle hill to a small town square, still hung with Christmas lights. In the middle of the square, a small group of warmly-wrapped women were protesting the war: 8 BILLION A MONTH read one placard. Another said BRING THEM HOME. It was unclear whom they were protesting *to*, exactly; the Karma Café, just opposite, didn't look like the staunchest of Republican bastions. I pulled up in front of the church.

"I won't be long," said Kelsey, reaching for the door.

"Where are you going?" I asked, but he was already gone, pulling his coat tight as he made his way through the protesters, coming to a halt on the other side of the square, waiting for an aquamarine pickup truck to get out of the way so he could cross the road to the liquor store on the other side.

The liquor store.

I could barely believe my own stupidity. But of *course*. What an *idiot*. His central nervous system was probably on fire, every cell in his body screaming for more, and still more—an agony of dis-satiation that would not stop until his poor pulverized liver made one last push of half-purified Jack Daniel's, before fluttering, finally, to a halt. Craning forward in my seat, I saw Kelsey look right and left, waiting for the pickup truck to get out of the way. When it had passed, he jogged across the street—he *jogged*—then stopped briefly to glance in the window of the liquor store before pushing inside the bookshop next door.

It was my turn to collapse, my head slumping forward onto my arms, which were still clutching the steering wheel. I stayed like that for some time, feeling suspiciously close to tears. A few minutes later, the car door opened and Douglas climbed back in.

"Thanks," he said. "Someone I haven't seen in a while."

I restarted the car and pulled out onto the road taking us back down the hill, past the liquor store, the bookstore, a pizza parlor, a café, a bank, a supermarket, a golf course. It wasn't long before we had left town and were driving through the countryside again, the fields frosted with white, the sun low in the sky, strobing the interior of the car with flashes of light through the trees. We were five, maybe ten minutes into the drive when I said, "I need to talk about what happened, Douglas."

He was sitting with his elbow resting on the window, staring into space. "You didn't have anything to do with it," he said.

"What are you talking about? I took you to a bar; we got drunk. . . ."

"I seem to remember the bar was my idea."

"But the auction. The pressure I was putting you under."

He harrumphed. "Didn't have anything to do with anything. I had that one coming to me for a long time, believe me. You have no idea how long. I've been waiting for this nightmare to be over."

"What nightmare?"

"Sobriety. Oh, I thought it was interesting at first. That someone like me should find himself stuck in a room with all these cops and firemen and doctors who knew not the slightest thing about my work. Just heaven. To be given the anonymity I'd craved for so long, just like that? I would have *paid* to hear them talk about their lives. The *material*. Did you know I once heard a man who'd gotten off a drunk driving charge because the person he hit was another drunk driver? Isn't that something? Another drunk driver."

He laughed.

"But do you want to know what's really funny? What's really funny is that I didn't once think this all applied to me. Oh, I sat there, drinking it all in, thrilled to find myself shoulder-to-shoulder with the kind of people I would ordinarily have been dismissing, in a single phrase. A small cameo, a bit player, maybe, in a forthcoming book. 'Hello, my name is Douglas and I am an alcoholic.' Out of all the sentences that I've written, the idea that this one summed me up best. My life's work, literally. It seemed like a joke to me: I would sit there laughing at this joke because the timing and delivery were so goddamned exquisite, don't you see? That I, of all people, should find myself dependent on the very clichés I'd once abhorred. I mean, if that isn't proof of the existence of God, then I do not know what is. He's one twisted fuck. I've always known it. And all the time—I can't quite believe I've just realized this—but all the time I was sitting there, I was waiting for someone to come to me and say, 'It's okay, Douglas. You've been a good sport, but really, the joke's over. You can go home now. Things can go back to the way they were before.'"

He shook his head, incredulous.

"That would be me," I said.

"I'm sorry?"

"That would be me. That's exactly what I did say to you. I came to you and I said everything can go back to exactly the same as it was before."

"You tried to get me a book deal, that's all."

"It's not all, Douglas, because I lied to you. I lied to you about who I was. I made a mockery of everything that kept you healthy and alive. I faked everything, and I didn't stop to think for a second what effect I might be having on you."

"And what effect was that exactly?"

"When I told you, the shock, I mean, look at what happened."

"Had nothing to do with it."

"But—"

"Look, nobody does what you did for a writer. I don't care how many times you read my books in college."

"What are you saying?" I asked, uneasily.

"I'm saying that the only people who find themselves attracted to twelve-step programs are those who feel their lives to be out of control in some way."

"I did it to get ahold of you."

"I'm not going to sit here and argue with you about it, Patrick. The lies to other people are one thing—we usually get caught out in those. But the lies to ourselves? Nobody clears those up for us. We're on our own with those. They stick around for a long time, if you're not careful."

He gave me a look—grave, imploring.

I felt suddenly tired of this conversation—his questions, his insinuations. Up ahead, I saw the first signs for I-87 south. Douglas's hand flew to his head.

"Fuck! Billy!"

"Billy's fine, Douglas."

"What do you mean, 'fine'? How can he be fine?"

"Your landlord's looking after him. We got him out when I was looking for you. Took him for a walk, gave him water, food. . . ."

"You did?"

"Yes, he's in great shape."

"But I've never left him like this before. I promised her I would never do that. I cannot. Fucking. Believe. I *did* that to him."

"You didn't do anything to him, Douglas, Billy is fine. . . ."

His face was all knotted and red, as if something had a tight hold of him inside and was twisting, slowly. He looked like a man who had just remembered he'd murdered somebody. This had nothing to do with the dog. It had to do with whatever had just plucked him out of a bar, like King Kong reaching into that hotel room, and deposited him, three days later, on the side of a mountain in upstate New York, with no memory of how he'd gotten there or even why he was there. It was scary. What must that feel like, to have someone occupying your body, going around doing things in your name, opening your mouth and saying things with your lips, things you had no memory of ever having done or said? Or to completely make up things that had never happened, like going to a second bar with me, some place with loud music and red walls, when I had never been in any such bar in my life? It was scary that someone could be so utterly lost to himself.

"It's okay, Douglas," I said. "Everything is going to be okay."

Up ahead, the road cut through the top of a hill, the verge rising up steeply on either side of us before descending again, down through a deep gorge, the land dropping away and fanning out at the bottom into a dusty white patchwork of fields, bisected by the Hudson River and the long concrete ribbon of I-87 south to New York.

chapter twenty-eight

IT WAS DUSK BY the time we got back to the city, the lights from the buildings starting to show up against the retreating blue of the sky. Emerging from the Holland Tunnel, I cut down through TriBeCa, the roads surprisingly empty, before turning up Broadway. The church sat in the middle of the block, on its own patch of land, surrounded by the impassive mirrored surfaces of the banks and brokerages, like a grandmother at a disco. Most people ignored it, filing past on their way to the subway station or bus stop. I pulled up outside, put the car into park. Douglas was asleep against the window, his head curled against his arm.

"Douglas, wake up."

I shook him gently.

"Hmm," he said, coming to. "Where are we?"

"We're back in the city."

"We are? How long have I been out?"

"The last hour or so."

He sat up in his seat, looked around. "Where are we?"

"There's a meeting here that starts at six o' clock. We've only just missed the beginning of it."

He looked up at the church, horrified.

"You've brought me to a *meeting*?"

I nodded.

"You're joking, of course."

"No, I'm not joking."

"I want to get back home and see my dog."

I squared off opposite him in the car. "Just do this one thing for me. Please. Then I will be on my way and you need never see me again. I really don't think that I am the person to sell your book, not after all that's happened. But I promised myself that the least I would do is get you back to a meeting. Will you do that for me? Please?"

"Take me home immediately," he said, crossing his arms.

"Douglas, please."

"I don't want to go to a fucking meeting, you little fucking idiot. I want to go home."

He tightened his arms.

I looked at him, sighed, unlocked my door, and began to get out.

"What are you doing?" he asked.

"Getting out. I've been driving for over two hours. I'm tired; I need a break. You can sit in the car or you can join me, but either way, this car is not moving anywhere."

He remained resolute. I got out of the car, stretched, shivered, and made my way through the gates. They creaked as I swung them open and clanged shut behind me. The grounds of the church were much bigger than they seemed at first glance: almost an acre of snowy parkland, with trees and gravestones and statues wearing little skull-caps of snow.

Approaching the entrance to the church, I heard the familiar sounds of a meeting under way—bursts of applause punctuated by laughter. It reminded me of a flock of birds, the sort you see switching back and forth in direction, seemingly on the turn of a dime, but all at exactly the same time, with not a single bird out of place. How did they do that? How did they know? I was just beginning to get cold when I heard the gate creak and turned, to see Kelsey striding up the path toward me. He made no acknowledgment of my presence, just swept past with a curt "Fuck you" and disappeared inside.

For a while I just stood there, too cold to feel much of anything. Now what was I supposed to do? Wait in the car for his lordship? Drive home? How did "Fuck you" communicate any kind of recognizable plan, let alone one I could sign off on? I pushed inside the big oak doors and was enveloped with warm air. It smelled of candle wax and old books, like just about any other church I had ever been in. This one was large, with a big vaulted sky blue ceiling, two aisles running on either side of a central nave, which ended with a circular stained-glass window. Everyone was sitting in the front three or four rows of pews; at the front, a woman with long gray hair was talking into a mounted microphone, in a heavy French accent, about an attempt she had once made to throw herself from the roof of her apartment building. She hadn't thrown herself from her building, in the end. She was too worried she wouldn't finish the job. "Knowing my luck, all I would do is break a leg and then I would 'ave to lie there wiz my broken leg until my 'usband come 'ome," she said, her voice echoing around the church, amplified by a tinny PA system. "And then I would 'ave to explain what I was doing there. On zer floor. Wiz a broken leg. Which I did not want to do at all, no, no, no, so I did not jump. My 'igher power 'ad other plans for me. As you can see . . ."

Kelsey was sitting in the back row of seats, next to one of the big stone pillars. I went to the end of his row and tapped the pew to get his attention. He turned and saw me, his face dropping. *"Why are you here?"* he hissed.

"To tell you I'll wait in the car," I whispered.

"Just go home."

"How are you going to get home?"

Two old ladies in the pew in front turned and glared at him; he beckoned for me to come closer. A round of applause swept the church and an amplified male voice boomed out, "Any more day counters?" The air filled with hands as I reached Kelsey.

"How are you going to get home?" I whispered.

"I'll catch the subway."

"Are you sure?"

"Yes, I'm sure."

"I feel bad about leaving you."

"Just go."

"Only if you're sure."

"Yes, I'm fucking sure."

"Okay, okay," I said, standing up again as the Frenchwoman at the front pointed to the next speaker. Everyone's hands descended. I turned to make my way back along the pew, only to find everyone in the pew in front all turned to face me. "Sorry," I said, as if I was at the cinema, making my way past everybody's knees. "Sorry. . . ."

"Yes, you, at the back!" said the Frenchwoman. "The young man in the corduroy jacket!"

I froze, looked up, found myself looking out over a sea of faces.

"Me?" I said, my hand going to my chest.

"Yes, you!" called the Frenchwoman.

"No, no, not me, I was just going."

"Can't hear you!" someone shouted from the front.

"Can you speak up?" called out someone else.

"I said I was just going," I called back. "You don't want to hear from me. I was just . . ."

"Someone pass him the microphone!"

"No, you needn't—"

But it was too late. The microphone was being handed from person to person, hand to hand, head over head, toward me. The entire congregation had swung my way, a sea of bright, eager faces, beaming and nodding their encouragement, all except Kelsey, who had shrunk into his seat, his head cradled in his hands. Finally, the mike was handed to me by a florid-faced guy with curly red hair.

"Thank you, but I don't need this," I said into the mike. "I was just going. I'm not supposed to—"

"Turn it on!" shouted someone.

The guy took the mike back, flipped the on switch, and handed it back to me with a firm nod. This time, my voice echoed throughout the church, like the great and powerful Oz.

"I don't need the mike. I was just going. I'm not here for—"

"Name!" called someone.

"I'm sorry?"

"What's your name?"

"My name? It's Patrick."

"Hello, Patrick," boomed the whole church as one. It was quite a sound. It hit you somewhere between your chest and the nape of your neck. What last vestige of resistance I had dissolved and fell away. I took a deep breath and started again.

"I'm not an alcoholic although I don't expect any of you to believe that. I don't expect anyone to believe anything I say. If you had told me a few months ago that I would get up to half the stuff I've done, I wouldn't have believed you. I've shocked even myself. I always thought of myself as a pretty nice guy."

A round of laughter swept through the church.

"I'm not saying I'm Gandhi. I just mean I had a basic sense of right and wrong. Compared to some of the guys I work with, I have certain standards."

More laughter, softer this time.

"That's how it always starts, I guess. The absolute certainty that you can do no wrong. I suppose you're right. That's how I've always looked on it, I guess. Wrong is what other people do. I mean, I knew what I was doing wasn't especially good, but I felt it was for a good cause. Literature. Books. A great man's career. The way I saw it was that you people were holding him back, trapping him in virtuous poverty. He didn't need a higher power. He needed a better agent."

More laughter.

"But it had nothing to do with him. Lola was absolutely right: It had nothing to do with him and everything to do with me. It wasn't his career that needed saving; it was mine, so much so that I was willing to put his life at risk—"

Down to my left, I saw Douglas shake his head.

"No, Douglas. It's true. I cared more about closing this deal than I did about you or your bloody book! And forget your health. That didn't even come into it. Don't you see? She tried to tell me all this, she tried to warn me, and I ignored her because I was angry with her. Because I was heartbroken."

I snorted derisively.

"I can barely believe she was even willing to talk to me. After what I did. I mean, even I knew that lying in AA meetings was pretty low. I feel truly poisonous. I really do. I feel like *I'm* the bloody disease."

The church giggled. One of the old ladies in front leaned over to her neighbor. "What did he say?"

"I think he said *he* was the disease of alcoholism," replied her neighbor.

She thought about it. "Well, it's nice to put a face to the name."

About halfway down the nave, next to the aisle, I saw a familiar dark curtain of hair shaking gently. A tight fist clenched and unclenched in my chest.

"I'm sorry for interrupting your meeting," I said. "I'm going to go now. Thanks for listening."

I shoved the microphone back to the guy with the curly hair, turned, and almost ran toward the exit as the church broke into loud, rapturous applause. *Please don't let it be her. Please God don't let it be her.* Reaching the big oak door, I closed it behind me with a clunk and set out toward the car, pulling in lungfuls of cold air that did nothing to ease my burning face. It was dark now, the trees and gravestones dark charcoal masses against the bluish snow. I was almost at the gates when I heard her. The moment I heard the voice, I knew who it was.

"Hey! Wait up!"

I slowed to a halt next to one of the tombstones, resting my hand on it as I heard her steps coming up behind me.

"Patrick," she said.

I turned, and there she was, Wellington boots planted in the snow, her hands on her knees, catching her breath. *"Whoo,"* she said. "You were moving *fast*. . . ."

"I'm sorry, I . . ."

"Great share," she said.

"I had no idea you were there."

"Oh, *otherwise* it was okay?"

"No, of course not."

"I was sitting at home, going, Should I go to the meeting or should I stay home and watch TV? It was cold out. I wanted to stay home, but you know what? I came. The meeting was a little boring. I was like, Maybe I should have stayed home after all, and then up you popped, sharing from the back!"

"I was trying to offer Douglas a lift home."

"And you just thought you'd share your thoughts with three hundred people while you were at it?"

"There were never three hundred people in there."

"Two hundred and fifty."

"Christ."

"How do you feel?"

I inhaled and exhaled, slowly. "A little sick."

"You've got share shame. It happens. You spill your guts in front of two hundred and fifty people, you're going to feel a little vulnerable."

"I had no idea it would feel so . . . *awful*."

She laughed, then wiped the smile from her face.

"You didn't have anything to do with what happened. You know that, right?"

"I took him to a bar, Lola. I watched him get drunk."

She shook her head. "It doesn't work like that. I know a guy who picked up a drink because his wife had a hard labor. You see? There's no logic to it. Douglas was in trouble long before you came on the scene."

"What do you mean?"

"He was coming to about one meeting a week, never getting his hand up, and when he did, it was always very dark, angry stuff. He was not a happy camper. That's why I was so eager to push you on him, I thought, Great, a sponsee. Just what he needs."

"Right. Instead of which, he got me."

"It's not all about you, Patrick," she said, her impatience showing. "You're just not that powerful, I'm afraid. If Douglas got it into his head to drink, there was not a single thing you could have said or done that would have made the slightest bit of difference."

"Do you want to know what the worst thing was? He was being so foul, I actually *wanted* him to drink."

"There you go. Where did you find him?"

"His old house in Woodstock."

"How did you know he'd be there?"

"I'm not really sure. I got lucky, I guess."

"Well, you did a good thing in getting him back. You know that, right?"

"Yeah, maybe. . . ."

Her face crumpled in sympathy. "God, you look so unhappy," she said, laying a hand on my arm. "I don't think I can bear it."

"I *am* unhappy, Lola—with myself, the way I acted. I can barely believe you're even talking to me."

"Oh, I'm a sucker for the rats."

She laughed, then saw my face. "I don't think you're a rat. I think you're a good guy. You just don't believe it. I wish you did."

I stared at her, incredulous. For a moment, we just stood there, our breath pooling between us, her hand on my arm.

"How did you get like this?" I asked her.

"Like what?"

"So nice."

"I'm not so nice. You'll find that out one day."

"So forgiving, then."

She looked me dead in the eye and said, "Because I know who you are."

"Well, do you think you could tell me?" I said, and laughed. "You know, it's funny. People have always said things like that to me. 'Be yourself.' 'Know yourself.' All that stuff. It always seemed to me that the only people who ever told you that had very nice selves to go away and be. Of course they'd say that. They're nice people. But what if you turned out to be an arsehole? What happens to them? Are they supposed to spend quality time with themselves and pour rose-scented baths for themselves, too?"

"You're not an asshole, Patrick."

"Then why have I been acting like one?"

"You'll figure it out."

I examined her face. I got the distinct impression she knew something more, something that she wasn't telling. I just didn't know how to go about getting it out of her. It was very strange.

Like I didn't even know what questions to ask, let alone what answer I might get. From the church came a distant round of applause.

"Lola, about what happened between us . . ."

"No," she said, pulling the lapels of my coat together and dusting them off. "You don't have to say anything. We're good."

"It doesn't feel that way."

She thought about it. "No, it doesn't, but nothing we can say this evening is going to change a thing. Will you promise me one thing, though, Patrick? Will you not delete my number?"

I frowned. "I wasn't going to."

"Good," she said, looking over her shoulder. "I'd better be getting back. You must be bushed."

"Yeah, I am."

She leaned over and kissed me on the cheek.

"Call me sometime," she said. "Let me know what's going on with you. And if I don't pick up, leave me a message, and I will call you back."

"Sure," I said, confused. I knew how phones worked. She wanted to give me a lesson?

She turned and walked away, and amazing as it might seem, I didn't call out, or run after her, or try to get her back. I did the right thing and walked back to the car. It didn't feel like the right thing to do at the time: My legs felt like they were made of cement. But it felt like the right thing when my face hit the pillow, one hour later, and I fell straight to sleep.

chapter twenty-nine

Leo didn't fire me—not immediately. Instead, he summoned me to his office for a long talk about industry ethics.

He didn't mention the expiration of my contract in April, or its renewal; he didn't need to; it was perfectly clear to me what was going to happen. I spent my days beneath a gathering storm-cloud of personal doom. Around the office, the story of what I had been up to spread quickly. The other agents divided up into two groups, those for whom what I had done seemed an amazing jape, and those for whom it remained just that little bit too strange to normalize with joshing camaraderie. I actually had more respect for this group. For one thing, I agreed with them: What I had done was not to be rewarded in any way. For another, at least they didn't put me through the agony of their conversation. I found all of it pretty unbearable, to be honest, and began to dread going into the office every morning. My fantasies about returning to England rose to an all-time high, and I sought out my English friends for a series of mopey conferences on what was to be done. In the second week of February, I even went to lunch with Ian Horrocks, who was in irrepressibly chirpy form: He'd started dating a girl he'd met at Saul's party. He'd rung her up to apologize for his behavior and ended up asking her out on a date. So he told me as he sat in the window of Salt, in SoHo, kitted out in a rust-colored roll-neck sweater, a jacket, and jeans: her doing.

"Finally managed to fool someone with the accent, then," I said.

"Actually, all it buys you is a few extra seconds of time. They look startled for a few extra seconds, and in that time, you can either get away with more bullshit than you ordinarily do or disappoint them. One of the two. Bullshit or disappointment."

"That sounds about right."

"You okay, mate?"

"What?"

"You seem a little down."

"Yeah, I guess."

"What's the matter?"

"I don't know," I said, picking up my menu as if it might offer me some clues. "Do you ever wonder whether coming to this city has changed you, Ian?"

"Changed me? How?"

"Have you found yourself doing things you wouldn't ordinarily do? Saying things you wouldn't ordinarily say? Feeling like you're letting yourself down?"

He thought about it. "My first year, I did feel something a bit like that. 'Kid in a candy store' syndrome. You know, it's America, isn't it? It's Disneyland. It's pretend. If you screw up, you can always go home."

"Right, right. That's it, isn't it? You have a fallback."

"Right, a safety net."

"So what happened?"

"I got into a fight with my landlord and he threw me out on

the street. For two weeks, I didn't have anywhere to live. I ended up on the couch of my editor at *Time Out* for two weeks while I found a place."

"You should have called me."

"Oh, this was before you got here. Long time ago. That seemed to settle the matter for me, somehow. This place was real, all right. It wasn't a dress rehearsal!" He laughed. "My shrink says I was testing the boundaries so I could stabilize myself."

"I didn't know you saw a shrink."

"Yeah. Twice a week. When in Rome."

"When in Rome," I said distantly.

"You're not thinking of going back, are you?"

"I have been toying with the idea, yes, actually."

"No."

He put his menu down. I had broached the most guarded taboo among English immigrants in New York. We were like birds: We had to do everything together; the thought of one breaking away from the flock was unbearable. It was like saying you had been thinking about suicide. You didn't voice such thoughts.

"Things don't seem to be going very well for me here, Ian, to tell the truth. My contract's up in April and I don't think Leo is going to renew it."

"What are you talking about? Why not?"

"I've been fucking up quite royally recently."

"But you can't throw in the towel. Not after one year."

"It's better than struggling on, prolonging the agony. Some people just aren't meant to be here. Maybe I'm just one of those people. . . ."

At which point, the waiter arrived to take our orders. Ian ordered steak frites. I ordered some red snapper and green beans. The waiter scribbled it all down, then said, "And would you care for some wine with your meal?"

"I will if you will," said Ian.

"Do we have to?" I asked, suddenly pained.

"We don't *have* to. . . . Do you *want* to?"

"I don't know," I said, my stomach roiling. "God, why does it always have to come down to this?"

"Down to what?"

"Drinking. Can't we go one day without it?"

"Of course we can. I was just . . ."

"I just think it's kind of pathetic that we have to drink every time we go out," I said, angry now. "Can't we just leave it alone this once?"

"I already said we could."

"Okay, thank you."

"Diet Coke for me."

"And for me, too."

The waiter wrote it down, but he still hovered, as if waiting to see if we would change our mind. I stared at him.

"The menu," he said, holding out his hand.

"Oh. Right," I said, handing it back to him. "Sorry."

I watched as he returned to the open-top counter. He placed the menus in their holder and shouted out our orders to the chef. When I turned back to Ian, I found him replacing a green folder inside his duffel bag.

"What's that?"

"It's just that proposal I was talking about, but if you're going back to London . . ."

"Let me have a look at that."

"I don't want an agent who's in London."

"I wasn't serious. Give it to me."

I motioned with my fingers until he reached down and brought up a green folder containing thirty or so pages of foolscap, neatly bound, the title page bearing the words *Talk to the Hand: A Short But Rapturous History of Applause,* and underneath that, "A proposal by Ian Horrocks." For some reason, I felt a sting of tears. "I did not know that," I said, leafing through it. "They clap and boo at the same time in Germany, do they?"

"Italy, too."

"This looks very interesting, very interesting indeed."

The waiter arrived with our Diet Cokes. "Actually, you know what, I think I will have that glass of wine after all? A glass of Pinot Grigio, please."

"Me, too."

"Why not make it a bottle?"

"Coming right up."

That evening, I went out with Saul and Natalie. Saul had just sold his optimism book to HarperCollins; seven o'clock found the three of us bouncing around in the back of a cab en route to some bar on the Lower East Side he had just discovered over the weekend. They did most of the talking. I gazed out the window at the city streaking past: the passing lights of a bodega, apartment blocks, the lights of a movie shoot on the corner of Sixth Avenue and Bleecker, the silver trailers all lined up in a row. My thoughts slipped back to Lola, the church, what she had told me. It made no sense to me how she could be so warm. Why did I get the impression she was hiding something from me? And what had that business been about the phones? Nothing added up. My insides felt knotted.

The taxi driver was gunning it, slaloming from lane to lane as he tried to make each intersection before the light turned red; with each intersection, we shaved it ever closer; each time I imagined the cross-traffic ploughing into the side of the cab, my door buckling upon impact.

"He's very quiet."

"I don't think we should ask him."

"Hey, Patrick," said Saul. "Are you with us?"

"I'm sorry . . . What?"

"Wow, you were really far gone," said Natalie.

"We were just taking bets on what had you staring out the window."

"Oh, nothing. I was just . . . spacing out."

"Was it her?" asked Natalie. "What was her name again, Saul?"

"Lola."

"Was it Lola?"

I looked back out the window again. A couple of actors stood bathed in lights, surrounded by technicians, makeup artists, microphones, cameras, booms—and then they were gone.

The taxi driver really was going too fast. He was talking on the phone now; it really was unconscionable. I began to rehearse what I would say to him when I tapped on Plexiglas and asked him to slow down.

"I told you," said Natalie quietly. "I told you it was her."

"He saw her the other day," said Saul. "They ran into each other at some church."

"A church?"

"That's where they have the meetings. In churches."

"I can hear you, you know," I snapped. "I am in this cab with you."

"You could have fooled us," said Saul.

"I'm perfectly happy to talk about it, but there's nothing to talk about, is there? I fucked everything up by lying to her. She ended it. End of story."

"I thought you said she told you to call her."

"She did, but . . . you have no idea how important the truth is to her, Saul. Or how poisonous a lie. It goes against everything she stands for."

"I thought you said they had no rules in there."

"The fact that there are no rules against something doesn't mean it's not bad to do it. There are no rules against flying planes into buildings, either, but that's not really encouraged."

"Oh, so now you're as bad as a terrorist."

"I'm just saying that the fact something doesn't have a rule against it doesn't mean it's a good thing. The opposite. It's a sign that something is so bad, nobody has even thought to come up with a rule against it. It's like that physicist guy said to one of his students—what was his name?"

"What physicist guy?"

"Hang on . . ."

"Einstein."

"No."

"Heisenberg."

"No. Oh God, this is really going to annoy me."

"Bohr? Pauli?"

"That's it! Wolfgang Pauli! That thing he said to one of his students. 'Your theory is so off, it isn't even wrong.' That's what I did. Something so off, it isn't even wrong."

We hit a pothole and were bumped out of our seats into the air. "We're going too fast," I muttered. "Don't you think we're going too fast?" I asked louder. I raised my hand to tap on the Plexiglas. "Excuse me, sir, but I think you're going too fast. . . ."

At which point we screeched to a halt outside the bar—an industrial-looking single-story building, sandwiched between a bodega and a bowling alley, with a hooded awning bearing the words GROCERY and FAST DELIVERY, FAST BEER. It looked more like a superexclusive warehouse and seemed weirdly familiar to me, which was nonsense of course—we never drank in the Lower East Side. Inside, it was hot and noisy, and I found myself almost instantly wanting to be home, but I followed obligingly as Saul pushed through to the bar, inset with small daisy chains of disco lights, packed with a downtown crowd sipping low-calorie beer. He found a place and parked his elbow, a twenty between his fingers. Natalie turned away in embarrassment.

"Please don't do that, Saul," she said.

"Do what?"

"Wave money at the bar."

"It's to get his attention," he said, wiggling the bill at the bartender. She turned to me, pulling her cardigan around her, nuzzling my side.

"Make him stop, Patrick."

"Don't pay him any attention," I said. "Then he'll stop."

"Okay."

On the opposite side of the room, a low corridor led through into another, smaller room painted a deep bloodred. I had been here before. But that was impossible. I hadn't known it even existed until Saul brought me here. But I had been here before. I knew it. Sensing something in me stiffen, Natalie came away from my side. "What's the matter?"

"Nothing," I said, my heart going like a jackhammer.

Inside the room were a series of small cuboid leather stools, on which people were perched uncomfortably. I had sat on one of those stools. I could remember how easy it was to slide off. I had been very drunk. At one point, Douglas and I had leaned in together, propping each other up. I had been here with Douglas. The night of the fight. We had come here afterward. It had been my idea. I'd heard the music and brought us in. We'd sat in that room, and drunk some more. At one point, Douglas had cried, upset over what we were both doing. I told him to pull himself together and ordered more drinks. He wanted to go back to Woodstock, he said. Was he serious? Yes, he was serious. He wanted to go back to his house in Woodstock, where he'd last been happy. With his wife and her dog in Woodstock. Wasn't it a little far? Probably. I was probably right. Did I want to get another round of drinks? Yes, I did. It had been almost dawn when we left. The birds were singing and the sky was a treacherous blue.

That's how I'd known he was going to Woodstock.

He'd told me himself.

"What are you having, Patrick?" called Saul from the bar.

chapter thirty

I WOKE UP THE next day feeling as if someone had irradiated my internal organs. My heart, my liver, and my kidneys all felt like they were glowing. I dry-heaved over the toilet for a little while, clutching the bowl like an old friend, then cracked open a Coke from the fridge, downed it, and went back to bed, where I phoned in sick. I didn't have to say much to Natalie: She'd seen the state I was in the night before; the two of them had dropped me off in a taxi. I fell asleep, and dreamed about a man trapped in the trunk of a car, and awoke at just after one with a dry mouth and rumbling stomach. I pulled on some clothes and went to forage for food at McDonald's. I downed an Egg McMuffin and some fries and decided to go for a walk. I needed to get some thinking done, and I always did my best thinking while I was walking.

It was a bright, blustery day, the kind that sends loose garbage skittering down the streets—the outer edge of a hurricane currently parked one hundred miles off the coast. I followed West Tenth Street out to the West Side Highway and crossed the eight lanes of traffic to the waterfront, where briny water lapped at the piers, the moorings like teeth stumps, while gulls circled overhead. In the distance, the matchstick figure of the Statue of Liberty, always smaller than you imagined her. Coming here had been a mistake—that much was clear to me. I was only supposed to have come out here on a work placement. I was never meant to have stayed. I wasn't cut out for it. I felt like a soft-shelled crab scuttling around to avoid people's feet. My efforts to make up for that missing layer had only resulted in behavior that was so unlike me that I didn't recognize myself. Getting into that fight. Getting drunk with Kelsey. Getting so drunk that I couldn't remember the rest of the evening. None of that would have ever happened in London. I needed to go back there or worse things would happen to me. I knew it. I could hear them coming around the pike. I could feel the rumble.

I reached Chelsea Piers, decided to press on north, alongside the High Line, the stretch of overhead railway they were busy turning into a public park; you could just see the tops of the tractors and backhoes. I thought of calling Ian's shrink. He might be able to help. Maybe it wasn't as bad as I thought. "Mr. Miller," he would say, polishing his spectacles, after listening to me chatter on for thirty or forty minutes. "I don't normally say this to patients, since I obviously stand to lose money by doing so, but there's nothing very much wrong with you that a change of pace and a little more exercise won't solve. Do you have any hobbies? I would suggest you widen the net of your interests a little." Maybe I could join a church choir. There were plenty of them around. I'd once sung in one as a boy, a plaintive soprano piping up from the back at our local church in Falmouth. That was what my existence lacked—friends, fellowship, roots, something to break the bonds of my appalling selfishness. Maybe I could volunteer for a soup kitchen, or become a big brother to one of those inner-city kids who needed someone to teach him Shakespeare.

I had always wanted a younger brother. A small black brother from Brooklyn, whom I could take to museums and art galleries and teach not to be afraid of Shakespeare. Gradually, his grades would pull up and his teacher would call me into the school to speak to the whole class. "Who dat?" they would jeer. "That's my big brother," little Jamal would say proudly, for that would be his name: Jamal. "He's from London, Ingerlund." The way they said it here: *Ingerlund*.

This struck me as such a good idea that I immediately turned around and headed back to my apartment, where I typed the words "Big Brother," "Sponsorship," and "New York" into Google, and read the following.

> Right now, our need is for volunteers willing to mentor *pregnant and parenting girls; children born or with parents born outside the U.S.* (particularly China) who are struggling with bias or adjusting to their new lives in NYC; *children with disabilities or chronic illnesses; children who lost a close relative on 9/11;* and *youth who are at risk* simply because their parents or siblings are in jail, or because they made some poor choices, got involved with the wrong crowd, or were in the wrong place at the wrong time, succumbing to negative influences in the absence of positive role models to guide them.

Pregnant? *China?* I didn't want a pregnant Chinese kid. I wanted a black brother from Brooklyn, whom I could take to museums and art galleries and teach not to be afraid of Shakespeare. Upon further examination, it transpired that they meant something funny by "inner city," too. They didn't mean Brooklyn; they meant Queens and the Bronx. That was an hour's subway ride at the least, two hours to get there and get back. How was that "inner"? Did the subway even go out that far? Not only that but you had to sit through an interview. I knew how that would go.

"Mr. Miller, we see from our records that you suffer from blackouts."

"Black*out*. Just the one."

"That's not what it says here."

I would lean forward, trying to get a glimpse of their notes. "Why . . . what do you . . ."

"It says here that you lost your job in London because you mislaid a manuscript while drunk."

"Yes, but that wasn't technically a blackout. Eventually I remembered what happened."

"Which was?"

"Look. I went out to celebrate. You've heard of Richard Blomkamp, I assume. He's a very important South African writer. He writes about postapartheid South Africa. I say that because. . . . Never mind. His manuscript came in. I went out to celebrate. Woke up the next morning and the manuscript was gone."

"Gone?"

"Yes. Somewhere between the Groucho, where I had it in my bag, and the cab ride home, it disappeared."

"You don't remember."

"Ah. But that's the thing. I did remember. I can remember lots. Flicking peanuts at the Damien Hirst painting. Ordering more drinks. The taxi rank. I can remember it all. I just can't remember what happened to the manuscript."

"Does this happen to you a lot?"

"What?"

"These blackouts."

"Blackout. Singular."

"What about doing Borat impressions at Leo's birthday party. You don't remember that, either."

I tried again to get a look at those notes. "That was just, that was just, uh—"

"And drunk-dialing Caitlin the night before you made the

amends. You don't remember that either, do you? That's three blackouts in the last three months. The period *you* say you were sober."

"This is ridiculous," I would say, getting up. "I've never been so insulted in all my life. Call yourself a charity for children? And you keep these kinds of records on people? It's an assault on my civil rights is what it is. It's disgusting what they let you get up to in here, absolutely disgusting."

And then I would storm out, pretty confident that they were not about to put me in charge of a six-year-old.

When I next looked up, it was almost dark outside, the city all lit up like a giant supercomputer in one of those movies where computers were represented by a thousand points of light, with each apartment and office representing a single point, a single cell, not sentient in its own right, but relaying small jolts of electricity that, when linked up, formed a single thought or picture. I don't really remember deciding to go to the liquor store. I just came to and there it was, the bottles stacked in the window, the window gated with cast-iron mesh, the bottles lit invitingly from below. When had I decided to come here? The door gave a tinkle as I entered, and the store owner, a middle-aged Indian guy with round cheeks, kindly eyes, and a graying beard, came up from under the counter.

"How have you been, sir?"

"Good, thank you, Deepash."

"I haven't seen you in a while."

"I know, I've been on a health kick."

"I'm sorry to hear that, sir."

"That's very funny, Deepash. You're getting very good at this."

"I try. So, what'll it be this evening?"

I left the store a few minutes later, grateful for the cardboard strips Deepash always inserted between the bottles so they wouldn't clink when you walked—an almost British level of tact about the small shames and embarrassments that make up an average day. I added it to my list of ways in which Britain and the United States sometimes swap reputations. We abolished slavery first. Their *Times* is the paper of record. We invented reality television. Their chocolate tastes lousy. By the time I had gotten back to my apartment building, I had decided that it probably didn't matter where I lived. What was I worrying about? Wherever I chose would be fine. Everything was going to be okay. Hearing the lock click behind me, it struck me as the most beautiful sound I had ever heard.

chapter thirty-one

THE NEXT DAY, I called in sick again. The day after that, it was the weekend. And by the time Monday came around, I wasn't feeling all that great about returning to the office, so I called Leo and asked him for some of the holiday time I was due before my contract was up. Did he realize what I was doing? He may have. I was beyond caring by that point. I knew I was finished at the agency. I went on a lot of walks that week—to clear my head in the mornings but also to figure out what my next move should be. I became intimately acquainted with the city's statuary. I walked the length of the West Side Highway, up as far as Riverside Drive and the Soldiers' and Sailors' Monument at Riverside and Eighty-ninth Street. I walked the length and breadth of Central Park, where I stood spellbound by the statue of the angel spreading her wings, *The Angel of the Waters,* at Bethesda Terrace, and also the sculpture commemorating the sled dog Balto, who led the team of twenty dogs that delivered an antitoxin to the inhabitants of Nome, Alaksa, to save them from a diptheria epidemic. I found myself in Madison Square, where a statue commemorated a congressman, Roscoe Conkling, who had frozen to death while walking in a blizzard. At first my routes were entirely random, but gradually, certain preferred routes began to emerge by a process of evolution, like gulleys forming in mud. A long, wide loop that took me all the way up to Madison Square and then back down Broadway and through Washington Square to the West Village proved an enduring favorite. I'm not sure what it was about this particular route that drew me in. It certainly had little to do with that final pass through Washington Square, past the stone lions and the copper plaque to one side, which read GRADUATE SCHOOL OF ARTS AND SCIENCES. It was the only awkward part of the whole walk. The thought of running into one of those people gave me the shivers. I would sometimes see them coming out of their meetings, talking and laughing, and I would curse them, once audibly enough to catch the attention of a woman walking in the opposite direction. I took to walking past the building, belligerently, making no effort to hide, almost wanting to run into one of them, just to see what would happen. One day, I turned the corner, and there at the bottom of the steps was Lola, wearing that same herringbone-check coat she had been wearing when we first met. She had her back to me, talking to a friend. I was feeling particularly hungover that day, and the shot of adrenaline she sent through my system made my temples feel like they were going to explode. I froze, about twenty yards distant, then crossed the street to the park, flipping up the lapels of my raincoat as I passed them. I was almost clear when I heard her call my name. I kept walking. She called it again, louder this time, but I ignored her, kept my head down, and carried on until I hit Sixth Avenue. I didn't stop until I reached my apartment, and when I finally got the door closed behind me, I noticed the red light flashing on my phone. I had been ignoring messages from Saul all week, but eventually it wore me down and I played the message.

"Hi, Patrick. It's Lola. I think I saw you today. I called you, but you didn't stop. Maybe it wasn't you. I really want to know how you're doing. . . . Look, I could be way off here—in which case, my apologies—but I'm guessing you're not having too good a time of it right now. I want you to know that it doesn't need be like this. There's no need for you to be in this much pain. I know it's probably very difficult to imagine anything other than the way things are right now but it's not like that, I promise you. Things can be different. They don't have to be like this. . . . Anyway, this is one long-ass message. I should probably stop. I just . . . I'd like to hear your voice. Call me and let me know how you are. Or just call me and say nothing. I don't care. Just call me. I—"

There she broke off.

What does she want from me? I thought angrily, wiping the tears from my face. Why is she torturing me? Why *leave* a message like that, for God's sake, if not to torture me? She was only interested in signing me up for her wretched cult, to sit in rooms and hold hands and say prayers for the rest of my life. It wasn't even about helping people; it was just about recruiting them. They filled your head with garbage, and the last bit of garbage they put into your head was an instruction to repeat it all to the next person you could lay your hands on, and so endlessly on. "You're a wonderful guy, Patrick, you just don't see it." She had never been interested in me. She was simply trying to lure me back. I played the tape again to see if I could hear a crack in the mask. She kept it up really well, injecting just the right note of concern into her voice, even seeming to fight back tears at the end. Oh, she was good. She'd done this before. They'd probably lured in many men this way. She was a front, a cover, a shill. The alternative—that she meant what she said, that she and everything she stood for represented my last shot at happiness—was too dreadful to contemplate. That evening I got hammered. I knocked down one bottle of wine, then another, only this time it didn't work. I felt a little hazy around the edges but my thoughts had a stone-cold clarity: Still I could see her face outside the church, imploring me to stay and be safe with her. "I know who you are." I paced the apartment, my panic rising, before heading out to buy a third bottle, with which I finally managed to eke out a small corner of oblivion, unbothered by thoughts of Lola or the message she had left or how swiftly she had moved into position and destroyed my life.

chapter thirty-two

A ROOM. THAT'S HOW the stories always ended. A man in a room, doing things to himself that he does not want to do. Outside the room, life goes on as normal. Mothers push prams. Street vendors sell hot dogs. Delivery bikes weave in and out of the pedestrians. But inside, everything is quiet and still and dark. The blinds are drawn, and if that is not enough, then towels are tacked up at the windows to keep out the light. Household objects—lamps, taps, sinks, fridges—seethe with silent reproach. They know that it was not always this way. When the story began, it was full of people and light and color and movement. There were families and wives and boyfriends and brothers and sisters. But gradually, over a period of time, by a process of attenuation so subtle that you don't even notice it happening, all that falls away like flesh from the bone. "Do you ever see those canvases Rothko did before he killed himself?" Kelsey once asked me in one of our late-night conversations. "He completed a series of black canvases. Small and smaller, darker and darker, until finally he ended up with just a small black cube. Three days later, he slit his wrists. It always makes me laugh when you hear critics talking about his 'appreciation of negative space.' Our lives start out as Renoirs and then end up Rothkos."

Was I honestly comparing myself to Douglas Kelsey? Every time I thought of what he had been through—the loss of his house, home, wife, career, until he was left baying at the moon—I winced at the comparison. What did I have? Three blackouts, plus a week of solitary binges—a pathetic attempt to induce a bottom that never quite arrived, a half-baked experiment, designed to lessen the burden of my guilt, because I simply could not face the damage I had done. I could try to go back to those people, like a bank robber returning to the scene of the crime. "Okay, Patrick. Uh. Thanks for sharing," they would say. "But here's the thing. There's alcoholism. And then there's what you've been doing. And I'm not sure quite what it is you've been doing, but . . . do you think you could do it someplace else?" I wasn't even get getting fucked-up right. I'd even fucked *that* up. That's how much of a fuckup I was.

I woke up one morning in the second week of my impromptu sabbatical and something seemed different. My head was not so bad that morning; the light coming in through the window was just that little bit less painful. I actually felt good about myself. My experiment seemed to have yielded a result. Either I could summon the decency to develop a proper drinking habit or I could stop my whining, snap out of it, and go back to work. I looked around my apartment, got out a bucket, a mop, bleach, soap, and sponges, and set about whipping the whole thing into shape. Whoever had been sneaking into my apartment and messing it up had been extra busy of late. My toilet, in particular, was a disgrace, lined with a stange fur the color of rust. I was halfway through cleaning it—it came away quite easily, like lichen—when the buzzer sounded.

I actually jumped, it had been so long since an outside sound had entered my apartment. I stopped what I was doing and listened.

BZZZZZR.

I got up from my hands and knees, dusted myself down, walked over to the buzzer, and peered at it.

BZZZZZR.

I picked up the handset.

"Hello?"

"Patrick?"

"This is he."

"Patrick . . . It's Caitlin."

I ran my hand through my hair.

"Caitlin! Good Lord, wow. . . . How are you?"

"Can I come up?"

"Up here?"

"I need to talk to you."

"Of course, uh, give me a minute," I said, buzzing her in, then racing around the apartment, trying to get it looking vaguely habitable. In what seemed like no time at all, there was a knock on the door. Should I change? I wondered, too late. Pulling my shirt down over my boxers, I opened the door. There she was, looking like a million dollars—neat, glossy, polished, her nails an immaculate maroon. "Hi," she said.

"Please," I said, opening the door. "Come in."

The door jammed on some mail. I kicked it free and she stepped into my apartment, looking warily around her. I felt suddenly mortified by the mess.

"Can I get you anything? Tea? Coke?"

"I'd love some water."

"Some water."

I opened the fridge, which was empty but for a few Cokes and a hardened block of Parmesan cheese. "I appear to be out of bottles," I called out. "Do you mind tap?"

"Tap's fine."

I came back from the kitchen with two glasses of water, to find her perched on the sofa, still in her coat, as if she might catch something.

I took the chair opposite her and took a sip of my water, which tasted warm and stagnant. "Sorry about the water," I said. "It's nothing to do with me. It's the chemicals they put in it to keep it clean."

"Patrick."

"Hmm?"

"Why aren't you at work?"

"Work? Oh, I'm on a sabbatical."

"A sabbatical."

"Yes, a sabbatical. I had a lot of holiday time owed to me, so I thought rather than waste it, I should just take it. Even if I'm not going anywhere."

"Why?"

"Why? Because . . . I . . . well, actually, I needed to do some thinking."

"Some thinking."

Why did everything sound so strange when she said it back to me? "Yes, some thinking. I needed to do some thinking about work. It hadn't been going so well for me at the agency lately, Caitlin. In fact, I'd been fucking up royally. I doubt very much that Leo is going to renew my contract in April. So I need to plan my next move."

She looked stricken. "Why do you think that?"

"Because it's true! They're going to fire me!"

"No, Patrick. They're not going to fire you. They're all very worried about you."

"Worried about me? Why?"

"How's your grandmother?"

"My grandmother? What's she got to do with anything?"

"Leo said you were going back to the UK to see your grandmother before she died. She was sick with something."

I stopped.

"Are you okay?" asked Caitlin.

"Yes, I'm fine," I said, cradling my forehead. It felt warm and prickly. I was beginning to feel very strange. "Look, the long and the short of it is that there's nothing wrong with my grandmother but Leo is unlikely to renew my contract, so I'd better be looking for a new job sometime soon. You know how quickly things move here. I lose the job, then bang goes the visa, and once the visa goes, I'm out on the street and I'm no longer legal. And once I'm no longer legal, then things start to get ugly very fast. Very fast . . ."

"Patrick."

"I want to go back to London."

"Patrick—"

"Things haven't gone well for me since I left, really. In fact that's almost exactly when things started going wrong for me."

"Patrick, stop."

"Stop what?"

"The same thing happened to you in London, didn't it."

It wasn't a question.

"I'm not sure I—"

"The same thing happened to you in London."

"No, it wasn't the same at all, not in the—"

"Stop, Patrick."

"I—"

"Just stop. I want you to stop."

And then I stopped.

I was breathing extremely fast and extremely shallowly, like a family dog I had once taken to the vet. The heat I was feeling in my face seemed to have spread to my chest and was funneling out through my arms and legs. It was a little like the feeling I had felt running up my spine at the church, but this time, it had run on, reaching every extremity. Touching my forefinger and thumb together, I found them to be piping hot. Had they always been that way, or was I just noticing it for the first time? My apartment was a mess, every available surface crammed with bottles and take-out cartons, a warm, close smell in the air, like the overrecycled air in a plane. I looked up at Caitlin. Her eyes were brimming with tears.

"I appear to have let things get away from me a bit," I said, and laughed.

She actually winced.

I hung my head. "I've been lying to you, Caitlin," I said. "I've been lying to everybody."

chapter thirty-three

"He can't win."

"You don't think?"

"He'll get the nomination, but the Republicans will make mincemeat of him. Once they get ahold of that pastor of his. Men like that don't get to be president, Patrick, and it's probably just as well."

Kelsey pointed to the newspaper on the table, which showed a picture of the president cantering on the White House lawn. "Did you see this? Even *he* can't wait for it to be over. I'm not seeing much in the way of peacekeeping missions for this one."

He shucked another oyster and swallowed it whole, the arterial vein in his neck standing to proud attention. I felt sick, hungover. It had been three weeks since Caitlin's visit to my apartment and my promise that I would start going to meetings again. I'd fully meant to the first day I arrived back at work, but my desk had been so piled high with unopened mail and manuscripts that my plan went immediately out the window. It didn't have to be done the first day I got back to work, did it? It didn't happen the second day, either, because by then I had the precedent of the first day to work with: I hadn't drunk anything at lunchtime, I'd had only a few glasses of wine after work, and I felt fine in the morning. Maybe I was in the clear again. There was no need to overreact. By day three, I was absolutely convinced the whole thing had been a complete aberration, a mirage, the result of stress and the move and God knows what else. Of course you're going to drink if you take two weeks off work and give yourself no structure for your day. By the end of the week, I was back to normal—or not quite normal, because I had Caitlin to deal with. Eventually I had no choice but to lie to her and tell her that, yes, I had started attending meetings again, and had put together five days of sobriety. Was she happy now? Yes, she was. Very much so. Very happy. And so a double life of sorts started up again, with me getting drunk every night while pretending to Caitlin that I was as dry as a bone. I hated her for it: for making me lie like that. I couldn't drink now without feeling lousy almost instantly, which meant I had to drink more to stop feeling lousy. My spell in recovery had had, I realized, the exact opposite effect to the one it was supposed to. It was like the Catholic Church: They filled your head with such interminable guilt that you had to drink more, not less, just to silence the voices. If anything proved that I was simply an average Joe who had accidentally wandered into a minefield, it was this. Normal alcoholics drank less when they went into recovery, not more. Plus, there was the very fact that I was asking myself these questions all the time. Wasn't I supposed to be in denial? I was in the opposite of denial: I was in wretched, neon-lit twenty-four-hour superawareness. Then one day, inevitably, Caitlin came into the office. I had just been out to lunch with one of my authors and had polished off the better part of a bottle of Valpolicella. I gave her a polite hug, my breath locked in my lungs, and then, as soon as it was over, sprang away from her. She spent the best part of the next hour attempting to get close to me, the two of us embarking in this absurd little dance around my office, until finally she cornered me by the window. She didn't even have to smell my breath. The moment she managed to look me in the eye, the whole thing fell apart. Game over.

"You sure you won't have one of these?" asked Kelsey, holding up an oyster.

"No, thank you," I said, my stomach churning.

"They're very good."

"I'm not that hungry."

He stopped, looked at me. "So what's on your mind, Patrick? I'm sure you didn't call me up to watch me eat lunch. If it's to apologize again for what happened, please don't bother. We're through with that."

"It's not that," I said. "That night when we went out drinking, after we got thrown out of that bar . . ."

"I thought you said we weren't going to talk about that."

"You said we went into a second bar and drank more there, but I couldn't remember it. Do you remember me saying that?"

"Yes, vaguely. It was a long time ago now, Patrick. . . ."

"But I can now. I can remember going to the second bar. It was my idea to go in there. I heard the music and suggested we go in."

He looked at me blankly.

"It was noisy and hot—a young crowd. You said you were old enough to be their father, do you remember?"

"Yes."

"And we found this little room, away from the main bar. The stools were difficult to sit on. We fell off a couple of times. We were both very drunk by that point. You were very upset about what we were doing, and I . . . I kept on buying drinks to calm you down. You told me about how much you missed your house in Woodstock. How you regretted ever having sold it. How you were happiest there and wanted to go back, do you remember?"

"It's completely untrue, by the way; I was miserable there. But go on. I still don't . . . Why are you telling me all this?"

"Because I remember now," I said quietly. "I remember, and I couldn't before."

"Your point being?"

My head felt like it was going to snap off my neck under the sheer weight of the shame it contained, and roll away into the corner of the restaurant to be used as a football by the waiters during their lunch break.

"It's not the first time that's happened to me. A blackout. I had one in London. I went out one night and lost a manuscript. I almost lost my job. Then the work placement came up and, well, I think we all saw it as an opportunity to save face. So I moved out here. A clean slate. I was determined things were going to be different. And they were for a while. I was in love with Caitlin and that was enough to keep me from drinking too much, and it was for a bit, but I was a complete nightmare to be around, I think. I was horrible to her. That's why she threw me out. She couldn't take it any longer. That's when I started to drink again. Not very much at first, but then the Christmas parties started in and I was doing it pretty much every night. And then I ran into you in Washington Square and I . . ."

I hung my head. For a while, neither of us said anything; then I felt his hand on the back of my head. "Sweet boy," he said. "I'm so sorry. . . ."

"It's gotten so much worse than it used to be. I mean, I was drinking in London, but at least it was with people. Now it's . . . It's so much worse."

"You made it angry."

"What did I do?"

"I would have thought that was obvious. You got sober. When

it came back at you, it had to come back with twice the force. What you have to imagine, Patrick, is a grand chess master with the instincts of a vandal. Just pure, hellacious chaos, thinking five moves ahead. It was sitting there taking notes. You made a move. It made a countermove. Checkmate."

He spread his hands as if to demonstrate that they held nothing: thin air.

"You're saying . . . that if I hadn't gone to meetings, I might have been able to carry on for a little longer."

"You can either quit the game early, while you still have a few pieces left on the board, or you can quit the game later, when you have none. Either way, you were in checkmate."

"I'm not sure I understand."

"It's okay," he said. "It's over."

After that, everything just fell into place. Kelsey asked if I wanted him to go with me to the meeting, but I said no, I wanted to go alone. Something about telling Kelsey seemed to have secured me to the Earth so I couldn't go flying off of it. It was a little like getting my first line out during the school play. You are terrified that you're going to freeze, forget your line, blurt out someone else's, faint, fart, anything but remember the goddamn line you've just spent the best part of four weeks trying to remember. But then by some miracle, you manage to get it out, and the kid playing Melchior says his line, and the kid playing Balthazar his, and you know what your line is after *that,* and soon there you are, performing the play. It was like that. I paid for lunch, left the restaurant, turned right up Broadway, left on West Fourth, and reached the southeasterly corner of Washington Square, the fountain in the center sending up spumes of water into the air, the trees in bloom, the triumphal arch in the distance, the beginnings of Fifth Avenue visible through its legs. The air felt warm on my skin, the exact temperature, it seemed, of the molecules inside my body. I felt almost boundaryless, my insides and outsides the same. The other people in the square paid me no attention. They had no idea of what I was about to do. They saw only a thin, slightly undernourished-looking Englishman in a corduroy jacket making his way past the fountain, underneath the legs of the triumphal arch, then stopping and looking for traffic. He looked right, then left, and crossed the road, turning right along the row of rust-colored brownstones on the north side of the square. He stopped in front of one of them, paused for second, then pushed through the gate and jogged up the steps to the door. It was buzzed open for him and he disappeared inside.

chapter thirty-four

I DIDN'T SEE ANYONE I knew at that first meeting, thank God. I just sat there and let the words wash over me. I can't remember anything the speaker said, just the steady march of blood around my head. It was the opposite of a blackout—a whiteout. Instead of feeling terrible afterward, I felt twenty pounds lighter. You know when you stand with your hands pressing against a doorway and then, stepping away from the door, feel your hands tugged up from your sides? That's the only way I can think to describe it. But I felt like this all over. I became aware of having borne a huge weight whose existence I wasn't aware of until it was lifted, in much the same way that you only become aware of the density of fog you are driving through after you've left it. On the second day, I saw Felix, who barely batted an eye at my presence, but who immediately started pressing me for my opinion of one of the girls who sat at the back, knitting. Two rows a minute. Never dropped a stitch. Did I think she wanted to be talked to? Why didn't he speak to her and find out? In some weird "stopped clock tells the right time twice a day" kind of way, I think he always expected me to show up there again sooner or later.

Prudence was a little pricklier when I ran into her two days later. "Are you sure you're not just overreacting?" she asked. "Have you always been this much of a hypocondriac?" I told her I was sorry for all the confusion. She told me it happened all the time. Wives came for husbands and ended up staying for themselves. Had I seen Lola yet? I told her I hadn't. I put off calling her for a day, another day, until I got to the end of my first week without calling her. I don't know why I had such a block about it. Finally, it got to be too much. We'd gone to about six or seven meetings without running into each other. She knew. I knew that she knew. She knew that I knew that she knew. So I called her up and asked her to meet me for coffee. She suggested a café not far from where she lived, in Chelsea, not far from the West Side Highway, on Eighth Avenue.

Spring was definitely on the way: The sun was out, the trees in blossom, people had on shorts, T-shirts, flip-flops. She was already there when I arrived, sitting on a bench, talking on the phone with someone. She was wearing jeans, flats, and a navy blue halter top, her hair down, just brushing her shoulders, which bore a trace of pink from the sun. "No. . . . Uh-uh. . . . I think you should take it . . . You won't see any better. . . ."

She saw me and made a "Won't be long" face. "Okay . . . okay, I hear you. . . . All right, let's do that. . . . Tomorrow, then. . . . All right. . . . Bye-bye."

She closed the phone, putting it away. "Why do people want to keep on looking at apartments when the place they want is right there in front of them?"

"They think there'll be something better around the next corner."

"Right. So someone else ends up getting the apartment."

She got up, and for a second or two we stood there, sheepishly, before embracing, like two five-year-olds who have been told to make friends but don't know how to go about it. I hated our awkwardness but accepted it: This was how things were going to be between us.

"It's nice to see you again," she said.

"You, too."

"Do you want to go for a walk?"

The café was packed. We started walking up Eighth Avenue, past cafés and diners, parking lots, billboards, garages. Behind metal fencing, new tires were mounted in tall, teetering pikes; a new season of *Lost* was coming to NBC. The closer to the edge of the city you get, the less thought through it seemed, like it had been thrown together at the last minute by someone in a hurry.

"How are you sleeping?" she asked.

"Badly."

"It gets better. Have you told anyone at work?"

"Not yet, no. Although I think they've guessed."

"Oh yeah?"

"I'm gone at lunchtimes again. And I come back in a much better mood than when I left. At first, I told them I was going to lunch with clients, but they know I don't have that many clients."

She laughed, and I felt something in me relax. There she was, the girl I knew, the one with the tattoo at the base of her spine, who slept like a baby and spoke like she was getting rid of loose change. A familiar ache started up in my chest.

"How's Douglas?"

"He's just about gotten over the shock."

"I always knew you were a drunk."

"You did? How?"

"You mean apart from the fact that you were attending AA meetings and lied to me about drinking lemonade when you were drinking vodka? You seemed to be taking it all so personally. I was like, Who cares so much? Nobody cares about that stuff, not unless they're imagining it for themselves. Plus, you seemed to be in New York but didn't seem to have the faintest clue why you were here."

"It was that obvious?"

"I don't know about obvious, but it was clear you were pretty lost, yeah. You shook me for a bit. But . . . I don't know. You never struck me as someone who could bring off that kind of lie. You were so traumatized by it, for one thing."

"I felt awful."

"You see? What kind of person lies and then feels awful about it? Then you showed up at that Sunday meeting, and that's when I knew you were in real trouble. I knew I had to stand well back or get hurt myself. You understand that, don't you?"

She pulled up on the sidewalk, beneath what looked like a metal bridge or stretch of overhead railway running across the street.

"I think so."

"You needed to work it out for yourself. You wouldn't have listened to me. You would just have resented me."

"I resented you anyway," I said, looking down at the sidewalk between us. "A bit of me knew. A bit of me always knew I was in trouble. That's what made it so painful. If I had completely fooled myself, then there wouldn't really have been a problem, would there? But it wasn't like that. There was this little chink, letting in light. I could see what I was doing. A bit of me was sitting back, observing all the bullshit I was feeding myself, not buying any of it. And then I met you and that chink got a little bit wider."

"I'm just glad you're okay," she said.

Somehow the distance between us closed and we embraced. "I was so worried," she said. For a while, we just stood like that, in the shade from the bridge, holding each other tightly, and when we came back from the hug, she wiped something from her face. "Jesus," she said. I reached for her chin, brought it up, saw the tears streaking down her cheek, and kissed it. Then we were kissing properly, my hands finding the small of her back, hers the back of my neck. This time, when we let go, we stayed in each other's arms, her head on my shoulder, my cheek against her head. The bridge in whose shadow we stood was held aloft by massive steel girders, the girders studded with rivets as fat as beetles.

"I've just realized where we are," I said.

"Standing next to a parking lot on Eighth Avenue?"

"We're underneath the High Line."

She looked up.

"Let's go up," I said, taking her hand and leading her toward the steps. A small ice-cream kiosk stood to one side. We stopped for two cones, then made our way up the stairwell, emerging into the middle of the tracks. They'd planted bushes and trees, creating an avenue of green that cut through Chelsea, the apartment buildings and hotels rising up on either side. One building looked like it hadn't gotten out of the way in time; the tracks simply plowed right through it, creating a big arched tunnel. The air above the grass danced with dust motes and no-see-ums. We began walking north.

"You know we're going to have to wait, don't you?" she said.

"You beat me to it."

"Oh, I did, did I?"

"I was going to say that one of us has to step up and act responsibly. And since I'm not sure it can be you, it's probably going to fall to me."

"Is that right?" She feigned outrage.

"Yes, it is. I've seen the way you are with newcomers. You see one you like, you just jump. Like a lioness on an antelope haunch."

She took a swipe at my behind.

"*Someone's* landed on his feet."

"Does that mean I get to kiss you before a year?"

"No. In fact, you have to wait two years."

"Since when?"

"Since you turned out to be a hoser."

I took her by the hand, pulled her to me, and kissed her again against the steel balustrade that marked the edge of the track. Her lips felt cool with ice cream.

"I'm serious," she said.

"I know. So am I."

"It's not that long. Just stay away from the other newcomer girls. Hey, I know what I wanted to ask you."

"What?"

"What's your name?"

I looked at her. "What are you talking about? You know my name."

"Not your first name, dummy. Your last name."

"Oh . . . right. Of course. Miller. Patrick Miller."

"Patrick Miller," she repeated.

"And yours?"

"Mathisson."

"Lola Mathisson."

"Miller and Mathisson."

"Sounds like a firm of personal-injury lawyers."

She took a lick of her ice cream and we began walking again.

"So a year," I said.

"A year."

"A year from now or a year from December?"

"From now."

"The time I got before doesn't count."

"Uh-uh."

"So what was that just then?"

"What was what?"

"What happened against the railing back there."

"That was a slip."

"A slip."

"Yes, a slip. Now the thing about slips is not to beat yourself up about them too much. You just have to get up, dust yourself off, and get back on the horse."

"Back on the horse."

"That's right."

This was going to be hard, I could tell.

chapter thirty-five

DEAR DOUGLAS,

First I'd like to thank you for letting me write out my fourth step like this. I know it's not the way they want you to do it. I saw how they want you to do it in the book.

I'm resentful at:	*The cause:*	*Affects my:*
Mr. Brown	His attention to my wife.	Sex relations. Self-esteem (fear).
	Told my wife about my mistress.	Sex relations. Self-esteem (fear).
	Brown may get my job at the office.	Security. Self-esteem (fear).

I mean, come *on*. I'm telling my life story here, not filling out my tax returns. I've tried to tell it the only way I know, which is how it seemed to me at the time. I've heard people in meetings, and there's always so much retrospective wisdom going on. "I was born an alcoholic, and drank alcoholically from the get-go. From the earliest age, I was restless, irritable, and discontent. . . ." Not me. My story goes: *Drinking like a normal person, drinking like a normal person, drinking like a normal person, drinking like a normal person—Shit, I'm an alcoholic!* That's how it was. I had no idea. I could never write one of those memoirs, with their endless binges and blackouts and overdoses and rolls in the gutter. I hear about people injecting their toes, or losing their house, or flatlining on the dance floor and—okay, I'll say it, I get a little jealous. I know, I know. I shouldn't compare. My story is my story. You've told me all this. Can I say, by the way, that the way you did it in your book was stupendous? I'll be giving you my full notes in a week or two. You already know I think it's better than the first *Freefall.* But here's something I appreciated, which I don't think I would have gotten before: the lack of alcohol in the book. I mean, it's there, but it's not in the foreground, and if you're not looking out for it, you barely notice it. I know how much you were really going through, of course, which only made it all the spookier that Frank Leary seems to drink so little. You just *know* that guy's going to end up in a drying-out clinic, but not until it happens, if you know what I mean. Maybe it reminded me of myself. I don't know. Either way, it's a great book, and I can't quite believe I'm the one who gets to sell it for you. Leo's so proud we're representing you, he's even making jokes about making me a senior partner by the end of the year. We'll see. He still doesn't know about my return to the rooms. The only people who do are Saul and Natalie. They both guessed. "You're so much . . . lighter," Natalie told me, "so much easier to be around"—which was both sweet and sad at the same time, since it told me how difficult I was before. The one person who's reacted badly to the whole thing is Ian Horrocks. He's pleased I sold his book, of course—*Talk to the Hand* went to HarperCollins for a handy sum—but not so pleased that he's lost his pub-crawl buddy. I think he thinks I've been in the country too long, or watching too much *Oprah*. I get a lot of "Do you believe in God yet?" and "Are you really sure about this?"

The weird thing is, I'm happy to let the whole subject lie. *He's* the one who keeps bringing it up. So this weekend? I'm going to that softball game I told you about, the one Lola is playing in. After ragging on it all week—"Sober softball? What's *that*?"—Ian now says he wants to come along. He wants to mock, but he wants to mock from the sidelines. Did you know that Lola was captain of the UCLA team that went all the way to the Women's College World Series at the Hall of Fame Stadium in Oklahoma in 1995, where they beat Arizona 4–2? Isn't that something? And all through a permanent hangover. We've been trying, Douglas, we really have. Both of us want to wait until I have my year, but whoever came up with that rule has absolutely zero understanding of basic human nature. You're telling me that you're going to take a whole bunch of young men and women, some of them highly attractive, and stick them in a room together, every day, after years of isolation, in a hormonally charged environment that resembles nothing so much as high school, and ask them to speak honestly about their lives—giving up the kind of information that normally only a boyfriend or girlfriend gets to hear—and ask them *not* to fall in love with one another? How is *that* supposed to work?

Seriously. That is what I recommend if you wanted them in bed with each other by the end of the week. That hasn't happened, Douglas, I'm not saying it has, but since we're on a big honesty kick these days, I should tell you that there may have been some coffee dates, and a movie or two.

Okay, look. Since we're on such an honesty kick these days: After the movie, I walked her home. It was late at night. It was warm out. I couldn't just let her walk home by herself. I hate saying good night without talking about the movie you've just seen. It's so abrupt. So we saw *The Wrestler* and I walked her home and there was some kissing under the scaffolding outside her apartment, okay? Not just the kind of kissing on the railway track, either, like "Welcome back; I'm glad you're okay," but proper kissing.

There. Confession over. There really is nothing more to say. I didn't go up to her apartment, didn't spend the night, although it does occur to me that were it to have happened—and I'm not saying it did—but were it to have happened, it wouldn't be the absolute end of the world, not for someone with as high a bottom as mine. The way I see it is, the lower your bottom, the more fried your brains are, the more important it is to avoid emotional entanglements for the full year. But when you're the kind of effete, three-blackout drunk I was, then obviously that time comes down a little. Four or more blackouts and I would probably have had to stay the course. But three blackouts? It should be half a year tops. I'm almost at four months now. That's just another two to go, no?

Okay, okay. Let's talk about it some more, the next time we see each other. It really was just kissing beneath the scaffolding though and *The Wrestler* is a good movie. No lie.

Love,

Patrick.